DAUGHTER OF THE DRAGON

Wrath of the Stormking
Volume 2

By

Michael G. Manning

Cover by Christian Bentulan
Map Artwork by Maxime Plasse
Editing by Keri Karandrakis
© 2024 by Michael G. Manning
All rights reserved.
Printed in the United States of America

ISBN: 978-1-943481-50-7

For more information about the Mageborn series check out the author's Facebook page:

https://www.facebook.com/MagebornAuthor

or visit the website:

http://www.magebornbooks.com

Lystal
BONDGRAD
T E R
Kemp
T R E N D H A M
TALMA
F
A
R
E
S
H
Tumpton
EDAL
Fareth Desert
PRAKA
DELGATH
S H I M E R
Grath
Dinath
2019

HERCYNIA
Tharntum
INIA
aham
Maldon
Barrowden
Branscombe
ERRIA
DARROW
MYRSTA
ela
BARSTA
BERN

CHAPTER 1

Moonlight caressed the tips of the wavelets that moved across the waters surrounding the port of Baricia. It was a calm night with only a light breeze and with the humidity, it would have been a miserable evening but for the mild spring temperatures. In two more months, summer would arrive in full force, and any day without a strong wind would be uncomfortable to say the least.

For tonight, though, the weather was merely warm and sultry, suitable for a seaside romance or a pirate adventure, if Will had been living in a storyteller's fiction. Unfortunately, he was not, at least not as far as he knew. *Does the mind of a dreaming god count?* he thought idly. Whenever he mused about such things, the thought always came to him. He'd spoken with Marduke once, and while the details of the conversation always remained firmly beyond his grasp, certain thoughts resulted in firm convictions that he couldn't quite explain. One such conviction was the fact that the world they lived in was all part of a dream.

He could only assume it was something that the god had told him, since he didn't recall reading such a thing in any of the books he'd studied. Will blinked to clear his mind and focus on the world in front of him. He'd been motionless too long and had allowed his attention to wander.

Across the water, fifty yards from the dock he stood beside, was an elven trade galley. He'd been watching it, and a few other trade ships like it, for more than a week. This ship in particular had moved away from the dock close to sunset and was now moored in relatively open water. It was following a similar pattern to the other elven ships he'd watched. The elves never remained moored dockside at night, presumably because they were being cautious.

No one from Trendham was allowed aboard, not even briefly. There were humans that moved up and down gangway when their ships docked, but those men were directly employed by the elves. They weren't dockworkers from Baricia.

As a result of the tight security, Will had to be extra careful in how he attempted to board. His options were limited, and he had to be either entirely unseen, or he would have to take the place of one of the elves' employees. His skill with auditory illusions was exceptional, but his practice with visual illusions was rudimentary at best. Besides, the elven captain was likely a spellcaster of some sort, and any illusion he could manage would be easily spotted by anyone with the ability to see turyn.

Physically altering his appearance—flesh-shaping, as Selene called it—was not something he had any ability with, and he wasn't willing to let anyone, even his wife, remold his features. The very idea repulsed him, which was ironic, since he was married to a lich who regularly practiced such magic with both living and dead bodies.

So remaining unseen was his only real option, and when he saw the ship weigh anchor, he knew the time had come. Will stepped off the dock and dropped to the water's surface, but his legs didn't sink in. As he'd dropped, he'd cast a water-walking spell. The surface held him up as though he stood on stiff but slightly spongy ground. The spell strengthened the water tension nearby such that the water's surface acted as if it were a stiff carpet. It still swayed slightly with the movement of the rest of the water in the bay, so it did require him to pay some attention to his footing lest he fall over.

A camouflage spell hid his outline as he crossed the moonlit water and stepped up to the back of the galley, where he scaled the rear end of the ship like a lizard, his hands and knees adhering and releasing from the painted wood as though it was the most natural thing in the world. Will's familiarity with the climbing spell was such that if anyone could have seen him, they might have thought he'd been born scaling walls.

The elves' paranoia regarding their security was exceptional, and consequently, the ship was warded. Will had noticed that before touching the wood, and he'd matched the frequency of his turyn to that of the ward before starting his climb. He could only hope that they hadn't warded the interior of the ship as well. He didn't want to have to regulate his turyn for days on end.

The trip back to the gate the elves used to travel between their realm and Hercynia might take weeks. No one knew, and despite Will's investigation, he hadn't been able to find anyone who had an idea how long it would take. While a number of men had taken employ with the elves, and some had even gone with them to live in their realm, none had ever returned to share any details of what they had seen.

It sounded ominous when put like that, except that the human deckhands on the elven ships seemed happy enough. They were healthy, well fed, and apparently well paid. Will had spoken to a few when they came ashore and had been frustrated by their singular unwillingness to answer any questions regarding the elfhome. All they would say was that they were happy with their choice, and if he truly wanted to know, he should sign up to work for the elves as they had.

Will didn't trust their words, not for a minute. Given what he'd seen before, he had little doubt that at the bare minimum the human workers had had their minds altered. They might truly believe what they said, or they might be under some sort of geas, but whatever the case, he didn't believe the elves were benign.

Pulling himself over the railing, Will was relieved to find that the ward didn't cover the interior as well. As easy as it was for him to fool wards, maintaining the deception for days on end was probably beyond him. He had to sleep sometime. That thought led his mind down a tangent of what might be possible with a custom spell design. He'd crafted so many new spells over the past decade that the exercise was almost a habit, but he forced himself to push the ideas aside. Now wasn't the time.

His next task was to find a quiet place to set up a nest of sorts, and as much as he disliked the notion, the most likely spot would be in the bilge. Moving slowly and deliberately, he walked across the deck until he reached the cargo hatch. Once he was sure no one was watching, he used a heavy-duty telekinetic spell to carefully lift the heavy wood and iron cover, then dropped down. The hold was dark and full of wooden crates, but he needed to go farther. Working his way toward the stern, he found a stair that led down to the ship's lowest level, the cramped and curved bilge.

That area was completely dark, but that was no obstacle. Will was pleasantly surprised to see that it was almost entirely dry. Enchanted pumps kept any water that made its way down from above from accumulating, and only a tiny amount of water that was below the pump's inlet managed to remain. Whatever he felt about the elves themselves, Will couldn't fault their ship design.

Using a selection of specialized spells he'd designed over the past week, Will created a small cabin at the bow end of the bilge. The spells were simple enough, based on the same elemental air magic he used to create temporary cookware. More specifically, he had adapted a spell he sometimes used to create a magical bread oven. Within a minute, he had a small compartment with walls and a floor composed of invisible yet solid air. He could control the temperature and humidity within, though he had changed the range of values to match those compatible with human comfort (as opposed to baking). He had another spell ready to create an air mattress when he was ready to sleep, but he was hours away from that.

To avoid discovery, for someone was sure to check on the bilge eventually, Will set up a nearly undetectable ward that would trigger an illusion contingency. The illusion was very simple, meant to simply hide his tiny cabin, and the ward was set to trigger it if there was any change in the lack of light. As long as whoever was sent to the bilge wasn't a mage, he would be relatively safe from discovery.

In the meantime, Will's biggest challenge would be boredom. To that end, he'd brought plenty of reading material and had a number of spell projects he intended to work on, but he had little doubt that weeks in the dark and tiny space would be oppressive anyway. With a sigh, he summoned a book and adjusted his vision until he could read despite the lack of visible light.

***

Oliver glanced over at his aunt curiously. It was perhaps the tenth time he'd done so in the past five minutes, and the count would be much higher if one considered the last hour of traveling. They were riding on an elemental travel disk, zipping along the north road that led away from Bondgrad. Sammy made a fresh turn and took them off the road and into the forest.

"Where are we going?" Oliver asked once more.

Sammy glanced at him. "Did your previous employer let you nag him like this?"

"He didn't listen to me at all. Maybe if he had, he wouldn't be dead."

His aunt smirked. "This lip on this boy," she muttered. "I didn't want to say anything until we were well away from the city, but we are going to meet with your stepmother."

"My stepmother," he muttered reflexively, though he knew full well who his aunt was referring to. He had met her once, but he'd never actually spoken to her, and considering the fact that his father had beheaded and burned her to dust the last time he met the Queen of Terabinia, Oliver couldn't help but feel nervous. "Is she really my stepmother?"

Sammy shrugged. "Will says they're married still, and even though he said exactly the opposite for most of your life, I'm inclined to go along with whatever they say. Selene isn't the sort of person you argue with."

"Is she that bad?"

Sammy looked at him, then slowly brought the travel disk to a stop. "I should probably explain a few things before we reach the meeting place." Oliver nodded and she continued, "Your dad married a princess, and she's now queen, that much is simple enough, but since you grew up in Trendham, you probably don't appreciate the social differences. You can think of her like you might think of one of the oligarchs, but that doesn't fully encapsulate the difference. In Terabinia, the social classes are fixed, and royalty is as far from commoners like us as the sun is from the ground beneath your feet.

"Selene has always done her best to minimize that aspect of her upbringing, but that's easier said than done. You'll notice when she speaks that very often, she will assume obedience without even giving an order. Given your relationship, she'll probably make allowances, but be prepared anyway. Don't argue with her unless you've a very solid reason to do so."

Oliver nodded again. "I wasn't intending to, but you make it sound as if she's going to stay with us."

Sammy grinned. "No. You'll be staying with her or traveling with her more likely."

Oliver felt his skin grow cold. "I thought I was supposed to be your bodyguard."

"For now, you'll be hers," said Sammy. "I'm sure Alex will be sufficient until she no longer needs you."

"Couldn't Alex do this instead of me?"

His aunt shook her head. "I think part of the reason she asked for you was *because* of your father. She wants to get to know you, and as nervous as that makes you feel, I think she's right. Despite everything I've said, she's not as scary as you might think."

"Did the two of you get along back then, before Dad left?" asked Oliver.

Sammy paused, dismissed the elemental travel disk, then answered, "I got along best with your Aunt Tabitha. Selene was older, and I was still rather immature. We got along, but everything fell apart before we could really cement our relationship. She was really close to Tabitha and Will, so I felt comfortable with her because of them."

"Aunt Tabitha told me she doesn't trust the queen."

Sammy nodded. "That's because she could tell something had changed and then Will left. I'm sure once they're all together again, the two of them will be able to clear the air. Selene was like an older sister to her before things fell apart." She studied him for a moment, then added, "Relax. She's a queen, not a monster. I'm sure you'll discover you like her once you get past your jitters."

A sharp crack rang out to the east, as though something heavy had snapped in two. More noise and sound followed, and the entire forest began to shake. Oliver had a blade in hand and his shield out before he was consciously aware of it. The trees in that direction were whipping back and forth. He glanced at his aunt, but she seemed calm. "Something big is coming," he warned. "Maybe you should recast the travel disk."

"No. I think that's her," said Sammy.

"What?" Oliver's neck whipped back around just in time to see an enormous head emerge from the trees, followed by heavy, reptilian shoulders. The monster was wider than a wagon and he could only see part of it, but his mouth went dry. It was a dragon, he knew that, though he'd never seen one before, and its mouth was large enough to snap him up in a single bite.

There was no fighting such a colossal enemy. Young as he was, Oliver knew his days had come to an end. "Run, Aunt Ess! Run!" Despite his fear, he stepped forward, thinking perhaps he could distract the monster long enough for her to recast the travel disk spell.

The dragon froze, and for a moment no one moved. Then the dragon's mouth opened, showing a jaw full of teeth as big as short swords. "I thought I heard you over here. Thank you for bringing him, Sammy." The deep voice rumbled over them, vibrating through Oliver's chest and rattling his teeth.

Sammy nodded. "No problem at all. Sorry about last time. Will told me what to do, but he didn't have a chance to explain until after. I hope it didn't hurt."

"I hardly felt a thing," reassured the dragon, but its eyes remained fixed on Oliver. "Olly, I'm glad to finally be able to meet you, without pretending to be someone else for a change."

The tension and fear coursing through him was almost too much to bear, and now it seemed he had misread the situation. Taking a deep breath, Oliver lowered his sword, trying not to let the unspent adrenaline make his arm shake. "You're—you're her?"

The dragon's chin dipped slightly. "I'm Selene. Your father's wife, your stepmother, I suppose, though I know I'm essentially a stranger to you."

"But you're a dragon," muttered Oliver, struggling to organize his thoughts.

The dragon's face shifted, exposing teeth in frightening ways as Selene's human instincts caused her to instinctively move her facial muscles in ways that no true dragon would. After a second, she responded, "Your father and Sammy, they explained my unique circumstances, didn't they?"

Sammy spoke up. "Actually, I left out the part about you meeting us in a dragon body." When Oliver glanced back at her, she simply smirked. "I couldn't help it. You should have seen your face. An opportunity like this only comes once in a lifetime."

Selene's draconic eyes narrowed, which made her appear even more terrifying. "I had hoped you would have matured by now, but I should have known better."

Sammy's features hardened. "I'm here because Will asked me to do this, but I also hope we can mend our fences. Tolerance runs both ways. I am who I am."

The dragon stared at her without blinking. "At the very least, the girl I remember has developed a strong spine over the years."

Sammy glared back. "It runs in the family."

"And we're all family here, right?" announced Oliver suddenly, feeling a need to break the tension.

"Of course," said his aunt.

Selene answered apologetically, "I hope you'll both forgive me. This body affects my emotions in unusual ways, and the biggest casualty seems to be my sense of humor. I didn't mean to be so prickly."

Sammy exhaled, relaxing, and Oliver felt the tension recede. "I have to admit your current form makes me a little nervous," Sammy replied.

"Can I ask why we're out here?" said Oliver.

"This body isn't suited for a meeting in the city," said Selene drolly.

"It's about the elves," answered Samantha, getting to the heart of the question. "They haven't left Terabinia."

Selene dipped her massive head in agreement. "I've spent the last couple of months in Lystal, waiting to see what the return of the dragon would cause the elves to do. I'd hoped they would withdraw completely, but that doesn't appear to be the case."

"They've withdrawn from Trendham," announced Sammy, "but it seems that they're simply concentrating their numbers in Terabinia. They must know you aren't the real dragon."

Oliver had been staring at Selene's scaled hide with morbid curiosity the entire time. "She seems very real to me."

"I wear this body as you might put on your clothes, but I am far from the creature the elves truly fear. Dragons bear the fires of creation within them. This body is a pale shadow of that, a dead husk. If the elves somehow figure out the ruse, they won't fear this form any more than they fear me," said the queen.

"But you're immortal, right? And you're in a dragon's body—what's the difference?" asked Oliver.

Sammy sighed. "She doesn't have her father's power."

Selene's dragon form wasn't much for showing a proper smile, but it excelled at displaying annoyance. A wave of menace made Oliver flinch instinctively as Selene glared at Sammy. "Don't call him that. He may have raised me, but that creature wasn't my father." After a moment of silence, Selene glanced at Oliver. "She's right, though, I don't have his power."

The difference wasn't clear to Oliver. "You're a wizard, though, like Dad, and he was able to kill the dragon. Doesn't that mean—"

"No," replied Selene flatly. "I have nothing like the power your father has, or even your aunt. My transformation keeps death at bay, but it also weakened me. I will likely never have the same strength as a third-order wizard, unless I live for millennia, and even then, I'll lack their special talents."

"The dragon was more powerful than your dad," added Sammy.

Oliver still had clear memories of what he saw the day the Stormking revealed himself and put a stop to the war between Trendham and Terabinia. Despite the terrifying immensity of the dragon in front of him, his aunt's pronouncement didn't seem possible. "But he won," argued Oliver.

"Does the strongest warrior always prevail in battle?" asked Selene. She didn't wait for an answer. "Of course not. Tactics and cunning play a strong part in the outcome, and your father didn't win by himself. He capitalized on the preparations Grim Talek had been making for thousands of years." After a moment, she moved on. "The important fact is that the elves obviously know I'm not the real dragon. They remain in Terabinia, and I am certain they are still working to consolidate power there."

"What's your plan?" asked Sammy.

"Janice still rules in my place, so the elves aren't strong enough yet to claim power openly. Thanks to Will and the two of you, I'm currently able to act as a free agent, so I plan to capitalize on that. I'll return to Terabinia, acquire a new body, and uproot the parasites attempting to use my nation for their own benefit."

Oliver had one important question. "When you say, 'acquire a new body,' what does that mean exactly?"

Selene answered directly. "It takes a strong spine to ask me that the first time meeting me, especially in my current form. You definitely take after your father. Hopefully I can earn your trust, but for now I can only give you my promise—I have no intention of harming any innocents. The simplest way to acquire a new human form is to steal a dead body, the fresher the better. Such a form is capable of meeting almost any of my needs, but during the course of our project I may need an actual living body as well. In that case, I'll take one from our enemies. Is that acceptable to you?"

"As long as Olly agrees with your choice at the time," said Sammy.

Selene nodded, but Oliver was frowning. "I appreciate you respecting my feelings, but I'm not sure I understand why. Why do you need me there, and why would a queen care what I think?"

"We are family," said the dragon. "That's important to me, therefore *you* are important to me. Aside from that, I do actually need your help. Obtaining a new body while in this one presents several challenges that I'd rather not discuss now. Suffice it to say, I need helping hands, and that fact that yours are exceptionally strong hands is even better. This isn't something I can trust to a stranger, and your father is currently occupied."

Oliver looked to his aunt, then back to Selene. "I'll do my best."

With a hug and a lengthy goodbye, Sammy left Oliver with the dragon.

CHAPTER 2

Flying was a nightmare. Oliver wasn't a naturally fearful person; quite the opposite, in fact—curiosity and adventure seeking had been defining characteristics of his nature throughout childhood and adolescence. Cautious people didn't seek to become wardsmen. Their very motto was 'Live fast, die young.'

Clinging to the back of a flying dragon was an extreme test of that philosophy. There was no saddle, only a rope tied around the base of Selene's thick neck for him to hold onto. That had seemed good enough when they were on the ground, but once they were in the air it felt woefully inadequate.

Selene was aware of his distress, but she was having problems of her own. A change in the air caused her to drop several feet suddenly, and she pumped her wings furiously to compensate. She'd only recently learned to fly and hadn't had any practice during the last couple of months while she was in Lystal with Will. Her sharp draconic hearing picked up the muffled 'eep' that escaped Oliver's lips as she struggled to compensate for the change in air density.

She'd *really* wanted to make a good impression on her stepson, but she was floundering, figuratively *and* literally. This wasn't the smooth, bird-like flight she'd hoped to demonstrate on their trip to Terabinia. *Not unless the bird is suffering from a seizure disorder,* she thought.

It hadn't been this hard last time, when she'd flown from Cerria to Lystal. The air had been different, smoother, more supportive. But that had been months ago, and the weather had changed. Or perhaps she was flying at a different altitude. She really wasn't sure. All she knew was that the air was turbulent and seemed to be full of warm and cold spots that offered different levels of support for her wings.

Would it be better higher up? She didn't know, and she wasn't sure it would be safe for Oliver either. Perhaps lower would be better, but every time she tried that, it seemed to increase her problems.

What she did know was that she was using an enormous amount of energy just staying in the air. Most of that was due to her clumsiness, and the rest was probably due to the difference in the air currents. Bending her neck slightly and swiveling one eye, she got a fair view of her passenger, and to his credit, Oliver was hanging on without complaint, though he was tight-lipped and white-knuckled. *He must be terrified,* she thought. *I would be.*

She flew slightly higher and found a region where the air seemed to be steadier, and there she stayed until they passed over the mountains and into Terabinia proper. Then, she allowed her altitude to slowly drop. "How about a break?" she asked.

"That sounds good," Oliver shouted back. The wind carried his voice away, but her hearing was able to discern his words despite the wind noise.

A broad river was on the horizon, and with it the city of Fernham came into view. The region had been devastated by the troll invasion in prior years, but with help from the crown, it was rebuilding. The elves had *graciously* donated a generous sum to assist with the recovery, which was somewhat ironic considering she now had strong reason to believe they were the ones behind the troll disaster.

The river allowed easy access to Fernham, and the elves had been very helpful in transporting goods upriver. Though she felt embarrassed to consider it, Selene had been on the verge of granting land and titles to some of the elves in consideration for their help. It had seemed like a good idea at the time, especially considering how well they seemed to get along with everyone, including Count Fernham, who had first suggested the idea.

Now she recognized how strange the plan was. Robert Fernham would be the one surrendering some of his lands to make such a thing happen, something no nobleman would willingly countenance. Not if he were in his right mind, and Selene was now certain he had not been. The elves had almost certainly subverted his will, as they had done with her.

The frightening thing was how subtly it had been done. She hadn't suspected a thing and all her normal desires and drives had been left untouched. She'd left at certain intervals, sneaking off to visit William, and returned without the elves knowing. They'd apparently even been unaware of her undead status, and yet they had still managed to control her, or at least subverted her reason in matters pertaining to their goals.

How they managed such a feat was still an open question. She hadn't noticed any strange magic being used, and while she knew the elves could have strange effects on humans due to their pheromones and unusually attractive features, those things shouldn't have affected her.

For one, her primary body had been thoroughly dead, unable to smell and barely able to feel. Sight and hearing were the only senses that worked reasonably well in such a body.

She had presumably escaped their influence when Will had destroyed her body, so whatever magic they used didn't seem to be linked to her soul, which was a bit of a relief. Selene had spent most of her life chained to her father's commands with the heart-stone enchantment, and being enslaved like that again would be a horror.

If it wasn't magic that affected the soul, and it wasn't something specific to living bodies, then the only likely possibility was some sort of mind magic. Such magic had long been forbidden, not just over the history of Terabinia, but even before the civil war, when Terabinia and Darrow had been united under the flag of Greater Darrow.

She intended to be exceedingly cautious the next time she interacted with any elves. Which might be sometime soon, given where they were landing. The area around Fernham was sparsely populated these days, but if the elves had ignored her warning, it was quite possible they still had a substantial presence in the region.

Selene would find out soon enough, but first she needed a body.

After landing, she gave Oliver a solid ten minutes to rest his nerves before discussing her plans. "This is a good place for us to start," she began.

"Where are we?" he asked.

"About fifteen miles west of the city of Fernham. Are you familiar with the name?" Oliver shook his head, so she continued, "It was a sizeable city, before the trolls overran it years ago. Your father had a hand in putting that problem to rest."

Oliver snorted. "At the time, he told me he was going on a buying trip to Bondgrad."

"He did his best to protect you," she responded.

The young man grimaced but said nothing.

"It annoys you, doesn't it?" she asked, sensing some common ground between them.

"He's just doing his best for me," said Oliver.

If Selene had been in human form, a smile would have been sneaking in at the corner of her lips, but her draconic body was too limited for such expressions. "It's admirable of you to refrain from criticizing him."

Clearly irritated, Oliver replied, "It wouldn't be criticism, just selfish complaint. He's a good father."

A long sigh escaped the dragon's mouth. "He was the same sort of husband. I admire him, but he made me so angry with his continual efforts to protect me from everything, especially when he kept secrets for my own good. It wasn't just me, either. That's the biggest part of what came between him and his best friend."

Oliver knew she was baiting him into the conversation, but his curiosity wouldn't be denied. "The duke? Sir John?"

The dragon nodded. "His friends call him Tiny, his peers 'Sir Tiny,' and the rest call him the Black Duke."

"After seeing him in his black armor, I can understand why," offered Oliver, then added, "Dad tried to protect him too?"

A series of choking coughs came from the dragon as Selene tried and failed to laugh with her unfamiliar anatomy. "Yes. He went to save his mother and Tiny went with him. They met the lich and Tiny was rendered unconscious. When they returned a few days later, poor Tiny thought he was coming back with Will, but it was actually Grim Talek playing your father's part." Oliver frowned as she continued, "Your father made a deal with the lich, and he kept it secret from everyone, including Tiny. That led to all sorts of friction."

"Why would he do that?"

"To keep the dragon"—she gestured to her own scaled breast with one claw—"from discovering his plans. We didn't know how Lognion was getting his information, but we suspected everyone and everything. Your father took it a step further by keeping his secrets away from us as well. He knew we would hate that, but he did it anyway. Your father is perfectly willing to make everyone hate him, even his loved ones, so long as it keeps them safe."

After a thoughtful pause, she added, "It's probably the only thing about him that I despise. But I guess it's why I'm still here."

Unsure what to say, Oliver responded, "Because he protected you?"

She growled. "No. It worked for the others, though. If I had been willing to accept my fate as the recipient of his continual sacrifices, maybe I would have lived, but then again, I might have died anyway. No, it was my spite that kept me here. I thought he was dead, and I wanted vengeance. But later, when I found out all the details, I was angry—not as angry as he was, though, when he discovered what I had done to myself."

"And yet you weren't content to let him go."

There was a spark in the dragon's eye as she replied, "I'm the only woman who could be married to him."

"Because he makes you angry?"

"Because I'm willing to tolerate his actions. I was raised a princess, with the implicit understanding that everyone around me should devote themselves to my protection, and while I never fully accepted that, it does make it easier for me to accept his behavior, even his lies. I was raised on logic and political calculus. My way of thinking is far from normal, but it's why I can accept his actions when a normal woman would be unable to accept his betrayal of trust."

She waited, and after a minute, when Oliver still hadn't replied, she asked, "What do you think of me?"

"I'm not sure," said Oliver hesitantly. "You're not what I expected."

"What did you expect?"

He shrugged. "I don't even know, to be honest."

"You're worried about offending me," she pronounced. "That's not what I want. I'm well aware of how unusual my circumstances are, but you're one of just a few people who knows the darker secret of my continued existence. I'm happy about your father's acceptance, but I want to be a family in more than name. Please be honest with me. I'll accept anything, if you'll grant me that."

Oliver held his breath for a moment, then answered, "I'm having trouble thinking of you as a queen, a wife, or even as a person right now. Every movement, every breath, anything you do puts me on edge. My brain knows you're you, but that body triggers an instinctive fear response, so I'm not sure I can give you good answers right now."

"Oh." Selene had let herself forget about the effect her current form might have. She had smelled fear but had been thinking in more human terms when considering the cause. "Well, the first thing we need to do is fix that. That was a big part of the reason I landed here. It's also why I need your help."

Oliver took a step back, suddenly wary. There was only one human body in the vicinity—his. "That's not..."

Selene chuffed, sending out an exhalation of hot air. "No, not you. Not that it would hurt you, but I know very well what your father's reaction would be. Besides, I prefer female bodies when possible."

Oliver stopped. "You've tried both?"

She nodded. "Curious?"

"Well..."

"No need to be shy. I don't mind sharing, but for now it's probably best if we solve the problem at hand," she told him.

"I'm not sure what you think I can do to help."

"I normally make arrangements well in advance to avoid these awkward situations, but I didn't have any alternatives left after my last volunteer, and I needed to bring *this* body back to Terabinia, in case it's needed. My phylactery is hidden, so we can't use that to—"

Oliver interrupted, "What's a fill act—what did you call it?"

"Phylactery," she repeated. "It's the relic I created that keeps my soul bound so it won't pass over. You could think of it as a chain that makes it impossible for me to finish dying."

"Finish? Aren't you already dead?"

Selene tried and failed to shrug; the gesture instead looked like some sort of prelude to a pounce. "It depends on your definition. My source—my life—is gone, but my spirit is bound to the phylactery. I can leave it to possess other bodies, living or dead, but there are certain strict limitations. I can't go beyond a hundred yards or so from the phylactery unless I'm within a physical vessel—a body. Without my phylactery nearby, I dare not leave this body without having another close by to inhabit, otherwise I'll wind up drawn back to the phylactery, and you'll find yourself alone in the wilderness here with nothing but a dragon corpse for company."

Oliver nodded, still unsure what she might want his help with.

She sighed, then explained, "I cannot enter a town or village like this, or I'll cause a panic."

"Definitely," agreed Oliver, nodding again.

"If my phylactery was here, you could simply carry it into the city, but it isn't. So I'm stuck here," she added.

"I see."

Selene's dragon head canted slightly to one side. "No, I'm not sure you do. I can't go into Fernham in *this* body."

"And you won't use mine, since neither of us wants that, so we're stuck here, until—what? Someone wanders by?"

The dragon's massive eyes rolled up toward the sky. "It might be quicker if someone brought a body here, someone strong and healthy enough to carry a grown woman."

Oliver took a step back. "You want me to kidnap someone?"

"Absolutely not! A dead body will be sufficient, provided it's—"

"You want me to kill a woman? Are you—"

Selene growled loudly, cutting him off. She wasn't fond of being interrupted, especially by someone assuming the worst. "Dead doesn't mean you have to kill them. Recently dead is sufficient." She waited to make sure she had his attention, then finished, "Fernham has a sizeable cemetery. I'm not asking you to commit murder. The appropriate term would be graverobbing."

"Oh." Oliver felt a bit embarrassed. "Sorry. I'm not used to this sort of thing."

"Trust," she said, putting emphasis on the word. "Trust is what I'm hoping to build. I realize this is an odd situation for anyone to be put into, but please give me the benefit of the doubt before making accusations in the future. Can you do that?"

He nodded. "I'll do better."

"You barely know me, so I can't blame you for being suspicious," she admitted. "I won't pretend to have a conventional set of morals, but I am not evil, and I have no intention of asking you to do anything against your own conscience."

Steeling himself, Oliver met the dragon's gaze evenly. It was getting easier the longer they were together. "I jumped to conclusions, but I'll listen first next time." After a pause, he asked, "So, *any* body will do?"

"The fresher the better," she responded. "Bring back a skeleton and I can make it function, but it won't help the situation much. A rotting corpse might even be worse, but if you can find something that hasn't started to bloat, I can restore it to a condition that will allow me to pass unnoticed in the city."

Oliver was nodding and began removing his armor. "I think I've got the idea now."

"There are likely elves in the city. Should you be removing your armor?" she asked.

"It's heavy. If I have to carry a body any distance at all, I'd rather do it without all that metal weighing me down." Oliver checked his purse to see how many coins he had. Glancing up, he explained, "Hopefully I can find someone with a shovel to sell, or if not, I'll steal one and leave payment. How much do you think a shovel is worth?"

Selene had absolutely no idea. Unlike most sovereigns, she had posed as a commoner on many occasions, but none of those had involved heavy labor or buying tools. "I'm not sure, but I'll return your money to you later."

Oliver shrugged. "Family, right? I'm not worried about it. I'm just making sure I have what I need."

She watched him preparing, and after a moment she said, "Thank you. Try to find one that died in the last day or two. Anything past three will be impossible for me to restore to a condition that will pass."

He nodded. "Got it. Three days or less, otherwise just kill someone." He waited, and as the seconds dragged on, he began to reconsider the wisdom of making a joke to a dragon.

Finally, the dragon coughed. "Sorry," she told him. "I haven't figured out how to make this body laugh, or if it's even possible."

"I was getting nervous," he admitted.

CHAPTER 3

Will stood in the midst of the wide ocean, which was an even stranger experience considering how far from land he was. The waves were larger but milder, causing him to bob slowly up and down by several feet as he watched the elven ship burn. There was nothing else to see in any direction, for the land had passed beyond the horizon the day before.

"Well, shit," he muttered to no one in particular. "This is really inconvenient." He'd been napping, his favored activity while living in hiding as a stowaway, when one of the sailors had woken him up by stepping into his small, warded living space in the forward bilge. Will had paralyzed the man, then killed him, but others had come looking for the sailor soon after. One of them had been a mage, and things had escalated rapidly.

After the captain and most of the crew had gotten involved, someone had started using fire spells against him, since nothing else worked. Will had suppressed the elemental magic, but a momentary distraction had caused his concentration to waver, and things had gotten out of control. Not that it mattered; from the moment he'd been discovered, his plan had been ruined. He would have to find another ship. With a sigh, Will cast a force travel-disk spell and lifted himself above the waves. He couldn't see land, but he knew the coast was to the north, so he checked the sun and headed roughly in that direction.

It was hours before he sighted the coast. Will followed it north and east, but night was falling before he came to a true city, Karda. He found a dockside inn called The Lazy Mermaid and got a room for the night. He'd start looking for another elven ship in the morning. For now, all he wanted was a warm bath and some rest.

"We have a washtub, but you'll have to draw your own water," the innkeeper told him. "I don't have the time or help to spare doin' all that for you. The pump is next to the kitchen door. There's a bucket next to it."

Will had already used Selene's Solution to clean himself; he just wanted to soak in some hot water, but after seeing the rough and rusty tub the inn had to offer, he declined. It wouldn't be comfortable, and he'd have to make a show of hauling the water himself. Instead, he went to his tiny but private room and used another of the vast array of utility spells he'd memorized to lock the door since it didn't have a latch.

Privacy secured, he modified a spell he'd originally designed for cooking soups and stews. It created a vessel of air to contain and heat liquids for cooking. The spell was fairly complex, since it included built-in adjustments for setting temperature and varying the volume of the container, but it still didn't quite meet his needs. But Will had become a master of spell design over the years. After a minute's thought, he put the spell construct together, including changes to make it a comfortable shape and size for a grown man to lounge within. He started to fill it then, but paused, and after a moment, he sighed. Summoning his current working journal, he recorded the new spell in its pages.

That done, he started to summon several large jars of water from his limnthal to fill his tub of air, but once again he changed his mind. For his trip to unknown lands, Will had learned a few new elemental water spells, but in the back of his mind he'd been mulling over an idea he'd gotten while studying them. Most water spells relied on the presence of liquid water to serve as a substrate for the magic. Earth and air never had to worry about a lack of material, and fire was generally just an energetic phase change involving air, but elemental water spells came in two main varieties. One type assumed the presence of liquid water already, and the other type was meant for instances where liquid water wasn't available.

That second type was essentially a reversal of spells that created fog, instead drawing the invisible water present in the air out and condensing it into liquid form. Those spells were very limited in number and generally restricted their function to things that required only small amounts of water. The only spell Will knew that used that sort of function was a water-missile spell.

While he'd been holed up on the elven ship, he'd partly occupied himself by working on a spell design to produce drinking water using just the condensing portion of the battle spell. There were probably already spells made to do just that, but he didn't have one handy, and he enjoyed the challenge. Over the years, he'd often found that reinventing the wheel wasn't always a waste of time. He might be repeating someone else's work, but in the process, he learned things that paid dividends when he was designing other spells.

Thumbing through his journal, he checked his notes and tested the new spell to produce drinking water. He hadn't dared do so while on the elven ship. It worked, but took more turyn than he expected, so he added a quick note to the page, then quickly drew up a new version that would hopefully provide enough water to fill his temporary bathtub.

Will looked it over once, then revised two runes before he was satisfied. Wasting no time, he created the spell construct and poured his strength into it. A decade ago, such an action would have been beyond foolish, but his skill had progressed to the point that he rarely encountered outright failure anymore, and when he did make a mistake, his mastery and strength of will made it almost impossible for a failed spell to injure him.

The only real risk was that of property damage, but he was confident enough that he tried the spell anyway. It worked, but Will observed several things that surprised him. First, the room's temperature dropped precipitously even though he was supplying all the energy the spell required. Second, the air became suddenly and uncomfortably dry, though he had a hard time describing the sensation. Fortunately, that wasn't too much of a problem once he opened a window to let in fresh air.

It was the third unexpected effect that surprised him the most. While the air had briefly become intensely cold and dry, the water that filled his tub was hot to the point of boiling. When he'd tested his drinking water spell it had been warm, but not scalding.

Will stared at his air tub, then adjusted the temperature setting so it wouldn't add any additional heat. As it was, it would take a considerable amount of time for the water to cool down enough for him to get in.

He sighed. Without realizing it, he'd already spent more than an hour designing his tub filling spell, and now he would have to wait some more. Will had an abundance of spells for heating water, particularly for cooking, but none for rapidly cooling it. In fact, the only cooling spell he knew was the one he used in conjunction with his sonic shield to prevent being flash cooked while diverting dragon's fire, or Sammy-fire as was mainly the case when practicing.

Thinking about it made him realize there were a number of similarities between the cooling spell and his water-producing spells. Intrigued, he sat down on the small bed with his journal and started comparing the spells, studying the parallels between them.

Hours later, Will discovered he'd forgotten all about his bath, and he was too tired to care, so he diverted his now cold bathing water into the street, dismissed his tub, and went to bed. The next day, he began looking around the docks, hoping to find another elven merchant.

There weren't any available, but a few of the dockworkers he met assured him that one would be along sometime in the next week or so. Will was tempted to go home for the time being, but since he couldn't teleport back it wasn't practical. He returned to the inn and negotiated a room for the week, then finished perfecting his new bathtub-filling spell.

Once that was done, he filled it and enjoyed his first proper soak in some time. Then he turned his thoughts back to the problem at hand.

"Their ships are heavily warded, within and without," said Will, speaking quietly as he organized his thoughts. "They check their personnel when they leave port to make sure everyone is aboard, and I'm guessing they do the same again before they dock." That made replacing one of the crewmen a difficult task. Worse, while he'd been aboard, he'd spent some time examining the dormant wards that were present throughout the interior—although they hadn't been used, he suspected they were meant for a fairly simple task, confirming the count of men or elves aboard. "They stumbled onto me by accident, but even if they hadn't, that ward would have given me away if they'd used it." He supposed it was something that would be activated only at particular times, such as the midpoint of the journey.

Given time and effort he could probably create solutions for those problems, either subverting or tricking the wards that the elves used, but there was a far simpler way to tackle the issue. He didn't actually *need* to be on their ship, so long as he could follow the elves back to wherever the congruence point was that they used to travel between realms. Will's eyes stared at the invisible boundary of air that contained and insulated his steaming bathwater. He'd already mastered the magic for creating containers of air and controlling the temperature within them—and a bathtub had a lot of similarities to a boat.

"A travel disk would work, but it would be tiring trying to stay atop one for days or weeks on end," he muttered. "Not to mention having to continually direct it." Will could draw and maintain enough turyn to manage such a task indefinitely, but he was still human—the need for sleep would eventually cause him to fail. But a passive spell, one imbued with the energy necessary to last for hours or days, that would be quite practical. A simple boat of air was entirely possible, so long as it could somehow keep up with the elven ship while remaining unseen. Much of that would be mitigated by the invisible nature of air, combined with distance and a bit of camouflage magic. More importantly, his spell-boat would have to follow the elven ship even while he slept.

A smile crept across his features as Will imagined a dinghy, tied to a larger ship by rope and being towed along. He could certainly replicate something like that with magic. He only had to make sure it couldn't be detected by the elven sailors.

Growing more excited, Will forsook his bath and dried himself. Even dressing was too much of a bother, so he summoned a robe from his limnthal and threw it on before sitting down to sketch out his ideas in his journal, the first step in creating a set of spells to enable him to shadow the next elven ship without actually boarding it.

His first solution was simple, and he could have crafted the spell for it in less than an hour, but Will was already familiar with the many problems of living in a small space for days on end. He wanted better. Being constantly under the sun would be a problem—he would need shade. Bodily needs also were a concern. His next design was more complex but wouldn't fix everything.

His tongue was forgotten, sticking slightly out of one side of his mouth as he considered whether to do everything with one overly complex spell or split the job up into multiple spells. The lamp in his room ran out of oil as he worked, but Will never looked up. When the room grew too dim, he adjusted his eyes to the light available without even thinking about it. There was no moon that night, so when even adjusting his vision wasn't enough for reading, he created a quick spell light.

The sun was rising again when he finally put his head down and fell asleep. Though he'd forgotten to put up his customary sleeping wards, no nightmares visited him. Will's mind was filled with visions of his newest project, and he dreamed of testing his new spells in the bay before using them on his final target.

***

Oliver crept around the outskirts of the city of Fernham for more than an hour before realizing stealth wasn't really required—he wasn't a grave robber—yet. No one could see into his mind and read his intentions. The time wasn't wasted, though, as he discovered the city's main cemetery on the southern side. It was massive in comparison to the much-diminished city itself, a natural consequence of war. *Or rather, of a troll invasion,* he amended mentally.

Fernham's outer wall remained, but the population was more that of a market town than what most would consider a city. Oliver studied the people as he walked, observing that the populace seemed very young as a whole. That was to be expected wherever war had touched, but unlike a city recovering from a human conflict, this one didn't have any elderly to complement the youths who had been too young to fight. The trolls had eaten everyone unable to run. Very few of those living in Fernham now were original citizens. Most were young families given incentives by the queen to move there and repopulate the region.

As a result, despite the relatively small number of people occupying the old city, it had a feeling of robust activity. The city had two gates, one on the north side and a larger, more frequently used gate on the south side. Like most cities, the gate was open and was probably only shut once or twice a year to make sure it worked properly. Unlike most cities, Fernham's gate was of relatively new construction; it had been rebuilt after trolls had ransacked the city and eaten most of the inhabitants. Ironically, the old gate hadn't failed the citizens; the trolls had simply used their long limbs and incredible strength to climb over the twenty-foot-high stone walls. Destroying the gate had been an afterthought. Once the trolls had sated their incredible appetites, their full and bloated bellies had made climbing too much of a hassle, so they had ripped the gates down from the inside.

One benefit to such a rapid defeat was that the walls and most of the city's major infrastructure had sustained only minor damage. A lot of homes had been torn apart, but larger establishments only had to replace door frames or fix a few walls where a window had been spontaneously converted into a door while the trolls were extracting their 'treats.'

In the aftermath, Queen Selene's administrators had facilitated the sale of now empty farms to freeholders while the city buildings went to enterprising merchants and businessmen. A good portion of those entrepreneurs had been elves, and the new Fernham was the first place in Terabinia to feature a mixed populace. Count Fernham had been a strong proponent for allowing the foreigners to move in, and at the time Selene had thought the nobleman's only motivation to be the possibilities for a new level of prosperity, and the wealth that would accrue to the lord of such a successful city.

Oliver considered entering, but then went back to the cemetery. Most of the graves there were very old, dating to before the troll disaster. The trolls hadn't left any bodies behind for burial when they had come through, and what remains were found had been largely unidentifiable by the time Terabinians returned to assess the damage. As a result, the cemetery hadn't seen much use, and the new citizens were still young.

And yet, luck smiled upon Oliver as he spied freshly turned soil on the far side of the cemetery, in the portion farthest from the city itself. A small wooden marker had been thrust into the soil, and it bore only a name and a short inscription: *Sasha, the sweetest girl and the greatest gift ever graced to me by the Mother. Forever loved and never forgotten.*

"Perfect," Oliver muttered, "now I just need to find a shovel." His first thought was that he might need to go into the city after all, but as he walked back through, he saw a small stone building that he'd thought to be some sort of mausoleum at first. Drawing closer, he realized it was some sort of utility building, likely for the groundskeepers. A sign over the door was marked, "Sexton's Office." Oliver frowned at it. *Why would they need an office at a graveyard?*

"It's a joke," said a deep voice, causing Oliver to start. Somehow his acute senses had failed to alert him to the other man's presence. Turning, he saw a lean older man sitting on a bench beside the small building. The stranger's clothes were a drab grey, matching the stone wall he leaned against, and he'd been so still that Oliver had missed him. "Most can't read it anyway."

Unsure what to say, Oliver responded with a simple, "Oh." A long silence stretched out between them as he tried to think of something to say.

"Saw you looking around over there. Were you a friend of Sasha's?"

"Umm."

"It's all right. She made friends all over. She was especially fond of young men." The groundskeeper gave him a quick wink, though his expression remained flat.

Oliver shifted from one foot to the other. "I just wanted to pay my respects. Do you live here?"

The other man frowned. "People always think gravediggers are odd, but no, I don't live here. I've a place at the Mother's temple." The older man jerked his head in the direction of Fernham.

"At the temple?"

"Where else would a sexton live? No, wait, don't answer that. Maybe if I'd had a family, but Sasha was all I had."

Oliver looked down. "I'm sorry for your loss."

The other man stood up and put a hand on his shoulder. "Thanks. I wasn't sure why I was waiting around here. I've plenty of work to do, the bushes don't trim themselves after all, but I'm glad to have met you—a sorrow shared and all of that." He waved his hand and started walking toward the city. "We'll all be sadder with her gone."

Oliver watched the man leave, taking his place on the stone bench. He wasn't sure what to make of his encounter, but he was already feeling guilty. *I'm about to dig up that poor man's wife.* He sighed, then studied his surroundings to make sure no one else was nearby. It wouldn't do to be surprised again. Once he was certain no one else was within view, or earshot, he got up and tried the door to the building.

It was locked, but that wasn't much of an obstacle. He gave the door a hard rap with one hand to test its sturdiness, and the latch snapped immediately. With a shrug, he stepped in. As he'd expected, the interior revealed a lot of dust and dirt as it served as a utility shed for the cemetery. A variety of tools adorned the interior walls, sickles and shears for keeping the grounds, as well as shovels and wheelbarrows for the actual burials. He gathered up two different shovels and left the rest. He planned to return the soil to the grave when he was done, so he wouldn't need anything else.

Since the grave was fresh, the hardest work was already done for him; the ground had already been broken, and he didn't have to worry about roots or stones. He didn't lack for strength, so once he'd double checked to make sure he wasn't being observed, he began quickly excavating the grave. The simple exercise felt good, but it did nothing to alleviate the guilt he felt. Oliver worked hard, piling the soil neatly to one side so it would be easy to replace. After digging down just four feet, he found the top of what appeared to be a fairly small wooden box. It was perhaps three feet in length and less than two feet wide. His feelings of shame doubled as he realized Sasha must have been the old man's child rather than his wife.

The easiest thing to do would be to open the casket and take just the body, but Oliver didn't want to see the girl inside. He felt bad enough already. With a little more digging he was able to reveal the edges, and eventually he had enough space to lever the shovel beneath one side and pry it loose from the ground. Although it was small as coffins go, it was still an awkward size to carry, and he wished he'd brought some rope. Fortunately, he remembered seeing some in the sexton's utility shed, so he went back and cut a length from it.

With that, he tied a loop around each end, using hitches to snug them tight and ensure that the box didn't fall open, then he used the remaining rope to create a strap he could put across his chest while carrying the box. It wasn't his best ropework, but it was nothing to be ashamed of. In the past he'd seen someone do a better job resulting in two shoulder straps rather than one, but he couldn't remember the particulars. In any case, it was good enough for this job. He tidied up the ground, returning the loose dirt to the grave and packing it in place as best he could, then he returned the shovel and closed the broken door to the shed.

Feeling guilty about his vandalism and rope theft, not to mention grave robbing, he left two gold crowns inside where they would be easily noticed. Guilt somewhat assuaged, he eased the coffin onto his back and pulled the rope loop across his chest where he could hold onto it. It wasn't perfectly stable, but the size and weight weren't great enough to make it a problem for Oliver. Turning his back on Fernham, he headed away from the city for twenty minutes before realigning his course to take him back to where he had left his dragon stepmother.

Dragon stepmother, he thought. *Heh, never thought I'd be stringing those two words together!* He'd once heard a man in Lystal refer to his mother-in-law as a dragon, but Oliver was pretty sure his situation was unique.

Chapter 4

Selene stared down at the furry body her stepson had brought her. Given her current massive size, it seemed even smaller than it might have otherwise. "Is this an attempt at humor?"

Oliver looked even more naïve and clueless than usual. "Say what?" he replied.

She sniffed the dog's body, then turned her head to stare at him with one large eye. "I'm asking if you were trying to make a joke." Oliver stared back with a blank expression, so she continued, "Is this a jest? Should I be laughing? If so, this body is a poor candidate for laughter."

"N-no!" he stammered in response. "I thought it was a girl. I even spoke to the groundskeeper."

"And he told you it was a girl?"

"Well, no—but it sounded like he was talking about his daughter, or a friend, or something—not a dog!" After a moment, he added, "Although, now that I think about it, it does sort of make sense, especially the way he said she loved men. That seemed a little odd at the time, but now I can see—"

Selene cut him off with a brisk exhalation that blew him back a foot. Realizing she might say something she might regret later, she quickly got her frustration under control. "This isn't what I expected, but I can work with it."

"This isn't a prank," said Oliver. "Honestly, I didn't realize it was a dog."

"I know," said Selene. "I wasn't thinking at first, but I understand. Thinking about what your father told me, I should have realized immediately that it wasn't a joke."

"What does that mean?"

"He said you're very literal and that you don't have much of a sense of humor."

Oliver gaped at her. "I have a sense of humor!"

Now it was Selene's turn to backpedal, which wasn't easy given the limited options the dragon form gave her for emotional expressiveness.

"I didn't mean it quite like that. Just that he told me your taste in humor is simple."

"Simple?"

"Uncomplicated," she corrected.

"He said I'm stupid," accused Oliver.

"No, of course not! Just that you don't do well with sarcasm." Oliver stared at her without saying anything, clearly offended. "He meant you prefer an honest sort of humor. I'm not communicating this very well."

"No, you aren't."

"Let me try again," she offered, then stared down at the canine corpse. Glancing back up, she fixed him with one large draconic eye. "Woof!" The sudden shift in demeanor, combined with the ridiculous sounding bark, coming from a dragon, caused Oliver to snicker. Unable to help himself, his snort turned into a loud laugh. Selene capitalized on that by letting her tongue hang out and pretending to pant.

Oliver took a step back, laughing so hard he almost fell and was forced to sit down suddenly. The sight of Selene's terror-inducing dragon body pretending to be a dog was too much for him. After a minute, he begged her for mercy, "Stop, I can't take any more."

"Now you understand?" she asked.

"No, not really."

Simple humor, she thought. "Exactly," she responded, turning her attention to the body in the box. "As much as I'd prefer a human body, this is merely a steppingstone."

"You're going to use it?" asked Oliver.

Selene nodded. "It needs some work, but that would have been the case with a human body too. Once I've gotten it into an acceptable state, I can use it to travel into the city with you and find something *fresher.*" When Oliver blanched, she quickly added, "Someone deserving, preferably an elf."

Relaxing slightly, Oliver had a different question. "What sort of work will you do with this one?"

"The carcass is relatively fresh, which is why you see the swelling there. Soon it will either deflate or it will pop in a more dramatic fashion. I have a plethora of spells to prevent that and either stop the decomposition or accelerate it. I'll also use spells to clean the exterior and get rid of unpleasant smells."

Her stepson was frowning. "Why would someone accelerate decomposition?"

She tried to laugh but all that came out was an odd chuffing sound. "As a lich, I've had to learn a lot more about necromancy. Other than its use in healing, there are a number of more unsavory uses for death magic, including some specialized techniques suited for battle. One of those is a rather novel spell that causes decomposition so rapid that a corpse will explode." Oliver turned a little green at her description, but she continued, "I've never had cause to test it, mind you, and I hope I never will. I'm a little skeptical of its effectiveness in combat anyway."

Looking away from the dog's body, Oliver asked, "What should I do while you're working on this?"

Selene could see his desire to escape for a while, so she went along with it, even though it would probably take her less than an hour. "If you want to explore Fernham, you can. Come back tonight and tomorrow we'll go back together. Just make sure you give a wide berth to any elves you come across."

"All right."

***

A short time later, Oliver was walking down the main street that ran through the center of Fernham, from the north to the south gate. Lord Fernham's keep was located on the western edge of the city so it didn't interrupt the flow of the main street, which was named, as might be expected, 'Main Street.' The road that branched off near the center and headed west toward Fernham's keep was labeled Fernham Boulevard.

Even to Oliver, it was obvious the city planners hadn't been very original in their name choices, but it did make it easy to explain the layout to newcomers. He strolled along Main Street, hoping he could find a public house that offered something appetizing. He had plenty of camping supplies, but a cooked meal was always preferable and he was pretty sure neither dragons nor dogs were well equipped for cooking.

As for himself, he could boil peas and make porridge, but his cooking skills were far below the level to which he was accustomed. For that matter, even the cooks at Roc's Roost weren't quite up to his father's daily fare, though they came close. His Aunt Ess hired the best she could find, but his dad was exceptional.

He stopped and asked a woman hauling water, "Excuse me, is there a good place to get something to eat here?"

The woman glanced at him with tired eyes. "Keep going up the street and you'll see a sign with a red crown on it. That's the Red Crown Inn and they do serve a simple stew at any hour of the day. If you show up near sundown, they also have roast meat on occasion, but it's still not as good as a home-cooked meal."

Oliver smiled. "You sound like my father."

"Your mother's a good cook?" asked the woman.

"Dad is," corrected Oliver. "Know a good cook who might be willing to share a meal with a stranger? I can pay."

"There's an alewife over this way. She doesn't usually sell food, but I hear she might have an extra place at her table today. Follow me. I'm hauling water there now," answered the woman.

"What's an alewife?"

She looked him up and down. "You must not be from Terabinia. Around here, some women make extra money by brewing ale and selling it to their neighbors. Today you're lucky. Gemma's got a cask ready, and her door is open."

Oliver nodded. "How do you know she's got extra food?"

The middle-aged woman shrugged, then lifted the wooden bar from her neck. "Take this if you're going to have me stand here answering questions." Oliver took the bar and set it across one shoulder, easily balancing the heavy water buckets. Then the woman motioned for him to follow. "The reason I know is because I'm Gemma. Pleased to meet you."

"Oh! Good to meet you," he said immediately.

"I'm not giving you a cheaper price for carrying the water," she returned. "You're lucky you ran into me."

He shook his head. "I wouldn't ask for that. I'll just be glad to eat good food."

Gemma grunted, then pointed to a house on the right-hand side of the road. Two makeshift tables had been cobbled together using wide boards laid across sections cut from a tree trunk. Three grey-bearded men sat at one of them already, sipping from wooden cups. "What took so long, Gemma?" called one of them, waving an empty cup.

The alewife walked over and took his cup. "I found a new customer, one that probably pays better than you, Harold."

"Now, don't be like that. You know I always pay. Heck, I'd even marry you if you gave me a second look. Then you wouldn't have to ask strangers to haul water for you," returned Harold.

Gemma smiled at him and replied without looking back, "You'd never pay if I married you, and then we'd both be broke." She glanced at Oliver. "Find a seat. You *do* have money, right?"

He lifted his coin purse and shook it. "I have coin, if the food is good."

"Pick a seat. I'll be back," she replied.

Oliver glanced at the empty table, but before he moved, one of the old men called out, "Sit with us and I'll stand you a cup of ale for news of wherever you came from." It wasn't an unusual offer. People everywhere wanted news, and travelers could often barter fresh stories for food, drink, or even a bed for the night. A traveler's tales were more valuable in villages and less frequented places, but Fernham seemed more isolated than most cities of its size, probably due to the recent troll disaster. He took a seat.

"Thanks," he told them, tipping his head and touching his brow, though he wasn't wearing a hat. "Not sure I've got anything worth telling, but I'll do my best."

"Don't stress over it, lad," said the man sitting directly across from him. "Gemma will give you as much as you can drink for two pennies."

A shout reached them from the house. "Not for him! That boy could drink all three of you under the table! I'm not in the business of losing money."

The man to Oliver's left was skinny and had a wind-worn appearance, while the one sitting on his right was heavier and mostly bald. Both were grey haired, and they started laughing at Gemma's words. The skinny one pointed at the man in the middle. "Damn! Gemm's got ears like a hawk! You shoulda kept your voice down Raf."

The one in the middle, presumably named 'Raf,' replied, "It's eyes like a hawk, Tom. Ears don't make no sense."

"More sense than eyes," said Tom.

"You can't hear with eyes," argued Raf. "Besides, maybe hawks have good hearing too. How do you know?"

The bald man to Oliver's right shook his head. "You're both fools." Then, he fixed his gaze on Oliver. "I'm Clive, that's Tom, and the one who tried to get you a good deal is Raf."

Oliver dipped his head again. "Oliver."

Raf replied first, "You're a real talker, aren't you, Oliver?"

"Not really," said Oliver apologetically.

"Well, where are you from?" asked Raf. "What are the roads like? See anything interesting out there?"

Having spent most of his life in Trendham, Oliver didn't bother trying to lie. He wasn't any good at it. "I came here from Bondgrad."

Tom leaned in, a serious expression on his face. "You're Trendish?" He looked at the others. "He's a spy!"

Everyone froze, and Oliver had no idea what to say, but Clive broke the tension a few seconds later. "They're just twisting your pubes, lad."

Oliver frowned. "What?"

"Having you for a laugh," clarified Clive. "Besides, half the new families in Fernham are Trendish immigrants. Nobody cares if you're a spy."

"I'm not a spy," he protested.

"Nobody gives a shit," said Raf. "You're too big to be a spy anyway. What did they feed you back in Bondgrad? You look like your mam bedded an ox to birth a giant like you."

His mouth opened slightly, but Oliver was unsure how to reply. Before he could think of a response, Tom piped up, "You'd best hope he don't have a temper, talkin' like that, Raf. The lad looks like a soldier if you ask me. Were you in the recent pissing match between the queen and the oligarchs?"

"Actually, I was at Karda," admitted Oliver, "but luckily they called it off before things could get bad."

"I heard the Stormking showed up and told 'em all to pack up and go home," interjected Clive. "Is that true, lad?"

Oliver nodded. "Pretty much, but..."

"Don't worry about offending us. We all owe a lot to the Stormking, those of us that survived the trolls," added Clive.

A cup appeared in front of Oliver, placed there by Gemma. "Let him talk if you want to learn anything," she chastened the men. "Half a penny a cup, or five pennies if you plan to drink a lot and don't want to keep count."

"That's hardly fair," complained Tom.

"He's the size of two of you put together—at least—not to mention young," snapped Gemma. "Stay out of it."

Feeling generous, Oliver pulled out a silver coin. "This enough?"

The alewife winked at him, the coin disappearing almost as quickly as it had appeared. "I'll bring your change when the food's ready."

As soon as she stepped away, Clive spoke up. "Back to the Stormking—how much did you see? Did he summon a storm? I heard the thunder was so loud it made ears bleed."

"Yes and yes," answered Oliver, taking his first sip. "I can try to describe it, but it was like nothing you've ever seen. Words don't really do it justice. Luckily, I was far enough away that the noise didn't hit me. But the soldiers trying to advance on the city suffered badly from it. A lot of them had their eardrums ruptured."

"Did he really attack the queen?" asked Raf.

"It wasn't really the queen," said Oliver.

"Yeah, yeah, we know, but still that must've taken some balls," responded the older man. "Hard to believe things didn't fall apart after that."

Oliver wasn't much of a storyteller, nor was he good at lying, but the basic events of that day were hardly a secret, so he just gave an honest account without going into anything beyond what he'd seen from the walls of Karda. There was nothing to be gained by mentioning his close and personal adventure fighting against the Black Duke or the elven fighters. They certainly didn't need to know about his close ties to both the Queen of Terabinia and the Stormking.

Gemma brought out a bowl of stew, and while it wasn't the best he'd had, it was good enough that he asked for a second helping. Cups of ale washed it down, and his hostess was good to her word that he could have as much as he wished. While Oliver felt relaxed and faintly tipsy at points, if he stopped drinking, the feeling faded quickly. The built-in antidote function his father had added to his tattoos prevented him from getting properly drunk.

He had only enjoyed alcohol on a few occasions, and the realization that he'd never be able to get properly drunk again made him feel a little sad. To maintain his faint buzz, he ordered cup after cup of ale, drinking them as quickly as he could manage.

"I stand corrected, Gemma," announced Tom, "you were right. Olly here drinks more than any two men I've ever seen in all my years."

Oliver belched and smiled, then his eyes focused on a newcomer approaching. The stranger walked down the street but was obviously heading for Gemma's door as his attention was on them. With a start, Oliver realized at the last moment that the man was an elf. He hadn't been paying attention, but the pointed ears and knife-edge features were plainly obvious.

"Lolly, you here for a drink?" asked Raf in a familiar tone.

The elf grimaced but shook his head. "I came to meet your new friend." His eyes moved to Oliver and then he added, "Lalleigh Glavenstren, are you enjoying Gemma's ale?"

Oliver nodded, but Tom answered first, "He's drunk gallons but it hasn't fazed him in the least!"

A strange vertigo swept over him as Oliver met the elf's eyes, but it passed after only a moment. Lalleigh frowned. "Where are you from?"

"Bondgrad," said Oliver. It felt odd that the elf had asked after his origin rather than his name. A sense of pressure made him rub the bridge of his nose. It felt as though he had a headache coming on.

Gemma stepped out, a look of faint concern on her features. "Do you want ale, Lalleigh?"

"Just a cup, Gemma. I brought wine," said the elf. He looked at Oliver. "Ever had elven firewine? I'm happy to share." The old men at the table perked up, but the elf shook his head at them. "I've only one bottle, so I thought I'd share with our guest."

"I've never tried it," lied Oliver, though he had indeed had it on a few occasions back at Roc's Roost. He drained his cup and handed it over. Lalleigh uncorked the bottle and filled it halfway.

"It's strong," explained the elf when Oliver raised one brow.

It was strong, which surprised him. The elven wine Oliver had tasted at Roc's Roost was light and sweet with a mild floral scent. The drink passing his lips now was strong and bitter, more similar to what he thought dwarven spirits might taste like, though he'd never tried any. Oliver tossed it back.

Lalleigh took a small sip, then offered the bottle. "More?"

He shrugged and held out his cup. Something about the elf irritated him, and though he didn't like the drink, he hoped it was expensive since it was obvious the newcomer meant to get him drunk.

"Is that a tattoo?" asked Raf, pointing at the side of Oliver's neck. Subtle lines ran from the collar of his tunic up behind his ears and on to his hairline; they continued unseen beneath his hair. Oliver nodded. "Never seen one like that," said the other man.

"Because you've never been anywhere, Raf," interjected Tom. Leaning forward, he stared at Oliver, then asked, "Are you a wardsman? I hear they're tattooed all over."

"I am," admitted Oliver, emptying his cup and holding it out for Lalleigh to fill again.

The elf obliged, a look of resignation on his face. "What brings a wardsman to Fernham? Seems suspicious after the recent conflict."

Oliver hadn't expected to use it, but he'd already prepared an answer to avoid having to improvise. "I'm traveling to Barrowden to visit family."

"You're from Terabinia?" said Lalleigh.

"I was born here, but we moved away when I was small."

The elf nodded, then looked ruefully at his empty bottle. "I've never seen someone drink so much. Does it run in your family?"

Oliver shrugged. "I've always been a little different." In truth, the strong spirits had made him lightheaded, but the feeling was fading fast already. It was interesting to think that he could win any drinking contest now, but he still wished there was some way to turn off the antidote functionality of his tattoos, or at least have them ignore alcohol. He'd never considered himself much of a drinker, but he'd like to have the option once in a while.

The conversation meandered for the next hour, and Oliver began pretending to be a little tipsy, even going so far as to stop asking for more ale. He felt a little bad for Gemma that he'd drunk so much of her ale already. Lalleigh left at some point, and as the sky grew steadily darker, Oliver decided he should probably do the same. He wasn't worried about getting lost at night, but he didn't want to worry his stepmother.

As he reached the city gate, he wasn't surprised to see Lalleigh waiting for him there. The elf was armed and armored, with a six-foot-long spear in one hand. He was flanked on either side by ten more armored warriors. Oliver was empty-handed, and the only weapon he'd brought was a modest belt knife meant for eating or general use. He'd left his mail back at the camp as well to avoid drawing attention. He nodded at Lalleigh.

"Lord Fernham would like to meet you," said the elf, an evil gleam in his eye.

"Is that so?" replied Oliver. "Seems sudden. Why didn't he come himself if it was so urgent?"

"It's not my place to question orders," said the elf with cold eyes.

Oliver felt a strange pressure in his head, and he knew without a doubt this time that the elf was attempting to use magic against him. He took two steps forward as the world flowed around him like a lazy river. Heart calm, Oliver reached out, bare-handed and slapped away the spearhead already driving toward his midsection. It was held by one of the elven warriors, one who apparently possessed extremely quick reflexes, for the others were just beginning to react.

Ordinarily, being unarmed and clothed in nothing but a simple tunic would mean a hopeless fight when facing multiple armored and lethally armed opponents. For a wardsman, the odds weren't as bad, though most wouldn't expect to do better than to make the enemy pay a steep price in blood. Oliver had no such concern—words no longer existed for him, and things such as doubt, fear, and hesitation were gone as well. He shifted direction, his third step pushing him toward the elf whose spear he'd just turned aside. Getting closer would complicate the angles of attack for the rest of his enemies.

With a fist that had become hard as iron, Oliver struck. He would have liked to target the elf's midsection, but the breastplate there would have broken his hand, regardless of his magical fortification. The neck would have been nice, but the gorget and helm made that impractical— in fact, striking someone in plate armor was typically a fool's errand no matter where you aimed—but Oliver didn't need to cut or stab, he merely needed someplace without a rigid plate in his way. None of this passed through his head, however; he acted without the inefficient trappings of conscious thought getting in his way. His fist found its own target, slamming into the gap beneath the elf's left arm. There was mail there, to prevent a dagger or spear from doing the same, but it wasn't meant to protect against the bludgeoning force of a mace.

Oliver didn't have a mace, of course, but his fist struck with the power of one. An audible crack resounded as ribs broke. Dodging another spear, Oliver pivoted around the warrior he'd just incapacitated. Whether the elf was dying or not hardly mattered—he wouldn't be fighting.

Ducking under a slow-moving sword blade, he pulled the spear shaft free of the wounded warrior's grip, then whipped it across the face of his closest foe. The elf flinched back instinctively, though there was no way such a slash would have endangered him. Sweeping the point past, then down, Oliver brought it back to catch the elf's foot as it lifted from the ground. As that foe crashed backward, he thrust the back end of the spear into one of the others, preventing the warrior from flanking him.

That was his moment to escape. Unencumbered and much more fleet of foot, they could never have caught up if he took the opportunity to slip through and run.

But Oliver was too powerful for that. The lion did not run before jackals, and the Stormking's son had little to fear from such weak opponents, armored or not. He'd fought elven warriors before. He knew them. He was too fast, too strong—and too dumb to do the wise thing.

He pretended to run, but only for a second, long enough to draw the closest warrior into a mistake. Oliver's new spear darted forward, sliding up across the top edge of the elf's breastplate and into the slim gap beneath the gorget. The mail stopped the point from penetrating, for Oliver hadn't used much force, but it was enough to bruise the throat. It might have even collapsed the windpipe, not that it mattered—the warrior fell back, choking and clawing at his neck. Oliver's second thrust was delivered to a different warrior. It struck with similar precision, but much more force, driving into the mail skirt that draped over the elf's hip. The point punched through the mail and padding to impale the elf just above the thigh plate and below the bottom edge of the breastplate.

The head was caught in the elf's mail, so Oliver abandoned the spear and zigged forward to put his shoulder into the warrior coming at him from the left side. Avoiding a rather skillful sword swing, Oliver stole the elf's misericorde from his belt, then overbalanced the foe, causing him to fall.

He didn't know what the elves called the long, narrow knife he held, but it was called a rondel by Terabinian knights and a misericorde by the Trendish military. The handle was simple, and it only had a small, circular guard. The blade was shaped like a foot-long needle with a triangular cross-section. The edges could cut, with enough effort, but it wasn't meant for that. It was a stabbing weapon, specifically designed to drive through mail and padding, provided there was enough weight behind it. Typically, it was the easiest weapon with which to dispatch a fallen knight in heavy armor. Fall on top of the foe and keep him down with the weight of his own armor, then drive the tip home through a gap. Popular spots included the neck, eye slits, groin, and the gap beneath the arms.

Oliver couldn't afford to grapple, though, but he didn't need to. With inhuman speed and strength, he could drive the metal spike home without bothering to stop his enemy's movements. Dancing forward, he wove in an out, dodging blades and spear points for tense seconds until he found his openings. Each time he spotted one, he would dip in too quickly for them to stop him, driving the rondel home with his left hand braced against the pommel.

Fire danced in his eyes, and joy filled his heart as he killed one after another. The armor made it challenging for him, and for that he was grateful.

"Cast your spell, damn it! Why is he still moving?" yelled one of the elves, one who was mere seconds from becoming the next victim.

"I've been trying!" screamed Lalleigh. "It's not working!"

"Then do something else! Kill him, for fuck's sake! Before—" the elven captain's words were cut off by a wet gurgling as Oliver drove the rondel through his aventail and into the side of his neck.

It caught on something, and Oliver released it rather than fight to withdraw it. Instead, he blocked an incoming sword with his left forearm while pulling the captain's rondel free from the elf's belt. The sword cut through his sleeve and bit into his forearm, spilling some of Oliver's blood for the first time since the fight had begun. It had been a solid blow, and if his skin hadn't been hardened, it likely would have sheared through bone and muscle instead of just creating a serious cut. Oliver brought his injured arm up, catching the elf's right elbow in his grip before taking a step to the side and driving his new weapon into the warrior's armpit.

Blood ran freely down his left arm, but the skin was already closing as Oliver roared and charged into his next opponent. There weren't many left, and it made him sad to think the battle might end too soon.

His feet sank into deep mud, and he fell forward, suddenly off balance. Lalleigh had finally switched tactics and was using earth magic.

"Is that the best you can do?" yelled one of the warriors. "Mud?"

"I'm a secretary! I wasn't trained for war!" replied Lalleigh, his voice tight with fear. "Get him while he's down."

"Don't you have an attack spell?"

"No!"

Oliver was dragging himself free of the mud, but he wasn't able to dodge or even turn. In a panic, he struggled to move more quickly, which only made matters worse. Searing pain struck as something slid into him from behind. Roaring, he pulled himself forward, until something hard struck the side of his head. The world reeled madly about as he continued to fight his way free, then everything went black.

CHAPTER 5

Selene sighed, consciously trying to release the tension that had built up while she worked. She'd been in the dragon body for almost two weeks, and the thing that frustrated her the most was the extra difficulty that created for her when she was spellcasting.

Creating a spell construct didn't have any particular physical requirements, but most mages started initially by creating them above one hand. With time and practice, they could do the same at any point close enough to the body, but mental habits were tough to change. Most of the bodies that Selene had inhabited were human, so the differences were insignificant, but the dragon body was so large that it made her feel as though she was casting spells while being trapped inside a haystack. The difference in limb count was also confusing, since dragons had six limbs rather than just four as humans did.

Despite the challenges, she had done her best to prepare the canine body Oliver had brought her. Over the past ten years she had become an expert not only in healing, but also its darker twin, necromancy. The apparently opposing disciplines were two sides of the same coin, though the dividing line between one and the other was far from being well defined. The long-standing taboo against necromancy had inhibited a lot of potential progress in the field of medical magic, something she had done a lot to correct since taking the throne in Terabinia. It was no stretch to say that Selene was likely the foremost living authority on the subject of both healing and necromancy. Well, perhaps not the *living* part.

The dog, formerly Sasha, had been thoroughly sterilized to stop any further decomposition. Selene had taken the extra step of removing the innards to simplify matters. If she had intended on using the body for a longer period, she would have retained them, restoring them to limited function, but that wasn't necessary in this case. She intended to discard the canine form within a few days at most.

No one appreciated the complexities that came with lichhood. Selene could possess almost any recently living body, but there were extensive considerations to be managed if she wanted to maintain a body for a lengthy period of time. A fresh body still functioned in most respects—the muscles retained the ability to operate for hours beyond the point of death—but older corpses were only marginally different than trying to possess a doll or some other inanimate object.

The only real difference between an old corpse, say a skeleton for example, and an inanimate object was the fact that she couldn't anchor her spirit in objects without a certain amount of preparation, whereas corpses retained a natural affinity for the spirit. That affinity decreased with time and decay, however, and a long-dead skeleton was only marginally better than a scarecrow.

Living bodies were the best, naturally, but they came with the added complication of a resident soul that would resist cohabitation. Even if the host volunteered, long-term possession put such a strain on the mind-body connection that they eventually died after a period of weeks or months.

Necromancy provided the best solution to the problem. A fresh body could be maintained in a state so close to life that the differences were academic. Organs could be made to function, metabolism continued, and normal processes such as eating and elimination of waste were not only possible but necessary. That level of maintenance was only possible with a body that had died within minutes, and it required extensive spellcasting to prepare and maintain a corpse in such a state. If she casually took over a dead body, it would become unusable in a day or two unless she took some time to repair it.

For Selene, freshness was a matter of real significance, for it directly impacted the nature of her existence, specifically her perception. Possessing a living body was a poignant reminder of when she had been truly alive, for she could then fully experience things like joy and pain, both physical and emotional. In a well-prepared and properly maintained dead body, she could get close to that, but it was never quite the same. Her emotions were muted, sensations were duller, and food lacked the same flavor it held for the living. What she could experience faded along a continuous spectrum the more decrepit the body was.

At the far end of the spectrum, when she retreated fully to her phylactery, she lost all sensation and became a creature of pure intellect. She could think, but not feel, and the choices and urgency of the living world became a distant concern. Selene could easily imagine losing interest in everything and watching centuries pass without boredom or concern if she allowed herself to remain in such a state. When she was in a living body, she sometimes had nightmares of falling into such a dull state and waking to find everyone she had known was dead and gone.

The dog's body would last her a day or two, but without the ability to eat (since she had removed its organs), it would gradually become less hospitable and more difficult to move. That was all right, though; she intended to claim a more suitable form at the first opportunity. *As long as I can avoid meeting any elven mages,* she thought wryly. An ordinary person, human or elf, would be relatively easy to possess, but magical practitioners were a different matter.

Selene wasn't comfortable admitting it to anyone, but her will was drastically weaker than it had once been. In life, she had completed the third compression, and her will had been considerably stronger than any except some of the other new third-order wizards, but after becoming a lich, she felt weak as a kitten. For living wizards, the link between mind, spirit, and body was natural and effortless. It was maintained by the living source, and that was also the reason compressing the source beyond the third compression was impossible—a certain fraction of the source's output was required to maintain the link between spirit and body, and—without it, separation, or death, was inevitable.

The enchantment binding Selene's soul to her phylactery substituted for the living source she had once had, but it was not without cost. Though it irrevocably anchored her spirit in the material world, it required a heavy investment of will to maintain. It wasn't something she was consciously aware of—the phylactery's enchantment took care of that—but it was still a price she paid. She had never directly contested another practitioner since her transformation, but she wasn't sure she still had the strength of will to overcome an ordinary sorcerer, much less even a first-order wizard.

Selene still had her skill, and the almost limitless turyn provided by the countless elementals she had inherited, but at her core she knew how weak she had become, and the knowledge made her feel ashamed. Whether she liked it or not, her father's influence still lived within her, and weakness of any kind was deeply abhorrent to her. Going by Grim Talek's example, it would be centuries or perhaps millennia before she approached her previous strength. In the meantime, her weakness was something to be hidden, and direct confrontations of will, such as attempting to possess another mage, were to be avoided at all cost.

Satisfied with her preparation, Selene took note of the darkness that had settled over the camp. Dusk had come and gone, giving way to full night, yet Oliver had not returned. *I told him to come back tonight. Did he think I meant at any time? Surely, he wouldn't want me to worry,* she thought.

Oliver hadn't mentioned any problems after his first foray into Fernham. Even if his tattoos were noticed, it shouldn't be an issue, and if they did create some hostility, the young warrior was too fast to be caught. Mentally, she reviewed what she knew of the enchantments tattooed on Oliver's skin and hidden within his body. She knew the basic functions most wardsmen had, and Will had told her about the changes and additions he had made. They'd talked long into the night about it, since some of the changes were built on Selene's innovations— research that had originally been meant for Terabinia's Iron Knights.

Will's son was one of a kind. Being naturally gifted, he hadn't needed the strength or speed enchantments that were foundational for most wardsmen. Instead, Will had used the exterior tattoos merely as a map of Oliver's body. The skin tattoos channeled and anchored magic from the more complex enchantment hidden within the young man's chest. He had shown Selene a large book detailing the enchantment, and she'd been amazed at the breadth and complexity of it.

She hadn't had a chance to study the methodology fully yet, but it all hinged upon an innovation that came from Will's brother-in-law, James Wellings. The university professor had come up with a way to use a new device he termed the luxpress to miniaturize enchanting runes, enabling vastly larger texts to be put in areas with limited physical space. Sophisticated magical jewelry such as rings and broaches had been the first use for the new technology, but Will had used it on a metal plate that he'd implanted within his son's chest.

The plate served both as a physical barrier to protect Oliver's heart, and an ideal place to hide the extensive miniaturized script that replaced the crude enchantment regular wardsmen had. A good portion of it was directly copied from the enchantments Selene had designed, originally with the hope of incorporating them into the armor of Terabinia's elite soldiers. Those efforts had been unsuccessful in armor, but they had worked when tattooed directly on and within the flesh. Will had added other things as well, a new type of defensive magic based on phase spiders, sensory improvements, and a few other tricks, but the bulk of what was inscribed was the healing enchantments Selene had designed.

She stared at the dog's corpse, reluctant to use it. Her stepson had to be safe. His body was a miracle of magic, making Oliver a combination of warrior and artifact. It would take much more than a random fight or bad luck to keep him from returning safely.

It was late, probably close to midnight. He would have returned if he could, and she knew there was no chance of Oliver getting drunk and passing out somewhere. The enchantments in his body made that impossible. Something had happened.

Relaxing her hold on the dragon, Selene fought against the sudden pull of her distant phylactery. Unless she retained her focus on her present location, it would instantly draw her back to where it was stored in Cerria, and if that happened, she would have no easy way back. She quickly moved into the canine body, claiming it as her own. The dead flesh was far different than her own, but it accepted her, and once her hold on it was established, the pull of the phylactery faded into the background of her awareness.

Her vision changed. It was better in the dark than human eyes but wasn't quite the equal of the dragon eyes. In the daytime, she suspected it would be worse than human or dragon eyes, which excelled at color perception, but in the current low light conditions, canine vision was acceptable. Everything was louder now, and her sense of smell was so great it was positively distracting. She had thought the dragon's sense of smell was acute, but the dog's nose was on an entirely different level. *This will take some getting used to,* she realized.

To begin with, she did *not* like her own smell. She smelled dead. The spells she had used to clear up unpleasant odors were calibrated to human standards. As a dragon, she had noticed a difference, but with a canine nose, it was both obvious and uninviting. Over the past ten years, she had noticed that dogs and cats avoided her well-preserved human form, and now she knew why. As queen it had been an easy problem to deal with; once her subjects learned she wasn't fond of animals they kept them away from her.

Now that she effectively *was* a dog, the problem was more immediate. Selene resolved to experiment with canine bodies in the future. It should be possible to recalibrate her spells to get rid of the unpleasant smell; she would just have to perfect them while in dog form. For now, she had more pressing concerns. Standing, she went to Oliver's pack and stored it within her limnthal. His armor was inside, and assuming she found him in good health, he would probably want it. Then she padded into the forest, following the scent that she now recognized as that of her stepson.

She loped through the underbrush with an easy pace that ate up ground more quickly than would have ever been possible as a human. The dog's body was built to cover distance and difficult terrain, and she arrived at the outskirts of Fernham in a fraction of the time it would have taken a human to walk. Oliver's trail was obvious to her nose, and she followed it around the city and into the cemetery. It was strongest there, near a freshly disturbed grave and a small stone building. That fit with her stepson's story about how he had acquired her current body.

Moving on, Selene circled the area once more, finding several more areas with Oliver's scent. Two were probably related to his comings and goings, but a third, and importantly the strongest, indicated he had entered the city through one of the gates. *Just as he said he would,* she observed.

The trail led into the city, but a more interesting scene drew her attention before she got very far beyond the gate. Two men were sweeping up sand that looked to have been recently scattered across the cobblestone roadway. Her nose picked up an overpowering smell of blood. Men had bled and died there, and Oliver's scent was mixed in with that of sweat, armor, and—elves. *It wasn't men that died, but elves,* she corrected herself mentally. Looking beyond the cleanup crew, she spotted a wagon thirty feet farther down the road. A man stood beside it, but the quality of his clothing and the strangeness of his body smell informed her that it was no man, but another elf. The man's ears were obscured by a simple wool hat, but his fine-boned features and the way he stared at the men cleaning the road gave him away. *That would be the one in charge of the cleanup.*

Padding closer, Selene smelled the stench of blood, death, and metal in the wagon. Beneath a canvas tarp, the bodies had been piled. How convenient.

The elf beside the wagon took notice of her and moved to shoo her away. "Beat it, bitch! You're too late if you thought you'd get an easy meal. Filthy mongrel."

Selene froze, debating her choices as the elf interposed himself between her and the wagonload of flesh. The simplest course would be to take the elf, but if the man had any training at all, she might fail, resulting in an abrupt trip back to her phylactery in Cerria. The other option was slightly messier, but it guaranteed success. Leaping forward, Selene sailed toward the bed of the wagon. Cursing, the elf tried to kick her but missed.

She was past him, and with a second leap, she made it into the bed of the wagon. In the meantime, the wagon's guardian had drawn a truncheon from his waist and was now swinging it down at her. She ignored it, already preparing to leave her body. Dull pain shot through her as the club smashed into her shoulder, breaking bones and ruining her ability to run.

She didn't care, though. The pain was temporary and disappeared the moment she released her form and slid into one of the dead elven warriors. A little time to pick and choose would have been nice, but the body she chose at random turned out to be in remarkably good shape. After a few seconds securing her hold on the body, she examined the wounds from within—a few broken ribs and a bruised heart. Something hard had struck the elf beneath one arm, and the power of the blow had likely shocked his heart into failing. Aside from the broken ribs, there was nothing really wrong with it.

The elf who had struck her was lifting the dog's body out of the wagon. Selene remained still beneath the tarp. Once she was fairly certain he had turned away, she restarted the heart and repaired the broken ribs. Doing so wasn't necessary, but keeping the body as close to normal as possible meant she would need to use less turyn to animate it. A beating heart and flowing blood meant cell function and metabolism would continue, and that meant the body's muscles could supply all the energy necessary for movement. Fundamentally, it was the difference between using magic to move the limbs or simply needing to tell a living body what to do.

The body was dead in the sense that it no longer had a source and a soul, but physically the flesh had little wrong with it. Keeping it functioning made everything easier, and there was no one in the world with more expertise on doing just that—except Grim Talek of course.

Taking a slow, careful breath, Selene was pleased with her acquisition. It wasn't perfect—perfect would be taking a truly living body, and second best would be taking hold of a body in the first seconds after death—but this was close. The elven warrior had died just hours ago, and there wasn't much in the way of tissue damage that she couldn't fix.

Bonus, it was the body of a strong, fit warrior, and it was already armored. Weapons were piled up on one side of the wagon, meaning she wouldn't need to look far to arm herself either. She smiled beneath the canvas. Killing the elf overseeing the cleanup would be simple, but first she needed information.

If she had been dealing with humans, she might have considered sitting up and pretending to have been merely wounded rather than dead, but dealing with elves meant language and accent would be a problem. She had lived among the elves for a year, but that had been over a decade ago. Despite dealing with elves as queen, her fluency in their language was far from perfect and her accent would be a dead giveaway.

That might not have been a problem if the body was truly alive, since she could access memories of living hosts and borrow instinctive skills, but her current body's brain had deteriorated too much for that to be possible. Given time she could still dig through some of its memories, but it would be slow and there was no chance of borrowing something as sophisticated as language skills. *Brains are always the first thing to lose function,* she sighed mentally. The gut was the first to decay, but the brain would begin losing information and function within minutes of death.

So, her best choice was to wait and listen. Her proficiency in elven was more than sufficient for that. Soon the humans would be done with their work and the wagon would be taken—somewhere. She wasn't sure what elven burial customs were. None of them had died in Terabinia while she had been dealing with them diplomatically, and while quite a few had perished during the brief conflict with Trendham, she hadn't been around to see how they dealt with the aftermath.

As far as she knew, they might take the wagon straight to the cemetery and dig a mass grave. Alternatively, they might take the bodies to Fernham's keep, preserve them with magic, and ship them home.

Half an hour passed while she quietly worked on her new body. She was careful not to do anything overly noticeable, since she wasn't sure if the elf nearby was turyn sensitive or not. In truth, her work might even be a waste of time, since there was a fair chance she'd be switching again before too long, but she had nothing else to do. Eventually, she heard the elf climb into the driver's seat while the two humans who had been cleaning the street got into the back close to where she lay. Soon, the wagon began rolling away.

Much to her relief, they headed toward Lord Fernham's keep rather than out to the cemetery. She wished the elf would discuss things with his helpers, but the humans apparently weren't worth his time. Oliver's body wasn't in the wagon, so she had high hopes that he'd been taken prisoner.

A short while later, the wagon came to a stop, and the elf driving it jumped down before issuing orders to the two human workers. "Stay here. I must consult Strasyn. When he's ready I'll be back, and you can help me bring them in one at a time."

"Yes, sir," answered one of the men, and then Selene heard nothing but silence for several minutes. Eventually, she heard the man speak again to his coworker, "Can you believe this shit?"

"I heard he wasn't even armed," said the other man.

"He was a wardsman."

"Was? They brought him in alive."

"You think he'll stay that way for long? Better for him if he was already dead."

Selene listened to their chatter for several minutes but learned little more. She needed specifics—most importantly Oliver's location—but the men didn't seem likely to mention that detail. Gently pulling at the tarp, she got one corner down far enough to see, then cast a sleep spell on the two men. Their bodies swayed, and then the two sat down abruptly before falling over.

She sat up slowly and looked around. The wagon was in a walled courtyard, presumably a courtyard within Fernham Keep. The inside of a gate stood ten yards distant, and an armsman stood guard near it, but he wasn't paying attention to the wagon, or its suddenly sleeping stewards. Wincing at the loudness of her armored body, Selene eased herself out of the body pile and climbed carefully out.

Her sword belt had gotten tangled and twisted, so she took a moment to straighten it and get it properly oriented. The scabbard was empty, and she noticed there was also an empty dagger sheath. A quick rummage through the weapons in the bed of the wagon found suitable replacements. She felt awkward during the search, for the helm she wore restricted her vision somewhat, and she was forced to raise the visor if she wanted to see anything in the vicinity of her waist. It was tempting to remove the helm altogether, but that would have required unbuckling at least one strap, and that would have meant removing her gauntlets first, since she couldn't manage such a task without being able to feel properly.

All in all, the armor made her feel awkward and clumsy. Now that she was on her feet, it felt fine since the weight was well distributed and her new body was strong, but doing anything that required manual dexterity greater than drawing a blade would be difficult.

Looking around, she oriented herself and headed toward the main keep. It was relatively small, meant to house only Lord Fernham, his family, and a few select servants. The keep was roughly sixteen yards in width and had been designed as a broad central tower with three slightly taller square towers equally spaced in a triangular arrangement around it. The main body of the keep was thirty yards in height, and the square towers that framed it stood another four yards above the roof of the central keep. The courtyard that surrounded it was circular and lacked any subdivisions. The outer wall had been badly damaged during the troll attack, and it was visually evident which sections had been repaired in recent years, since the stone was of a slightly different color and the mortar was much newer.

Most of the soldiers who protected the keep were housed in the barracks that were built against the outer wall. The main kitchen, storerooms, a stable, and various other necessaries were built against the rest of the curtain wall, between the towers.

All of this meant that the central keep was primarily a residence. It was five stories tall, and the upper two floors were where Robert Fernham and his family lived. The lower floors and the outer keep towers housed rooms for servants, a chapel dedicated to worship of the Mother, and an audience chamber for court functions. Thanks to the compact design, most heavy goods were stored in the outer buildings, other than a certain amount of food. Because of that, the main entrance didn't need to be large, since nothing large was transported in and out. It was elevated ten feet above the courtyard, and reaching it meant climbing a small stone staircase.

That fact alone was the main reason Count Fernham and his family hadn't been eaten by trolls—as his soldiers and most of the rest of Fernham's population had been—the human-sized door had been elevated and easily defensible once the trolls had breached the courtyard. That defense was improved when the trolls, in their fury, had destroyed the stairs and the stone landing in front of the door. Only a few dozen people had been within the keep at that time, and most of them weren't armsmen, but the trolls had sought easier targets after finding the keep too difficult to quickly enter.

As queen, Selene had been told the story by Count Fernham himself once things had settled down. She hadn't personally visited the keep since before her ascension to the throne, but she still had a rough idea of the internal layout. Climbing the stairs, she found the door at the top closed but unlocked. Given the guards at the outer gate, it might even be unguarded.

Sure enough, after pushing it open, she found the bottom hall was busy with activity, but the people moving back and forth were all servants. Several of them gave her strange looks, probably because of the closed visor. In Cerria, her guards wore open-faced helms when on duty, and the knights removed their helms when within the walls—if they bothered to wear full armor at all.

Selene caught one of the servants by the arm as he started to pass by. "Where is Lord Fernham? I have news."

"He and Lord Strasyn are with the prisoner, milord." The servant dipped his head politely. When Selene released him and started to the left, toward the stairs leading down, he spoke up again. "Not the cellar, upstairs. He's in the cell on the second floor."

She silently cursed her mistake. She'd forgotten that Fernham didn't have a dungeon below. The city had a jail, and Robert Fernham wasn't the sort of lord to regularly keep personal prisoners. She headed for the stairs, but the servant stopped her again.

"Not the main stairs, the ones next to the kitchen. That way," he told her, a puzzled expression on his face.

Damn it. Selene glanced at the room. The others had all paused to watch and listen. With a sigh, she cast another sleep spell, putting several of them to sleep. She had to repeat the spell twice more to get the rest. The main floor was now littered with sleeping servants, thirteen when she counted. She went back to the door she had entered through and put the bar down to keep anyone else from coming in and discovering what she'd done. *At this point, I'm committed to incapacitating everyone else I find within the walls,* she observed silently.

With that in mind, she took the cellar stairs anyway, to see if anyone was below. She discovered two children playing and put them to sleep as well. Then, she went back up and explored the kitchen area until she found the small stairwell leading up. Since the kitchen was built into one of the square portions of the outer towers, it was likely that the stairwell led up into an isolated room. *Or a private prison cell.*

She heard voices as she climbed the steps, confirming her suspicion. "Who sent you?" demanded a harsh voice. A few seconds later, she heard a pained groan that sounded like Oliver. "I'll keep cutting until you tell me."

Selene picked up her pace, though she had to be careful not to fall on the narrow stairs. A second voice commented, this time in the elven tongue, "He heals like a troll. Have you ever seen magic like that outside of a regeneration potion? Are the tattoos doing that?"

"Possibly, though I can't see how. They're too simple for something like this."

"Cut off his fingers. Let's see if they grow back."

Selene took the remaining steps two at a time, and when she reached the top, there was no door, the stairs terminated in a ten-by-ten room that was subdivided by a steel grate with a door in it. That door was open, and within the crude cell, Oliver was chained to one wall. His clothes had been stripped away, and fresh blood ran down his chest and legs. More blood had dried on his skin in various places.

Two elves stood within, one holding a small but obviously sharp implement, while the other was richly dressed and obviously giving the orders. They both turned to see who had just entered. The elven lord's face took on a glad expression as he saw the design on the breastplate Selene wore. "Thalonyr! They told me you were slain."

The air was turbulent with turyn, and by the way it moved around the two elves, she was sure that both were wizards of some degree, so she didn't dare try a magical attack, much less attempting to possess one of them. They probably expected her to reply in elven, and her accent was unlikely to be convincing, so she lifted the visor and uttered a dry croak while pointing to her throat.

The noble elf opened his arms as if to embrace her, but Selene coughed and bent at the waist as though something pained her, using the movement to hide her hand as she drew the dagger from her belt. She straightened after a second, to accept his welcome, then drove the point forward, angling up. It struck the elven lord just below the sternum and went on to pierce first a lung and then the heart. Her victim let out a strangled cry as he started to collapse.

She didn't bother removing the dagger. Instead, she released the handle and drew the sword before turning and slashing the second elf who was only just registering what had happened. The blow was ill-aimed and cut deeply into the man's right arm rather than anything vital, but she remedied that with a frenetic flurry of swings. The torturer tried to ward the blows with his arms, so the next few strikes chopped deeply into them, causing him to bleed profusely. Her following swings were lower, catching his thighs until the damage caused him to fall.

The elf screamed the entire time, until she finally managed to get the point against his chest and drive it home, skewering his liver and one lung. The man's screams grew wet and lost much of their volume. After the third and fourth thrusts, he grew silent entirely. Selene took a moment then to stab the elven lord a few more times—just to be sure. When she looked up, she saw Oliver watching her warily.

"Who are you?" he asked, lifting his head to study her.

Despite the seriousness of the situation, or perhaps because of it, she responded in an unusual fashion. Selene barked. "Woof!"

Oliver stared at her, unable to reconcile the sight of an elven knight panting and pretending to be a dog, but at last his brain kicked into gear. "Your Majesty?"

Selene winked. "I'd prefer you use my name unless I'm holding court. We've been over this already."

"Selene?"

"You didn't think I'd stay a dog forever, did you?" she replied, but she didn't wait for an answer. "How did you wind up in this mess?"

Somewhat embarrassed, Oliver hung his head. "Would you believe someone slipped something into my ale?"

"No," she answered instantly. "I know precisely how a good portion of your tattoos work, particularly the healing and poison prevention portions. You're even worse at lying than your father." She graced him with a crooked smile. "Besides, you left a pile of dead elves in the street. That's not something I'd expect if you were somehow drugged and unconscious."

Oliver's eyes grew wide with alarm. "They're coming!" he hissed.

She hadn't heard anything yet, but she knew Oliver's hearing was enhanced. Knowing she didn't have much time, she retrieved her dagger, then placed her sword in the noble elf's hand. "What are you doing?" demanded her stepson. "Set me free. They'll be here in less than a minute!"

Selene shook her head. "Even if I had the keys in hand already, it would take that long just to start unlocking your chains. I'm not going to risk a fight with you naked and chained to a wall. I'll handle this my way." Lifting the dagger, she opened her visor and pressed the point into her mouth, driving it slowly back until the point pierced the back of her throat. She was careful to avoid hitting the large blood vessels there, nor did she go too deep. It wasn't as if she could kill herself that way, and she could easily repair her flesh, but too much damage would impair the efficiency of her body and make using it more work.

Oliver watched her with horrified eyes as she slumped to the floor near the stairs, spitting blood from her mouth to cover her chin and add to the effect.

Another elf and three human guards wearing mail hauberks stormed into the room. The elf saw Selene's body first, then turned and spotted the dead noble. "Lord Strasyn!" He glanced around the room, muttering, "What the hell happened here?" The elf's gaze turned to the prisoner chained against the wall. "Explain this!"

As soon as their backs were turned, Selene studied the distribution of her foes. To her disappointment, she wouldn't be able to easily leap up and stab the elf. He was too far away, and the sound of her rising to her feet would give him and the armsmen too much warning. She considered putting the humans to sleep, but the elf had the obvious aura of a magic user—she needed to handle him first lest he stop her spell from taking hold.

Wasting no time, she changed her plan. Letting out a gurgling moan, she reached up and pulled feebly at the dagger lodged in her throat.

Her eyes rolled dramatically while she pulled the blade free. "He's still alive!" exclaimed one of the armsmen.

The elf's eyes widened, and he quickly knelt beside Selene. Speaking in elven, he reassured her, "I'm going to heal your throat, Thalonyr. Don't try to talk yet." The elf's eyes went wider still when she took the blade she'd just removed from herself and jerked it upward. The point struck the elf under the chin and went into the back of his neck.

The wound looked fatal, but whether it was or not was an academic question as she jerked the steel from side to side before withdrawing the blade and climbing to her feet. One of the human guards shrieked in terror as he fell back against the wall, but the others retained enough discipline to draw their weapons and attack.

Selene didn't bother trying to fight them as a warrior. With the elf out of the way she resorted to simple magic. Force-lances would have been faster, but it had been years since she'd seriously practiced battle magic, and she'd lost the ability to reflex cast the spell. Elemental water spells had always been her favorite, though, and she was still more than capable of using several of those spells without needing a spell construct. With a thought, she created a circular water blade from the ample moisture (provided by all the spilled blood) and sent it scything into the armsmen. They still got several sword strikes in, but the elven armor on her arms was enough to stop the cuts as she lifted them to protect her head.

The armsmen did not fare as well against her water-blade. The water within the circular formation was spinning at incredible speeds, and it sliced through the hardened leather that was guarding their lower arms and throats. The iron mail that covered their torsos and upper arms was another matter, but losing an arm at the elbow was still a quick way to bleed to death, and decapitation was even quicker. The fight went on for a little over a minute until she had removed their ability to fight or walk. Three were still conscious as they bled to death, and they continued to scream and cry for help until she took the time to cleanly remove their heads with her spell.

The floor was covered with blood, and red spattered the walls on every side, giving the place the feel of an abattoir. Selene moved to the elven lord, Strasyn, who had been in charge when she arrived, and quickly built a specialized spell construct before using the spell on his head. With that done, she created another water-blade and removed the lord's head before storing it in her limnthal.

"What are you doing?" asked Oliver. "I'm still chained."

"Gathering information," she replied without looking up from her work. Once the head was safely stored, she created a force-wall across the doorway that opened onto the stairs. It was the only entry to the room. Satisfied that they couldn't be easily interrupted, she began searching the bodies. Strasyn was first, but other than a purse full of coin (which she stored in her limnthal), he had nothing of interest. The keys turned out to be on the belt of the elven torturer, and after trying several, she found the one that unlocked the manacles around Oliver's wrists and ankles.

Finally free, Oliver rubbed at the skin of his wrists while surveying the blood and bodies that surrounded them. "How does taking a grisly trophy count as information gathering?"

Selene gave him a rueful smile. "Once upon a time, the word *trophy* quite literally meant taking someone's head as a souvenir." She waited, but Oliver didn't reply, so she answered his question instead of dragging things out any further. "There are necromantic spells that can deliver answers from a fresh corpse. A living necromancer could use them to learn quite a bit from the recently dead, but given the special state of my existence, I can do better than that. The spell I cast will preserve the brain. Later, when we aren't battling to maintain our freedom, I can possess the head and explore the elf's memories in a more direct fashion."

The look of disgust on Oliver's face said everything, but he kept his words to himself. Selene produced his pack and gestured for him to open it and put the armor on.

"Shouldn't we make haste? It's going to take a few minutes to get into my mail," he told her.

Selene shrugged. "They probably know we're here. We might as well finish what you started. For that, I'd rather you wear armor, for the sake of safety." Oliver raised one brow, so she continued, "Your father is going to kill me when he finds out I let you fight ten armored knights barehanded and wearing nothing more than simple clothes."

Oliver pulled out his mail, wrinkling his nose at the familiar stench of iron, sweat, and leather. "You know, I *did* defeat them. If I'd just used my phase spider defense there at the end, they'd never have caught me."

"Which is why your armor includes a steel cap," she reminded him. "You're lucky they knocked you out rather than cutting your foolish head from your shoulders."

Oliver glanced away, suddenly sheepish. "I think they did run me through with something."

A worried look crossed Selene's features, and she grabbed Oliver's arms to stop him as he started pulling on his gambeson. "Wait. I need to give you a thorough examination."

"Don't we need to hurry?"

Selene's eyes were grim and determined when she answered him. "I'm more concerned about your wellbeing than how many people I'll have to kill when we leave. Any elves still in Terabinia have forfeited their lives by remaining after my edict of expulsion." Silently, she added, *If there's anything wrong with him that I can't fix, Will may never forgive me.*

CHAPTER 6

Selene spent nearly ten minutes checking and rechecking Oliver's body with spells meant to reveal hidden problems and injuries, but she found nothing wrong. Even the entry and exit points were difficult to find as the healing enchantments built into his tattoos worked so close to perfectly that only the faintest of lines could be seen from his most recent cuts. The scars were so fine, they would probably disappear entirely in a matter of months.

She couldn't help but feel a great deal of pride in the results. In person, she performed such healing just as well, but to create a fixed enchantment capable of such precision work over the entirety of a person's skin—that was a different matter entirely. In large part, that was due to her design of the original enchantment, but it was greatly aided by the topological advantage the tattoos provided, enabling the magic to 'know' exactly what area it was working on. Most non-healers didn't appreciate how specific good healing spells needed to be when it came to what was being healed.

In Oliver's case, the enchantment was designed to handle skin, fascia, muscle, and bones; and it did so by utilizing a small library of spells meant for hundreds of specialized tasks. As she had originally created it, the enchantment was to be engraved on the interior surfaces of a knight's armor, but it had failed for two main reasons. The first was that they were unable to miniaturize the runes enough to fit within the available space, and the second reason was that the armor wasn't actually physically a part of the wearer.

James' luxpress had solved the space problem and had done so well enough that the entire thing was made to fit on a single plate implanted behind Oliver's ribs and in front of his heart. Will had solved the second problem by redesigning the enchantment to integrate with the tattoos that covered Oliver's body. Selene had been skeptical at first, since making even minor changes to such a complex enchantment was a major task for even advanced artificers, but the proof was before her eyes now.

Oliver's skin and bones had healed so well that most would think he'd used a regeneration potion.

While the tattoo enchantment's healing was not *quite* as perfect as regeneration, it had several advantages over a regeneration potion. First, it was always on and would work whether Oliver was awake or unconscious. Second, it was vastly more energy efficient and didn't exhaust the user—Oliver could continue fighting even while he healed from small wounds. Third, it didn't carry the risk of tumorous growth in the way that potions did.

There were some disadvantages too, though. Oliver's tattoos couldn't be designed to handle the infinite number of ways a person might be injured. While it could handle skin and muscles (including the heart), it would do little to save him if his vital organs were damaged. Brain, liver, spleen, kidneys—direct injury to his organs could kill her stepson as easily as anyone else, and depending on the injury, it might not be immediately noticeable.

In this case, he'd been lucky. Something sharp had passed completely through without touching his vitals. His intestines had been damaged, but the fascia portion of the enchantment had resealed them, and the blood-cleanse portion had kept him from developing a fatal infection. If the blade had passed through his kidneys it might have been otherwise, though it was early enough that she could probably have fixed that herself.

She let out a sigh of relief, and Oliver interpreted that as a sign that all was well. "See? I told you I was fine."

She gave him a stare meant to nail him to the wall. "Listen carefully," she said, placing her hands on his belly, "anything that passes through here could kill you. Your tattoos can't fix everything. Your organs, and your brain"—she rapped a knuckle against his skull—"anything that hurts those could kill you."

Oliver started shrugging into his gambeson and mail byrnie once more. "It seems a little odd that you're more worried about my safety than your own," he commented. "You said you needed a bodyguard."

Selene shrugged. "I'm immortal, so my needs are different. I can't really be hurt, but I'm a lot weaker than almost anyone realizes—even your father. What I really need is your strength, and you need to be hearty and hale for that."

He cinched his main belt tightly at the waist, then picked up his sword belt. "You just invaded a keep and slew a considerable number of men, and you think you're *weak*?"

"Compared to almost any living wizard, yes, I am. I might be stronger than one who hasn't undergone any compressions, but I'm not confident in that assertion. Elven mages are all older and experienced. They're guaranteed to be stronger, and I suspect they do some degree of source compression, but no one really knows. I had to pick my targets carefully to rescue you," she explained.

Oliver frowned. "Well, if any of them are like my dad"—he shrugged for effect—"we're screwed. I couldn't do much to someone like that."

"We have a unique combination of gifts," countered Selene. "Plus, I'm sneaky. Trust me, we can handle this, and as far as I know, none of the elven mages are on par with your father. If they were, they would have killed the dragon themselves instead of fleeing all those years ago."

Someone's head appeared coming up the stairs, but the newcomer quickly ducked back down and retreated. "It's going to be harder for me to outrun them once we get outside. The weight of the mail saps my endurance."

She smiled. "Oh, we're not running. Since we've made a good start, we should finish the job and clear out this rat's nest."

He frowned, "You mean…"

Selene nodded. "We kill them all."

He gaped. "Everyone?"

She sighed. "I meant the elves." Oliver looked at the three dead humans that lay around them, and she added, "I'm not perfect. Would you rather I left you chained up?"

"No."

"They're gathering down below, and there's at least one mage with them. I'm sure they're preparing a trap, so don't be squeamish when we get started. We'll kill all the elves and try to minimize how many humans get hurt, but don't try to be too careful and get yourself killed by hesitating. Is that clear?" Oliver nodded, and she continued, "So this is what we're going to do…"

***

Elven knights and human armsmen encircled the stair entrance on the first floor, and the elves had been protected with quick spells that would prevent possession and more importantly, sleep spells. The caster stood back and was hidden out of sight behind the corner leading to the outside entrance. It wasn't much of a trap, but it was thoroughly practical and probably more than enough to give them serious trouble if they tried to come down via the stairs.

Selene had used an eye plucked from one of the dead men to scout the room below. She hadn't possessed it, but had instead used an old necromancy spell to cause it to float and send back visions of whatever it could see. It had worked well up until someone had noticed it, and then the elven mage had dispelled the magic animating it. He'd also seized control of the turyn within the keep, making it difficult for her to cast anything else, aside from force spells.

That necessitated altering her original plan a little. Selene had intended to use her water-blade spell to cut a hole in the heavy wooden beams that formed the floor beneath their feet, allowing Oliver to quickly drop into the midst of the enemy. Force-lances were great for shattering stone, but battering through ten-inch wooden beams would require far too many castings since wood was more elastic, and since she couldn't reflex cast the spell anymore, the time required to do it would negate any element of surprise.

Glancing around the room, Selene's eyes fell on the hearth. It wasn't a full hearth, merely a sheltered opening into the chimney leading up from the kitchen hearth below. On other floors, there would be a place to build a fire that vented into the same chimney, but the prison room only required enough of an opening to borrow the minimum heat from below to keep its occupants from freezing to death in the winter. An iron grate was secured across the front to keep someone from falling into the chimney itself. Escaping that way would be pure foolishness since the main hearth below was kept ablaze year-round.

She pointed at the grate, and Oliver unsheathed his enchanted shortsword. She shook her head. "Let me. You be ready to jump down the instant it's clear so we can surprise them."

Studying it, she didn't see any signs of weakness; the four corners of the iron grate were solidly mortared into the wall, and it hadn't rusted through anywhere. Breaking it free from the mortar was probably the best method, but if the force was applied from within the room, it would push the metal against the stone. A better choice would be pulling it into the room, or pushing from the inside of the chimney. After a moment's thought, she selected an adjustable force-sphere spell. Assembling the spell construct was a matter of seconds, and then she cast the spell, placing it just on the other side of the grate before she started expanding it. As it swelled, it put pressure on the metal grate, and seconds later, it popped free with a loud metal crack and flew across the small room to smash into the far wall.

He'd already re-sheathed his sword and hooked his buckler onto his belt, so without a word, Oliver encased himself in a shimmering silver defensive layer and dove feet-first into the chimney. He dropped into the fire below, kicking aside two simmering pots and a wide metal spit that held them up. Orange embers and yellow sparks flew outward, giving the impression that a silver demon had just emerged from some infernal pit.

The sound of the upstairs grate breaking had given the warriors below some warning, so they weren't caught unaware, but it hardly mattered. At least a dozen crossbows fired, and while a few missed, most hit solidly as he leapt out of the fire. The shimmering silver magic that covered his skin stopped them all.

The men holding spears were still repositioning, but a few still managed to bring their points in line, not that it did them any good. Oliver had his feet under him now, and he spun in place as he drew his shortsword and took the buckler from his belt into hand. Most of the points missed, and those that did strike true failed to penetrate.

With his defensive magic up, in an enclosed room, there wasn't much hope for his enemies. He had weaknesses—in particular, elemental air spells could strip his protection from him—but it was doubtful that the sole caster in the room knew that, or knew the spells that might save them from him. Their only chance lay in Oliver exhausting his turyn, which wasn't likely in a short fight. Failing that, the only option would be to ensnare him, or weigh him down under sheer weight of numbers.

Oliver knew that as well, but he didn't bother wasting time and energy killing those already within his reach. He was surrounded, and though his strength was greater than those around him, avoiding a grapple was paramount for his success. Trusting his magical defense, Oliver did the one thing he'd been cautioned many times never to do in battle—he leapt into the air.

With their incredible speed and agility, it was natural for wardsmen to want to leap over their enemies, and quite often the surprising move might pay off, but the reality was that it was usually a foolish and dramatic way to court death. Once in the air, a wardsman could no longer dodge or change direction; he was stuck following a set path until his feet were once again on the ground. The iron-body transformation, even with armor on top of it, wasn't enough protection against spears and crossbow quarrels to prevent serious injury.

But Oliver's defensive magic was a significant change in that equation. He sailed up and over the heads of half a dozen men, holding his sword and buckler ahead of him in his hands. His body was stretched out as he passed the top of his arc, and then he pulled his arms back slightly and tucked his head, falling into a somersault that brought him rolling to his feet halfway across the room. A mace slammed into his chest before he got his bearings, sending him falling sideways, but other than the shock of the blow, Oliver was unhurt.

He feinted in the direction he'd come from, acting as though he meant to jump again, then jerked around to run for the entrance where the caster was still hiding just out of view. Catching the guards on that side of him off-guard, Oliver slipped between two, shoving them off-balance, then tripped the man behind them. Another heavy blow slammed into his back, but he went with the momentum and fell forward, rolling over the man he'd just tripped. It had only been a few scant seconds since he'd emerged from the hearth, but he was close to his goal.

The sounds of more fighting arose behind him as Selene emerged from the stairs to engage the men who had initially been waiting for them there. Unable to use most of her magic, and unschooled in combat, her entry to the fight was a distraction at best. She got in a few ineffective swings with her weapon before she was overborn and the guards with spears began forcing them into the weak points in her armor.

Oliver ignored that as he cut the legs out from beneath the man in front of him and charged forward at the now vulnerable mage.

The elven caster, seeing his death approaching, panicked and did the worst thing possible. The mage went for the only spell he was familiar enough with to reflex cast. Flames bloomed around Oliver, exploding into a fiery ball that burned and maimed half the men in the room. Unfortunately for the mage, the flames did nothing against the liquid- and force-like spell that protected Oliver. He leapt out of the blaze and swung at the caster.

Sadly, his sword rebounded from a defensive force-dome, so Oliver was forced to do things the slow way. Pressing his hands against the force-dome, he began pushing his way through. The strange magic of the phase-spider defense dissolved holes in traditional force spells. The elven mage stared wide-eyed at him, horror written on his face as Oliver's arms slowly passed through. Before the hapless mage could think to do anything else, Oliver's hands reached his shoulders and throat.

The elf died quickly, neck broken and throat crushed. Oliver turned back to help Selene, but with the elven caster's demise, that was no longer necessary. The men steadily stabbing spears into her body began to scream and claw at their armor. It wasn't immediately apparent what had happened, but seconds later, blood and liquified flesh began to leak out of the guardsmen's clothes and armor. Those few who were standing farther back, who hadn't been unfortunate enough to be burned by the fire ball, were frozen by the horror of what they were witnessing.

"Throw down your weapons," ordered Oliver from behind. "If you want to live, surrender now."

Weapons fell from their hands as the men turned to look at him in shock. Oliver motioned them toward the other side of the room, and they stumbled in that direction as Selene's mangled body struggled to sit up. Oliver helped by pulling out one of the spears that had gotten stuck after being forced through the mail just below the bottom edge of her breastplate. "Are you all right?" he asked.

She tried to answer, but one of her opponents had forced her visor up and jammed something in that had broken her jaw and ruined the bottom half of her face. She gave up and held up a hand, indicating she would need some time.

Oliver turned to the eight still able to move, then gestured to those who had been burned by the fireball. Many of those were dead, but some still moved, those who had been lucky to be far enough away and had not been inhaling when the blast struck. A few escaped with only burns to exposed skin, while others were worse, burned over large swathes of their bodies. "Help your fellow soldiers, but put hand to weapon or move toward the outside door and I'll put steel through your heart," he told them. Then he moved to that very door and replaced the bar to keep anyone else from entering.

After a few minutes, Selene was able to speak. "Help me get this armor off. It's easier to work when I can see what I'm doing." Oliver moved quickly to help, and once she had the majority of the armor off, she continued, "If I'd been smarter, I would have saved one of the ones that was stabbing me and just switched."

Oliver looked at one of the semi-liquid enemies, then grimaced in disgust. "What did you do to them?"

"I like to think of it as a reversed healing spell, but according to most magical scholars it's necromancy. It's something I designed myself. Used in a controlled fashion it can create painless incisions for surgery by unlinking connective tissues at a cellular level. Used with a bit more energy and a disregard for the consequences, *this* is what happens." She gestured to the fallen armsmen.

"It melted them."

Selene shook her head. "No, just parts of them. Skin and fascia and other connective tissues. The muscles and bones are mostly intact if you feel around a bit."

Oliver fought hard to keep himself from retching.

She'd finished sealing her wounds and repairing the major functional problems like broken bones and severed muscles. Selene considered doing more, but it was highly likely she would be finding a new body soon, so she decided to focus her energies where they might do more good. Rising slowly to her feet, she moved toward the burn victims. "Show me the ones who got the worst of it first," she ordered.

A thickset man who appeared to be in his late thirties and sported a heavy moustache moved to position himself between the wounded and Selene. "You've done enough. Spare them." The armsman had removed his helm so his features were clearly visible, and fear was written on his face. It must have taken considerable courage for him to speak. "I probably can't stop you, but you'll have to kill me before I let you do that to them." The armsman gestured toward the ones she had melted.

Oliver looked uncertain, but Selene's masculine elven face softened. "I didn't burn them, nor do I have any quarrel with you. I can heal some of them, if you will allow me."

"He betrayed Strasyn," said one of the other armsmen. "Don't trust him."

"I am not Thalonyr, though this was his body," replied Selene. "I know that's confusing, but the only thing you need to consider at the moment is that I can help some of these men." When the man didn't move, she asked, "What's your name?"

"Raskin Leyton, sergeant, and now that you've killed Captain Brighton, I'm responsible for these men." The sergeant's hand displayed a faint tremor betraying his fear, but he kept his stance firm.

Selene nodded in acknowledgment. "Sergeant Leyton, you can call me Isabel. Before I became as I am now, I was a healer of some skill. I'm an enemy of the elves but a friend to Terabinia. That man"—she pointed to the burned soldier behind the sergeant—"I can save his life. I would like to, but if you refuse me, I will respect your decision. Choose quickly, though, for I cannot work miracles."

Raskin studied her face for a long moment, then stepped aside. One of the other men protested, "Sergeant, you can't—"

"Shut up, Liles," barked the sergeant. "We've already lost, and Carson won't make it otherwise. We'll see what Thal—Isabel can do."

She had already moved around the sergeant and knelt beside the worst of the burn victims. Carson had been covered by a gambeson, but it had had short sleeves. The man's head, neck, and arms had been roasted, and most of his hair was gone. If he hadn't been exhaling when the flames hit, he would have died already, but as it currently stood, he had several days of pain ahead while his charred skin slowly peeled away, and the ensuing infection would run rampant until he died.

But Selene had other plans. Before anything else, she cast a preservation spell to prevent decomposition of her patient's dead skin. It wouldn't do anything for the charred and blackened parts, but there was much more that, while technically dead, still looked like skin and functioned as a proper barrier to dirt. She used several spells to check his condition, within and without, and then began the real work. With a combination of spells to spur healing and reshape flesh, she took small portions of his still living skin and seeded it throughout the dead regions.

Necromantic spells would keep the dead skin whole and semi-functional until living skin could replace it. Selene's work was something she'd perfected while working with children in Cerria. She'd taken a combination of older spells and reworked them to achieve better results. Her first attempts had been crude, clumsy even, but she'd saved countless children and adults from death and crippling injuries. Over time, she'd gotten better, and she'd developed better spells and the finesse to use them.

Was it healing or necromancy? She'd long ago decided those were meaningless questions that weren't even fit for an ethics discussion. It was the same magic, and the labels were academic. The simplest definition would be that necromancy dealt with dead flesh while healing dealt only with living tissue, but she knew that the lines were constantly being crossed. Necromancy had once been forbidden because of the terrible things that could be done with it, like the vampires Grim Talek had created. Selene could easily imagine much worse being done, but she could also envision nightmares created with pure healing alone.

With the necessary skill and knowledge living flesh could be molded, shaped, combined and reconfigured to create all manner of monstrous abominations. Was that any better? No. She'd made her choice when she'd sacrificed others to give herself the chance to survive beyond death. Her actions had been evil at one level, but it was her intention and the results she had achieved that mattered. Since then, she had personally saved hundreds, maybe thousands, and as queen she'd done even more for the entire kingdom.

"Doesn't make it right to steal someone else's life." Those had been William's words the day he had confronted her. He'd since forgiven her, but those words had shaken her, and they came back to her daily.

Intent and results. That was what mattered. Her intent had been good, was still good, and as long as she proved it with results, none could gainsay her choices. All this and more fluttered by unspoken in the river of her unconscious mind, a constant backdrop to her everyday thoughts, to her work. She would spend the rest of however long her life lasted proving it to herself.

She moved from patient to patient, using spells to stop the wounds from worsening until she could take the time to properly attend to each of them. It was two hours before she finished, and when she did, those with the lightest wounds were whole and unblemished. Those who had been more badly injured were swaddled in bandages made from boiled linen, but they would be well again within a day or two. The very worst might have some odd-looking areas, where the skin and hair patterns didn't quite match up with what they should be, but they wouldn't be crippled or disfigured.

Mentally, she couldn't help but tally the numbers. *I killed five, but saved seven.* Of course, she hadn't injured the seven, and she'd killed the five in self-defense, but the fight itself was ultimately her responsibility. The real justification was the greater good. She had to eliminate the threat posed by the elves, otherwise greater harm would fall on the people of Terabinia.

Or would it?

Selene's thesis rested on the assumption that her rule would be better for the people of Terabinia than that of the elves, but did she have any proof that such was truly the case? So far, the little bit of Fernham she'd seen seemed to be well administered, though since the city was still rebuilding, it probably would be hard to judge yet. When she had lived with the elves for a year, their realm had seemed almost a paradise. What if they could do the same for Hercynia?

She was under no illusion regarding the opinion of her people. Thus far, they had loved her reforms, but public opinion was fickle and ultimately proved nothing. In reality, most saw little difference between one lord or another. Did it really matter if she ruled, or some elf? Technically, she wasn't human anymore, so she couldn't make that argument in her favor either.

Glancing around the room, she saw the armsmen gathering the dead bodies and organizing them to one side. If the elves could offer a better life, then those deaths had served no purpose. The entire fight was a pointless exercise in vanity. Selene wondered how she would feel if she were a normal person, for she still had no doubt and little remorse.

Something was missing in her heart, and it wasn't something she'd lost since becoming a lich. It was something she'd lost as a child, living under her father's cruel rules and ruthless logic. Certain feelings simply didn't work for her. Love, joy, anger, loneliness, those she understood well, but guilt and remorse were notably absent most of the time.

Deep down, I'm not even good, she thought, *not like William.* She tried, but it was an intellectual exercise for her. It was something she'd decided for herself long ago, an act of rebellion against the monster that had raised her. But if the elves were the better choice, then her actions were based on a falsehood and even her attempts at *acting* good were a failure.

A touch on her shoulder roused her from her grim thoughts. "Are you done?"

Selene realized she'd been sitting still, staring at her last patient in silence for an unknown time. She stood up. "I am. I was lost in thought."

"What do we do now?"

"I need more information. Can you keep an eye on them while I interrogate Strasyn?" She remembered the dead mage. She would have two heads to question. She drew her sword to decapitate the body, though it was a poor tool for the job. There was a butcher's cleaver hanging near the kitchen hearth, but if she used that, the people probably wouldn't want to use it for cooking any more.

A second later, she realized she was being silly. A water-blade spell was far easier than using the sword. Someone across the room struggled to keep from retching, but she ignored them and claimed her prize. Then she went to the stairs that led up to the prison cell. "I'll need half an hour, maybe more." Turning her attention to the sergeant, she added, "If you're hungry feel free to use the kitchen, but don't attempt to leave."

CHAPTER 7

Back in Oliver's recent prison cell, Selene found a place near the wall that didn't have blood all over the floor and sat down, crossing her legs and leaning her head against the wall. From her limnthal, she brought out Strasyn's relatively fresh head and put it in her lap. It was tempting to use a spell to probe for answers, but that method was slow and relatively crude compared to what she could do directly.

It wasn't a pleasant task, but she'd never allowed herself to be defined by what was pleasant and what was not. Letting her breath out slowly, she released her current body and focused on Strasyn's lifeless head. The body she had been occupying went still, returning fully to death as her consciousness took up residence in the skull of the elf lord.

As places to inhabit, heads without bodies were low on her list, but she didn't plan to stay any longer than necessary. Settling in, she sent out feelers and began teasing Strasyn's memories out of hiding. She felt cold without a heart and warm blood, and the dead brain responded sluggishly at first, but as she focused her will and energy, the world shifted, and she began to get a sense of who Strasyn had been.

Another life drifted before her, full of images, context and meaning, a bewildering blur that threatened her sense of self. Although she had a rough fluency in elven, Strasyn's thoughts were beyond her competency initially, until she made herself at home with the mental machinery the dead elf's brain had used to process language.

The span of another person's life was too great to encompass within the small amount of time she had, but this wasn't her first time combing through the memories of the dead. Focusing her attention, she brought herself closer to the present, searching for information that was pertinent to Terabinia. She'd never been through the mind of an elf, but the structure felt similar to that of a human.

Silently, she hunted through Strasyn's life and what she found was far different than her expectation. Her first revelation was that the elven home plane was not the paradise she remembered. If the elf's life was typical, then what she had seen had been a carefully curated world meant to portray a false reality.

After an unknown time, she opened her eyes, looking around the room as she reflected on what she had learned. She was startled to find the ghostly image of her husband standing a short distance away, watching her. Their eyes met, and he asked, *Are you awake now?*

Feeling flustered, she abandoned Strasyn's head and returned to Thalonyr's body. Technically, she didn't need lungs or a physical voice to talk while in the astral realm, but it felt more natural. "I wish you didn't have to see me like this," she responded.

Will's spectral form smiled. *I have to confess it wasn't what I expected. Why are you holding an elf's head?*

"Looking for clues, but there's so much. Have you found their crossing point yet?"

He shook his head sadly. *They noticed me again. I had to destroy another ship. I just made it back to land.*

"Maybe you should leave it alone," she suggested. "Given time, I can probably find out everything we need to know. There's no need for you to risk yourself trying to infiltrate their plane." She'd voiced that opinion previously, before he'd left, so she anticipated his response, but she couldn't help but say it again.

I'm feeling stubborn now, Will told her. *I've also learned a few things about their spellcasters during the short battles I've had before sinking their ships.*

"Oh?"

Their wards are exceedingly sensitive and highly sophisticated, but none of the mages I've faced were third-order. If I had to guess, they're only going as far as the first or second compression.

"That's good news, considering they seem to have a lot of mages among them compared to us."

How is Oliver?

She winced mentally, and though it didn't show on her face, Will felt her reaction. Before he could ask again, she answered, "The healing from his tattoos is very good, but he gave me a scare today."

Will frowned. *What happened?*

"One of the elven warriors put a sword all the way through him from back to front."

What! How? What about the defenses provided by—

"He wasn't using the shield—"

Why not? What was he thinking? Will's ghostly form paced back and forth in agitation. *I need to have a word with him.*

"It won't happen again," she replied. "I didn't expect him to get into—"

What happened? interrupted Will.

"Will you let me finish?" Selene waited for several seconds, then gave a quick account of what had occurred.

When she was done, it was obvious that Will wasn't happy. *How could he be so reckless? He should have just run. You're sure there was no permanent damage?*

She nodded. "I examined him thoroughly. Unfortunately, I can't change the fact that he's young and he takes after his father. Perhaps you've forgotten some of the things that happened to you?"

That's not pertinent to this.

"Will, you've been run through in almost the exact same way *twice,* and it scared me to death each time. Trust me, I know how you feel. Sometimes when I think back, it seems as though I spent half our years together worrying about what new way you'd find to get yourself mangled or blown up."

I still need to talk to him.

"He isn't astrally sensitive. He couldn't see or hear you. Let me handle this. That's the whole point of him helping me, isn't it? I need to develop a rapport with him. We're family now."

Will struggled with himself for a moment before finally responding, *All right. I trust you.*

"Do you," she asked, voicing her secret fear, "after all these years?"

I do.

She sighed. "Then I need to get back to work."

Contact me if anything happens. I don't keep myself blocked off anymore, except when I sleep.

Selene chewed her lip. "Actually, about that."

Yes?

"I can't leave my body the same way you can, at least not now."

But you have to move through the astral in order to move between bodies, don't you? Will asked.

"I'm anchored to my phylactery. I can't move far from it, unless I'm using a body. If I tried to cast myself out into the astral the way you do, I'm pretty sure I'll get drawn back to it, and it isn't here. If I tried and failed, I would likely wind up accidentally abandoning Oliver here."

Have you ever tried?

"During the years we were apart, yes, but I never succeeded. You were always shielding yourself with that anti-possession spell, though, so I couldn't test the idea. Not to mention, back then I always had my phylactery close by. When I'm away from it like I am now, it pulls at me. It feels like jumping into a fast-flowing river and trying to swim against the current. I wouldn't feel comfortable trying it until we get back to Cerria."

Will's ghostly visage sighed. *That's inconvenient, but not insurmountable. I'll try to look in on the two of you daily. If you need to reach me sooner, have Oliver use the enchanted tablet I gave him.*

She nodded, then gave him a wistful look. "I miss you."

He smiled. *It hasn't been that long since we parted.*

"After the last ten years, even a few minutes is too much," she teased. "I love you. Please be careful."

I will, and the same goes double for you and Olly. Keep a close eye on the knucklehead. Give him a hug for me. Will's spectral form faded away. Selene crossed her arms, and clasped her shoulders with her hands, an unconscious response to the lonely feeling that swept over her.

She sent the preserved head back into her limnthal and got to her feet, then headed down the stairs. Below, she found Oliver at the base of the kitchen stairs, vigilantly watching the armsmen. A few of the servants she had put to sleep on the way in had returned and were busily preparing a meal. Ignoring the tense atmosphere, she could almost pretend the violence of an hour ago had all been a dream.

The stench of burned flesh and the bloodied floor reeds that had been swept to one end of the room belied that dream, though.

Oliver looked over at her when she reached the main floor. "There were servants hiding in the cellar. The guards woke them up and sent them down while they were preparing their ambush."

She nodded approvingly, glad that they hadn't been in harm's way when the fight was underway. "Is there anyone outside?"

Oliver shook his head, but it was Sergeant Leyton who answered from where he was standing a short distance away. "What you see is most of what's left of us, aside from the city guard, and I'm guessing they've decided to leave matters to us unless Lord Fernham calls for them." The sergeant gave her a sardonic look and glanced toward the keep entrance. "Don't suppose you'll let me take a stroll so's I can call for help, would you?"

Oliver couldn't help but smile faintly. The sergeant was brazen in the face of his fear, a quality he admired. Selene showed no expression, however, as she asked, "Where is Lord Fernham? Earlier, one of the servants said he was upstairs, but I saw no sign of him."

The sergeant frowned. "Wasn't he?"

"Would you like to see the bodies?" she asked.

A few minutes later, she stood in the makeshift prison with Sergeant Leyton. The man grimaced as he looked over the faces of dead armsmen, some of whom he'd likely been close to. With an air of resignation, he looked back at her. "He's not here, but I could have sworn I saw him in the keep earlier." The grizzled veteran paused, bracing himself, then asked, "Mind if I send the men up to bring the bodies down so we can put them with the others?"

"Do as you wish," said Selene. "We will be leaving soon. So long as you are loyal to the queen and you don't obstruct my path, I will cause you no harm."

Leyton's face showed puzzlement. "I don't understand the cause for all this." He stared at her face. "And you're an elf…"

She shook her head. "I am not, but I do not expect you to understand." After a moment, she went on, "The elves should not be here. The queen ordered them out of Terabinia over a month ago. If you seek a root cause, look there."

"That's not what Lord Fernham told us," said Leyton, frowning. "The elves are our friends."

"Then he was in their thrall, as I believe many of you were," she replied. "When was the last time you saw Lord Fernham?"

"I told you, not long before you came—"

"No," she interrupted. "Or he would be here. I suspect you will not find him, or if you do, it will be as a moldering corpse. You have seen only what they wanted you to see."

"Who?"

She gestured to her ears. "The elves. Haven't you been listening?"

Leyton's face showed a vague confusion, and she was reminded of her own cloudiness when Will had first tried to explain the problem to her. At first, she had struggled to even remember the topic, that the elves were the enemy. Later, her mind had cleared, though whether that was a function of time away from them or the fact that she had changed bodies, she still wasn't sure.

"Who are you?" he asked again.

"To you? I am no one, but to the monsters that would prey upon Terabinia, I am a nightmare made manifest." She turned back to the stairs and left the sergeant with his muddy thoughts.

CHAPTER 8

An hour later, they stood before what looked to Oliver to be a general store. After they'd left the keep, they'd encountered no resistance, and Selene had led them on a deliberate walk through the streets of Fernham, ending at the current address. "Wait here," she told him as she moved to enter. "Make sure no one enters behind me."

"Are you buying something?"

She shook her head. "An elf owns this establishment. Hopefully this won't take long."

Oliver's hand found her shoulder. "Wait, you're going in there to…"

"To kill him, probably in cold blood if I can catch him unsuspecting," she answered without any trace of shame. She had made a mental list of elven businesses while exploring Strasyn's memories, and with luck, she could remove the majority before the news spread to them of what was happening in the city.

"But, that's mur—"

"No, it's a purge. I do regret the setback this will cause Fernham. The people here are still recovering from the troll disaster, but this is necessary."

Oliver frowned. "You're a queen. You shouldn't be—if you must, let me do this."

Thinking of William, she shook her head. What she had to do was distasteful enough, but if she turned her stepson into an assassin, she'd never be able to face her husband. "A ruler must be prepared to answer the call of necessity, and for now, I am not a queen. I am a tool in the service of the people." She headed for the door once more, glancing back only once. "Wait," she commanded.

Inside the store was a cheerfully organized array of sundries. Dried beans, flour, salt, and various other necessaries were lined up and arranged in rows that struggled to bring order to the chaos of so many different goods. The sights and smells spoke of industry and hope. Behind the counter, a beautiful elven woman greeted her. "Thalonyr! The news I've heard today, is it true? They said a man was captured but many of our knights were slain. I feared you might be among them."

Selene gave an enigmatic smile, walked casually around the counter, and then stepped up to the woman. "It's worse than that," she said, and then without warning, she drew her dagger and drove it into the woman's midriff. The powerful muscles of the elven warrior whose body she wore performed the task perfectly. Her arm punched in and out to a rapid, frenetic beat as she plunged the blade home multiple times.

She was no expert with a blade, and it wasn't until the fourth or fifth strike that she punctured the lungs and silenced the dying woman's terror-filled screams. The elf was dying, but she still hadn't hit the heart. The woman's arms scrabbled weakly, trying to push her away.

A deep voice called from the back room, the words spoken in elven, "What's wrong?"

"It's murder!" called Selene, answering in the same tongue as she wiped her hand and blade on the shopkeeper's skirts. "Help!" Glancing up at the doorway she painted her features with a picture of surprise and dismay.

When the elven woman's husband appeared, he rushed over, never thinking to suspect the actual culprit. Selene wore the guise of a man he knew. "What happened?" He had already dropped to his knees beside them and only belatedly did he wonder at Thalonyr's bloody appearance.

It was too late, though. Selene put a hand on his shoulder to brace herself as she stood, then drove her knife into his unsuspecting back. The elven man let out a strange gasping sigh as the point passed down through his upper shoulder and into the top of his right lung. Before he could react, it had withdrawn and returned again, striking many more times in rapid succession. A weak gurgling cry escaped his lips as the man collapsed, kicking at the elven knight who had seemingly betrayed them.

She watched and waited, but despite the terrible wounds, both of her victims continued to stare at her, their chests rising and falling with desperation as blood filled their lungs and suffocated their impotent cries. As the seconds drew out, she became impatient. The two were too weak to resist now, so she carefully slit their throats. Death came more swiftly then, a welcome relief to their spastic movements.

Finally certain of the end, Selene moved beyond them to search the back of the building. A staircase led to living quarters. Feeling strangely trepidatious, she went up, hoping she would find no children. Their spawn couldn't be countenanced either, distasteful as the task might be. A voice in the back of her mind offered unhelpful commentary. *It isn't as if you haven't killed children before.*

She found no one, so she went back down and dragged the two bodies into the back, where it would hopefully be longer before they were found. Then, she returned to the front entrance where Oliver waited. The look on his face made it clear he had heard her doings. "Are you all right?" he asked.

Selene nodded. "Let's go. There's quite a few more to go, and it will be easier if we can get to them before the word spreads throughout the city."

"Hold on," said her stepson, removing his pack. He sorted through it for a moment before withdrawing a blanket. "Here. Wrap this around yourself to hide the mess. You're covered in blood."

She glanced down, only then realizing that her victims had sprayed her with blood when she'd cut their throats. Without a word, she wrapped the blanket around herself. "Thank you," she said absently.

The day didn't get any less bloody after that. They visited several more small businesses, and each time, she asked Oliver to wait outside. Each time, Oliver's sharp ears caught the sounds of struggles and the occasional scream, although with each stop, he noticed that her kills were becoming quieter as she improved in choosing the best spot for her first thrust. Every time she emerged, he saw more blood on her skin and clothing. She said nothing when he stopped her to wipe blood from her cheeks or forehead.

At first, Oliver was quietly horrified. He had seen death, but it had never performed in such a methodical, dispassionate manner. When he had first learned his father's identity, and the fact that Selene was his stepmother, he'd wondered at the way his father had kept him hidden for years. Even after the events of the abruptly terminated war, he hadn't quite understood. The Queen of Terabinia hadn't seemed like a particularly intimidating figure, even after everything he'd been told.

Now he understood.

It wasn't her unnatural existence, the fact that she was an unliving immortal. It wasn't even the disturbing bits of necromancy, like the spell she had used to melt her enemies from the inside out. What scared him, and what probably had scared his father, was her inhuman pursuit of her goals. Selene seemed to have the right goal, the health and happiness of her people, but she was willing to stoop to anything, no matter how reprehensible, to achieve that goal.

But he also began to see cracks in her seemingly unflappable demeanor. Whether she was aware of it herself, he didn't know, but Selene's eyes were haunted. "You don't have to do this," he told her when they reached the fourth place, a dockside warehouse.

"Hmm?"

"You don't have to do this," he repeated. "You've taken their leaders, cut the head off the snake."

"You aren't 'people' to them," she answered.

Oliver frowned. "You?"

"Humans. I'd say 'us,' but I don't think I deserve to be included any more. My point is that I lived with them for a year, and I started to suspect it then. Today, I saw Strasyn's memories, and it confirmed my suspicion. They don't see humans as people. You're chattel. Livestock."

"Does that justify this?"

She shrugged. "I don't know. I'm a monster myself, but I've chosen my side. They won't learn, they won't relent—and neither will I. I will remove them from my country, stem, branch, and root—if I have to cut and burn every single one of them myself, I will have them out."

Oliver didn't know what to say, and though her words bothered him, he felt sad as he listened to her speak. He didn't want to, but still he offered, "Let me help."

Selene shook her head. "Wait here." Then, she went inside.

The first people she met were dockworkers, all of them human. There were nearly ten men working inside the warehouse, so she put them to sleep. None of them realized she was a threat yet, but there were enough that she worried they might come to the aid of their elven master, and she wanted to avoid killing innocents.

She searched the main floor and found no elves; even the small office was empty. At first, she was mystified, but when she went out the large doors in the back to examine the dock itself, she noticed a broad wooden stair leading up to a second floor. At the top of the steps she found a balcony decorated with plants and flowers. A brightly painted door gave her the impression she had found a home rather than a place with some more industrial purpose. Opening the door, she stepped inside.

The first room was a modest sitting room with a couch and several chairs. A door across the room led into a hall that led off in two directions.

Selene went right and opened the first door on that side. Within she found two occupants, or perhaps three depending on how one counted, for there was an elven woman and a human maidservant, but the maid was very obviously pregnant.

"Thalonyr!" The elven woman was shocked at Selene's bloody appearance. "I heard you were slain."

She'd had time to master the language centers of her current host, so Selene answered in perfect and unaccented elven. "Fortunately, the news you heard was faulty." She stepped toward the lady of the house, but the elven woman took a step back. Some instinct had warned her that all was not as it appeared.

"Run!" commanded the elf to her human maid, as a spell construct began to take shape above her open palm.

Selene leapt forward, dagger in hand, intending to slay the elf before she could finish her spell. But a movement from the corner of her eye caused her to turn. The human maid was charging forward to stop her. The elven woman saw it all and ran toward Selene from the other side, shouting, "Marissa, no!"

The three of them collided and went down in a heap with Selene in the middle. She landed atop the pregnant woman, and she felt the dagger in her hand slide into the woman's body. Furious at the unintended casualty, she shoved herself up from the ground, her heavier masculine form shedding the lithe elven woman who had fallen on her with ease.

In her rush, Selene had lost the knife, but the elven lady collapsed to her knees at the sight of her dying maid rather than resuming her spell. It was a fatal mistake, as Selene's current body was far stronger and more dangerous, even unarmed. She seized the elf by the neck with both hands. With a strong, sure grip, she squeezed. The woman's throat collapsed, but Selene held on until she was certain of her death.

Then, she stopped to survey the scene, puzzled by what had just happened. The two women had tried to protect each other. The maid she understood, for the woman was likely enthralled, but the elven woman had tried to protect her servant as well. *Was it because she was pregnant?* Selene wondered. *Why would she care?*

She stared at the two dead women for long seconds, trying to understand, until a choked cry of alarm came from behind her. "No! Sylara! Fiend, what have you done!"

The elf standing in the door was well dressed, clearly wealthy, and obviously the dead woman's husband. Before she could react, he stretched out his hand and reflex cast a spell. A roaring gout of flame struck an instant later, and she was wreathed in flame.

Before her transformation, she would have resisted it once it reached her skin. Back then she'd been strong enough that the flames might have died a foot away, sparing her hair as well, but now her will was no longer sufficient, and the elven mage was exceptionally strong. As Will had mentioned previously, he was likely a second-order caster. The flames chewed into her flesh and began to devour her body as the enraged husband poured every ounce of his rage into destroying her with fire.

She had no hope, so she released her body quickly, saving herself considerable pain as she sought a new home to shelter her spirit. The mage continued to roast her abandoned flesh, screaming as it burned. Selene watched it all from her new vantage, while she carefully healed her damaged throat.

It wasn't until the distraught husband had emptied himself, and Thalonyr's corpse was nothing but ashes, that she sat up, moaning. Seconds later, the bereaved elf rushed to her. "Sylara, I thought you dead!" His eyes searched her up and down, looking for injuries. All they found were the bruises at her neck, but she was quite clearly still breathing. "Are you hurt? Your neck…!"

Selene gave him a tight smile, then waved her hand dismissively. "Merely a bruise. I'm fine, but you, you've cut yourself." She reached out with a slender hand, touching his lips tenderly. "Let me heal that."

When her turyn began to move, the elf didn't resist, and by the time Kellemar realized something was wrong, his flesh had already begun to melt. He stared at her in horror as he collapsed and died in ignorance, uncomprehending of the betrayal that had ended his life.

She stepped back to avoid the sack of skin puddling at her feet. Words came to her mind, but she withheld them, not for the sake of the dead, but out of respect for the task she had set herself. *I've more work yet to do.*

The past few minutes had left her disquieted, but she wasn't sure why. It wasn't because of the grotesquerie of the man she had slain, or the charred stench of her recently vacated body—it was the behavior of the elven woman and her maid. But she now wore the lady's flesh, and the simplest memories to retrieve were those that had just occurred before death. She turned her attention inward, and a second later Selene gasped. *Her child? How?*

She went still, completely still, as only the dead can do. Minutes passed before she returned to the present. Her chest filled as she remembered to breathe, then she turned and left, walking with quick strides. Back through the warehouse and past the sleeping workers she went, and she hardly stopped when she exited and saw Oliver. "We need to go."

Oliver had been watching her suspiciously, not sure whether she was a stranger or his stepmother until she spoke. "Where's the next one?" he asked somberly.

"We're returning to camp. I need to think."

"What happened?"

"I'll explain after I understand it myself."

CHAPTER 9

Hours passed while Oliver kept watch over her motionless form. She reclined against her dragon body, but if a stranger examined her, they would have been convinced she was dead. Selene had used spells to prevent decomposition and yet more spells kept her heart and lungs moving, though it was so slowly as to be undetectable. All she cared about was maintaining the function of her newest brain while she explored the elven woman's past.

The sun rose and fell again while she reflected on someone else's life, and Oliver began to grow worried she might have lost her hold and been drawn back to her phylactery, leaving him alone in the wilderness with two empty shells. He wasn't sure what to do if that was the case. Did the dead dragon need guarding? Would it be eaten by wildlife? He had no idea whatsoever.

When she suddenly sat up, drawing air into her lungs with a heaving gasp, it almost caused him to jump into the air. Selene's eyes locked onto him. "Is something wrong?"

"No!" he declared in embarrassment, but he corrected himself immediately. "Yes. You! You nearly scared me into next week. Can't you at least wake up like a normal person?"

She arched one brow. "What did I do?"

"It's how you breathed, the way you sat up."

"My breathing? Really?"

"It was a gasp, as if you were about to yell."

"But I didn't yell, did I?"

"Well… no," he admitted sheepishly. Running a hand through his hair he shifted topics. "Did you learn anything?"

Her eyes unfocused again, but just for a second as she considered what she had seen. "Enough to know we cannot coexist with them. Their methods of reproduction are an abomination."

Oliver lifted both brows.

"I said before that they don't see humans as people, and that is still true, but in another sense it's false. They don't see us as a truly separate species. They require us to survive, to create children. Whether it was that way from the beginning I am unsure, but throughout the extent of history that Sylara knew, elves have survived through parasitism."

"Paras—what?"

"Parasitism. They are parasites; however, unlike mosquitoes, they aren't using us for food, but rather to reproduce. That's why they're so attractive to us."

"Slow down," complained Oliver. "I thought the word 'parasite' referred to how something feeds. What does parasitic reproduction mean? Are they eating…?" He glanced down at himself, then looked away, his cheeks flushing red.

Selene sighed. "No, you twit." *William should have sent him to Wurthaven.* Pausing, she drew a slow breath. "Parasitism can involve any resource. In this case, it's reproduction. They're also enslaving people, but that's a social engineering problem. Back to the matter at hand. Have you ever learned about the cuckoo bird?"

"Like in fancy clocks?"

"Yes, but I'm not talking about clocks. I'm talking about the living bird. In nature, it doesn't rear its own young. Instead, it waits until another bird leaves its nest to find food. While the bird is away, the cuckoo sneaks in and destroys the eggs before replacing them with one of its own. The original bird returns, and when the cuckoo egg hatches, she thinks it is her own chick."

"But people don't lay eggs," put in Oliver.

She nodded, then placed a hand over her stomach. "For humans, our nest is here. We call it the womb. Women do have eggs, but they are fertilized and nurtured within the body. You only see the final product, when a baby is born."

"So what are they doing?" Oliver looked thoroughly confused.

"Physically, I *think* they're similar to us," said Selene. "But female elves don't bear children. They might have in the distant past, but they don't now. They're implanting their fertilized eggs into human women, using them as incubators." She held up a hand as Oliver started to ask another question. "Let me finish. Sylara's knowledge doesn't contain the scientific particulars I would really like to know. Despite her long life, she was somewhat ignorant, at least when it comes to medicine and magic. She did, however, know the process. She and her husband indulged in coitus, much like humans do, but after conception, she would feel a change. A week or two later, they would repeat the act, and the tiny embryo would attach itself to the father's member."

"To his member…" repeated Oliver, his voice empty of understanding.

"His phallus," clarified Selene. "They use a spell and either that draws it in, or it somehow climbs into the urethra."

"I didn't understand half of that, but I'm starting to feel nauseous."

"You don't have to worry anyway," she told him. "If it happened to you, it wouldn't survive. Apparently, long ago they tried it with human men, but the result was similar to an ectopic pregnancy."

"Ectopic?"

"The fetus would gestate inside your body, but without a method of egress, it would eventually die, killing you with it. Something similar can happen to human women even under normal circumstances. It's very rare, but it's always life-threatening. Anyway, back to the elves. No, the male elf, the father, he accepts this role, but then turns around and has sex with someone who will become a surrogate mother. With another spell, he implants the embryo within a human female."

Her stepson seemed a bit green, but he tried his best to hide it. "What brought this up? Does it have something to do with why you changed bodies?"

Selene spent a few minutes describing the events within the dockside warehouse. Once she had brought him up to date, she continued, "The pregnant woman was carrying their child, which is why they were both so protective of her. It wasn't the woman they cared about, but the babe in her womb."

Frowning, Oliver had an odd question. "Are you sure it wasn't voluntary? The people I met in Fernham seemed relatively happy. What if she volunteered to have their baby?"

She shook her head. "I saw enough of her memories to know that. Sexually, they are almost irresistible to us. That part seems to be biological, though I don't know if they changed themselves to be that way somehow or if it's a product of some weird sort of evolution." Selene had uncomfortable memories of her own time living among the elves. She'd almost succumbed to temptation herself, and while she'd always been proud of her self-control, now she wondered if she had gotten away unscathed because of Aislinn's deal with the elves. Pushing that thought aside, she continued, "Pheromones and good looks aside, they've also mastered magical manipulation to an astonishing degree. Their personal servants love them, and their menial slaves are rendered incapable of disobedience. We aren't seeing the ugly side of it here because they're still on their best behavior. Back on their world, things are much worse."

Another thought passed through Selene's mind. "Your question makes me wonder something else, though. I'm unsure whether they are obligate or facultative reproductive parasites, but though Sylara was too ignorant to know, I believe I can find the answer in her flesh."

"Obli-what?"

"Obligate or facultative. By that I mean whether they *have* to use us for gestation or whether it's a choice. At some point in the past, they must have had their own children, although Sylara has no memory of it. But even if it was in their distant history, the question remains whether they still can or whether they've lost the ability."

Despite his better instincts, Oliver couldn't help but ask, "How can you tell that?" Selene was already withdrawing something from her limnthal. Oliver saw a flash of metal, and a split second later, his eyes identified the object in her hand as a surgeon's scalpel. He took a step back. "Oh no."

Selene's eyes locked onto his. "This would have been easier if we had brought a second body back, but since I only brought back heads, I'll have to operate on myself." Seeing how pale her stepson was, she added, "Why don't you go stand on the other side of the dragon? There's no need for you to watch this."

Oliver moved so quickly that all she saw was a blur before he was gone. Selene sighed as she removed her dress and lay down. *I didn't expect to expose him to any of this. Now he'll never be able to accept me. I can only imagine what he'll say to William.*

Schooling her thoughts, she began to cut and hissed as the pain hit her. The body she was in was in such perfect condition that it was almost as sensitive as it would have been if she had possessed someone. She couldn't withdraw because she needed fine motor control of her hands, so instead she used a spell to crudely block the nerves in the lower half of her body. For a real patient, she could have been more specific, but she was using magic on parts of herself she couldn't see.

Once the problem of pain was solved, she resumed cutting. As far as surgeries went, the limited angle of her view and the awkwardness of working on her own body made the incision somewhat crude. She cut through skin, fat, fascia, muscle, and more fascia, until at last she had access to her organs. As expected, they began to escape almost as soon as she had fully breached the peritoneal cavity.

What a mess. She still had to go further, and she strained to see past her bladder and colon. *In a normal person, the uterus will be here, protruding into the base of the cavity.* Blood and viscera made it difficult to see, so she felt around with her hand to get a better understanding of what was there.

Frustrated by the lack of visibility, she finally gave up and began cutting out organs. Bladder, colon, liver, spleen—the more she removed, the more the remaining organs sagged down to interfere with her investigation. Swearing, she put aside any pretense of salvaging the body and completely gutted herself. Once that was done, she was sure. Sylara's uterus was vestigial, too small and undeveloped to gestate a child. For a moment Selene couldn't find ovaries, either, but eventually she found them among the viscera she had discarded.

Her hands were growing clumsier as time passed. The body she currently occupied was no longer even remotely alive. The heart was still in place, but most of the blood was gone, so keeping it beating did nothing. Without the organs to support a myriad of vital functions, her magic had to take up the slack. Sylara's body at that point might as well have been made of clay.

She was about to clean up the mess when she heard retching noises. Oliver had come around and snuck a peek at her doings. He'd retreated immediately and was now vomiting on the other side of the dragon. "I'll tell you when I'm finished," she yelled, though she wasn't sure he could hear her over the sounds of his gastric distress.

Looking at the scene, she could well understand Oliver's squeamishness. It looked like a cross between some foul ritual and a torturer's most extreme labor. Blood soaked the earth, and organs were strewn about her on every side. She didn't bother trying to replace anything; she'd done far too much damage for that. Instead, she sealed up the skin, leaving her abdominal cavity empty. With the skin closed, it gave her a grotesque and sunken appearance. Clothes would help that. She cleaned away the sanguine mess with her signature cleaning spell, making sure to include her clothing, then redressed. Aside from her sunken belly and clumsy, awkward movements, she could almost pass as a living person now.

"I'm presentable now," she announced.

"Are you sure?" her stepson called back, sounding hesitant.

Glancing around, Selene realized she needed to do a little more, so she summoned an earth elemental and had it scour the ground clean and bury her discarded bits and pieces. "Definitely ready now."

Oliver's head peeked around the end of the dragon's snout. After a quick look, he came fully into view. He seemed embarrassed. "Sorry about that."

"About what?"

"I shouldn't have looked—or rather, I reacted as badly when I did."

She raised one brow. "*You're* apologizing to me? For being normal? I think it should be the reverse."

"I've been in battle." He seemed to be struggling to find the right words. After a second, he went on, "Blood shouldn't bother me so much."

"Blood in battle and blood in a surgeon's tent, they're two separate things. Most soldiers I've known couldn't stand to see a leg amputated, much less this—" She waved her hand at the now clean ground.

Oliver seemed thoughtful. "You've known a lot of soldiers?"

"Your father told you how we met, didn't he?"

"Some."

With the earth elemental, she quickly constructed an earthen bench they could sit on. "Let me tell you about it, from my perspective." She sat down, and Oliver followed her example. "Back then, when this thing was still alive"—she pointed at the dragon—"I was posing as a commoner. Your father knew me as Isabel, a nurse and medical assistant at the army camp in Branscombe."

"The dragon was king then, right?"

"Yes, but no one knew he was a dragon. He possessed the empty shell of the man who was my father by blood."

"But he wasn't your actual father."

She shook her head. "My true father was essentially dead and gone before I was even conceived. I had a brother, but he 'died' when I was young. The dragon took him and used his body to replace his former human host, so for much of my life the man I knew as my father was technically my biological brother. But the creature inside them was *that*." She nodded toward the dragon once again.

Oliver was at a loss for words. "I'm sorry."

"Don't be. I'm well past it now, thanks to your father. Anyway, so when I met William, I was working on wounded soldiers and—"

"I hate to interrupt," said Oliver, "but weren't you a princess? Why would you be there, doing that?"

She offered up a sad smile. "As I'm sure you've noticed, I'm not normal. Even when I was alive, my cruel upbringing had changed me. I knew I wasn't like other people, but I also hated the man I knew as my father. I didn't want to be like him. I wanted to be good, to be kind, to be everything he was not. But I didn't really understand how, not the way you do. The best solution I could come up with was trying to help people. Medicine and magic were my best skills, so I tried to use them for the benefit of others."

"That makes you a good person then," stated Oliver with all the sure confidence that comes with youth. "If you help people, that's good."

"Trust me, it's not that simple." Selene waved her hand dismissively. "Let me finish the story." She went on to describe the years before he'd been born, and unlike Oliver's father, she had no reservations about painting William in a good light. Will might have doubted himself, but she knew the truth of the matter, and she was more than willing to share.

Oliver listened raptly, hearing his father described in a new way.

CHAPTER 10

They moved camp after that. Selene switched back to the dragon form so she could fly, storing the dead elf woman's body in her limnthal for future use. She regretted having done so much damage to it, but hopefully she would soon have a chance to replace it with a fresh body. After putting ten miles between them and Fernham, she set them back on the ground.

"I thought you might go on to Cerria," observed Oliver as he climbed down. "We've hardly traveled at all."

"I just wanted some more distance before investigating the information stored within Lord Strasyn's head," she rumbled. Her dragon voice felt deep and cumbersome after only a short time in a humanoid body.

Switching back to the stiff and ungainly female elf's form, she took out the head she'd referred to and settled into a comfortable position with it in her lap, once again using the dragon's body to recline against. Oliver was already setting up a campfire as she closed her eyes and shifted to Strasyn's head.

Sylara had given her a broad picture of the elves, but the elf lord had more detailed information regarding their plans in Terabinia. She'd garnered hints from the woman, but she wanted more. Unfortunately, she still had to sift through years of memories to find the things that were important to her, and another day and night passed as she focused on her search. Unbeknownst to her, Will appeared briefly, checking on them, but she was so rapt in the memories of the past, she failed to notice him.

The next morning, she came back to herself and the face of Sylara's dead body formed an expression of anxious concern. Oliver noticed the change before she had said a word. "Did you learn something?"

"You need to contact William," she announced.

"What is it?"

"Now!" she snapped, struggling to unwind the stiff limbs of her newly animate body. "This is an emergency." Her stepson stared back at her with an uncomfortable look. "What? Where's the tablet he gave you?"

"I think it's in Fernham."

Aghast, she gaped at him. "Why?"

"Well, you both told me to keep it with me at all times, so I did," he answered slowly.

"And?"

"I had it with me when they captured me, but when you came to rescue me, you brought my armor and other things, so it didn't occur to me that I was missing the one thing I'd had with me before that. It's probably in the keep somewhere."

Stifling the urge to scream in frustration, Selene went still. Outwardly, she was calm, but within her, heart was lost in a storm.

"What's wrong?" asked Oliver anxiously.

"He's walking into a trap."

"Who?"

"Your father," she snapped. Taking a slow breath, she tried to regain her composure. "The elves have had spies in Terabinia for many years, since before I took the throne. Apparently, they were stymied by a counterintelligence force commanded directly by Lognion. They know he's dead, and they know I'm a fake. That's why they didn't withdraw from Terabinia after I tried scaring them. They haven't been worried about me at all. I'm playing games with myself, totally irrelevant to their plans."

Oliver frowned. "That sounds annoying, but how does that translate into a trap for Dad?"

"They're focused on the only credible threat to their invasion—the Stormking, and they've guessed that he's overconfident enough to bring the fight to them. They've got something waiting for him on the other side of their congruency, or gate, whatever it is they use to cross between the worlds."

Oliver was on his feet, having picked up her anxiety. "So, where do we go? Back to Fernham to get my tablet, or is there one in Cerria?"

"I'm sure he gave one to Tabitha. Fernham is closer, but we don't know where they put yours. If we can't find it quickly, we'll have wasted time," she replied. "I think the capital is a safer bet, but I need to fly faster."

"I noticed you were flying a little faster when we came here. I think you're improving," offered Oliver.

She grimaced. "I need to be better, much better, and I also need more information. I'm thinking I should do something I probably should have done years ago."

"What's that?"

Her eyes went to the dragon's fierce-looking head. "Examine *his* memories. If I delve into his brain, I can access his natural flying talents, as well as find out how he organized that covert network. If the elves couldn't subvert it while he was alive, it must have been formidable."

"How long will that take? You said we need to send a message soon."

"Too long. I'll just tap into his motor skills for now. The information can wait until later," she replied, already switching bodies again.

A random thought struck Oliver. "You had to use spells to preserve those heads you took. How were you able to manage that with Lognion's corpse? Dad said you were missing for a few days after he killed the dragon."

Selene answered with the dragon's voice, startling him. "I'm loath to admit it, but I didn't have to do much work on the dragon body. Everything that wasn't eaten by the dragon whelplings refused to decompose on its own, and as soon as I channeled turyn into the flesh, it began to heal."

Her stepson's eyes widened. "It's still *alive*?"

"In a sense, but his spirit is long gone."

"You're sure?"

"Lognion died. It was some time before I could get back to clear the nesting chamber and examine the carcass. It wasn't healing on its own, and the heart-stone enchantments he held were no longer attached to his soul," she explained. "That wouldn't have been the case if he lived. I would have had to untie them before claiming them myself."

"Heart-stone enchantments?"

"A forbidden magic used to bind souls and create elementals. Lognion had thousands, and your father is still disappointed in me for not freeing them all." Oliver didn't respond, but his lips pressed together into a firm line. Selene took that as a sign of disapproval. "Yes, I'm still in possession of many of them, though I did free quite a few. Currently I command a thousand elementals, and each of them represents an enslaved soul. Still think I'm a good person?"

Oliver stared up at the dragon, meeting her eye. He'd finally gotten used to its intimidating appearance, and he felt only a faint shiver when he answered, "Dad thinks you are, or we wouldn't be here together."

"He'll put an end to me if I don't free the rest of the elementals," she stated flatly. She said it calmly, but inwardly, she wondered at her actions. *Why am I saying these things? I brought Oliver to try and build trust, but instead I'm sabotaging myself at every turn.*

Her stepson didn't back down. "You really think so?" he asked in a challenging tone. She glared down at him, but said nothing, so Oliver answered his own question, "It sounds to me like you're trying to convince yourself of that. He's forgiven you, but it feels like you haven't done the same."

I don't waste my time and energy on guilt, she told herself, but she didn't say anything. After a minute, she told him, "We don't have time for this. Give me a few minutes to tap into the dragon's motor skills. Then we'll head for Cerria." She closed her eyes and turned her attention inward.

Selene wished she felt the same confidence she had pretended to when she told Oliver her plan. While she was very certain of Lognion's death, the prospect of delving into the memories within his brain sparked a deep fear in her heart. The monster had hollowed out and possessed her ancestors for generations. She didn't want to see what he'd done to her mother, or her brother. Most of all, she didn't want to see what he'd thought of her. The cruelty of her childhood was enough on its own; she didn't need to experience it from the perspective of the thing that had pretended to be her father.

Up until then, she'd controlled the dragon by tapping into the brainstem, connecting herself directly to the body while avoiding any of the higher functions. She didn't want to see, hear, or feel anything remotely resembling one of her father's thoughts. *He's dead,* she told herself. *It's nothing but information.*

She tapped into the cerebellum and immediately felt a difference in her control. The dragon's limbs were her own at a more instinctive level now. But she could do better. Higher up in the brain were movement centers that assisted in planning the body's movements, portions of the mental machinery that helped translate formal thoughts into actions to be performed. She reached for those as well.

As her soul expanded and her thoughts and turyn spiderwebbed into the higher portions of the dragon brain, she began to feel echoes of other things, hints of memories and thoughts. *That's far enough,* she thought.

Selene?

Electric fear obliterated all thought in her mind. It was Lognion's voice. In a panic, she began to withdraw, but she could feel a fire spreading through the dragon's brain. Like dry tinder, the touch of her soul had ignited something, and even as she pulled away something else began to fill the empty space she left behind.

She abandoned the brain entirely, but something was fighting her for control of the brainstem now, threatening to erase her control of the body itself. Struggling to master her fear, she fought back, but the will that opposed her was gaining strength with each second that passed.

It is you! How can this be?

Unbidden, she remembered her father's human face. In her mind's eye, it was animated as a sadistic smile crept across Lognion's lips. She fought harder, but terror undermined her efforts. She lost control of the body entirely, and then she felt grasping tendrils diving into her soul, trying to claim her.

She'd spent much of her life bound by a heart-stone enchantment. She wouldn't go back to that, and she didn't have to. She had bound her own soul to a phylactery; all she had to do was release the dragon's body and it would pull her back, a flawless escape.

Who is this you brought with you? A friend perhaps?

No! she screamed.

Leave and I won't have anyone else to talk to. Is he important?

Tendrils continued to dig into her inner self, questing for knowledge. Selene cut and burned them as they stabbed into her, but there were always more. More than she could count. More than she could see. More than—*No!* she shouted. *That's my fear talking.* In the realm of thought, speed was an abstraction, and so were numbers. She redoubled her efforts and maintained her boundaries.

His son! What a precious gift you have brought me.

She fought on without answering, but she felt the body shift in spite of her efforts. One eye opened, and she saw Oliver clasped within one clawed foot. *His life is in my hand, daughter. What will you do?*

What do you want? she asked in desperation.

Everything. But I will begin with you. Let me in, and I will allow him to live.

Liar!

You know me better than that. Open your mind to me.

No. But then she heard Oliver's scream as one of his ribs snapped.

It was over in an instant. Despairing, she surrendered, and her father's fire flooded into her mind. Everything disappeared in a flash of endless pain.

***

She woke in bed and sat up with a start. It was her old bedroom, the one she had lived in when Lognion had been king, before Will had turned her life upside down. Glancing to the left she saw sunlight coming from the other room. The window Will had climbed in through was there. Was she reliving the past?

"This is no dream," said a deep voice, sending shivers down her spine. Lognion sat on the bedside to the right of her. She'd been avoiding looking at him without even realizing it. "Look at what you've become. Pathetic."

"Leave me alone."

"Of all my human pets, you were the one that surprised me most. I almost believed you could have been born a dragon yourself, but your weakness betrayed you in the end. A lich? What foolishness! I admired the fight in you. Better you had died than turn yourself into a worthless shadow."

Gritting her teeth, she stared straight ahead. "I would rather be weak than be like you."

Lognion laughed. "Yet, like all rebellious daughters, you married the closest thing to me you could find, a man with the soul of a dragon."

"Will is nothing like you. He's stronger than you, and despite what you believe, his kindness makes him stronger still."

Her father nodded agreeably. "He's definitely strange, but despite his bizarre personality, he is still a dragon."

Rage swept through her, and Selene met his eyes. "He's the First Wizard. You just can't accept the fact that a human beat you."

Lognion smiled. "That look suits you better, but your opinion doesn't change the facts. Your husband may have been born human, but only a dragon can do what he did."

"You're dead," she spat. "Your soul was gone. This cannot be real."

"I am the *only* thing that is real. Don't you understand? Dragons do not have souls, we do not have bodies, we do not die. We are the very foundation of existence itself. Allow me to give you a lesson, an explanation of this world you live in."

"I don't give a damn what—" Pain obliterated her senses, and for a moment, Selene could do nothing but scream in silence. A moment later, the world returned, and she found herself panting and sweating.

Her father watched her with a faint smile. "Ready to listen?" He waited several seconds, then he stood and opened his coat. Inside was a black void which swept out and devoured the room. Selene found herself disembodied, floating in a vast emptiness. Lognion's voice spoke beside her. "This is reality, an endless sea of nothing." A tiny light flickered in the distance and as she watched, it grew—though whether that was because she was getting closer or because the light was getting larger, she couldn't tell, but she felt no sense of movement.

As the light grew, it became a blazing bonfire that filled her vision. At the edge of her perception, she could still see the darkness that surrounded them, and as her view shifted she saw more lights in the darkness, like a sprinkling of stars. "The fires you see are dragons. We are the only light, the only support. Without us, there would be nothing. You and your kind are like fireflies, drawn to the warmth and living in the flickering interplay between light and shadow. You are ephemeral, a fleeting wisp of consciousness, but I am eternal."

She surprised herself when she heard her own voice. "You are not a god."

"There are no gods. They are a fairy tale for children unable to bear the truth. The truth is that we exist in a biting darkness. The world, the universe, everything you know, is but a tiny speck floating in a cruel uncaring void, and the tiny, almost insignificant lights you see, that is all there is. Those are the dragons."

"You claim to be the sun, or a star?"

"In this metaphor, yes. In the world you know we are not anything so simple as stars, but our existence gives birth to the energy that powers them—and everything else."

"And yet you died," she said boldly. "Why didn't the world vanish if what you claim is true?"

"The pillars of creation cannot be destroyed so easily. My children subsumed my flesh, but my power did not vanish. What they devoured went with them, and what was left remained in this body. I spent countless ages acquiring that power; now much of it is in the hands of my ignorant children. Do you understand now why newly hatched dragons fight to consume one another?" She didn't answer, so he continued, "They strive to consolidate the spark of power given to them. Each one is insignificant, but together, they begin to be something meaningful. They fight until only one is left, and then they move on to eat and grow elsewhere. Through cycles of destruction and regrowth, the dragons slowly grow and expand, and with them existence itself grows."

In spite of herself, Selene was awed by the vision she saw. Though it made her feel small and insignificant, it also made her feel equal, for even Lognion was tiny in comparison to the vast emptiness. "Even if this is true, why show me?"

"To punish you for your folly."

"Because we took your place," she declared.

"Because you were too weak to deserve it. You were always destined to fail, but you could have been so much greater. Instead, you gave in to cowardice and chained yourself into eternal mediocrity."

"You can't kill me."

Lognion laughed. "Has this living death addled your wits? Once, I respected your intelligence. Where has it gone? My child, I will educate you. From here, you will watch and despair. Weak as I have become, I will yet reclaim everything taken from me, and while I do, I will destroy everything you thought you loved. You wanted to know how I dealt with the elves? You will see! And while you learn, you will also see what I do with the imposter you placed on the throne in your stead. You will watch as I destroy the friends who rightfully no longer trust you. I will tear down everything you made and rebuild according to my own desires.

"I have no need to kill you, daughter, for you have done that yourself. You will study at my elbow, child, until you surrender hope and gain true wisdom. Once there is nothing left in your heart, you will transcend fear. *Then* you will be purified. *Then* you will give up the pathetic cowardice of your undying weakness.

"I have no need to kill you. You will release yourself." The dragon laughed again. "Learn quickly, for the longer it takes to understand this final lesson, the more you will suffer."

The vision winked out, leaving her in darkness. Alone, all Selene could do was scream.

CHAPTER 11

Lognion sealed Selene inside himself, leaving her only the ability to see and hear. Then, he studied the boy he held in his claws. The lad was strong and sturdy, though being human, he still seemed ridiculously frail. Having only just reawakened, Lognion yearned to vent his frustration and crush the child, but he restrained himself. Only one rule ever bound him, and that was his own word.

He released the young man. "How badly are you hurt?" he asked, knowing he had squeezed a little too hard while persuading Selene to behave.

The youth looked back at him without fear. "I'm healed already."

Lognion liked what he saw in the young man's face. Fear only garnered his disdain, but Oliver seemed to have none. "Healed?" Lognion studied the currents around the warrior, then consulted Selene's memories. What he found surprised him. "You are a most unusual type of wizard, aren't you? You have magic but you can barely use it."

"I'm a wardsman," stated Oliver.

"You're defective," countered Lognion, "yet your softhearted father let you live. He should have put you out of your misery."

Oliver ignored the remarks, instead observing, "You aren't Selene."

"At least your mind works." The dragon considered Oliver carefully for a moment. "The enchantment carved into your body is quite clever. For all his strange choices, your father certainly has a gift for taking flawed materials and reforging them into something useful."

"What happened to my stepmother?" asked the young warrior.

Lognion's lips drew back to display lethal teeth. "She's still here. I'll be keeping her with me until she's learned an important lesson."

"Who are you?"

"Has the world forgotten my name so quickly? I am the one who will destroy your father."

Oliver's brows tightened in consternation. "Lognion?" After the dragon nodded, Oliver added, "If you're dumb enough to face him, my father will tear you apart."

Lognion chuckled. "What a delight you are! I'm starting to understand why your father didn't eat you. Perhaps you have some worth after all."

"If you eat me, you'll never know."

"I'm feeling very hungry. Perhaps you should run." Oliver's eyes had already surveyed the area around them, but he didn't move. Lognion's estimate of him went up another notch. "You aren't afraid?"

"I wouldn't make it," said Oliver. "I can tell you're faster than before. I promise I'll give you the worst case of indigestion you've ever had if you try to swallow me, though."

"Nothing gives a dragon indigestion."

Isn't that how he killed you, thought Oliver, *from the inside out?* It didn't seem wise to say that, though. While he was calm outwardly, inside he was struggling to master his fear. With his stepmother no longer in control, it felt as though he was swimming in deep water with a predator beneath him. At any moment, he could be torn apart.

"I'm leaving," announced Lognion.

"What do you plan to do?"

When Lognion answered, it was more for Selene's ears than Oliver's. "I have a number of debts to repay. I will start with Trendham. Since they embarrassed the Terabinians in the recent unfinished war, they deserve a small lesson. Burning Bondgrad should suffice." After a second, he added, "Samantha Cartwright lives there as well." When Lognion spotted Oliver's grimace, he took a moment to review the memories he had gained. "Your aunt—and your lover is with her, isn't he? Alex, that was the name."

Oliver's eyes bored into him, but he responded with a simple request. "Take me with you."

"For what purpose? Do you think you can save them?" Then, the dragon's eyes narrowed. "You don't imagine you can inflict a crippling blow if I let you ride my shoulders, do you? I assure you, you cannot."

"I can't do anything if you leave me here."

The dragon smiled viciously. "You amuse me, child." Lowering one shoulder and extending a wing as a ramp, he offered his back. "Climb up, but I'll only give one warning. Try your steel on me, and my forbearance will come to an end."

Walking up the wing and taking his place just in front of them, Oliver considered his reply. Something Tiny had told him during their brief time training came back to him, but he used his climbing spell to anchor himself in place first, then answered, "Violence is a tool that always comes with a cost. If you feel the edge of my blade, it will mean I've found a way to make you pay the price. That or there's something worth paying it myself."

"Good words," rumbled the dragon, "but the true test will be whether you can live up to them." Stretching out his wings, he tensed his haunches, then sprang into the sky with a grace that was both exhilarating and frightening for his passenger. Inwardly, Lognion projected his thoughts to Selene. *The boy's wisdom is something you should learn from. If you had followed such a precept, I would not have to train you so harshly.*

I would be dead and gone, she returned bitterly. *I made my choice with open eyes, and the price was worth what was saved.*

Better to have died proudly, the daughter of a dragon, than survive like this, Lognion replied. *You sacrificed your power in return for scraps. In life, I was proud of your resolve, but in the cowardice of your undeath, you have earned only my disdain.*

It was worth it, she insisted.

You will learn otherwise.

Lognion gained altitude, then circled briefly as he gathered turyn from the currents in the sky. In the past, he wouldn't have needed to delay, but his strength had been much greater then. If he'd still been in possession of his elementals, he could have used them, but he preferred relying on his own power. His accrual of so many elementals back then had been more a side effect of his strategy than a goal.

Several minutes passed while he prepared himself to create a gate. Before the hatchlings had devoured most of his power, it would have only taken him seconds, but Lognion would remedy that problem soon enough. With a final push, he opened a passage wide enough for him to dive through, and the terrain beneath them changed.

Oliver had no idea how difficult gates were to create, or how much turyn it took to make one big enough for a creature the size of Lognion to pass through. If he had, he might have been impressed, but as it was, his attention was focused on the view below. It took a moment since he wasn't used to the aerial perspective, but then he recognized where they were. A large river threaded through the countryside to bisect a large city. A massive bridge spanned it, connecting the halves, and in the center was a building he knew well, Roc's Roost.

Lognion had brought them back to where he and Selene had left from, Bondgrad, the capital of Trendham. Anxiety filled Oliver's heart. He'd thought the trip would take days, but it appeared Lognion's retribution would begin much sooner.

The dragon's flight slowed as he climbed, gaining altitude as he performed a seemingly lazy circle around the city. Meanwhile, Oliver could only observe with a growing sense of horror. Far below the tiny specs of people in the city paused in the streets as they tried to make sense of what they were seeing in the sky. A sense of urgency swept over him, and Oliver released the magic holding him to Lognion's back, the vague idea of dropping and using his special shield to survive the fall in the back of his mind.

Lognion's voice came to him as they reached the relatively quiet apex of their flight. "Do not consider jumping. Your tattoo magics won't prevent the fall from killing you. Even if your bones and skin were somehow as strong as steel, the impact would reduce your brain to jelly. No shield can prevent that." The dragon's body gradually pitched forward, and they began to pick up speed as they fell back toward the earth. "Watch and despair."

Terrified, Oliver reestablished the climbing magic and held on tightly. The wind grew louder in his ears as they raced toward the distant city, until he could hear nothing but a constant roar. He tried activating his phase-spider shield, but he immediately discovered its weakness as the air ripped it away from his body. All he could do was activate his iron-body transformation to spare his skin from the abrasive wind and hope that his ears would survive.

Bondgrad had been small, a distant vista at the height of their flight, but now it was growing in front of them with alarming speed. The people who had been staring up were now large enough that Oliver could see the moment that they realized what was happening. They were no longer pointing and calling to one another. Panic reigned as the citizens began to run, trampling one another in their efforts to find cover. Some of those on the causeway gave in to terror and leapt to their deaths.

Less than fifty yards from the top of the tallest buildings, Lognion shifted the angle of his wings, and their dive became a horizontal glide at speeds too great to contemplate as they swept over the eastern half of the capital of Trendham. The dragon's jaws opened, and a gout of flame so hot it blazed almost white swept over the buildings and people beneath them.

Oliver feared the rushing air would sweep it back onto him, but somehow the dragon's breath emerged with such fierce velocity that it outpaced them. Screams began to rise through the air to meet them, but they were not from places the fire touched. Stone buildings melted like butter, wooden beams exploded as though made of flash powder, and people vanished, turned to ash in an instant without even time to register their deaths.

The screams came from those on the fringes, those close enough to have their skin instantly blistered by the heat wave, yet far enough back to retain enough of their lungs to cry out in pain. They came from those wounded by collapsing buildings farther back, and loudest of all, they came from those untouched yet close enough to see what had become of their neighbors.

Shocked and paralyzed, Oliver witnessed it all, as one of the largest human cities went from civilized to the depths of hysteria in a span of seconds.

The dragonfire cut a swath nearly twenty yards wide through the oldest part of the city, but Lognion did not relent after one pass. As he reached the edge, the dragon went into a wide banking turn that brought them a quarter of the way around. They were moving at a more leisurely pace when they turned back inward, this time heading perpendicular to the river to follow the line of Breville's Causeway. Roc's Roost was prominent in the skyline ahead, and it would pass directly beneath them.

Gauging by what the dragonfire had already done, the bridge would not survive, and the historic inn that defined the city was about to become a pile of molten rubble damming the Trent River.

Lognion's jaws remained closed until they were almost to the bridge, then opened, pouring out a river of fire that would transform the once-beautiful city into a scene of hell on earth. The citizens that normally crowded the causeway were gone, having fled into buildings or leapt to their deaths, but Oliver's keen eyes spotted a small figure standing atop Roc's Roost.

Even at a distance, her auburn hair made it easy to identify his Aunt Ess. Samantha Cartwright, known to the people of Trendham as Madeleine Brightblaze, had taken a stance atop her home at the heart of the city, atop the inn colloquially known as Breville's Cock.

Dragonfire touched the street, turning stone into an explosion of sparks, black smoke, and spattering molten rock, but when it reached the edge of the causeway, where the bridge met the street foundations, something changed.

From his view atop Lognion's back, Oliver couldn't see past the flames, but the smoke and sparks had stopped. The dragon flew on, heading directly for the tiny figure atop the tall building at the center of the bridge, and as they got farther out, Oliver could see that the dragonfire was floating above the causeway, arrested in midair by some mysterious force.

In a flash, understanding struck him, and as they drew closer, he could see the stern concentration written on his aunt's face as she worked to contain the blazing fire that Lognion left in his wake. Glancing back down, he saw the flames moving like a floating river of fire, flowing rapidly toward the center of the bridge. Against all expectations, it remained in the air, racing toward Sammy at high speed. It outpaced the dragon's flight and joined the fresh fire pouring from Lognion's mouth.

Realizing things weren't proceeding according to plan, Lognion cut off his fiery exhalation and closed his massive jaws as he pulled up to hover directly in front of the woman who faced him.

In that moment, the remaining fire gathered before her, forming a tiny ball of incandescent energy so bright that it hurt Oliver's eyes to look at it.

Deep within the dragon, Selene also watched, helpless to affect the situation. *Don't do this,* she begged.

The other Cartwright also has spirit, Lognion answered silently. *But she is close to her limit. Watch and learn.* Opening his jaws once more, a new gout of fire issued forth. It swept past the ball of captured fire that Sammy was holding in abeyance and rushed straight toward her. Her eyes widened, and Oliver saw the surprise written on her features for a split second before she disappeared, engulfed in flames.

Oliver screamed at the sight, but seconds later, the flames changed again, rushing inward. Where Sammy had stood was something that bore her shape, a humanoid body formed of distilled dragonfire. With a gesture, the burning wizard flicked her hand, and the blazing star that still floated a short distance in front of her launched itself toward Lognion.

Oliver felt a shiver pass through the dragon's body as the tiny shining sphere struck, and for a second, he thought nothing had happened. Could a dragon be burned? Not by fire, surely, but by dragonfire? Lognion shuddered, and Oliver felt a sudden foreboding. He covered himself with the spider shield with only seconds to spare as a hole erupted farther down the dragon's spine, and a column of fire exploded into the open air. The dragonfire star had burned completely through, and now the remnants were venting from the other side.

Lognion's mouth opened, but instead of a roar, only dim flames guttered forth. The dragon's wings fluttered, then lost their rhythm as the great reptile began to fall.

Oliver felt his stomach begin to float as he lost his sensation of weight. He released his hold on the dragon's back, but he was still fifty yards above the stone deck of the causeway. *So this is how I die,* he thought, strangely unafraid. *At least I got to see the dragon die first.* His eyes met those of the burning figure as he started down.

His view was suddenly filled with fire. Somehow, his aunt had appeared in front of him, and her blazing hand reached out to grab him. The spider shield stopped her from making contact, so he dispelled it. He was sure her hand would burn him, but he felt nothing when she reached out again, and then they were standing on the bridge. Sammy had teleported them.

Well, she was standing. Not being the one in control, Oliver hadn't been in the right position. He collapsed onto his side, but immediately rose to his feet again. They both stumbled when the bridge shook a moment later.

The dragon's body struck the bridge close to the right side, and the shock of it shattered the stone there. The arches supporting that portion of the deck collapsed, and the road fell away beneath the massive body. Slowly, the scaled body rolled slightly, then dropped, falling to the river far below. Lognion struck the rocks sticking up from the shallows and lay still.

Sammy looked at her nephew. "How did this happen?"

"She tried to use his memories and somehow he came back to life," answered Oliver. "I think she's trapped inside him, but I'm not really sure of anything." He had to squint while looking at her, for the flames she seemed wholly composed of were far too bright.

Sammy nodded, studying him with eyes of liquid gold. "Wait here."

"Where are you going?"

"To finish this."

Peering down from the broken roadway, Oliver glanced back at her. "He's dead."

Back straight and shoulders square, Sammy replied, "No. From what Will told me, this isn't enough. He will recover. I need to render him down until there's nothing left but ash."

Oliver had no answer for that, but he could see from the stiffness of her posture that his aunt was hiding her weariness. "Don't—" He started to argue, but she vanished. Looking down, he saw she had appeared on the rocks below. He also noticed Lognion's body was already beginning to twitch. *How can he still be alive?*

CHAPTER 12

Selene had a firsthand view of the fight. In fact, aside from not being in control, she saw, heard, *and* felt everything Lognion did. When she saw the dragonfire engulf Sammy, she screamed with impotent fury, unable to stop what was happening. It was with great relief that she saw Will's cousin emerge unharmed, and she felt pride and satisfaction when Sammy turned the tables.

But the pain was incredible. There was no doubt in her mind that the dragon's body was fully alive. Her sensations were every bit as vivid and real as when she possessed a living human, perhaps more so. Sammy's dragonfire star burned into her chest, boring through from front to back, and emerged from a place on her back just above her hips.

Lognion, and by extension Selene, lost awareness for some period of time, and when vision returned, they were crashing down onto the rocks beneath the causeway. The force of the uncontrolled fall broke ribs, eliciting more waves of pain.

From her perspective, however, the pain was worth it. *You deserve this,* she shouted at Lognion.

The younger Cartwright surprised me, replied Lognion. *If only you had learned the same lessons, my daughter, you would not be such a disappointment.*

Selene felt the dragon's vitality rekindle. It had guttered for a moment, nearly overwhelmed by the damage Sammy had inflicted, but already it was recovering. Worse, she could feel Lognion's excitement. He hadn't expected such a challenge, and the idea seemed to thrill him.

You're enjoying this? she asked, dismayed by the thought.

Immensely. There is no joy such as meeting a foe worthy of eating.

Opening one eye, they saw the blazing wizard appear on the rocks twenty yards away. Selene couldn't help but admire Sammy's poise. The young woman was shining with power and showed no sign of fear. But Selene knew the truth. It wasn't a fight Sammy could win. Even

Grim Talek, with millennia of preparations and some of the greatest ancient wizards to assist him—even he had failed. At most, he had created an opportunity, and it had been an incredible stroke of good fortune that someone like her husband had been there and had had the power to take advantage of it.

Selene would do anything for her people, but she didn't believe in fighting unwinnable battles. Faced with such a circumstance, the only wise thing for Sammy to do was to flee and fight another day. *Please, Samantha, please run,* she silently prayed.

"You are a credit to your family," rumbled Lognion. The flesh and organs inside his body had already begun knitting back together. Without warning, his tail whipped around from one side.

Sammy was well within its reach, but she teleported and reappeared even closer after the tail had passed by. "You made a mistake, *wyrm.* This is my home."

Lognion shifted his weight, struggling to rise to his feet as his body recovered. "You've grown strong. If you try to escape, I doubt I could capture you in my present state, but you cannot defeat me. What will you choose?"

"There is no choice," replied Sammy. "I will put an end to you." She was standing directly in front of the dragon, glaring at him with an imperious gaze and her chin high.

What is she doing? thought Selene, but she understood a moment later. *She's taunting him. Trying to get him to unleash more dragonfire.* Ordinary flame couldn't hurt Lognion. Very little could even wound him, but dragonfire was something more than ordinary fire. It held something more like the dragon himself, the spark of creation or the essence of the divine perhaps—whatever it was, it could hurt him. Sammy was still covered in it, but she obviously needed more.

"In honor of your choice, I will spare the city after devouring you," said Lognion. Lifting his head, he opened massive jaws and began to exhale.

Flame poured out, and Sammy seized it, but Lognion had seen through her ploy. His exhalation had been a feint, and he stopped after half a second. Meanwhile, his tail whipped back around at the same time, driving toward Sammy's back while his jaws opened wide and shot forward.

Sammy didn't attempt to teleport this time. Instead, she leapt forward, surrounding herself in a force-sphere. The tail slammed into it, driving her across the remaining distance, directly into the gaping maw, a place where no simple shield could save her.

But at the last instant, she released the shield, and as Lognion's jaws closed the dragonfire that covered her exploded outward in a searing flash.

Selene's awareness dissolved into pure agony as the dragonfire burned through Lognion's tongue and destroyed the flesh of her throat and sinuses. For a moment, she thought Lognion's head would be completely consumed. It was difficult to fathom, since Sammy hadn't seemed to be holding onto that much captured dragonfire. She had surprised Lognion once again. If he had been foolish enough to unleash his breath upon her again, as she had wanted, Sammy might well have had enough to destroy his head completely.

Whether that would have killed Lognion was separate question, one that Selene was less certain about after the events of the last two days.

Sammy dropped free, falling through the bottom of the dragon's jaw since most of the tissue had been burned away. The flames covering her body were gone, and Selene could read the expression written on her face as Sammy stumbled away from the half-burned dragon head. Anger, fear, desperation, and the sure knowledge that she had failed— all these were visible in the red-haired wizard's eyes.

You did your best, Sammy. There's no point in dying. You've done all you can, thought Selene, her heart crying for Will's younger cousin. *Please, Samantha, get away while you can.*

Sammy moved farther away, keeping her eyes on the enemy. Controlling the dragonfire had taken far more out of her than simple turyn; it had been extremely taxing on her will. If it hadn't been for her natural talent with fire, it would likely have not been possible at all, but now she was paying for it. She gathered turyn to her as rapidly as possible, but without Lognion's dragonfire, she had no good way to end the fight.

Lognion's tail whipped around once more, whistling as it aimed for her. Sammy blocked it with a hastily erected point-defense shield, and while she waited until the optimal time, when the tail was closest, the force of the blow almost overwhelmed her. She stumbled, almost falling. Teleporting away would have been the smarter move, but she didn't have enough turyn left for that. In truth, even if she had wanted to run, it was too late. She'd spent everything on that one last gamble.

Lognion lifted his head, the flesh already beginning to reform around his lower jaw, and Selene could sense his anticipation. Slowly, the massive dragon lifted himself back onto his feet.

Sammy struck at him with force-lances, but she might as well have saved her energy, for they did almost nothing. When the tail came at her again, she blocked it once more, and this time the effort did cause her to lose her footing. Falling to one knee, Samantha Cartwright looked up and saw one of Lognion's claws descending. The dragon had extended a single digit, stabbing downward to skewer her with it.

With nothing left, Sammy bared her teeth, snarling as death descended upon her.

And then something unexpected happened. Two figures dropped down, seemingly from nowhere. Madeleine Brightblaze had two wardsmen in her employ as bodyguards, and though she had deliberately left them behind, they apparently had a difference of opinion regarding that decision. Alex had found a long length of rope and secured it from the stone bridge rails so that they could slide down.

Now they had arrived, but it was almost too late.

Oliver threw his shining silvery body into the path of Lognion's claw, but he didn't rely only on his spider shield. His enchanted buckler was held high, and he used both arms to brace it. Meanwhile, Alex ducked low, charging at Sammy. Though she wasn't prone, he seized one of her arms and rolled, jerking her up and over his shoulder as he came back to his feet. Using everything that remained of his momentum, the young wardsman ran, carrying his mistress across his shoulders.

As quick as Alex was, the maneuver still wasn't fast enough. He and Sammy would have both been impaled by the descending claw, but he had coordinated his plan with Oliver's blocking tactic in order to give him the half second needed.

Oliver's part didn't go as well, but then again, his part was ridiculous to begin with. As large and strong as he was, the sheer mass and size of what he was attempting to halt was too much for any man. The supernaturally sharp claw pierced the enchanted buckler, tearing through the magically reinforced steel as though it was tissue, and it proceeded onward. The phase-spider shield failed as well, and the tip went through one of Oliver's forearms and into his right shoulder before the weight of it all smashed him into the rocky ground.

Alex was intent on running, so he didn't see what had become of his partner, and by the time he looked back, it was far too late. He kept to his mission and fought to contain the emotions that would destroy his ability to move forward.

But Selene had a much closer view. Mentally, she screamed, even as she felt the claw tear into her stepson. For a moment, she was beyond rational thought, and she threw the weight of her will against Lognion's mental prison. The dragon tried to withdraw his claw, but for precious seconds, she held him still. *No! He'll die if you pull it free.*

He is dead already, returned Lognion.

I can save him! shouted Selene. *Just stay still and free me.*

Free yourself. You already know the answer to your problem.

She knew what he wanted. In her mind's eye, it stood out as a green door, one she had created for herself the day she had crafted her phylactery. The imagery was symbolic, but it represented a knot in the enchantment that kept her anchored. If she used it, the magic would unravel, and her immortality would end. Free of that self-imposed prison, her strength would be her own once more—the portion of her will that was bound up in maintaining the phylactery would be unburdened.

She might even have enough strength of will to overpower Lognion, though she had no way of knowing without testing it. But even if she won, it would be a temporary victory. She might hold on briefly, but without her living source or the phylactery to anchor her, she would pass on. Then, Lognion would have his body back and she would be gone.

All this passed through her mind in an instant, for she'd been thinking about it since first losing control. She argued with him instead. *You said you would not kill him. I took you at your word.*

I warned him not to try his steel with me.

He was defending someone, not attacking. And you promised me that he would live. There was no condition regarding whether he fought against you or not. Let me save him!

Wretched child, you will save no one until you learn your lesson. But I will honor my words. Observe and do not distract me or the outcome will be on your head, replied Lognion. Turyn flowed from his other claw, forming a strange spell construct.

Selene watched him work, unsure what he was doing. The runes were unfamiliar, which was unusual in itself, given the breadth of her knowledge, but since Lognion was a dragon with millennia of experience, it went without saying that he'd probably learned and forgotten more runes and systems of magical writing than she could imagine. What truly had her stumped was the geometry of his construct. It made no sense to her, for parts of it were clearly unbalanced, as though there were portions she could not see supporting the parts that she *could* see.

That can't work, she murmured, but before she could say more, the world went black. At first, she assumed Lognion had sealed her in darkness to prevent her from distracting him, but a moment later, a new world filled her senses. Oliver lay in the center of her awareness with a light shining upon him. Lognion's claws were visible, one still buried in the young man, and the other open and close by, as though her father was working with magic, but she could see none of it.

Selene was startled when a voice spoke beside her. She turned and saw an unknown woman. "I've hidden parts of it from your view."

"Parts of what?" asked Selene.

"The magic your father is using is forbidden, a relic from a forgotten world, the world that birthed me long ago."

"He's *not* my father. Who are you? Why is it forbidden? What's happening here?" Selene was filled with questions and confusion. Though Selene didn't recognize the woman, she seemed intimately familiar somehow. The newcomer was of medium height with light-colored hair and warm brown eyes. A sense of peace radiated from her that made even Selene's panic fade into the background.

"I am one that remembers who you once were. The magic you cannot see controls the flow of time. My husband and I deemed it too dangerous for this new world. Lognion is using it to slow time around your son so that he can heal him without endangering his life." The strange woman looked at her with sympathy on her face. "As for what is happening, I thought perhaps we could talk for a moment."

Selene frowned. The feeling she got from the stranger was so empathetic that she couldn't help but wonder if that was what having a mother felt like, and that thought alone irritated her. "How does he know such magic?" she asked.

The woman smiled without showing her teeth. "He does not. When he thinks on it, he will believe it was from a dream, and if he tries to use it again, he won't remember how it was done."

"Who are you to manipulate a dragon?" Selene wondered aloud. Her eyes snapped back to the stranger. "Temarah? He said you weren't real."

"Am I? I'm not truly certain anymore," answered the woman. "Call me Penny."

"But you're the Mother, aren't you?" insisted Selene, hope beginning to stir in her heart. "You can fix this. Help me stop him!"

Penny's expression turned somber. "I will not."

Selene was stunned. "Why not?"

"What your father told you is true as far as he understands it. The dragons are necessary for reality to sustain itself."

"And you created them!" accused Selene. "Have you seen how sick and twisted Lognion is? Are you telling me that that is what you want?"

"I do not control him, or you for that matter. Despite my role, I do not control the world you live in. This dragon is necessary. It cannot be removed without unmaking a portion of reality, including the world you live in."

"It was doing quite well without him these past years," argued Selene.

"The dragon was never gone. It was merely changed. Parts of it were claimed by the whelplings, a part by your husband, and the rest has been in your hands all this time. You should consider how things came to be as they are now."

Selene couldn't accept the goddess's words. "You're blaming me? I've sacrificed *everything* to save my people! If Lognion, if this *monster*, is what you consider right and proper, then I would rather be wrong."

The Mother's expression remained unyielding. "On the scale of eternity, most acts of good and evil shrink into insignificance, nor do I presume to judge, but some things rise to a different level of importance. Your spark of life, the piece of the divine that connects us all, the eternal part of you, your soul—that cannot be treated lightly."

"I have accepted the consequences to myself," interrupted Selene.

Penny shook her head. "Your soul is not yours to bargain with, nor are those of the children you wronged."

Fury built within her as Selene glared back. "A few pay the price to alleviate the suffering of the masses. Don't dare compare me to Lognion. He would burn this city just to assuage his ego."

"An evil thing, to be sure," agreed Penny, "but life and death are fleeting and ephemeral. The soul has no number, it cannot be counted, for there is only one, but you have stolen pieces of it and imprisoned them for your own purposes. That is an evil that endures perpetually, and one that cannot be forgiven until it is undone. Do you not see, child?"

Selene turned her back on the goddess.

Penny sighed, then continued, "You will not listen, but you must know four things. There are three enemies that must be stopped, the corrupted dragon, the elves, and the Watcher in the Void. The fourth thing you must know is that only the power of the dragon can accomplish these things."

Exasperated, Selene turned back. "You just admitted he is corrupted."

"Not your father, the corrupted dragon you helped create when the whelplings were sent to Hell after consuming so much of your father's power."

"That wasn't even me," argued Selene. "And stop calling him my father!"

"I am not saying he is worthy of your love, but denying his role will not solve your problems."

"It must be nice, sitting around on a cloud or whatever it is you do and watching the rest of us struggle and suffer while you decide what you think is the best thing for us to do. Try living in this twisted world you created and then come back and tell me whether you think I'm doing the right thing or not. I spent most of my life trying to be better than that *thing* that you call my father, and I spent a lot of it trying to help the people in *your* church and the people of my country. If you want me to help your damned dragon, then we're done. I've done as much as I could on my own. So, either help me, or get out of my head."

The goddess watched her silently for several seconds, her visage firm and unyielding. "You remind me of myself. In my day, I was stubborn and given to anger. Those traits can be a strength, so long as you don't allow them to drive you to poor choices."

Exasperated, Selene replied, "If you won't leave, then at least explain who these enemies are. I have no interest in your moralizing."

"The first two need no explanation, and the third is hidden from my eyes. The Watcher wields a power that could unmake the world. Long before the universe was born, we knew that the power of the Void could destroy this dream, for that is how ours ended. To forestall that, the dragons were created. But now, the power of your father, the power of *this* dragon, has been divided. The greatest part of it lies with his corrupted offspring, a dragon in the pit of Hell. *That* dragon is unlikely to oppose the Watcher in the Void, and it might even choose to ally with her," explained Penny.

"It's a shame I'm trapped like this," said Selene dryly. "But even if I wasn't, I'm not sure what you think I should do."

"The Watcher must be stopped, and the power of the dragon is needed for the task."

"I truly hope you aren't saying that only Lognion can save the world," observed Selene.

The goddess held her gaze. "I had hope for you, daughter, but what you have done to yourself not only makes you unfit, it makes it impossible for you to touch the dragon's power. Your husband also showed promise. He defeated your father by using the dragon's power against it. Yet he also was touched by the shadow when he attempted to trap Grim Talek. He might very well defeat the Watcher only to fall prey to the same corruption."

"What about Sammy?" asked Selene. "Didn't she just touch the dragon's power?"

"You saw the outcome. She has the potential, but she couldn't best your father, even as weak as he is now. Lognion is ruthless, intelligent, and has millennia of experience. He is also willing to do anything to achieve victory, even if it costs him his own existence, something you have already proven you are unwilling to do."

Annoyed by the jab, Selene responded angrily, "Since I'm so unworthy, what *exactly* is it that you expect from me?"

"Your father is currently wasting precious resources keeping you contained. You are a drain on his will and his power, one he cannot afford." She pointed to one side, and Selene's green door reappeared. "You called yourself unworthy, but you do not have to be."

Selene stared aghast at her. "You're telling me to die? You want me to die so your demented champion will be a little stronger?"

"You are dead now. Free yourself, free the children you trapped; do this and I will welcome you home."

Selene's eyes narrowed. "Home? What does that mean?"

"Your spirit will rejoin the dream, the unity that all souls are part of," explained the goddess. "Reject this offer, and while you might persist for centuries, eventually you will be destroyed, and when that happens, you will disappear completely—cursed—never to be reborn."

"And Lognion will go on to murder and destroy everyone I care about," she countered.

Penny nodded. "He might, but their deaths are not permanent. Their souls return home, and new lives await those who are willing to be reborn. In any case, his choices are not yours."

Bitter, Selene answered, "My choices are not yours to make either. See yourself out."

"My offer will remain open to you until the final battle, but the longer you wait, the more difficult it will be to defeat the Watcher." The goddess faded from view, and the sights and sounds of the outside world returned.

From what she could see, almost no time had passed. Oliver still lay on the ground, impaled by the dragon's claw, but blood was no longer seeping from the edges of the wound. The spell construct Lognion had created had expanded and now hovered around the young wardsman, forming a hazy container of magic. Within those confines, nothing moved, and even Oliver's breathing had stopped.

Yet, the claw was able to move, and Lognion withdrew it. Selene started at that, wanting to yell, but she saw that the young man's flesh didn't seem to register the absence of the claw. The wound remained open, as though the claw was still there, and simultaneously, no new rush of blood appeared. Time had all but stopped within the dragon's spell.

New spells were rapidly cast, sealing damaged blood vessels and closing the holes in Oliver's lungs. In Selene's estimation, they were crudely done. Some of it would have been better done by Oliver's tattoos, and the more serious damage done to his lungs and heart needed a far more delicate touch. *You're botching it. You'll leave him permanently crippled, if he survives at all,* she argued. *Let me do this.*

But Lognion ignored her. Releasing the stasis field, he watched as Oliver collapsed, gaping and gasping. Blood still seeped slowly from his wounded shoulder, and the young man writhed in pain at the crudely done healing.

The dragon pulled back and set the tip of one claw against his own chest. Selene felt a brief pain as Lognion pierced his own hide. When he removed the claw, he held it out, examining the blood on it.

It was dragon's blood, but it bore a peculiar luster that Selene hadn't seen in the copious amounts of blood Lognion had recently shed. Somehow, it reminded her of the dragonfire that Sammy had briefly stolen. *What is that?* she asked.

A boon, one that Grim Talek once sought to replicate. His failure led to the sad creatures you knew as the Drak'shar. Unlike them, this child will receive the true blessing of my heart's blood. With that said, Lognion stuck the bloody tip of his claw back into Oliver's damaged shoulder, causing the wardsman to jerk, a cry of pain filling the air.

Stop! What will that do to him? demanded Selene.

Remember the egg guardians? This is how they are made.

In the dragon's nest there had been guards, almost human in size and proportions, yet draconic in nature. Grim Talek's vampires, along with Tiny in his demon-steel golem had fought a hard battle against them when they tried to destroy the nest and Lognion himself. The thought of Oliver being transformed into such a creature horrified her. *No! I could have saved him. This is worse than death!*

Silence, commanded Lognion. Oliver had gone rigid where he lay on the hard stone rocks. His back arched, and his mouth was wide in a silent scream, but his eyes remained open and they were focused on the source of his pain. "My gift will heal you," the dragon announced. "What it does to you beyond that depends upon the strength of your soul. If you are weak, do not blame me for what comes next."

You're trying to twist him into one of your servants, accused Selene.

Lognion's reply seemed to ignore her words. *You wanted to know how I stymied the elves' efforts to infiltrate Terabinia. The heart-stone enchantment was my most important tool for that, since they could not manipulate those servants that I commanded directly, but its original purpose was for this. The blood drives most who receive it to rage and madness, and much like a dragon, they cannot be controlled afterward—unless their souls have already been chained.*

You're saying he will go mad?

The dragon's body was almost whole now and his belly rumbled as he chuckled. *His mind is his own. He is free to do as he pleases, assuming he can control himself.* Speaking aloud, Lognion announced, "I tire of this place." He stretched his wings and tested his legs, making certain his body was hale enough for flight. Glancing down, he said to Oliver, "Your aunt fought well, and she did not flinch, even in defeat, though you prevented me from properly tasting my victory. I will leave the city intact. Tell her to grow stronger. The fight will be better once she has finished maturing."

Stretching out his wings, Lognion prepared to launch himself into the air, but Oliver managed to call out in a hoarse, trembling voice. "Wait." When the dragon paused, the young man added, "Take me with you."

"Your place is here."

"She's still in there, isn't she?"

"For now."

"Then I need to come with you. I promised to guard her."

Lognion's laughter erupted and grew steadily louder until it threatened to shake even the massive stone pillars that supported Breville's Causeway. "There is nothing that can threaten me that you could defend against, and your stepmother is hardly more than a ghost." But the young wardsman was already getting shakily to his feet, though the effort visibly pained him. Seeing the human's determination, Lognion lowered one wing to act as a ramp. "Very well."

Oliver stood slowly, his body weak as a kitten. His first steps were clumsy, and he struggled to keep from crying out each time a foot landed and sent a tiny shock from leg to collar bone. After only three steps, he collapsed, vomiting onto the ground while his entire body shook uncontrollably. Much of what he ejected was dark blood.

"I will leave if you insist on wasting my time," warned Lognion.

Oliver barely heard him, his awareness overwhelmed by searing pain that rushed through every inch of his body. It was almost identical to what he imagined it would be like to be burned alive. A slow groan escaped his lips as he tried again to rise.

"What you feel is your flesh being purified. I've been told it is an excruciating experience, but what is more important is whether you can function in spite of it. Once this burning subsides, you will have to live with a different type of fire that will persist in your heart. If you cannot control the pain, you have little hope of controlling the rage that will follow. In that case, it would be better for you to stay here. There is an entire city just waiting for you to sate your bloodlust. I have no use for monsters," said Lognion mercilessly.

Growling inaudibly, Oliver pushed himself up onto his arms and knees and scrambled up the wing on all fours. Reaching the dragon's spine he collapsed again, but managed to reactivate his climbing tattoo and fix himself to Lognion's hide.

Without waiting for him to adjust, Lognion's wings flexed and he launched them into the air.

CHAPTER 13

Where are we going? asked Selene.

I have several options that appeal. Clearing out this elf infestation, removing your doppelganger from the throne, and reclaiming my full strength. Which do you think I will choose first? returned the dragon.

Selene didn't fail to notice that Lognion's list was very similar to the one the goddess had given her, with the exception of the Watcher in the Void. She wondered if the Mother had implanted the ideas without his knowing. *The elves seem like the obvious choice,* she replied. *If you intend to kill Janice, you'll upset the balance in the capital. She looks like me and they think you're dead.*

Lognion chuckled mentally. *They'll never notice. I don't intend to return with my old face. I'll use yours. The only one who needs to die is your friend.*

She had anticipated he might choose the capital first, though she was surprised that Lognion intended to usurp her identity.

It will be quite the shock to them when they die by your hand, added the dragon.

He was trying to provoke a reaction. She understood that. It fit with his stated goal of tormenting her, but she wouldn't allow him the satisfaction of hearing her beg. She tried a different tactic. *Sammy was almost too much for you. Janice won't be alone.*

I've examined your memories. Janice isn't strong enough to challenge me, and that black golem you created won't be enough either.

Selene kept her tone neutral. *There are two other third-order wizards in Cerria, Emory Tallowen and Will's sister, Tabitha. Sammy has the means to warn them of your coming. Together, they might be too much for you. Especially if Sammy recovers in time and can teleport there to aid them. Are you really that confident after what just happened?*

There's no beacon linking Bondgrad with Cerria, remarked her father.

Will can teleport to people he's familiar with, she argued. *You saw Sammy reflex casting the teleport spell during your fight.*

According to your memories, he's the only one capable of teleporting to someone using an astral bond. Don't bother trying to fool me.

He's the only one I'm sure can do it, she corrected. *It's been over a decade. Just because I haven't mastered it doesn't mean Sammy or Tabitha haven't. I've had almost no contact with them to know.* She waited, but Lognion didn't respond, so she added, *I notice you are flying rather than creating a gate. You don't have the strength to spare for it, do you?*

Still the observant one, aren't you? said Lognion. *It's obvious that you're trying to delay the inevitable for your friends. But you haven't considered the difficulty of the third option. Facing my offspring in Hell will be far more dangerous.*

She'd been waiting for that, and Selene quickly slid her verbal blade home. *If you are too weak to face the younger dragons in Hell, then you're doomed to fail at the rest. You might kill my friends and allies, but you won't be able to handle the elves, and William will tear you to pieces when he returns.* She allowed her anticipation to show in her thoughts. *Next time, he won't leave the scraps to be eaten by scavengers. I'll make sure he has better options. You won't recover from that defeat.*

The dragon chuckled even as he flew. *You're hoping to buy time, perhaps even long enough for Will to return and save them.*

Would you prefer killing them only to be too weak to have a chance of winning when he catches you? she taunted.

Lognion's thoughts were full of sarcasm and mockery as he replied, *If I am as weak as you suppose, is it better for me to die facing my offspring? At the very least, I should finish teaching you the folly of your ways before my inevitable defeat.*

She ignored the sarcasm. *You would have a better chance if I help you.*

With what?

To regain your strength, she told him. *Keeping me prisoner is taxing your strength. If I help you defeat your offspring, you'll have a better chance at succeeding.*

You think you have something of worth to offer? You? A maimed and crippled shadow of your former potential—you think you have some value?

Selene decided to show her hand. *I still have a thousand elementals.*

There was a pause as Lognion checked the memories he had stolen. *So you do. You're proposing a deal?*

You leave them alone and I will help you.

Who, exactly?

Janice and her family, Tabitha and her family, as well as Sammy, Oliver, and anyone else close to Will.

That's not much of a bargain, replied the dragon. *You expect me to give up my revenge, and forget reclaiming my kingdom? That leaves me nothing but the joy of destroying the citizens of Terabinia.*

You weren't planning to do that! she exclaimed.

I wasn't, but I've changed my mind. You need more motivation to be helpful. His thoughts carried a palpable sneer.

I'll give you what you want after defeating the dragons in Hell, she offered. *I'll end my existence, so long as you give me your word not to hurt the people I named or the people of Terabinia. I'll even make sure you get your throne back—peacefully.*

You are not worth a fraction of that. Choose, Will and his family or Terabinia.

If I choose to save my people, that should include Janice. She'll retain the throne in my stead?

Certainly, he agreed. *Assuming she doesn't interfere while I'm enjoying the taste of William's relatives.*

Just his blood relatives? Not Oliver, or Tabitha's husband and in-laws?

Tabitha's family I will destroy entirely, but I've already agreed to let the boy live. However, if you wish to make this deal, I will need to use him as a guarantee. If you fail to follow through, his life will be immediately forfeit.

It wasn't the deal Selene wanted, but she knew her father, it was probably the best she could hope for. It would mean sacrificing Will's family, but Oliver would be safe, and the others at least had a chance of escape. Tabitha and Sammy were both powerful. The regular citizens of Terabinia would have no hope if she chose family instead of kingdom. In the end, it was hardly a choice, the lives of millions or one family. As queen, she had a duty, and she had never failed it. In the silence of her heart, she felt a small flash of pain. *I cannot ask you for forgiveness, Will, but at least I know you will avenge them,* she thought to herself. Then she addressed Lognion. *Let's clarify the terms, then I will agree.*

After a brief discussion, it was decided. Lognion would spare Terabinia and leave it in the hands of Janice, who would continue to rule in Selene's place. Tabitha and her family would be hunted mercilessly, as would Sammy and Will's mother. Lognion would also be free to eliminate anyone who interfered with that pursuit, including Janice or individual citizens. Only Oliver would be spared, though he would be used as a hostage to ensure Selene's compliance with her part of the bargain.

In exchange, Selene would freely assist Lognion in defeating his offspring in Hell, offering up all her skills, knowledge, ideas, and her power to make sure he succeeded. Once that was done, Oliver would be free and clear, and Selene would end her own existence, unravelling the enchantment that bound her soul to the phylactery.

We have a deal, she stated, and her father agreed. A moment later, she felt his power begin to move and a gate appeared in front of them in the air. As they flew through it, snowy mountaintops appeared below them. Her first thought, however, wasn't about the scenery. It was the fact that Lognion had just casually created a gate, proving that her first assumption about his relative weakness hadn't been entirely accurate, and the fact that he hadn't argued the point meant he'd purposely allowed her to deceive herself. *He intended to take this course of action all along,* she realized, *but he wanted me to bargain with him.* It would have been disheartening if she hadn't spent most of her life being similarly manipulated.

But could she have gotten more? Probably not. Lognion almost always had the advantage of negotiating from a position of absolute strength, and the most recent situation hadn't been any different. At the very least, she'd gotten a guarantee for her people. *And if he thinks William will lose, he's making a serious error in judgment,* she consoled herself.

Not curious about where we are? asked the dragon.

I'm assuming there's an intersection of ley lines here, she replied. *Beyond that it hardly matters. You'll need the boost to create a gate to Hell.*

Despite debasing yourself, you remain sharp as ever, my daughter. You aren't frustrated by my deception, are you?

She could feel him gloating, but she refused to give him satisfaction. *I expected there would be something like this, but I got what was most important to me, as did you.*

The dragon chuckled again. *We will need to separate for you to assist.*

In her prison, Selene tensed. For her to function, she would need a body and to access the one stored in her limnthal, she would need some control in order to summon it. If Lognion turned over complete control of his body, she might be able to reverse their positions. It would violate their deal, but she wasn't bound by anything other than her word. But if she failed a contest of wills, her father would imprison her again and then be free to do whatever he wished.

The dragon spiraled downward before landing on a broad stone platform that bordered a stone chasm. It was the same place that Will and Sammy had once used to create the gate that Will had used to travel to Hell. Moments after settling down, Lognion breathed lightly, sending a gout of what seemed to be normal fire out, melting the snow and ice that obscured much of the area. Once the stone was clear, he spoke aloud for Oliver's benefit. "You can get down now."

Oliver released his climbing spell and slid down the dragon's side. When he reached the ground, he didn't bother trying to sit or stand. He curled into a ball, making no attempt to hide his misery.

Meanwhile, Lognion withdrew slightly, allowing Selene to access the right side of his body. With fifty percent under her control, it would be an even battle, but she knew she wasn't strong enough to win. She activated her limnthal and summoned the barely functional corpse of the elven woman she had operated on. She deeply regretted not having saved a second body when she had had the opportunity.

Once the elven corpse had appeared, she let Lognion know she was ready. Silently he released her, and she transferred to the cold, stiff body. Without organs or any life at all within the flesh, it was barely better than a clay golem. Selene's senses felt dull, and her limbs were wooden and clumsy. Climbing to her feet, she immediately went to Oliver. "It's me. How are you feeling?"

She could see his jaw muscle move under the skin as the young man struggled to unclench and respond. "It burns. All over. Feels like I'm on fire," her stepson hissed.

"Does it feel better or worse than an hour ago?"

Oliver's eyes flew open, and Selene saw fury in them. "It's the same!" He closed them immediately after, but not before she noticed that his pupils had changed, becoming vertical slits, like those of a cat— or a dragon.

"I'm going to use a few spells to examine you. Try to relax if you can," she told him, and without waiting, she immediately began casting. What she found was disturbing. His heart was racing, his temperature elevated, and from the activity in his nerves and muscles, she could easily read the signs of extreme pain. It almost looked like what she might have expected in a patient suffering tetany, but she'd already seen that he could still freely move, if he had to.

The change to his eyes bothered her more, and beneath the surface, Selene could tell that subtler changes had happened within his body. Unfortunately, she had no idea how to help, and the only thing she could offer was some relief. "I can ease the pain a little if you'll allow me to block some of your nerves," she told him.

Before her stepson could answer, Lognion interjected, "Interfere at his peril. He must adapt to the pain. If you dampen it, he won't be able to react to the changing influence of my blood."

She looked up at the dragon. "What do you mean?"

"You saw the egg guardians in my nest. Most who receive my blood are transformed, and while that might grant him greater physical prowess, his spirit will become atavistic, and his mind will be controlled by savage emotions. Only by surviving and mastering the fire in his blood will he retain his former intelligence," answered Lognion.

The recklessness of what Lognion had done made her furious, but there was little she could do about it. "What about the physical changes?"

"They vary, but usually they seem to reflect the inner control of the recipient. The better he does at soothing and controlling his reactions and emotions, the more human he will appear—probably."

She looked askance at her father. "Probably?"

"There are always exceptions. My existence spans time scales you cannot imagine. Across so many worlds, places, and species, I've seen all sorts of things happen. Leave him alone; he will be fine," said the dragon.

"Fine? How is this fine?" she replied, her tone rising. "You've already told me he might transform into a monster!"

"Most do," agreed Lognion, "because they were meant to be such. My blood will burn away the dross and purify his flesh. If he is meant to be a monster, he will be, and he will be happier as such. More interesting, though, will be if he doesn't. Perhaps he will be more like William."

Oliver's eyes opened. "What does that mean? Did this happen to my dad?"

"No," answered Selene. "He simply can't accept the fact that he was beaten by a mortal."

"I don't lie, daughter," intoned the dragon's deep voice.

Selene glared at the great beast, her gaze furious. "He was never poisoned by your blood."

Lognion chuckled. "Somehow, he did it himself, before we ever fought. The spark was in him, and during our battle, he used it to steal some of my power. The fact that he didn't transform after that is all the proof I need. Only a dragon could consume my essence without being changed. The fact that it wasn't my physical blood is irrelevant."

"You're mistaken."

"You have existed for less than the blink of an eye from my perspective, yet you would argue about things you do not understand. You just witnessed his cousin do something similar, though she drew from my fire rather than my body. Either she somehow changed herself, or your husband found a way to acclimate her to my power before this."

Selene remembered Will telling her about the alien, amoral, and god-like euphoria he had experienced when using his power to control storms. At one point, he had confessed to fearing that he might lose himself completely. She'd consoled him and convinced him he could choose his own identity, but the conversation stuck out in her mind. His problem had arisen mainly after fighting the dragon, but he'd experienced the strange, god-like state even before that. Was her father really telling the truth? Evil, egotistical, and arrogant, Lognion had always been those things, but she had never known him to lie.

Oliver's body straightened out, and his muscles tightened painfully as a scream escaped his lips. His face was locked in a rictus grin as his body shook violently. Seconds later, he relaxed slightly, and his desperate eyes sought those of his stepmother. "What's happening to me?"

Selene studied him silently for a moment, watching the interplay of the violently turbulent turyn within his flesh and the orderly flows that were still regulated by the channels his tattoos created. The dragon blood was changing him, and some of the alterations were being rejected by the healing templates built into his tattoos. The changes to his organs were largely unopposed, but those to his skin, muscle, and bones were being rejected and repaired—over and over. What would that mean for the final result? She had to admit that she didn't know.

Since his inner battle might be even more important, she answered with a confidence she didn't feel, painting a useful fiction from partial truths. "The dragon's blood is making you stronger, but it's also trying to make you into a monster. Your power is struggling against that, and the tattoos your father gave you are helping you." Tears were leaking from Oliver's eyes as he listened. Selene put her hands on his cheeks. "Stay focused. Don't let the pain drive you mad. Try to stay calm and have faith in your father's magic. It will lead you through this."

"There's nothing but pain," said Oliver, his voice rising in panic. "I can't find a way through this."

His fear tugged at her heart. "Look for the calm and embrace it. That's your father, Oliver. You believe in him, don't you? He won't let you down, but you have to meet him halfway." The words were pure bullshit, but she had nothing else to offer, and if Oliver believed them, perhaps it would help.

"We've wasted enough time," said Lognion. "I want you to make the gate."

Selene's gaze caught fire as she glanced up at her father. "Not until he's through this."

"You made a dea—"

"And if you want me to honor it, you'll wait," she snapped, "otherwise we're done, and you may as well do what you wish without me."

"This—"

"I'm not negotiating. It's your choice."

The dragon snorted, exhaling sharply in disgust, but said nothing more. Turning away, Lognion curled up like a cat and closed his eyes. Selene made a fire and laid out Oliver's bedroll before helping him into it. Her stepson alternated between growls and whimpers, and while he didn't speak, she knew he wasn't able to rest.

Fortunately, she didn't need sleep anymore, but it was a long night as she kept a silent vigil over her husband's only child.

CHAPTER 14

The sea was beautiful at night. The moon shone down over black water, highlighting the tops of gentle waves that stretched out endlessly in every direction, but Will was hardly able to enjoy it. Though he thought of his family, his concentration had to remain on the task at hand. The elven trade ship was barely visible on the horizon, even with his enhanced eyesight.

He'd given up on attaching his spell-ship to the ship he was following. The previous attempt had ended in disaster, and he still wasn't quite sure how they had detected him. Without understanding their security measures, he couldn't find a solution to get around them. Instead, he had opted to remain at a distance.

Will had refined his temporary ship spells, and he now had a suite of different spells to accomplish everything he needed while at sea. Eventually, if he ever had free time on land again, he intended to consolidate some of them into larger, more all-inclusive spells. Currently he was maintaining more than a dozen separate spells, and while none of them required constant attention, it was still mentally wearisome.

Once he had a chance to refine them into one or two master spells and improve the efficiency, it would be much better, but for now he was forced to remain awake without sleep. This was his third night without the joy of being able to put his head to a pillow.

He'd overcome the issue by using a spell he'd learned from Doctor Lorentz, the wizard physician who oversaw his hospital in Lystal. It seemed that healers occasionally had times when they couldn't rest for more than a day or two, and the wakefulness spell had been created to help them accommodate the need to remain conscious and functional.

Of course, the physician had also cautioned him against using it except when necessary, and never for more than forty-eight hours, but Will didn't have much choice. He was beginning to understand why, though.

"You're beginning to hallucinate," said the doctor's voice from beside his ear.

"Shut up, Carl," said Will. He felt constantly irritated, but the voices only made it worse.

A flicker at the corner of his vision made him turn his head. "You're starting to see things too," said Dr. Lorentz.

"I know you're not real."

"Then why are you so out of sorts?" asked his imaginary companion.

Will sighed. "Because if I'm going to hallucinate, I'd rather it was someone else. Selene, for example."

"What about me?" asked James Wellings, his brother-in-law.

"You're an improvement, actually."

"Aww, that's kind of you to say," replied James.

"I was being sarcastic."

"That's hurtful," complained Tabitha's husband, but then the doctor's voice returned. "If you keep going, you'll have a stroke. Then you won't be any good to anyone."

"If I dismiss the spell and sleep, I'll pass out, and sometime after that my magical ship construct will fall apart. I might not even wake up while drowning. Is that a better option?" asked Will.

"People always wake up if they fall into water."

"Are you sure? Even people who've been awake for three days straight?"

"Well..." The doctor's voice was clearly uncertain.

Will snorted. "That's what I thought." Then, he blinked to clear his vision. The ship he was following was closer, and he thought he saw something on the horizon. It was too far to tell, but the turyn currents seemed to cluster there, indicating that something deliberate had been done.

He shook his head to clear it and shake off his imaginary companions, then he adjusted his speed. His magical ship was composed of nothing but air and turyn, and it was propelled by manipulating the water around it. Initially, he'd tried a submersible design, but it was too difficult to remain at any depth. Since the construct was air, encasing air, it had almost no weight, and even using water as ballast, it remained buoyant even if it was completely filled with seawater. To remain underneath the waves, he had to fashion rigid fins and maintain enough speed to create negative lift, and that had been too much of a pain long-term. If he used stone or some heavier building material, he could probably do it the easier way, but he couldn't do all that while at sea.

His current design relied on staying half-submerged near the surface, and since his ship was literally made of air, it was practically invisible. To avoid detection, he had simply been maintaining the farthest distance he could while still keeping the elven ship within sight. The plan worked for the simple reason that their traditional sailing vessel stood much taller in the water and was made of solidly visible wood, while the only part of Will that was visible was his body, and that was almost entirely beneath the waterline.

Over the next hour, he watched as the trade ship pulled up to a small, unassuming collection of rocky protrusions that pointed up from the water. Any ship's captain that spotted the rocks would likely give them a wide berth to avoid risking their hull. To ordinary eyes, that's what it appeared to be, but beneath a haze of illusion, Will could see it was actually a wide stone arch that stretched between two rock columns.

He'd expected to find a congruence point connecting the two realms, either at a point in open water, or possibly on some small, unmarked island, but this clearly wasn't that. From what he could see, it was some sort of permanent gate. Will couldn't fathom how it was powered, since the ley lines were down beneath the seafloor, and while there were turyn currents in the ocean itself, they weren't strong enough to maintain such a massive gate. *They might be maintaining it from the other side,* he realized. That made better defensive sense as well. If anyone from Hercynia located the gate and decided to attack, the elves could simply cut the power from their side and deactivate the portal.

The elven ship passed directly through the arch and vanished from view. Will relaxed slightly, no longer as worried about being spotted, though now he worried that the gate itself might have unseen protections that could alert his enemies. Moving slowly, he guided his magical vessel closer, keeping his eyes open for any sign of wards or observers.

The illusion itself was enough to protect the gate from being spotted, and its remote location far from any sea lanes that ships usually travelled through afforded it even more protection. Even so, if a skilled practitioner were to get close enough, the illusion would be immediately visible. Will knew he was better than most at spotting such things, so they would likely have to be significantly closer, but was that enough security for the elves? He didn't think so.

If a human sailing ship got close enough for a turyn-sensitive individual to spot the illusion, then the elves would need to eliminate it, to ensure no one reported the location of their gate. What would be the best way to accomplish that?

Will kept his ship still in the water several hundred yards distant from the gate while he thought. Nothing was immediately obvious to his senses, but the lack of sleep had left him feeling dull and stupid. What wasn't he thinking of?

"I need sleep," he said to himself.

He definitely couldn't sleep in a boat that might vanish after some unknown span of time. In the future, once he had refined the spells, he could test and improve them such that he would know how long they would last, but that wasn't now. The answer came to him immediately. He needed something simple that would keep him afloat, anchor him in place, and keep the sun off.

That was easy enough. He'd designed far more complex spells. Without pausing to think, Will imagined the necessary rune sequences and created an impromptu spell construct above the palm of one hand. After brief scrutiny, he decided it would work and pressed his turyn into it. A long, human-sized capsule made of opaque air appeared around him, and he dismissed the spells maintaining his ship. Suddenly in darkness, he felt a splash, and then his new container was bobbing along in the waves. A thin line of cohesive air ran down to the rocks below, keeping him from drifting away.

He still didn't know how long it would last, but it was similar enough to some of his cooking spells that he had a fair idea. It would be enough. Without thinking more on it, he dismissed the spell keeping him awake. His mind went from muddled to hazy and confused as waking dreams immediately began to intrude. With the motion of the water rocking him to sleep, he rapidly passed into unconsciousness.

All sense of time vanished, though he had the vague notion that many hours passed. If nightmares plagued him, they were forgotten by the time he became aware of himself again, though reality itself surged in on him like a blue wave. Salty water rushed into his nose and mouth, causing him to choke and cough. He almost inhaled more before he realized what had happened.

His spell had waned and finally vanished, dropping him into the cold sea. A bright sun was beaming down on him through several feet of water as he thrashed about without rhyme or reason. With effort, he oriented himself and kept his mouth closed until he could break the surface again. He coughed violently when he got his mouth above water, and his lungs and throat burned from the small amount of water he had already swallowed.

After several minutes, he had finally stopped coughing and spitting, and his swimming had fully stabilized his position. Now he was simply treading water, staring across at the veiled gate and contemplating the stupidity that had resulted in his current situation. *What was I thinking?* he thought as he remembered his final spell. *I created a new, untested spell on the fly and just assumed it would last longer than the one I was already using. I'm an idiot.*

Clearly, the sleep deprivation had impaired his reasoning. He was lucky that he'd slept long enough that he was able to recover his senses quickly after being unceremoniously dumped into the water. He was better now. *Cold, hungry, treading water in the middle of nowhere—sure, I'm definitely in better shape now,* he told himself wryly.

A water-walking spell, a drying spell, and Selene's Solution left him clean and much warmer, sitting cross-legged atop the rolling surface of the sea. What was next? Tackling the gate? No. He shook his head and began employing some of his cooking spells. With half an hour's time and some fresh supplies from his limnthal, he was soon eating a warm plate of bacon, eggs, sausage, and toasted bread—all supported by an air plate that rested upon an air table.

The only inconvenience was that he had to eat standing up. If he sat directly on the surface of the sea, the waves moved him up and down too much and he'd never designed an immobile chair for such a situation. He put it on his mental list of future tasks.

With immense satisfaction, Will finished the eggs, bacon, and sausage, then slathered the bread with fresh butter and jam, courtesy of the limnthal yet again. After inhaling the other food, he ate the jammy toast slowly, savoring each bite and chewing carefully while staring out at the gate. Somewhere in the back of his mind, thoughts were moving.

He'd finished the last bite when his thoughts crystallized. *Look below.* If the elves had a defense to sink ships that discovered their gateway, then the evidence should be on the sea bottom beneath him. Even if it was a rare occurrence, the elves had probably been using the gate for centuries. There would have been at least one or two incidents.

"Amazing what sleep can do for clarity of mind," he noted, then swallowed the last of his tea. He put away the few items he had out, sending them to his limnthal, then dismissed his magical dinnerware. A quick underwater breathing spell gave him enough air to last half an hour, and then he released the water-walking spell and dropped into the cold ocean water.

The second shock of cold water, so soon after the first, made him regret his decision, but it was too late to change his mind. He swam down ten or fifteen feet, then realized he couldn't keep himself down—his buoyancy was too strong to attain any real depth. The water was relatively clear, but the bottom was too far for him to get a clear view. He needed a weight, some sort of ballast to help him descend.

Fortunately, there was an easy solution. Along with food stuffs, books, clothing, and a variety of other supplies and sundries, Will kept a collection of weapons and armor in his limnthal. The first things that came to mind were the swords and hammers he'd prepared with the devastating ethereal switch spell that he and Selene had devised. The spell was designed to shift the blade or hammer head into the ethereal just before contacting the target. Once it was within the person or object to be destroyed, Will would release the handle, and the second part of the spell would transpose him into the ethereal while bringing the weapon blade back. The transfer while inside a person or other object meant that for a split second, two pieces of physical matter were occupying the same position in space—which would then result in a massive explosion.

Those weapons weren't bundled together, and he would need several to provide enough weight, so the simpler option was to summon the oilskin bag containing his mail byrnie. It weighed about twenty pounds. Or he could use the bag holding his hauberk, which was more than double that, since it was longer and also contained leggings, a coif, and gauntlets.

Either way, the salt water would get inside, and even if he dried it immediately, he was probably going to have to clean and re-oil the armor soon afterward to prevent a catastrophic amount of rusting. For simplicity, he chose the byrnie and hoped its weight would be enough.

The weight drew him downward immediately, and soon he had a clear view of the bottom. It appeared that the seafloor was rising toward the rocks, and closer to them, he saw that the bottom was flat and relatively level. The coral that grew there had been sheared off in places, indicating the bottom had been dredged. *They did considerable work here to form the terrain to their design,* he observed.

A few wrecks were visible on the bottom as well, making plain that some sort of defenses were in place. He couldn't tell exactly what had sunk them, but their hulls had massive holes in them that were probably below what would have been their waterline when they were seaworthy. *So the destruction came from below—probably.*

The turyn in the water flowed constantly, making it difficult for him to spot patterns the way he did in open air. Will thought there might be a network of wards on the bottom that served to detect ships, but he couldn't be sure. *Would they react to a lone person swimming by?* He didn't see any dead fish or dolphins to indicate that large animals were also being targeted, but he still didn't want to risk it.

On land, he was confident in his ability to slip through wards, but in the water he was less sure of himself. Swimming made it significantly harder to concentrate. On a whim, he shifted his vision, looking into the ethereal. The elves had shown themselves quite capable of working in both planes, but if they hadn't mirrored their work there, he would be able to easily see the differences between what had been done in the material plane and what remained unchanged in the ethereal.

Rather than a few rocks and an arch rising from the water, he saw a small island in the ethereal. It was still rocky and bare, but it made clear the fact that the elves had moved a tremendous amount of material, essentially the majority of the island in the material plane and piled it up in the ethereal plane. For their purposes that probably had several benefits, the chief one being they could sail their ships directly through the gate they had created.

The island had been worked on as well, but Will needed a better view. Having reassured himself there were no active observers in the ethereal, he used a spell to switch himself to the parallel plane. After examining it carefully, he didn't see any turyn traces or other signs of wards, so he walked across the water to the shoreline.

Apparently, the plan for the ethereal side was simply a passive defense. There had probably been a significant beach in the past, but it was piled high with rough stone now, as was the island itself. Almost as if a second island had been torn up and dumped on top of it. *Which is exactly what they did,* he realized. *They demolished the island in the material plane and dumped the rock and stone here.*

"A clever solution," he muttered. It was far easier than trying to transport so much stone, and it had the added benefit of roughly fortifying the ethereal side. Whatever the layout had been of the original island on the ethereal side, it was now buried under a vast amount of rock and rubble. No human sailors would be traveling in the ethereal, so the strange island would never be noticed, and if anyone did approach from that route, they would have to contend with a small mountain of stone covering the target. "So how do I get in?" he wondered aloud.

The stone was an obstacle, but if he was unobserved, it was far preferable to the actively defended gate on the material plane. Using a climbing spell, he scaled the steep rock pile and worked his way toward the center of the island. At a guess it was probably only two hundred yards across, and the highest point was around a hundred- and fifty-yards above sea level.

Once he was standing atop the center, he looked down. Beneath his feet was a jumble of tightly packed rocks and boulders with cracks that ranged from a few inches to feet in width. Ordinarily, his first idea for getting through manmade barriers would be traveling through the ethereal, or in this case, the material plane, but since that would simply drop into a well-guarded area and trigger all sorts of alarms, that wasn't an option. *They probably made sure the rock pile was solid all the way down, to prevent anyone from using the ethereal to get in,* he decided. He'd done the same thing at his own secret sanctuary, to prevent unwanted ethereal visitors.

For once, he wished he was a sorcerer with an earth elemental, but he'd never have admitted that fact aloud. If his special talents were earth oriented, that would be just as good, but they weren't. Lightning and storms weren't very useful against giant piles of stone, and while his sonic abilities could find resonating frequencies to shake and shatter, in this case he'd just be making big rocks into smaller ones. He needed a way through.

Fortunately, he had a fairly diverse array of elemental earth spells that he'd practiced to the point of reflex casting. His old favorite, the grave-digging spell, wasn't useful with solid stone, but he had alternatives that worked. *I can get there,* he told himself. The main drawback was that since he didn't have an elemental or a talent for it, he'd be far less efficient with his turyn and his time. There were no ley lines within reach, and unless he touched the sky and called a storm, he couldn't draw on the power that flowed far above.

He knew it was possible. As the Stormking, he'd touched that power without needing more than ambient turyn to bridge the gap, but it was still a difficult task for him to do consciously. Strong emotion or a lot of turyn seemed to be the two methods that worked for him most consistently. *Plus, a big storm might draw unwanted attention.* No, simple hard work would be best here. He had plenty of food and water. A few days' work would be the safest investment into this task.

Staring down, he began to cast, using a simple spell that could cut and move stone. It required a lot of turyn, turyn he had to replenish from the ambient currents around him, and half an hour later, he was forced to stop and regenerate his stores. He worked in cycles, half an hour of casting and five or ten minutes of rest whenever his activity drained him to the point of being unable to continue.

The real effort was the use of his will, casting and restoring his energy, but his will was strong—likely stronger than that of anyone alive. Morning came and noon passed, but still he worked, casting and resting. The afternoon sun made him sweat, but not enough to make him waste his will on a cooling spell. Night fell before he began to feel the strain, and he decided it was better to eat and rest. The shaft he had created went straight down more than fifty yards and was five feet wide at the bottom. At the top, it was fifteen feet wide, primarily because if he didn't include a taper, then the rocks above became unstable and tended to fall on his head.

With proper masonry, fitting the stones together, or simply using mortar, he probably could have made the sides straight and saved himself from removing a vast amount of material, but it would have cost him more time to be so careful. He had will and he had turyn.

After a quick meal, he set up his nighttime wards and fell asleep almost instantly. Tomorrow would be a long day.

CHAPTER 15

Selene was relieved when Oliver finally was able to sit up and eat. He didn't say much, and he was clearly exhausted, but he looked human. The only exception was his eyes, which now had pupils that were vertical slits. The constant changes and shifting beneath the skin had stopped. His will and the continual healing effect of his tattoos had won the fight, keeping him almost entirely human, inside and out.

Her diagnostic spells showed significant changes to his liver, heart, kidneys, and other vital organs, but they were still the same size and place as before. Oliver's muscles were subtly different, but any changes that violated the mapping of his tattoos had been rejected—repeatedly and with significant pain.

"How do you feel?" she asked him.

"Sore," said the wardsman, then added, "Angry. Angrier than I've ever been in my entire life."

"Angry at what's been done to you?"

Her stepson grimaced. "Maybe. I think I'm a little stronger, so I'm not too upset about that, I'm just furious—at everything. It's like an itch. I want to break something, or everything."

She'd expected something like that, but Selene still didn't enjoy hearing it confirmed, especially given what they were about to do. "You know where we're going?"

"Hell," answered Oliver, showing his teeth. "That should worry me, shouldn't it? But all I feel is anticipation."

"You'll have to fight your instincts," she reminded him.

"But there's nothing down there that isn't fair game, right?" he asked with an eager tone.

Selene closed her eyes and took a deep breath. "Whether here or down there, you can't let yourself go. It doesn't matter whether the enemies are deserving. If you let your bloodlust run rampant, it will change you." Oliver didn't answer, but she heard a low rumble coming from deep in his throat. "I'm not a warrior," she went on, "but I've known quite a few. I'm sure you had a variety of teachers. Some of them may have encouraged their students to tap into their primal instincts, but I imagine the more advanced teachers taught something different. Was that your experience?"

Her words brought forward memories from his time at the House of Ink. Before being sent to his final teacher, Daikor Sean, he'd been taught by an un-inked master, a martial artist he knew simply as Trainer Martin. The man had been older than most of the wardsmen, and his incredible speed and fighting prowess had been purely the product of a lifetime of training and dedication. Such skilled teachers remained without tattoos to preserve their lifespan and enable them to train more wardsmen. They obtained prowess that was nearly equal to the natural talent of a granling, prowess that sometimes surpassed the speed and strength provided by mere tattoos. Without magical defenses, they were far more fragile, but the lessons they taught were invaluable.

Most wardsmen didn't live long enough to benefit from that sort of intense discipline, but Oliver might live well into a second century of life since he was technically a first-order wizard. Deep down, he could feel a river of rage simmering, waiting for him to tap into it and fuel his fighting, but when he remembered Trainer Martin, it seemed like a shallow shortcut. *Like a more extreme example of my tattoos,* he observed.

I was born gifted, then made a wizard and eventually given ink, but those things were superficial, he told himself. The dragon blood offered even more, but it was the same sort of power, and it wouldn't truly be his own. The rage would bring strength and then transform him into a nearly unkillable fighting machine, but he wouldn't be himself, and he would never have mastery.

Trainer Martin had been better than most wardsmen, and it had been his own skill that made him so. Similarly, Oliver knew the dragon blood wouldn't give him anything he couldn't do better with skill and self-mastery. *"Fight cold, and use your mind,"* Martin had told him. *"If you fight with anger, you lose to yourself before you even step onto the battlefield."*

"Oliver?" asked Selene. The young warrior's eyes had grown distant, but they snapped up and focused on her then. The intensity in them was uncomfortable, but the hostility seemed to have faded.

"You're right," he answered. "I was given two different lessons back then, and this is no different."

She smiled. "You can handle this."

He nodded. "It won't be as easy as before, but the choice is the same." *I just have to become greater than the cheap and easy power offered by the dragon blood and my baser instincts.*

A deep voice rumbled over them, "As touching as this is, we've wasted enough time." The dragon's eye swiveled to focus on Selene. "Are you prepared to honor our bargain?"

Selene lifted her chin and answered, "I am. I can create your gate, but I've never been to Hell personally, nor do I have a link or target. You'll have to provide that."

"Construct the gate and power it. I'll provide the destination. Once it's open, we will all enter," commanded Lognion.

"I cannot hold it open there without a powerful source of energy," she warned.

"Don't waste your strength trying," said the dragon. "Once we have reclaimed my power, we can construct a new gate."

If Selene's face had not already been wan and bloodless, she might have visibly paled. "As I understand it, the turyn cost to ascend from the depths is much greater than creating the portal from this plane." Although the various planes didn't lie above or below each other in the ordinary sense, they did exist on some sort of gradient that made travel between them more expensive depending on where one initiated a portal. Hell was generally considered the 'deepest' or lowest level because it was easier to descend into but exponentially more difficult to leave. Her remark wasn't phrased as a question, but she hadn't said it idly. With her vast supply of elementals, she could probably create the necessary gate to return even in Hell. What interested her was whether Lognion would need her help to get back. If so, she could potentially escape with Oliver and leave the dragon stranded. She'd never deliberately broken an oath before, but she wouldn't hesitate if it would put an end to Lognion's threat.

The dragon stared at her in silence for a moment, and then his lips curled back to reveal dagger-like teeth the size of swords. "We both know you are capable of effecting our return."

Selene dipped her head in acknowledgement, never taking her eyes from her father's malicious gaze. "I am glad you trust me," she replied with venom.

"I well know what you are capable of, daughter, better than you know yourself. Keep that in mind as we proceed, lest you make any unfortunate mistakes," rumbled the dragon.

As she'd expected, her father had deftly avoided letting her know whether he was capable of returning on his own. One might be tempted to assume this meant he was hiding a vulnerability, but Lognion had also let her know that he knew exactly what she was thinking; his reticence very likely represented nothing more than his desire to keep her uncertain and off-balance. *This damnable game continues eternally, even though both of us have technically already died,* she swore to herself.

Moving to the center of the stone platform, she tapped into the ley lines that intersected beneath where she stood and began to draw on the massive currents of turyn. It had been over a decade since she first learned the rune construct necessary to create a gate, and though it wasn't something she practiced frequently, her skill with such complex magic had steadily increased. Even so, it took all her attention and required a level of focus that few could manage. It wasn't something she could do instantly—several minutes passed as she built up the runes and lines—but her mastery made it look as easy as breathing.

"Such skill," remarked the dragon as he watched her work. "A shame it isn't supported by a powerful will to match." His own magic stretched out to touch hers, filling in the final portion that would direct the gate to find its target.

Selene ignored his taunt, and once the connection clicked into place, she flooded the construct with turyn from the ley lines. It took all the power she could manage, pushing her capacity to its limit, but the gate opened and yawned wide, creating an opening large enough for even the dragon to pass through. "It's ready. Let's not waste time," she urged.

Lognion gestured toward the opening with one claw. "You first, little warrior," he told Oliver.

Though he'd just survived a serious trial, Oliver still hesitated. "Me?"

The dragon rumbled, "You're my guarantee, ensuring that my daughter remembers her promises. Go."

Oliver's eyes found Selene, and she nodded at him. "It's a hostile environment, but you can survive there. The turyn is inimical to life, but you're a first-order wizard. You should absorb and convert it quickly enough to manage."

With her assent, Oliver stepped through, and a second later, the dragon followed him. Selene went last, releasing her connection to the ley lines as she passed through. The gate shrank slowly, then more quickly, snapping shut completely a few seconds after she had entered.

They were in Hell now.

A grey, featureless sky stretched to the horizon, giving no visual from the harsh landscape of black stone and grey gravel. Large rock outcroppings stood out here and there, but while the ground wasn't smooth and level, it was bland and repetitive. At first, Selene found the unearthly terrain interesting, but as seconds passed, she realized that before long it would begin to grate on her nerves.

The ambient turyn was toxic to life, but that wasn't a problem for her. Sensing it reminded her of the first time she had encountered it and nearly died. That had been before she married, and though Will had told her he was a wizard, she hadn't truly understood the difference between what he was and what the instructors at Wurthaven had claimed to be. It had been his ability to absorb and transform turyn that had saved her life. She glanced at Oliver to see how he was handling it.

He appeared uncomfortable, and though the negative turyn was thin and relatively diffuse, his rate of absorption and transducing it was barely enough to keep it from damaging his flesh. From what Will had told her, he had also had trouble the first time he had traveled through Hell with the Cath Bawlg, but he'd been young and new to his power then. He'd needed the demon-armor spell to fully protect himself, but given the amount of turyn in the air, she couldn't understand why, since Oliver was only a first-order wizard, and he was managing.

"The turyn currents are faint," she observed aloud. "I know Hell is considered dead, but I thought it would have more energy than this since they steal life and turyn from the other realms they've parasitized."

"It is far more barren than it was the last time I was here," said the dragon. "Even Muskeglun seems rich with turyn compared to this."

Muskeglun was the native world of the trolls, best known for its fetid swamps and its low level of ambient turyn. Selene looked askance at her father. "You've been to Hell before?"

Lognion snorted. "I was not the *first* dragon, but the egg I hatched from was one of Caladrim's early nests. If you measured the years I have existed and compared them to the years I didn't, you would find that my life spans a significant fraction of the age of the universe. *This* Hell is but the most recent one I have seen."

Selene frowned. "There's more than one?"

The dragon's throat rumbled with laughter. "There is only one level of existence at the very bottom, and that one we call 'Hell.' As my kind grow in strength and number, more layers come into existence. The boundaries of the abyss are pushed farther back as reality grows and expands with us."

She hadn't wanted to believe her father's megalomaniacal diatribe when he claimed that dragons were the pillars of creation, the foundation of existence, but she was beginning to accept the truth, bitter as it was. "Does this mean the void grows weaker as reality expands?"

"No," answered Lognion. "Reality is never more than a speck of light against the vast darkness, no matter how large it grows. Dragons spawn, the universe expands, but it remains finite spark set against the backdrop of infinite nothingness."

Selene filed that away for future consideration; there were more pressing concerns. She eyed Oliver once more. The thin turyn would barely be enough to sustain him. Being first-order was both a blessing and a curse since it meant he still produced half the energy he needed to function normally, but he also didn't absorb the ambient turyn as efficiently and quickly as she did. If he started to suffer a deficit, she could attune to his frequency and top his turyn level up, but she didn't produce *any* turyn herself. Being dead, she had no source, so she was totally reliant on what she could absorb from the environment.

Currently, that felt as difficult as trying to breathe atop the tallest of mountains. She wouldn't last without tapping her elementals to replenish herself, and they would also have the same problem recovering their energy once depleted. Contrary to her previous assessment, if she used too much of her power, *she* might be the one dependent on Lognion to create a gate to get them home.

"There should be taps that link to other places," muttered Lognion. "The demons draw power through them. The turyn will be thicker near one of the taps. I can already feel the presence of the other dragon. It will probably begin to hunt us soon. If you are to be of any use, we should probably move to a place where the turyn can sustain you." He crouched and lowered one wing to the ground to form a ramp. "Climb on and we will search for one."

As they were settling into place on his back, Oliver asked, "What do these taps look like?"

"Some appear as pits, holes in the ground spewing turyn into the air. Others are small hills that expel turyn from their peaks. Usually, they are guarded by contingents of demons, but I suspect things have changed since my hatchlings arrived," replied Lognion. He took off, lifting them into the air with powerful downstrokes of his wings.

"You said you could feel another dragon?" asked Selene. "Is it only one?"

"Unfortunately, yes, which means it has already eaten the others and consolidated my former strength. It will be stronger than I am presently."

"Can you tell how far away it is?" she asked.

"Thousands of miles, at least a few days of flying," said Lognion, "but it may not matter."

Selene felt an ominous undertone in her father's words. "Why?"

"It might have learned how to create gates by now. If so, it could arrive at any moment."

Oliver yelled over the rushing wind, "Is it that easy? I was born a few years before it hatched. Shouldn't it need a teacher to learn something like that?"

Selene was thinking the same thing, but Lognion's reply dispelled that notion. "For my kind, certain magics are fundamental, much like breathing is for mortal creatures. As young as it is, it may not even have language. I doubt my spawn bothered talking to the demons before eating them, but creating portals is something it will learn instinctively, whether now or in a hundred years. It's impossible to predict, but it is inevitable."

"And it's stronger than you?" added Oliver. "This sounds hopeless."

"Likely twice as strong since I probably have less than a third of my original strength," clarified the dragon. "But I am much craftier. With age comes experience. I merely need to eat some of my child to even the playing field."

Oliver glanced at Selene to see if she was as surprised as he was, then yelled, "So what, the two of you will just come together and start eating each other? Whoever eats the fastest wins? That sounds bizarre."

"Your stepmother will think of something," Lognion said with a chuckle. "There, do you see that hill on the horizon? That's definitely a demon tap." The dragon banked slightly to fly directly toward it. "Be ready in case there are still defenders."

But as they flew closer, it became apparent that there were no demons waiting, and the turyn that should have been erupting from the top of the hill-like structure was notably absent. Lognion circled lower and landed near the top of the gently sloping structure. Now that Selene could see it up close, it looked to be made of rough stones piled into a gigantic cairn. The top was open with a shaft leading down, but there was no turyn or any sign of magic.

"It seems to be defunct," observed Lognion.

"What's supposed to be down there?" asked Selene, staring into the black pit, unable to see the bottom.

"A small artificial gate of sorts, maintained by an infernal engine made of demon-steel. Even if the demons were eaten, the machines should have kept running. They're built to last for millennia."

She studied the hole, thinking. Demon-steel was exceedingly rare and valuable. Will had bargained hard to get the supply they had used to make Tiny's black armor and the weapons used against Lognion. If she could salvage some of the equipment, it might come in handy in the future. Her limnthal had some spare room if she could find pieces that weren't too big to fit. "I'll go down and see what happened," she announced.

"Be quick," commanded Lognion. Oliver gave her a worried look, but Selene silenced him with a quick shake of her head.

Summoning one of her air elementals, she had it lower her carefully down the shaft while casting a light spell to enable her to see clearly. Down she dropped, ever farther, until she had descended at least a hundred yards, maybe more, and there she found the bottom, a round area with rough walls and a flat stone floor. The stone was torn up in places where something had been ripped free, and there was no sign of the infernal machine or the gate it had maintained.

The pit was empty, and the demon-steel machinery had obviously been looted.

She felt somewhat disappointed but also curious. There wasn't much she could do about it then and there, but it was something to think about. In the meantime, the shaft and the small room at the bottom were tickling her imagination. The shaft was just a little over thirty feet wide and would likely be a tight fit for Lognion's large frame. What size would his offspring be? With a mental command, she had her air elemental lift her back up to the top, and she stepped back onto the stone before dismissing it.

"How big will our opponent be? Does power determine a dragon's size?" she asked.

Lognion glanced at the stone pit, then to her. "Its size has more to do with age than power. Although a majority of my power was taken when they devoured the flesh from my bones, my body is still the same size. Having eaten its siblings, the dragon here will have fed well, and over a decade it may have grown considerably, but it won't be near my size for at least a century."

Oliver frowned. "Then how can it be stronger?"

Lognion glared at him briefly, then answered, "Size is the least important attribute for my kind. Being twice as strong, its body will be harder, tougher, more difficult to damage and faster to heal."

"But not as difficult to damage as you were the day we attacked the nest, correct?" said Selene.

"It will have increased its power independently to some degree," said her father, "but the majority of what it has will be what it devoured from me and its fellow hatchlings. So yes, it should be easier to hurt than I was then. You still won't be able to do significant damage, however."

"But demon-steel weapons hurt you," she clarified.

"Did you find some below?" asked Oliver, his interest piqued.

Selene kept her eyes on Lognion as she answered, "Someone already removed the machinery, but I had a surprise saved for Oliver." Turning to the young warrior, she held out her hand, and a spear appeared. "I had hoped to have a great-sword made, but there wasn't enough of the metal remaining. This is for you, though I had hoped to give it to you under better circumstances."

Oliver took the long weapon with both hands, feeling its heft as he moved it. It was eight feet long in total. The shaft was composed of a dark wood that was wrapped or inlaid with silvery metal vines and leaves that ran up and down the length reinforcing and decorating it simultaneously. The shaft was nearly six feet long, while the last two feet were made up of a long, black-bladed spearhead. The color wasn't from tempering or anodizing, but rather from the toxic turyn that suffused the metal. He glanced from the spear to his stepmother, then asked, "Is this…?"

"Demon-steel," confirmed Selene, "at least the sharp part is anyway. Back when I reclaimed Lognion's body, I also recovered Tiny's demon-steel golem body and the spear he used against our foe." Her eyes were filled with hate as they locked onto her father. "The head of this spear was the same that we used against him. Originally the entire thing, shaft included, was demon-steel, but that made it inordinately heavy and slow to wield, so I had it remade for you. At the time, I was deluded into thinking the elves were our allies, so I bartered with them for the wood and elf-steel that was used to make the shaft."

The young wardsman held it gingerly, tracing the metal vines with one finger. "Elf-steel?"

"They call it 'tendoril'," she replied. "It's lighter and stronger than iron or ordinary steel. It's almost as tough as demon-steel and has the added benefit of *not* exploding if you do stress it beyond its breaking point. The wood is from a tree they prefer for its strength and density, similar to the ironwood tree back in Trendham. They used the tendoril to reinforce the wood, and it also has an enchantment engraved into the inner side of the metal. Back then, I didn't know you'd become a wizard, so the enchantment is made to drain the demon turyn from the spear head and convert it into positive turyn." She guided his hand to a small metal bump that Oliver had taken to be a rivet. "Press this, and it will discharge a fiery missile that can travel for a dozen yards or so. It won't work unless the weapon has built up a certain amount of demonic turyn from being physically stressed during use."

"It's a beautiful weapon," said Oliver. "When did you make it?"

"Seven years ago," she admitted. "Back when I was still pretending to be Cora. And to be clear, I didn't do most of the work. I commissioned it and did the enchantment."

"That thing won't kill a dragon," stated Lognion looking down over them, "but with some luck, you might prick it enough to distract it while we're fighting."

Oliver glanced up. "How do we kill it then?"

"You can't kill us. Dragons don't die in the conventional sense. Our essence is eternal. To defeat a dragon, you have to consume it. That's where your father failed. He took a bite but left the rest to my children."

Selene saw the anger flare in Oliver's eyes, but the young man kept his tongue in check, asking instead, "If it's a simple fight of tooth and claw, how do you expect to win against a much stronger opponent?"

"Experience and cunning," answered the dragon. "But that may not be enough."

"I have an idea," said Selene, staring down into the demon pit.

CHAPTER 16

Oliver stood alone atop the rocky cairn. He was armored and held his new spear in one hand, but he still felt vulnerable without his shield. His first encounter with Lognion had shown him how inadequate his defenses were, but he still would have felt better with it. Glancing down at his feet, he wondered how thick the stone supporting him was. Selene had used an elemental to seal the pit, covering it with a layer of solid rock.

He would have asked her, but it was unlikely that she could hear him, since she was hidden below. According to Lognion, dragons were drawn together when in the same world. Lognion's corrupted spawn was likely already heading for them, but not only would it be drawn to Lognion himself, but Oliver as well. The small amount of dragon's blood inside him would also resonate with the other beast.

Oliver was bait.

If the two of them were in close proximity and only Oliver was visible, then the younger dragon would likely think the young wardsman was the main feast. He just had to draw it in and avoid being eaten until his stepmother could spring the trap. *Easier said than done,* he thought nervously.

He'd been waiting, alone, for more than half an hour since his stepmother had disappeared down the shaft and sealed the opening with stone. Now he had several important questions that hadn't initially occurred to him and no way to ask them. Should he be expecting to wait minutes, hours, or days? Should he make a fire and get comfortable?

Oliver was pondering this when a face appeared in the stone beneath his feet. Its mouth opened, and a rough voice spoke to him. "Lognion says his spawn is still a significant distance away, so you have hours to wait yet."

The face had startled him, and Oliver felt a rush of anger and adrenaline. He had to suppress an urge to stab the stone beneath his feet with his new spear. "Is that a spell? I didn't know you could do that," he complained.

"It could be done with a spell, but I'm simply using an earth elemental," answered Selene.

"How many hours do you think I have to wait? Should I plan on sleeping?" asked Oliver.

There was a pause while Selene consulted with her father, then she replied, "You can nap, but you need to be prepared to fight on a moment's notice. There's always the possibility the other dragon will decide to use a portal to cross the distance."

Oliver sighed. That meant he'd have to keep his armor on, and the armor meant he couldn't really sleep. At best he could recline and try to rest his eyes, and that would require a proper chair with support for his head and back. He explained that to his stepmother, and she responded with yet more magic. The rocky ground rose up on one side of where the pit had been and formed a small mound that shaped itself, forming a round, bucket-like depression on one side.

"Sit down," her elemental's voice told him. "Let me know what you think, and I'll adjust it until you're comfortable."

He did, and within a minute, the stone had shaped itself into the most comfortable non-cushioned seat he could imagine. It was so perfectly formed that he could lean his helmeted head back against a rest and relax despite the weight on his head and shoulders from that and his other armor. A light sleep might actually be possible. "Thank you," he told her.

"Lognion will sense when the other dragon is close, and I'll make sure you're awake and alert," she responded. "You'll probably have fifteen minutes or more of warning, but if it creates a gate, it could be as little as half a minute."

Oliver nodded. "That works. I'll eat and then try to rest a little."

He tried to do as he said, but it wasn't that simple. The dried meat he chewed sat in his stomach like a rock thanks to the nervous energy he couldn't shed, and while he was bored, even the comfortable shape of his stone recliner couldn't lull him to sleep. He sat, painfully aware of each breath, but unable to do anything that might ease his boredom. Minutes passed like hours while he studied the barren landscape. There was no chance he could nap.

Despite that thought, when Selene's voice returned, he realized he had somehow drifted off. His eyes snapped open, and he sat up so quickly that he nearly lost his balance. "It's here," she told him.

Glancing around, he saw nothing. "Where? I don't see anything!" Fear sent a chill down his spine, and some instinct caused him to look up.

The stone face near his feet answered at the same time, "Directly above us. It used a portal."

A massive midnight-blue form was diving straight down in complete silence, Oliver registered the dragon's claws mere seconds before they would have slammed into his position, crushing him into jelly. He dived sideways with only an instant to spare. Amazingly, the young dragon's reflexes were so quick that it managed to correct its course in the same time. It couldn't move laterally as quickly as he could, given its downward velocity, but it still hit the rocky hill just a few feet from where he had jumped to. Any hesitation or lack of speed on Oliver's part would have meant certain death.

He regretted not setting the spear, but while it might have inflicted a terrible wound, Oliver would have still been crushed. Without pause for thought, he dove in while the beast was still recovering its balance from the hard landing. Between and under the two forelimbs he went, stabbing his spear into a somewhat softer spot that would have equated to the armpit on a human. The demon-steel point met some resistance but still sank in almost two feet before being pulled out by his continued momentum.

The dragon reacted quickly, its head diving down and under, trying to follow him between its legs, and when the pain of his spear struck, the creature leapt up with its hind legs, causing the massive reptile to somersault.

Oliver had already reversed direction again, thinking the monster would try to spin and snap at him as he emerged on the far side, so now he found himself running directly toward the upside-down dragon maw. Black-stained, dagger-like teeth opened before him as the dragon rolled over its own head.

The dragon was more than half Lognion's size, and its quick movements and fierce eyes spoke of a feral cunning that had probably been the reason for the young dragon's victory over its late siblings. Oliver didn't try to change his direction this time. He was too close, and the momentary pause that would create would only allow the monster the perfect opportunity to crush him in its jaws. Instead, he whipped his spear head back in line at the last second and jabbed it into the roof of the dragon's mouth. He didn't commit fully to the attack for fear of losing his weapon, but the sudden pain accomplished his purpose. The jaws snapped shut at the same time he withdrew the point and took his next step—his right boot coming down on the beast's chin—and he ran up the underside of its jaw and neck, activating his climbing tattoo as he went to anchor himself in place.

Startled, the corrupted dragon finished its somersault by landing on its back and then flipping over onto its feet again. It swiped at its own throat to brush the offending human off, but Oliver had already run up and over its shoulder as it rolled. He stood now on its back, near the base of the wings, and drove his spear down hard in between the vertebrae of its spine.

So far, nothing had happened according to plan. The infernal dragon was supposed to have struck the thin stone covering the pit and fallen at least partway through. Selene was then supposed to use earth elementals to slow and trap it while Lognion emerged from below to rip into the younger dragon's belly and vitals. If Oliver hadn't dodged the dragon's dive, the plan would have probably worked, but he'd have also died instantly.

As things stood now, he was fighting alone, but now that things had started, his anxiety had vanished, and his confidence soared. His opponent was fast, but its size and mass imposed unavoidable limits on how quickly it could move. Oliver was far smaller, and his unique talents likely made him as fast, or faster than any other human alive. Combining that knowledge with the helpful magic of his tattoos and the raging dragon blood pulsing through his veins, he had no doubt left. He wouldn't fight to survive; he would fight to *win.*

"You fucked up." The words emerged from tight lips as his spear buried itself fully in the dragon's spine. The body beneath him spasmed, but the magic in his feet kept him solidly anchored as Oliver stepped sideways and pulled on the spear shaft, cutting laterally and ripping through flesh and muscle that seemed harder than stone. Black flame erupted from the spear as the metal cut, despite the tremendous strain resisting its edge.

A primal scream emerged from his throat as the infernal beast's hind legs collapsed and its forelegs jerked helplessly. He had won. Whipping the spear back in the other direction, he pulled it out and stabbed again, this time aiming higher up, closer to the base of the neck.

To his surprise, the dragon's legs moved with purpose almost the instant the spear point was freed, and its movement threw his aim off. His second strike lodged in the shoulder muscle rather than the neck. The wings beat downward, and Oliver felt heavy as the beast shot into the air. Looking down, he saw stone hands sliding impotently away from the dragon's legs. His stepmother had already been trying to help, but even stone couldn't prevail against the dragon's strength.

An electric spark shot through his heart—fear—but it quickly turned to excitement. The fight wasn't over.

The next minute lasted for an eternity as the dragon twisted and turned in the air, trying to dislodge him. Oliver had to move quickly to avoid wings and even claws as it curled and tried to scratch him off with its hind legs. The two of them caromed wildly through the air, and only the climbing spell of his tattoos kept him from falling to his death.

As he scrambled, Oliver continued to stab, but he was no longer able to put his full strength into it. The point still pierced the tough hide, but it didn't go deep, and the flesh healed almost as soon as he removed the spear blade. Somewhere in the back of his mind he registered the fact that his confidence had been misplaced. The intensity of the focus needed to remain attached to the dragon and avoid its attempts to kill him wasn't sustainable; he had strength and stamina to continue fighting for quite a while, but he was accomplishing nothing. His foe was inexhaustible, healed almost instantly, and would only need one slip-up from Oliver to land a blow that would end him permanently.

His death was all but inevitable.

Ignoring the feeling of rising panic, he released his spell's attachment and slid back several feet to avoid another bite attack as the dragon's head bent back toward him. He reactivated the tattoo a split second later to avoid falling to his death while simultaneously trying to see where they were. Far below, he could see the small hill that he'd previously waited at. While he might not be able to win the fight on his own, he needed to get the corrupted dragon back down to where his stepmother and Lognion waited.

Seconds passed as he dodged and moved, until at last he was between the beast's wings again. A quick slash showed him that there was no way he could hope to sever one of them. The bone and muscle were far too thick, and that was without considering the fact that he couldn't afford to put his full strength toward the task. A flicker of movement warned him almost too late, and he activated the phase spider shield and leaned to one side as the dragon's tail swept toward him from behind. It glanced across his back and ribs, and Oliver felt his magical shield come apart immediately. The barbed tail struck his mail but glanced off, having lost too much momentum to penetrate.

The force of the blow still cracked his ribs, though.

Pain shot through him, and he was no longer able to draw breath. His tattoos would likely fix the ribs quickly, but he didn't have time to wait. His injury would prevent him from moving fast enough to dodge the next attack.

Ignoring that, he shifted targets and aimed for the flexible membrane of the wing, sweeping the spear blade up and along the inside of the main bone. His weapon tore through the thin tissue, and although it tried to heal itself almost as soon as the blade passed, the movement of the wing and the intense air pressure held the edges apart. Oliver did his best to help by twisting the spear and cutting a second line perpendicular to the first.

A wide hole opened, and the next downbeat tore it open further. Another tail strike missed him as the dragon lurched sideways and began spinning uncontrollably. The ground was rising up to meet them, and all Oliver could do was hold on and hope he didn't land beneath the dragon. Seconds later, he felt the impact, and then the world went black.

***

Selene began cursing mentally as soon as her father told her of the corrupted dragon's arrival through a portal. A moment of hope came when she realized that it was diving straight for the weak point at the top of the hill, but that disappeared almost immediately as it changed course to follow her stepson's evasive maneuver. *How can something that big react so quickly?* she wondered.

Mentally commanding a dozen earth elementals, she directed them to form several stone hands to grab the dragon's legs and immobilize it, but the damn thing moved with impossible speed. She was using a stone-see spell to look through the rocky ground, but the blur it caused made aiming more difficult than she had expected.

When the beast stopped and turned, she almost had it, but then it somersaulted in place, slipping free of her grasp. Her massive stone hands tried again, but even those that managed to grab hold quickly lost their grip when the dragon sprang up into the sky. Its strength seemed irresistible. Selene's heart sank when she saw Oliver still clinging to the beast as it climbed into the air.

Tense seconds passed as she tried to see what was happening without emerging from the ground. Lognion's voice rumbled in her ear, "This plan was a failure." The ground shifted as his massive form began to climb upward.

"Wait!" she commanded.

"Without a distraction or you limiting its motion, this cairn will be my tomb," responded Lognion. "Once it senses me here, it will approach cautiously and I will be the one restricted by the ground while it tears me apart. I must get clear of this hole now."

"It's coming down—no, it's falling. He did something to one of the wings," she announced.

"I doubt it will land in the right place," countered Lognion.

"Let me worry about that," said Selene. "Just be ready. I'll drag it into position if need be."

"You have already failed at that."

"Silence. I have no time for your distractions," she barked. Her eyes unfocused briefly as she issued orders to yet more earth elementals, and her body began rising through the ground as though it was no more substantial than air.

The corrupted dragon landed fifty yards from the top of the hill and rolled. The impact did yet more damage as it landed partly on one wing, but the monster leapt up almost as though nothing had happened. When Selene's massive humanoid construct rose up from the ground in front of it, the dragon attacked without hesitation. Its legs were all in good shape, but one wing was limp, and dragged behind as it leapt to meet its new foe.

It tore the stone giant into two pieces as though the magical construct was made of mud rather than rocks, but the arms continued to function, and they clasped the dragon's neck while the lower half reformed into two smaller giants. The beast didn't seem to notice as Selene emerged from the chest and glided away on an elemental travel disk.

Her earth elementals continued trying to grapple the dragon while she quickly circled back and stopped next to the base of the broken wing. The bone had broken in the fall, but it was still attached by skin and muscle that were even now trying to tighten enough to bring the separated bones back into contact so they could heal. Dispelling her travel disk, Selene dropped onto the wounded area and held tightly with both hands. Drawing on yet more turyn from her other elementals, she used a quickfire succession of healing spells.

To her delight, the unwary dragon didn't react to her presence and its innate resistance to magic wasn't very strong. Despite its power as a dragon, it hadn't lived or practiced magic long enough to have a powerful will. In most cases, it wouldn't have mattered. The nature of its very being was to heal virtually any injury, but her intent wasn't to injure. Instead, she subverted the healing process, guiding it in a less productive direction.

With one spell, she isolated the turyn in the wing from the turyn in its shoulder, while with another more advanced spell she encouraged the bone sticking up from the shoulder to begin regenerating. Her trick didn't work completely, however, for the reason dragons healed so quickly was the fact that they existed in two planes simultaneously, the ethereal and the material. The corrupted dragon's mirror image in the ethereal served as a template for the healing that occurred in the material plane, and she couldn't prevent it from doing so. Fortunately, though, the regeneration she started was enough to start a complementary healing process in the ethereal. The result was that its body tried to reconnect the broken wing and regrow a new wing simultaneously.

The two healing processes interfered with each other, and while she wasn't sure if it could eventually correct the problem or not, for the moment it meant the corrupted beast wouldn't be flying.

Selene looked around, hoping to spot Oliver, but the dragon finished scattering her earth elementals too quickly, and it noticed her interference with the wing. She saw the tail sweeping toward her, but her slow, dead body wasn't quick enough to dodge. It struck with bone-shattering force, and she was sent flying away.

The damage wasn't really a problem for her, though. While a completely dead body was slow and clumsy, it also meant she didn't feel much pain, and she didn't actually need functional limbs to do her part in the fight. So long as the flesh and bone weren't completely turned to ash, she could continue anchoring herself to them. Selene didn't need hands or feet to do her work, and her inadvertent flight through the air gave her an excellent viewpoint of the area. She spotted Oliver's unconscious form before she finished falling to the ground.

She had an air elemental lift her stepson into the air before Lognion's voice spoke in her mind again. *I cannot wait any longer.*

You will if you want to win, she replied in the same way. Half of her attention was on reforming her earthen giant while the other half was on directing the air elemental carrying Oliver along a specific course. *Be ready. I'll have it in place in less than a minute.*

You're clearly losing, and my spawn has surely started to notice my essence is in more than one location.

Not for long, said Selene. *Quiet. I'm working.* She used a spell to turn her head and position it so she could see the battlefield better, but she didn't bother trying to piece together her shattered bones. She had too many orders to give to divert her attention.

Since her fallen body was dead and unmoving, the corrupted dragon gave no more notice to it. Instead, it was focused on Oliver's flying form. It knew the earth elementals were trying to distract it, for they continued to try and keep it from following after him. Their efforts were futile, however. Brushing them aside once more, it leapt after the human-sized piece of dragon essence, which was even now leading it toward a larger source of power, though not one large enough to be feared.

If her jaw hadn't been broken, Selene would have smiled. Using Oliver's limp form, she baited the dragon back to the site of their trap. As fast as the air elemental was, it was still carrying a heavy body, and the speed of the corrupted dragon shocked her as it raced after them. Thankfully, watching the chase allowed her to prepare perfectly for the instant of their foe's arrival.

The corrupted beast almost caught up, and it was a half second from clamping its jaws around Oliver's form when the ground disappeared beneath it. Selene's elementals removed the thin layer of stone, and the broken-winged reptile fell into the tight shaft. The space was large enough that it fell freely, but by putting out its clawed legs, the dragon halted its fall before reaching the bottom.

It felt the dragon essence below and realized the trap; it was scrambling to claw its way back up the shaft when Lognion's larger head emerged from the darkness below, and his massive jaws clamped onto the corrupted beast's right rear leg. The former king's sword-like teeth tore through scales, flesh, and muscle. The bone gave them pause for a second, but a shake of Lognion's head combined with the younger dragon's attempt to pull away finally created the stress necessary to break the femur. Lognion fell back into the pit, gulping down the severed limb as he fell.

Meanwhile, Selene had used another air elemental to fly her to the top of the shaft. Her earth elementals tightened the entrance as she descended, making it difficult for the younger dragon to climb out. Sending commands to more than a hundred earth elementals, she had them constrict the stone shaft around the dragon. Others lifted the platform that Lognion stood atop, and a second later, her father took another bite, this time ripping into the other hind leg.

Lognion's corrupted spawn was still technically stronger, but with a useless wing and missing two legs, it was clearly at a disadvantage now. Unlike the wounds Oliver had inflicted previously, Lognion's bites had taken effect in both Hell and the adjacent ethereal plane. The corrupted dragon's hind legs were already regenerating, but it was taking them much longer.

Unexpectedly, the younger dragon released its grip and tried to drop down so it could reach Lognion. It twisted and pushed with its forelegs and started to fall sideways. Lognion was coming up for another bite when it happened, and the smaller dragon latched onto his head and ripped away part of Lognion's jaw.

Flinching back, Lognion fell from his stone platform as he tried to get away from his spawn's snapping teeth. The smaller dragon landed on his back and caught hold with its two good legs, then tore loose another chunk of flesh from Lognion's shoulder. A bloody fight ensued, but with his jaws still wounded, Lognion was now the one at a distinct disadvantage. His four fully functioning legs would have made the difference, but the space at the bottom was too tight for the two of them, so he couldn't maneuver or gain space to allow himself to heal.

All Lognion could do was tear great bloody wounds in the corrupted dragon's chest and sides with his claws, while it in turn began to tear into Lognion's side and devour the flesh there. The fight had turned from a likely victory to probable defeat in a matter of seconds.

Selene did something no sane person would do. She dropped down onto the two fighting dragons. Her body was hardly more than a lump of flesh and broken bones, and she felt little pain, but she needed proximity if she was going to make a meaningful difference.

She couldn't hope to do significant damage, but she had already seen how well her ill-intentioned healing could work. She started with the smaller dragon's regenerating hind legs and encouraged them in unfortunate ways. Soon, the infernal creature was growing two legs on either side rather than one. Using an air elemental to plaster herself to the enemy's side, she healed the tears in its side, as Lognion tore them, but without waiting for the muscle and tendons to reattach. The fresh skin interfered with internal healing and prevented the muscles from reconnecting as they should.

It was a slow, brutal battle, but her efforts made the difference. The corrupted dragon's power healed it even faster than Lognion, but she turned every healing wound into a liability. Eventually, her father's jaw finished healing, and he began to take full advantage of the situation. By the time the smaller dragon twisted and smashed her tiny body into the wall, it was too late. It had lost a forelimb, and Lognion was now biting down on the back of its neck. It was all over except for a grisly meal.

Selene could no longer see, her eyes having been turned to jelly by the last blow, along with the rest of her. So she spent her time reconstructing what she could. Restoring her form to being merely dead was impossible, but she could reshape the flesh and bones into a vaguely humanoid shape. With that she could move around, but without eyes she was severely limited in what she could do.

Repairing and renewing existing tissue she could manage. Stimulating healing or reattaching skin and muscle were well within her purview, but regrowing entire organs was not. Her greatest achievement in living patients was the use of dead donor tissues to replace those that had been lost. She could graft them in place, and with some time and care, bring them back to life with the help of the rest of the patient's healthy body.

She couldn't create new eyes from nothing. She'd need a new body, or at minimum some eyes harvested from a corpse. Unfortunately, her ears somehow still worked, and she was forced to listen to the gruesome sounds of her father feasting on the still struggling body of the other dragon while she reshaped as much of her broken body as she could in the dark. *At least we won,* she told herself.

An hour later, Selene sat beside Oliver near the entrance to the pit. Lognion had finished his meal and was still below, napping while he digested his final offspring. She still couldn't see, but her ears worked, and she'd shaped flesh, skin, and muscle into a workable facsimile of a normal throat, tongue and mouth, as well as a basic air bladder in her chest to provide the necessary airflow so that she could speak.

Her voice was a sibilant, hissing whisper, but it likely matched the aesthetic of her horrifying body. After the reshaping, it qualified more as a crude flesh golem than as a zombie or any sort of normal corpse. She didn't have to look at it anyway.

"What happens now?" asked her stepson.

"We wait for him to finish resting, then we go back to Hercynia," she answered.

The frustration in Oliver's voice was audible as he clarified, "No, I mean how are we going to stop him?"

We aren't, she thought darkly, remembering her deal. She'd completed her side of the bargain. Terabinia and its substitute queen were safe, but Lognion would be free to hunt Will and his relatives— excluding Oliver. *I saved my kingdom and your son, William, is that enough? Will you hate me anyway?*

"Only your father can stop him now. He'll be back to his full strength now, or slightly stronger," she answered. "He's agreed to leave Terabinia alone—and you."

"What does that mean?"

"I made a deal for your life, and for the life of my kingdom, but that's all I could get from him."

Oliver's voice was puzzled but beginning to reveal some anger. "What about Dad?"

"It's worse than that," she said tiredly. "He'll pursue his revenge against the rest of your family. Sammy, Tabitha, even your grandmother."

"And you're fine with that?" demanded Oliver.

"No, but it's all I could do. Hate me if you wish. I won't be here to receive your anger, though. I have one last thing to do to complete my part of it."

"You're not going anywhere," insisted the young warrior. "You'll help me stop him or I'll kill you myself."

"No need," she told him. "I volunteered to do that part myself." In her mind's eye, Selene could still see the green door that represented her final task, the undoing of the enchantment that bound her soul to the phylactery. All it would need was a tug on that string to unravel the magic that kept her chained to the world of the living. There was nothing else left for her to do, and perhaps the Mother would still accept her soul rather than consigning her to complete dissolution. *Not that I deserve her mercy.*

CHAPTER 17

Janice stood at the head of a rather small table in what was sometimes called the 'war room' but was actually more of a large office where the real work of governing Terabinia occurred. People imagined the queen ruling from her throne, but in fact, the events that occurred there were mainly ceremonial. That wasn't to say they weren't important. Holding court and hearing the petitions of individuals—nobles and commoners—was a vital function, but most of the actual decisions were made in other places.

The war room was called so mainly because it excited the imagination more than the 'queen's study,' but most of the work done there was boring and administrative. The room included two desks, one for the monarch and a smaller one for her assistant, but currently Janice was sitting at the table with her husband John and one other, Lord Emory Tallowen. A map of Terabinia was unfurled before them, and Emory had placed several small tokens along the coast. All of them were within ten miles of the port town of Nerril.

Emory had just placed the fourth token and then glanced at Janice. Currently, she wore the face of the queen, and he hadn't been included in the secret, so as far as he knew he was addressing Selene herself. "I received reports from lookouts at all four of these locations just this morning. After responding with a request for more information, three failed to report. The fourth was more cautious and remained at a distance. We can only assume the other spotters were captured."

"If they were taken, the enemy probably knows we're aware of them," said Janice.

Tiny spoke next. "The enchanted tablets are made to melt to slag in the event that the proper owner loses it or has it taken."

Janice nodded. "True, but the elves are not newcomers to magic. I'm sure they'll realize what the devices were, even if the runes are rendered indecipherable. We have to assume they'll be preparing for our response."

"What did the scouts report seeing?" asked Tiny.

"Strange black beasts the size of a whale, Your Grace," said Emory.

The Black Duke held up a hand. "We're alone, Emory. You know better than to waste time with honorifics. When you say, 'strange black beasts,' that's not enough. What did they look like?"

"The first reports were that they saw military-style groups on the beaches, but no ships were in evidence. Two of them reported seeing large, dark shapes floating in the water nearby, but they didn't report back after that. The best description we have is from the one scout that didn't approach. He claims to have seen one of the monsters approach the shore and open its mouth. More soldiers stepped out from inside the creature. I can only assume he misinterpreted what he saw," responded Emory.

"You think they were some sort of underwater vessel?" asked Janice.

"That would make more sense than men emerging from the mouths of aquatic monsters," said Emory.

Tiny bypassed that issue and moved on. "One good thing about our recently aborted war is that we still have the army in a state of readiness, and we can easily recall the levies."

"My fear is that we may be missing important information," said Janice. "You've heard nothing from our agents in Darrow?"

"I sent queries, and all the responses were negative," said Lord Tallowen. "I can't rule out the possibility of a second attack there, but I would think they'd try and time it to arrive at the same time as the attack here."

"They know we have working teleport beacons between the two capitals. If they don't move simultaneously, we could move our forces from one place to another far faster than they could change targets," observed Tiny.

"Unless they're confident they can overcome everything we have, in which case a single powerful attack would simplify matters for them. Darrow is still recovering. Most of Terabinia's strength is here. If they've got the numbers and strength to break us here they can take their time with the rest. Darrow would be a fait accompli, and while Trendham might be more difficult logistically, with their subversive magics, that might not be a problem either," added Janice.

Tiny turned to her. "We should send word to Will's cousin. She has as much power as the oligarchs and might do better at convincing them of the threat than if we communicate with them directly since relations are still tense."

Emory's cheeks colored slightly. "Actually, I asked Lady Wellings to send a message to Samantha already."

Tiny frowned. "Before meeting with the queen? That's a breach of protocol."

"I was visiting at their home when I got the first report. I came here straight away, but I felt she should be warned. I apologize if I overstepped," explained Emory.

The Black Duke's countenance showed his irritation, but Janice put a hand on his arm to stay his anger, then she replied, "Duke Shaw is right. You should have reported to me first, but we can overlook that for now, especially since your decision aligns with my own. Did you receive a reply?"

Lord Tallowen nodded. "Yes, but according to what was written, not from Sammy herself. One of her armsmen responded, identifying himself as Wardsman Alex. The news isn't good."

Janice frowned. "One of her men is privy to her communications?"

Emory nodded. "The enchanted tablet that Lady Wellings uses to talk with her is a custom work produced by her husband, James. It doesn't have the same security measures we use on the devices given to our scouts. Of more importance, Your Majesty, is the fact that Sammy was unconscious, recovering from a battle with a dragon."

Tiny stared at Emory in shock. "A dragon? Why would she—," He paused looking at Janice. In a quieter tone, he asked, "Are we back at war? She didn't say anything about…"

Janice's eyes warned him not to say more, and she shook her head to indicate she didn't know anything either. She looked at Emory. "We'll need to know more to understand the importance of what you've just said. Perhaps Samantha can give us more clarity once she recovers enough to respond personally." She glanced over at Tiny. "Would you step out and send someone to summon Lady Wellings? Tell them to make sure she brings the enchanted tablet with her. We need to know what Samantha has to say as soon as possible."

Tiny and Emory looked knowingly at each other. Unspoken was the fact that Tabitha hadn't shown herself in court or more specifically to the queen in over ten years. She'd even ignored a direct summons, though Selene had chosen not to make an issue of the matter. Before they could say anything, Janice continued, "Tell them to be diplomatic, but let her know this is a matter of state security. She'll come or there will be consequences. Terabinia's safety may well hinge upon what Samantha Cartwright has to tell us."

After giving the obvious instructions to Lord Shaw to begin bringing the army into full readiness and for Lord Tallowen to try and get more information from his field agents, Janice adjourned the meeting until Lady Wellings arrived. As she waited, she thought about James Wellings and one particular project she'd set him to almost a year ago. She'd had him report on it directly to her, as Janice, so that hopefully the details would remain secret even from Selene herself, since he wasn't aware she often filled in for the queen. *Will we really need the dragon-killer?* She hoped not, for it wasn't ready and there were still many questions regarding how it could safely be used even if it was operational.

Tabitha appeared sooner than expected. Tiny and Emory were still away executing their respective orders, so Janice received Selene's estranged friend privately. She was sitting behind the queen's desk when the younger woman was ushered in. Tabitha curtsied, but once the servant had left and shut the door, she straightened up and gave the titular ruler of Terabinia a challenging stare.

Janice was fully committed to her role as Selene's stand-in and returned the stare with the confidence befitting a monarch, but Tabitha's eyes narrowed, and a frown appeared on her lips. Her next words were a statement of fact. "You're not her. What's going on here?" The ambient turyn in the room began moving in deliberate patterns as the third-order wizard's wariness increased.

After years of practice, Janice kept her aplomb and kept her features relaxed, but there was a stern warning in her voice. "This room is protected from eavesdropping, but you need to take more care with your words. If someone had heard you, we might have serious problems."

Tabitha's features didn't soften. "There will definitely be problems if you don't identify yourself and give a satisfying explanation for why you're sitting in a chair you have no right to be in." Her will had drawn the turyn tightly around herself, leaving an obvious paucity in the air around Janice, who hadn't attempted to contest the other woman's control.

Being only second-order, Janice knew she was outclassed in terms of strength, and any attempt at a direct confrontation would risk destroying her role as queen. "Since your acumen is good enough to realize I'm not Selene, I'm surprised you aren't able to identify me. We used to be friends."

"That isn't an answer."

"It's me, Janice," said the fake queen with a sigh. "I'm playing this role because of a direct command from Her Majesty."

Tabitha's eyes narrowed. "That face isn't an illusion. Explain."

"The queen is an accomplished sculptor of flesh." Janice gestured to herself. "This is her work, since an illusion wouldn't be sufficient to fool most of the nobility." She arched one brow. "That aside, don't you think your behavior is too bold? The way you've treated Her Majesty over the last decade has been difficult to reconcile with the fact that she has always thought of you as family."

Tabitha's expression hardened. "Your mistake is in assuming the creature issuing your orders is the same as the friend I grew up with. At least you're human. I'm not certain who or what she is."

"Don't pretend you're unable to recognize her. You know her well enough to spot the difference in turyn within seconds of entering this room with me. And I know you must have spoken with your brother as well. He couldn't convince you?" Janice kept her tone level.

The turyn in the room began drifting again as Tabitha relaxed her will. "I've argued with him about it. I'll admit my doubts about her identity are probably unfounded, but I still can't countenance what she's become."

"It must be nice to have that luxury," said Janice pointedly. "Some have to concern themselves with a more pragmatic reality." She lifted a hand to stop the other woman before she could respond, then added, "I don't expect to resolve this. The only question relevant to the present is whether you intend to recognize her authority and consequently the responsibility she has put on my shoulders."

"You expect me to bend the knee to you?"

Janice sighed. "I expect you to put Terabinia before your personal issues. I need your help."

Tabitha exhaled slowly, letting go of some of her tension. She pursed her lips, then answered, "You shouldn't have to suffer for my anger with her. I'm sure you've had to make some hard choices, and if this is an example of what you've been having to do for her, then it isn't fair for me to be judgmental." She lifted a cloth bag decorated with elegant floral embroidery and withdrew a square piece of rune-inscribed silvery metal. "I've had no more word from Sammy or her bodyguard."

"Bodyguard?"

Tabitha nodded. "Alex, the man who replied, is one of her most trusted guards; she hired him on Oliver's recommendation."

"I see," said Janice. "I'd like you to remain here until you get word."

"If the dragon is flying this way, it might get here before she wakes. You'd do well to make whatever preparations you can with that assumption in mind."

"Things are more complicated than that," Janice told her.

"How so?"

Despite the tension between them, Janice shared what little information she had about the elven landing. Afterward, she added, "You can see the quandary we're in. We need to respond as strongly as possible to the incursion, but if we have a dragon running loose in the country, that could be disastrous. The truly burning question is why did the queen attack Bondgrad?"

Tabitha frowned, but after a moment answered, "According to Alex it isn't her, it's Lognion."

"He's dead," stated Janice. "She's merely using his corpse."

Tabitha shrugged. "My tablet doesn't save the messages—they're overwritten by newer ones—but Alex spent some time relaying what Oliver told him during their brief time together."

"Oliver was there as well?"

Tabitha nodded, then explained what she had learned. During the face-off between Samantha and the dragon, the two young wardsmen had had a few minutes to exchange information while they tried to decide how best to assist their employer. "He didn't have time to fully explain, but he told Alex that Lognion had somehow come back to life and resumed control over his body. According to what he said, Selene is a prisoner within her father's draconic flesh."

"Do you trust his opinion?" asked Janice.

"I hardly know Alex, and Oliver is young," said Tabitha with a shrug. "At the same time, while I'm suspicious of what she's become, I find it hard to imagine Selene arbitrarily attacking Bondgrad, or attempting to kill Will's cousin."

"She's still the same woman she always was," put in Janice. "She still has the same soul, regardless of the body or object that houses it."

Tabitha met the statement with a flat, unemotional look. "Is she? You state something as fact without any way to prove it. She died and used an unholy concoction of soul magic—fueled with soul fragments from sick children—to reanimate herself. She obviously has the memories and knowledge of the woman I was once proud to call a sister, but does that mean it's still her? The Selene I knew before would never hurt a child; I don't know what to think of her now."

"You've seen the reforms she's put in place since becoming queen," pointed out Janice. "She's done more for children, for the health of Terabinia as a whole, than any monarch in history. Seeing her works, how can you doubt it's really her?"

"What would a soulless monster masquerading in her place do to maintain the illusion?" asked Tabitha, then added, "And no, I'm not casting aspersions at your current role. I'm trying to make an honest point. What does she do when she's out roaming in secret? While you maintain her façade as a proper ruler. Where does she get the bodies she uses?"

Janice's face reddened. "You know very well that they're paid volunteers—"

"That's what she told my brother," said Tabitha. "Do you know it for a fact?"

"I've been involved in finding and facilitating the arrangements, as well as compensating the women and their families. There's nothing nefarious here."

"Do the women know what they're agreeing to?" asked Tabitha pointedly.

"They're selling time. They have no memory of it or any need to know what—" Janice stopped with a frustrated sigh and lifted a hand as though she would run it through her hair—a thoroughly unqueenly gesture. She stopped herself. "We could debate this forever, but if you've already made up your mind, there's no shifting it. Your brother has accepted her. His judgment doesn't hold any weight with you?"

"Will has a good heart, but so does my James, and the same with your husband. How much would Tiny overlook if it was you instead of Selene? Men's judgment cannot be trusted when it concerns the women they love."

"Some men, perhaps," argued Janice, "but John once nearly broke things off with me when he thought I would excuse the killing of a dog. William took more than a decade to reconsider his decision. You don't give them enough credit."

Tabitha held up her hands. "I've already said I don't think she'd attack the city, whether or not it's actually her or a twisted copy. More importantly, it's your decision how our nation proceeds. I've accepted your authority for pragmatic reasons."

"Once John and Emory return, I'll decide based on their recommendations and whatever extra information they may have garnered," said Janice tiredly.

After that, they shared an awkward hour filled with long silences and punctuated by polite but brief chatter regarding their respective families. The one thing the two of them fully shared was a powerful grievance against the elves, Janice for the death of her oldest son, and Tabitha for both the near death of her husband and the violent invasion of her home.

When the Black Duke and Lord Tallowen had both returned, it was with some relief that they were able to face the problems of the nation again. Emory had received more reports of surreptitious landings, and it was clear that the elves were marshalling a substantial force on the coast near Nerril. It was an obvious and important location, since the port city controlled the nation's primary access to sea trade, with both the capital, Cerria, and another major city, located along the river, not to mention many smaller villages and towns. It made sense that the elves would seek to seize Nerril and then use it as a staging ground and logistical hub for a broader campaign to take the heart of Terabinia.

Their discussion was informal, but would be the basis for the queen's final decisions once the High Council had assembled for an emergency meeting. Janice looked to Emory to confirm a few key details. "Project Chrysalis is fully ready?"

Emory glanced uncomfortably at Tabitha since Janice was referencing a state and military secret. After Janice motioned for him to speak, he kept his answer short to avoid sharing anything more than necessary. "No, Your Majesty, it's still a work in progress in Darrow and some parts of Terabinia, but Nerril was a priority. Both the Driven and the new Arcane Corps stand ready."

Janice nodded, then turned to her husband. "Lord Shaw, in your opinion, will they be sufficient? How stands the army?"

Tiny's lips tightened briefly into a line. "From the limited reports we've seen, the elven force is insufficient. Lord Tallowen's force should be enough, and supported by the Iron Knights, I would anticipate a decisive victory for Terabinia. That bothers me. The levies will take at least a week to be ready, and even with Project Chrysalis, we can't expect to have more than two brigades in position for this operation."

"The prospect of a decisive victory bothers you?" asked Janice. "Clarify that for me."

"The elves have shown themselves to be highly competent thus far. We know they have plenty of wizards, with many of them being second-order. Their elite warriors worked alongside us when we invaded Trendham, and I was impressed by their organization and the high quality of their equipment, training, and magics. We also know that our information is incomplete. If anything goes wrong, this could turn into a disaster, and it might cost us our most effective forces at the same time," explained Tiny, his large brow furrowed with concern. He turned to Emory. "Surely you feel the same."

The third-order wizard rubbed his face absently, his fingers ruffling the previously neat beard on his chin. "Your points are valid, but everything we know about the elves up to now points to them not possessing a large military. They've lived in isolation, protected by secrecy, obviating the need for a large standing force. The quality of the warriors we have seen is further proof. It makes me think they've been putting most of their energies into creating small, elite units. They have also focused on subversion, espionage, and spells that manipulate the mind. If they had a large *and* superior military force, I can't help but think they would have used it years ago rather than bother with soft tactics.

"Fortune favors the bold. I think they've underestimated our intelligence and are hoping to gain a solid advantage before they think we can react. If true, our best course is to respond with speed and strength to crush them immediately. They've overreached, and we should take advantage of that to bloody their noses and teach them a lesson. If their military power is as limited as I suspect, losing their vanguard might make it not only impractical, but impossible to continue," finished Emory.

Janice was pensive, but after a moment, she asked, "What of evacuating Nerril, with the b—"

Emory took the risk of cutting the queen off before she could reveal sensitive information. "They're too close. We would need at least a week to get the population out."

Tiny was nodding in agreement. "The citizens would be exposed if they tried to abandon the city."

Janice frowned, "Can't we do both? Once our forces are in the area, they could protect the retreating populace."

Her husband shook his head. "They couldn't defend them, and the elves could use the chaos to potentially reverse our advantage. A strongly defended Nerril complements our operation. The city serves as an enticing target, meaning we know where our enemies will strike. It also gives us a strategic advantage by serving as a hard rock to crush the elves against. The people will be safer behind the walls."

"I'm inclined to act swiftly then," said Janice, giving a nod to Emory. "Any ideas how we can mitigate the possible risks if the elves are hiding a trump card, Lord Shaw?"

The Black Duke answered without hesitation, "Without knowing the unknown, no. But there are a few common-sense measures we should implement, particularly regarding how and where we deploy our limited reserves." He leaned over and used the map to explain his ideas.

Tabitha watched them lay out plans without attempting to contribute. She'd never had any real interest in military tactics, strategy, or even civil governance. Her focus had always been on her family, and even now it was her husband and children that were foremost on her mind. When the meeting finally came to an end, she interjected herself into the pause before they could leave to begin the meeting with the High Council. "I have a question." Once she had their attention, she addressed Tiny first. "My husband James served as an officer in the war for unification. If this does turn into a protracted war—"

Emory stepped in to answer first. "James is an accomplished wizard now, as well as an important academic." He glanced deferentially at Tiny. "He wouldn't be taken by the army this time since his talents would be much more important to the Arcane Corps."

Tabitha's eyes went to the false queen. "The crown still makes certain allowances for families, does it not?"

"Your sons aren't up for—," began Janice.

"Not my children, their parents," clarified Tabitha. When Emory frowned, she went on, "Let me explain…

CHAPTER 18

Tabitha spent the rest of the day at the palace. She would have rather returned home, but she had decided to play by the rules, even if the command came from a pretender. James had been working at Wurthaven, so he didn't discover her absence until that evening, and after making sure their family was settled, he came looking for her at the palace. Tabitha was in a restricted area reserved for the Driven when he got there, receiving a rough orientation from Emory. A messenger came for her, and she met her husband in one of the palace's many public areas.

It took some time to tell him about everything that had happened, and while James was generally an agreeable sort, he wasn't pleased that his wife was essentially restricted to the palace grounds. He accepted the logic of the queen's decision after a brief discussion, but even after she had explained Sammy's message and the news of an elven invasion, there were other questions on his mind.

"As alarming as all that sounds, I don't understand what it is that you're wearing. Are they drafting you?" He took a step back so he could gesture, waving his hand to indicate the full length of her body. She had exchanged her elegant dress for a form-fitting outfit of dark leather that no noblewoman would want to be caught wearing. A linen shirt was against her skin, but it was covered by a thick gambeson, a leather vest, thick leather vambraces, cops, and armor for the upper arms and shoulders. Farther down, she wore knit trousers that hugged her hips and thighs in a scandalous manner. On top of them were heavy pieces of boiled and waxed leather to protect her thighs, knees, and shins.

It was the sort of armor worn by the queen's special forces, the Driven. They'd originally been created by King Lognion as a secret guard of elite sorcerers. While Selene had stopped the creation of new sorcerers, she hadn't gotten rid of those already in her employ, and they were now supplemented by a few young first-order wizards recently graduated from Wurthaven.

The defiance Tabitha had shown in front of the false queen was nowhere to be seen with her husband. Her eyes were apologetic, though she kept her words firm as she replied, "I know you won't like it, but this was my decision."

James blinked. "I don't understand. I've served before. If war is really about to break out, I'm already on their lists. Does she plan to orphan our children?"

Tabitha shook her head, as she searched for words. "No. There's a rule in place, similar to the one about families that have already lost most of their sons. You won't be called to serve since I'm going."

Still in shock, he stared at her blankly. "This doesn't make sense. They can't ask this of you. You're a mother!"

She nodded, then wiped a stray tear from her cheek. She hadn't expected to become so emotional. "And you're a father, James, an exceptional one."

Anger finally appeared on his features. "What does that—"

"There aren't many third-order wizards, James. You know that. I can do things no one else can. Things that might well make all the difference in a situation like this. Your talents and knowledge make you far more important here."

"Don't be stupid," he snapped. "You don't have any experience with this. The children need you far more than—"

Tabitha pressed a finger to his lips, then pulled it away quickly. "There are many good mothers, James, but men like you are rarer than you realize. You're more important to us than you think. When you nearly died—I understood then. I didn't expect any of this, but when they were discussing their plans, I knew I was perfectly suited for what needs to be done. And I know this is selfish, but I also knew it would keep you out of harm's way."

"That's rubbish! I won't have it. What do you think you'll do?" he demanded.

"Reconnaissance," she answered. "Do you know anyone else who can turn into a hawk or an owl? Or a horse? I can be anything, even an elf, though I'm not planning to try that since I don't speak their language. The point is that my unique talents make me better able to scout out the enemy's positions than anyone else, day or night."

"It's too dangerous!" he hissed desperately.

"Who else can heal or regenerate the way I can? You *know* how difficult it really is to hurt me." She poked his chest with a pointed finger. "One dagger, one arrow, right here, that's all it would take for you. I'll never forget seeing you covered in blood that day. If it hadn't been for Rob, we wouldn't even be having this conversation."

James fell silent, hoping to think of an argument he could use. "Even with enchantments, that leather isn't enough. The elves have magical weapons, and we don't even know what sort of battle magics they've developed. You should have better armor, like the Iron Knights."

"Their armor takes weeks to be fitted, and besides…" She paused before continuing, "I won't be wearing this armor when scouting."

Her husband gaped at her.

Tabitha raised one hand and summoned her limnthal as a visible reminder. "If I transform, I'll store it here." She tapped the runes on one of the vambraces. "Part of the enchantment makes the armor self-donning. It only takes seconds. It's a handy trick for secret police, but it's well suited for someone like me who needs to redress after a transformation." She held out her hand, and hard ebon scales covered it, while wicked claws tipped her fingers. "If something happens while I'm scouting, I can grow better armor than anything you'd want me to wear."

James struggled for a moment, and then visibly deflated. "There's arguing which of us is more capable, but that begs the question, shouldn't defending our children be the higher priority?"

She remembered very well the horror of that day when their home had been targeted, but Tabitha didn't relent. "Your preparations were what made the difference then, and you've improved them since. I've no skill with enchantments, and you're probably better than me with battle spells, but my talent is ideally suited for this."

"And if you're caught?"

She arched one brow. "Since I revealed my talent, you've helped me train it. What do you think? Would you want to be the enemy that stumbles into me on a dark night?"

Her husband couldn't help but smirk. "No. That's the Mother's own truth, so long as you have the resolve to do what's necessary. This isn't like defending our home. You might have to kill in cold blood. Are you sure?"

"These are the people responsible for the attack on our home," said Tabitha. "I haven't forgotten that, and they'll regret it if I have anything to say about it."

James pulled her into a tight embrace, and Tabitha laid her head against his shoulder. "I don't like this," he told her in a quiet voice. "And now there's a dragon loose."

"Another reason we need to end this quickly," said Tabitha. "If Selene really has gone mad, there's no telling what she might be capable of." She leaned her head back and stared up at him. "You know what to do?"

He gave a small nod. "But if either of us had to face a dragon, you're the only one who could—"

"Sammy nearly died. I wouldn't stand a chance," she answered immediately.

"Just make yourself bigger," said James with a chuckle.

She laughed. "I don't think it's that simple, not to mention that much mass would take an incredible amount of turyn."

"I'm teasing," said James. "Please don't ever try that."

Tabitha pushed him away for a moment, then poked his chest again. "I won't, unless I have to get between the dragon and you or the children. Make sure that doesn't happen."

He smiled confidently. "You have my word on it."

***

Will rose from a solid night's rest and stretched languorously. He'd spent days working his way down through the fractured stone pile that hid the position of the elven gate on the ethereal plane. Yesterday, he'd put the finishing touches on the bottom of the stone shaft. The sides were smooth stone that had been fused together to prevent the danger of rockfalls. A stone stair followed the inside of the round shaft all the way to the bottom. At the top, he'd created a stone arch to support a stone ceiling and cut a horizontal shaft on one side to provide egress onto a relatively flat area near the top of the stone-rubble island.

At the bottom of the shaft, the stairs ended, and he'd created a round room with arches to support the weight above it. He'd crafted a stone bier to put his bedroll on, and when that hadn't been quite comfortable enough, he'd taken a little time to design yet another unique spell—one that would create a soft, compressible mattress of air. With that between his bedroll and the stone, he'd been almost as comfortable as he would have been in his bed at home.

He'd dutifully recorded the new spell in his journal, which was now full. He'd done so much bespoke spellcrafting lately that he'd had to start filling a new blank journal. Hopefully he'd be able to register them at the library in Wurthaven someday. He didn't care much about the potential royalties he would accrue from the numerous spells he'd designed, but he liked the thought that future wizards would learn his name for his contributions to domestic magic rather than the history of violence he'd accrued. Given enough time, history might forget the wild tales of the Stormking, but he couldn't imagine any wizard who wouldn't want an air mattress to sleep on when away from home.

That was his hope, anyway.

Will took a few minutes to check on Oliver and saw he was riding the dragon yet again. He wondered why they were flying yet again, but he trusted Selene knew what she was doing. At the bare minimum, they would have sent a message via Oliver's enchanted tablet if they needed him. Reassured, he returned to the task at hand.

The elves' use of so much stone to blockade the ethereal location of their gate had been simple and highly effective, but it also served to hide his efforts from them. Will's shaft and small room were hidden from any elven observers by all the broken rock. All he had to do now was position the final portion of his excavation where the gate was and cross back into the material plane. His appearance there might trigger alarms, but he could step through the elven gate a second later, presumably before they had a chance to deactivate it.

But assuming he did trigger an alarm, he'd have to be ready to fight his way clear on the other side. Considering how paranoid the elves were, there were probably considerable defensive measures in place on the other side of the gate. Once upon a time, he would never have considered what he was about to do, but he'd done so many ridiculously dangerous things in his life that this didn't seem so bad.

"Surely it can't compare to traveling to Hell and slaying the entire council of twelve demon-lords," he muttered to himself. "Still, it won't do to take the matter lightly." He summoned the oilskin bag containing his mail hauberk, wrinkling his nose at the smell of oil, steel, and sweat. No matter how he cleaned and treated the armor, it always stank.

Will undressed and then redressed from the skin out, donning a linen shift and hose, then a padded gambeson. A tight leather belt went around his waist, and the mail leggings were attached to it, putting that weight on his hips. He shimmied into the hauberk and tightened a second belt outside it at his waist, dividing the distribution of its weight between his shoulders and hips. A padded coif was followed by its mail counterpart, and then he spent a frustrating quarter of an hour fiddling with the lacing to make sure it was tight around his padded chin. A loose mail coif was worse than wearing nothing—it was a lesson his time in the army had driven home time and time again. The demon-steel breast- and backplate went over his torso, providing serious protection to his vital organs, and he completed it all by strapping a steel cap on top of his head. Mail was wonderful, but it wouldn't prevent a cracked skull.

All of it was enchanted to some degree, but Will hadn't updated the enchantments in years. The magic that imbued his mail made it stronger and more durable and reduced its weight slightly, but that was the extent of it. The rest of his armor was similar. Compared to what he'd made for Oliver, Will's mail was second-rate, though it was still miles better than what most could afford.

Feeling the weight and bulk of it all, Will was tempted to remove the armor. His magic had advanced far beyond what he'd had back as a young soldier in the army. He'd fought Lognion the first time in courtly attire, and he'd faced many similarly lethal foes with little more. Armoring himself to such a degree seemed like overkill. *I need to set a good example if I expect Oliver to be similarly careful,* he told himself.

Of course, Will's son would never know how he dressed for battle today, but Will would know. "It never hurts to be prepared," he reminded himself. Checking himself over one more time, he decided he couldn't be any more ready, short of having an army at his back. He cast the water-breathing spell as an added precaution. It wouldn't allow him to speak normally, but he could go for at least half an hour without breathing.

Just in case, he told himself silently. He cast a water-walking spell and then followed it with one to move his body back to the material plane. The elven gate stood right beside him now, and he stepped through before the elves could do whatever they might do at the sudden appearance of a stranger.

The transition was smooth, and he found himself standing on a still body of water in a different place. The water stretched out to form a quiet lake in a cavernous structure. Will might have called it a cave, but the ceiling fifty yards above came into focus, he could see it was in fact made of worked stone. The elven side of the gate seemed to be a small and very artificial lagoon enclosed within a solid structure.

A number of docking spots were lined up in front of him, roughly sixty yards from where he stood atop the unmoving water. Four ships were currently docked, but another ten or so spots were available. Will blinked and started walking forward. He had expected something larger, an open bay perhaps. Something that could hold more than a dozen or so ships. Given what he was seeing, the elves couldn't have much of a navy.

A loud noise was repeating, some sort of an alarm, though it was clear that the elves were using something other than a bell. A calm female voice carried clearly over the sound of the alarm, but since it was speaking in a language Will didn't know, he could only guess at what was being said. *Either a warning to me or instructions for their emergency response,* he guessed.

Despite feeling a sense of urgency, Will moved at a steady pace, his eyes studying the docks and the space beyond them. Rushing would do him no favors; neither would anxiety or fear. *Panic is for the enemy, not me,* he thought.

He reached the closest empty dock and jumped up a few feet to land upon a force-travel disk he cast simultaneously. It lifted him the rest of the distance, and he stepped onto the stone dock as he dispelled the disk. He anticipated needing to be able to cast force spells in the near future. The few dockworkers he had seen moving around the ships had taken off at a run soon after the alarm had started. They exited through four massive stone archways that stood roughly thirty yards beyond the docks. As the last of them went through, three of the openings were sealed by massive steel plates sliding down from some recess in the stone above. The metal doors boomed with an intimidating sound of finality as they hit the stone floor.

One remained open, though, and as the workers finished exiting, armed and armored guards entered. They carried a variety of weapons and gear. The first ones through carried heavy square metal shields and wore light armor; they formed a shield wall twenty men across while others in half-plate took positions behind them, lifting strange metal and wooden devices up to point in Will's direction. He assumed they were ranged weapons of some sort.

Behind the ones with ranged weapons were ten elites wearing the full enchanted plate that Will had seen when Trendham and Terabinia had almost gone to war. Those warriors moved to either end of the shield wall, prepared to cover the flanks or advance forward if it turned out the ranged attacks weren't sufficient to put him down.

Will's jaw tightened as he shifted course to head directly for them. His sonic shield was already buzzing, encircling his body at a distance of several feet. It was highly effective against physical threats, though it needed to be tuned to the proper frequency depending on what was coming at him. He'd originally developed it specifically to handle fire, but he currently had it adjusted to be most effective against iron and steel. Other things might be disrupted or potentially deflected, but steel-tipped arrows would disintegrate before reaching him. He'd adjust the shield frequency once he had a better idea of what the enemy's ranged weapons were throwing at him.

The first defenders fired, and their missiles struck so quickly that Will could barely register that they had released a volley. They timed their attack, so he used a custom-designed force spell with a hemispherical shape to block them all at once, placing it just within the boundary of his sonic shield. The missiles turned out to be slender, yet dense rods composed of some metal he was unfamiliar with. His sound shield shattered some of them but failed to have full effect, so it was the force spell that truly saved him.

The impacts were such that his force spell broke. It robbed the metal rods of much of their momentum, and when they hit his armor Will felt as though he was being pelted by rocks. Glancing down, he studied one of the pieces of metal, moving back just enough so that it was centered within his sonic shield. Watching it, he adjusted the frequency until the metal rapidly disintegrated into fine dust. *Whatever it is, it isn't iron based, but it's heavy and hard as hell,* he observed. It didn't matter now. He had taken its measure and adapted.

Breaking a force spell would ordinarily cause feedback, but one of the innovations Will had made in the years since leaving Terabinia was creating force spells with built-in load faults. Traditional force spells were all or nothing, and if the caster was short on turyn or the strength of will necessary, they could fail, causing injuries to the wizard's will. His new versions were made to fail by design, and so long as he didn't use a version with a load tolerance greater than he was currently capable of sustaining, there was no danger of will strain. He'd trained quietly for years to reflex cast the new versions in three distinct load levels.

Currently, he was fresh, so he'd used the strongest version, which meant the elven weapons were powerful indeed. It had only taken ten of them striking together to break his shield—after losing some momentum to his sonic shield.

He kept walking, and the elves fired again. This time, their metal missiles exploded into grey dust when they struck his sonic shield, and the powder drifted to the floor in a ring around him. Shock showed on their faces as Will came on without so much as a pause, a wicked smile forming on his lips.

They fired again, this time without cohesion as each of the defenders began to rush their shots. Will ignored them, advancing implacably. He was empty-handed when he reached the line of shields, and he didn't dare shift his sonic shield to rend flesh while the enemy was firing their strange metal rods at him so randomly. Instead, he summoned his sword-staff from the limnthal and set it to vibrating ominously.

His sonic shield created a horrific shrieking noise as it contacted the line of shield bearers, but their shields were made of something different than the missiles and survived the contact. Even so, the disturbing sound and jarring vibration caused the defenders to jerk away, and the defensive line fell into chaos. More missiles were fired at Will, but they disintegrated instantly. He moved into his foes and began testing their armor with his bladed staff.

The lightly armored shield bearers didn't fare well. They were disoriented and off-balance as his weapon tore through their leather and sliced into flesh and bone as though they were butter rather than living enemies. Red blood sprayed through the air and turned Will's vibrating shield pink as some of it became suspended in the air around him.

In a panic, the shield bearers and ranged defenders routed, dropping shields and weapons as they turned and ran. Only the fully armored knights kept their nerve, advancing on him from all sides with spears and heavy maces.

Will sent his staff back into the limnthal and let them come. With the threat of the strange metal rods now absent, he simply re-tuned his sonic shield—not for armor or any other type of metal, but specifically for bone. The change took half a second, and then he expanded his shield to pass through the advancing knights. The massacre was so swift that the elven warriors weren't even able to cry out as their bones turned to jelly. Only their armor kept them in some semblance of humanoid form as they collapsed limply to the stone floor.

Will reset his sonic shield to protect against their metal missiles and kept walking, heading for the still-open doorway that represented his only exit from the enclosed docks. He wasn't surprised when it was sealed shut right before he got there.

He stopped and glanced around, making sure there were no unexpected foes waiting to shoot him from behind. Just to be safe, he erected another force hemisphere behind him, trusting the metal door to protect his front, and then he extended his sonic shield until the edge met the door, and he tuned it for a few seconds until the metal began to turn to dust.

He didn't use it to go through the door, however. Instead, he pulled the shield in close to protect himself and left a tiny opening through which he placed one finger against the door. Slowly, he began sending vibrations into the door to match the frequency of his shield, letting them build. At first, nothing happened, but once the proper threshold of energy was reached, the door would explode.

That was the purpose of his sonic shield, to protect him from the violent explosion of metal shards. Hopefully, the enemy preparing for him on the other side would not be as ready for the consequences of their door's explosive failure.

As the door began to shiver, Will noticed a mist coming from holes in the ceiling and floor, making him glad he didn't need to breathe, as he presumed it was either a poison or some sort of soporific. An evil idea came to mind, and he paused his effort to destroy the door, letting it rest while the gas built up in the vast space of the enclosed dock. The fumigation system was built to handle the capaciousness of the area, and the place was filled with hazy mist within minutes. It didn't do much to hinder visibility, so he was certain it had to be laced with a drug of some sort.

Resuming his door-destroying effort, he soon had the large metal door humming. Seconds passed, and it started shivering. Finally, it began to emit a terrifying scream before violently exploding. Metal shards flew out in every direction at lethal speed. Another shield wall waited on the other side, and the shield bearers staggered under the impact. Behind them stood two men in military uniforms. Will recognized them as wizards by the way the turyn around them was held at the ready. One of them died instantly, however, as a piece of shrapnel went just over the tops of the shields and tore part of his skull off.

Will readjusted his sonic shield to prepare for the metal rods that had been fired at him previously, and then cast an elemental air spell to create a massive gust of wind, driving the gas from the dock area into the large room on the other side of the door. The remaining wizard and the soldiers in front of him ignored it, protected by some preparatory magic, but he was satisfied to see a large number of support staff take flight behind them. Most of them made it out, but a few collapsed after taking an ill-timed breath.

The wizard tried a spell and failed as Will stifled the turyn around him. Then, the elf managed one force-lance. Will blocked it with a point defense shield before attaching a source-link to the wizard and ripping the turyn from him so quickly that the elf went instantly unconscious. More metal missiles turned to powder as they struck his sonic shield. This time, the ranged attackers were spread out at the edges of the large room, and unlike the support staff, they were protected from the gas. The walls were nearly thirty yards distant, so Will didn't dare change his sonic shield to be anything but defensive. Instead, he switched to one of his more reliable long-range attacks, the light-darts spell. Each casting created five darts of deadly white light that were powerful enough to burn a pinky-sized hole all the way through a grown man. Leather was no real protection, but metal plates were effective against it.

Will wasn't wild with his attacks, however. He took a moment to pick each target and directed all five darts at a single elf each time, spreading them out just enough that one or two would find a vulnerable spot and burn through flesh. He rarely needed a second casting to end one of the defenders, and as the seconds ticked by, they fell one by one, their missiles exploding into dust as they fired back at him. One, two, five, ten—Will slew them methodically, his face murderously calm as they screamed and died. When the attacks against him stopped, he made a careful survey of the room.

With experienced eyes, he could read the turyn around the downed foes. Some were dead, but many were merely wounded, though if any were conscious, they did a good job of pretending not to be. Unfortunately for them, Will's turyn senses couldn't differentiate between those truly incapacitated and those merely feigning unconsciousness.

Now certain there would be no more missile attacks, Will switched his shield's frequency and made a quick tour of the large room, liquefying the bones of the living and dead alike. None of his enemies would rise to bother him again.

Taking a moment, he examined the room more carefully. It was largely empty except for the defensive barriers that had protected the ranged attackers around the edges. The floor showed signs of wear, and Will guessed that the elves had designed the big area to serve as a bottle neck for anything that managed to get past the docks. *Clearly, they didn't expect someone like me,* he observed.

Quickly shifting his vision, he examined the area for hidden traps and then checked the ethereal plane since the elves used it frequently. To his surprise, the ethereal on this side of the gate was also completely filled with stone. Will had hoped to be able to retreat there if things got too dangerous on the material plane, but they'd effectively sealed off that route of escape.

Good thing I didn't need a quick way out, he thought, but immediately regretted it as new enemies charged in through the two huge doors that stood across from the dock entrances. These appeared to be massive, armored combatants, but Will recognized them for what they were immediately—golems—magical constructs of unliving materials, in this case iron.

Of all the foes he could face, these were the most dangerous to him, for they were invulnerable to many magics. Unless they held still long enough for him to find and destroy the enchantments that empowered and controlled them, they would require Will to use raw destructive power—all while avoiding powerful strikes from oversized weapons that might potentially blow through a force spell if that was his defensive strategy.

Lightning was useless against such opponents and fire nearly so, unless he planned to invest the time and energy necessary to melt that much mass into slag. The explosive power of his ethereal phase-shifting weapons was ideal, but since the ethereal plane was completely filled the spell would detonate the moment his prepared weapons shifted, rather than when they shifted back—not to mention killing him when he was switched into the ethereal himself. Will sidestepped a massive swing and used a point-defense shield placed under an iron foot to cause the attacking golem to stumble.

He followed that with a force-lance to drive the off-balance construct into its companion. Two more were entering, but they hadn't circled around to reach him yet. Will used the brief respite to test his sonic shield against one golem. He tried the frequency for steel, then shifted it down slightly until it shattered part of the armor. The result was inefficient, and when he saw clay through the gap, he understood why. The constructs were built with a clay body protected by steel armor. Destroying them with his sonic shield would require him to alternate frequencies, and he wasn't sure what the resonant frequency for clay would be. He dodged two massive fists and the sweep of a long club held by one of the newer arrivals.

Despite their mass and size, the constructs were fairly agile. Trying to avoid all four was a fool's gamble that would eventually lead to disaster. Something tore through his sonic shield as he was experimenting and struck his demon-steel breastplate with enough force that it visibly darkened. The metal rod that clattered to the floor told him that the elves were taking aim with their ranged weapons through the doorway from the other room. If they'd hit anything other than the demon-steel, it might have ripped completely through his armor. Bare minimum it would have broken bones. If it weren't for the fact that demon-steel completely absorbed kinetic force and converted it to demonic turyn, it would have knocked him off his feet.

Shit.

He shifted the frequency of his sonic shield so it would protect him from their metal missiles again. The elves didn't have to worry about firing into melee, since the golems were nearly invulnerable to such missiles. With his shield tied up for defensive purposes, he would have to rely on spells to deal with the golems. Will's eyes went briefly to the stone floor. As with the main dock area, it was composed of solid stone blocks that were precisely shaped and mortared together. On dirt, he would have used elemental water to create mud, but spells that manipulated hard stone were far too slow for combat.

He continued to duck and dodge, using point-defense shields to trip the golems at every opportunity. Simultaneously, he was keenly aware that death was only a split-second mistake from finding him.

Will had been efficient in his use of turyn, so he still had plenty, but he had also noticed a paucity in the air similar to what he'd experienced in Muskeglun, where the trolls lived. Was that normal here, or had the elves engineered the environment around the docks as yet another defensive measure? How paranoid were they?

Either way, it was inconvenient. He sent a branching bolt of lightning through one of the doorways to disrupt the elves firing at him. Then, his foot landed on something, and he lost his footing for a moment. A massive fist clipped his leg, and pain shot through him. It was a grazing blow, but he could hardly put weight on the leg. At a guess, his femur had been cracked.

Knowing he was about to be pounded into jelly, Will released a powerful wind-wall spell, creating a temporary tornado around himself. It took a considerable amount of turyn and didn't hurt the golems at all, though it served its intended purpose and sent them falling and sliding a short distance away from him.

Out of options, Will tried the only thing he could think of. Shuffling forward, he reached down and grabbed an armored foot and reflex cast an ethereal translation spell, sending it into the parallel plane. The massive construct found itself sharing space with an equal volume of broken stone, and the resulting violation of physics resulted in a massive explosion on the ethereal plane. Will grinned and repeated the trick with a second golem. The last two regained their feet before he could send them to join their late brethren.

Will hopped back to avoid another swing of a club, then tested his broken leg. It ached, but held his weight, the bone already well on its way to healing. He wondered if he should tell Oliver that he'd had Dr. Lorentz test the majority of the new tattoo enchantments on himself before allowing them to be used on his son. The bone-mending enchantment had probably saved his life.

He dodged another swing while adjusting his vision to survey what had occurred on the ethereal plane. *I only need a little space...* It was there! Skipping forward and then to the right, Will used another spell to shift into the ethereal plane. The two golem detonations had created enough open space to hold him, although it was filled with choking smoke and dust. Thankfully, he wouldn't need to breathe for at least another ten or fifteen minutes.

Now they think I'm cornered, but am I? he asked silently. *Absolutely not.* Bracing the rubble above his head with a force spell, Will reached out to the shattered boulders hemming him in and began shifting them back to the material plane, creating more room. With his vision still adjusted, he could see the golems, and he timed the transitions to put large stones inside each golem in turn. They exploded with satisfying violence, and on the material plane, the force wasn't suppressed by a mountain of rubble. The exploding golems destroyed the room he had left, and the wall that separated it from the rooms on either side vanished, sending high-velocity pieces of broken stone into the elven defenders.

Looking at the wreckage, it was hard to overstate the immense power of an explosion resulting from two pieces of matter suddenly trying to occupy the same space. The room the golems had been fighting in was now a crater, and the shockwave had shattered the stone floors and walls in both the dock area and the room on the other side. Will waited half a minute before transferring himself back to the material plane. Again, he was grateful he'd thought to use the water-breathing spell in advance, for the air was filled with smoke and dust.

He advanced into the next room, which turned out to be a small warehouse. Most of the crates had come apart from the shockwave of the recent explosion, and there were dead elves scattered everywhere. Several sets of doors were located on the opposite side, a few being ordinary wooden doors sized for people and two being large enough for a wagon to be brought in for loading. Will picked his way through the bodies and debris until he was beside the leftmost door, which was sized for a person.

Using a succession of force-lances, he destroyed the hinges and sent the door flying away. Light streamed in, and Will realized he'd finally come to an exterior door. The sky outside was a light yellow-gray color, not the most appealing to his sensibilities, but he wasn't there to sightsee. With an elemental air spell, he brought in a steady stream of fresh air and recast his water-breathing spell.

Will didn't step out, but standing to one side of the doorway, he made a cursory examination of the area outside. The ground was cobblestone, and across a distance of some thirty feet, he saw a row of buildings, all built from the same grey stone. So far, his impression of the elven realm was nothing to write home about; it appeared grey and drab. He expected it would get more colorful once he escaped from the defensive military zone that had been built around the gate to Hercynia.

The turyn levels were still very low, and the area beyond the doorway was much the same. *Is it due to the enchantment that powers the gate, or is it a more general fact of this realm?* he wondered.

The alarm was still sounding, and the calm female voice continued to repeat warnings or instructions in elven. Will needed to move before reinforcements arrived. He checked the ethereal and saw that the area was still covered with broken stone here, so it wouldn't be accessible. Bracing himself, he tuned his sonic shield for the metal rods the elves favored, put a hemispherical force spell in front of himself, and stepped into the street.

The empty street changed immediately. Stone pillars began rising from the ground in the middle of the road at regular intervals every ten feet. Just beneath the road surface portion of each pillar was some sort of enchanted construct made of several intricate metal pieces attached to a cube-shaped central piece. A crystal-tipped rod extended from each one and in less than a second, Will realized he had more than a dozen enchanted weapons aimed at him.

He had barely any time to prepare, but he doubted his defense would be able to handle whatever the defensive turrets would fire at him. Unable to escape into the ethereal, he invoked his ultimate defense and activated the small ivory cube that he carried. It instantly deployed a defensive ward, and when he pushed turyn into it, he was separated from reality.

The ward was an adaptation of forbidden magic developed by a former First Wizard, the tenth to be exact. Will had used it twice in the past, once to try and destroy the lich, Grim Talek, and another time to escape a barrage of attacks when he was defending Trendham from a combined attack of the Terabinians and the elves. It was a last resort since using it would expose him to the void, which had apparently led to the tenth First Wizard's descent into madness.

The world vanished, and Will was secluded in a private rectangular space that was surrounded by absolute nothingness. He closed his eyes and covered his ears to avoid observing the void. Whether that mattered, he wasn't certain, but it was the only thing he could think to do that might reduce the risk of the magic he was using. He waited for an unknown period of time, and then prepared to cancel the defensive ward.

Hopefully, the long delay would have caused the enchanted defenses to stop firing. His reappearance would likely reactivate them, but if he moved quickly, he could hopefully get out of range. Ready to teleport, he removed the turyn from the ward.

Nothing happened.

It took Will a moment to understand. The ward was gone, and the cube in his hand was inactive. He wasn't spending energy to keep the ward active, yet he was still in the void—absolute blackness surrounded him. Reaching out, he felt his hand pass the boundary where the ward had been before. There was nothing.

Kneeling, he felt around his feet and was relieved to feel something there, though he could see nothing. Adjusting his senses got him nowhere, and he saw nothing but more darkness. A feeling of panic began to rise as he realized something had gone wrong. He was cut off from reality—trapped.

But he might not be alone. He heard a faint slithering sound of something moving across stone.

CHAPTER 19

A large owl swept through the window on silent wings and transformed smoothly as it landed beside the table where Emory's map was laid out. A variety of officers from the Terabinian military, from the Driven, and from the elite Iron Knights were arrayed around the table, and their eyes watched nervously as a lithe female figure rose from where the owl had been a moment before.

Tabitha had been in and out many times over the course of the night, and she'd discarded the idea of wearing armor after the reconnaissance run. Even with the armor's self-donning enchantment, the simple need to land, find a private spot, then transform and redon her clothing and armor was too time-consuming. Nothing was forcing her to transform into a fully human body. Fur, feathers, scales, any of these would serve to maintain a modicum of modesty. For protection, she'd made a habit of transforming into humanoid form with hard, tough scales and razor-sharp claws as long as daggers. For the briefings, she made her head and face human and recognizable, but with the rest of her body, she experimented, refining her ideas each time to make herself ever more lethal.

She thought she was close to an ideal for a nighttime ambush. Her armored form was human-sized but muscular with powerful legs that would enable her to sprint or leap across significant distances with incredible speed. Tabitha had added a tail after discovering how much it improved her balance, and when she wasn't in front of her allies, she would transform her head into a heavily armored saurian nightmare, though she didn't really intend to use her mouth. Tasting her enemies wasn't something she fancied, so she focused her offensive abilities on her limbs. The claws on her feet were shorter, primarily for increased traction and mobility, though they were also frighteningly sharp. Her knees and elbows featured nasty spikes, but it was still the long claws adorning her hands that were the primary threat.

From the neck down, there was nothing remotely feminine about her body, and the officers in the room made obvious efforts to avoid looking at her—at all. Probably so they would be able to sleep without nightmares.

Emory Tallowen nodded and met her gaze. He was one of the few who didn't flinch at her appearance, but then, as overall commander for the magical support Arcane Corps and the Driven, he couldn't afford to seem squeamish. Tiny wasn't present, as he'd already been quietly positioned in Nerril with half the Iron Knights and a regiment of soldiers from First Division. His second in command, Sir Kyle Barrentine, was present and would coordinate half the Iron Knights with the Black Duke and the defenders in the city through the use of enchanted communication tablets.

The Iron Knights would hopefully serve primarily as defensive support while the Arcane Corps and the Driven would rapidly eliminate the enemy threat, but no one expected the plan to remain unchanged. Things always shifted once battle was joined.

"Any change?" asked Lord Tallowen.

Tabitha shook her head. "They're still slowly making their way forward in two groups. I'm estimating between two and three hundred combatants in each. Their wizards are still using illusions to cover them. One group is advancing along the west bank of the river, while the other has finished circling around. They appear ready to start the final push, with the river group entering from the east side of the city and the second group attacking on the west side."

He nodded, then looked to Sir Kyle. That notable answered his silent question, "We're ready. We should hit them first while they're closest to our position. If we wait until they begin their attack, my men will have to advance across open ground and will take longer to aid the frontline attackers."

Emory's decision took less than a second. "Commence in five minutes. Send out the first orders. Everyone to your positions."

He started to leave, along with everyone else, but Tabitha snagged his armor with the tip of one claw. "Where do you want me?" she asked.

"You've done your part."

"My part isn't done until this is over. Where do you want me?"

Emory sighed. If anything happened to the noblewoman in front of him, he would have to answer to a lot of important people—the queen, James Wellings, and perhaps most worrisome, Will Cartwright. "Back in the air then. Keep an eye out for unexpected reinforcements or reserves. Do not make direct contact with the enemy."

"Where will you be if I see something?"

"Don't attempt to reach me. I'll be in the thick of it. Just use the tablet," he told her.

He just wants me out of the way, she realized, but she didn't bother confronting her old friend. *If they don't want to assign me, I'll assign myself.* She wouldn't do anything unless it seemed important, but she would judge that for herself. "As you wish," she answered. Emory left, and she transformed again, taking to the air once more.

***

The elven strike force made its way quietly along the riverside road that led to Nerril, relying on their wizard's illusions to hide them from observers on the city walls. Individuals encountering them was less of a problem, as they could easily eliminate them before they could escape to warn the humans.

Their plan seemed a bold one, as they were about to march straight up to the eastern gate and enter the city. The gates were only closed in times of war, but they obviously considered the chance of discovery to be low. The head of their column was within fifty yards of the gate when shadowy figures rose silently from the ground at many points. An instant later, hell broke loose as the Driven began the Terabinian response to the elven invaders. Closest to the city, the first thing that occurred was the rapid appearance of trenches and earthen barriers as the elite sorcerers used earth elementals to turn what had been an easy road into something virtually impassable for infantry.

The rest of the Driven were arrayed on either side of the river road for almost a hundred yards. They weren't great in number—they never had been, even during Lognion's reign—but they made up for that with the lethality and suddenness of their assault. Those closest to the elves used absurd amounts of turyn to launch force-lances across more than thirty yards of space to hit the elven wizards. Force-effect spells required relatively little energy when used up close, but at medium to longer ranges, something like a force-lance could easily exhaust a wizard with but a single casting, if it was possible at all.

The Driven in charge of eliminating the elven casters were instructed to spare no expense in turyn, however. Each one drained an entire elemental for that one spell, and if a second was required, they drained a second. There would only be one chance to catch the elven mages off-guard. After they realized they were under attack things like point-defense shields would make sniping them much more difficult.

The elven assault group had a ratio of roughly one wizard for every four soldiers, but most of them died in that first volley as force-lances blew fist-sized holes through chests, necks, and heads. There were less than seventy Driven for that half of the elven attack, and most of them were occupied with earth-moving or neutralizing elven wizards. The remaining ten used one very specific ranged light spell. Brilliant globes of light illuminated the road, pouring light straight down to blind the night-adjusted eyes of the elves and highlight them for the Arcane Corps.

A second after the blinding globes appeared, red sparks appeared in the distance, flying up and over in parabolic arcs as Emory's wizards launched long-distance artillery spells. In a frighteningly short amount of time, the sparks grew in size as they descended on the targets, making it apparent that what had seemed like sparks were in fact massive balls of flame.

Most of the Driven were spent, and they followed the plan by descending back into the ground, vanishing like wraiths as fire rained down on the elven column. Screams echoed as warriors were burned alive, cooked inside their armor. More than half the elves died in that first blaze, but five of the elven wizards had survived. It wasn't clear whether they had been missed or if they had been hiding their abilities somehow, but those five erected massive force-walls that deflected a significant portion of the artillery spells. Otherwise, the fight would have been over already.

The Iron Knights showed up then, having been hidden farther back from the road in shallow trenches disguised with more traditional camouflage. They'd begun a foot charge as soon as the Driven had lit up the area, and they arrived shortly after the barrage of fire to clean up what was left. But the elven wizards had preserved enough of their forces to enable a significant defense. Their fighters were well trained and well geared with enchanted weapons. They formed a defensive circle, and the Iron Knights found themselves in a solid fight.

It looked to be under control, though. Tabitha was about to fly to the other side of the city and see how things were going there when she noticed that the remaining elven wizards weren't participating in the battle. Instead, they'd withdrawn to the center, and three of them had taken position in a triangular formation. Turyn flowed inward, and the two remaining wizards assisted by drawing more from the surrounding area and feeding it toward the center three.

Some sort of ritual, she realized, and with that, her mind was made up. Tabitha flew out wide, gaining altitude with heavy downstrokes of her wings. When she judged her height to be adequate, she angled forward into a dive, her body shifting and becoming heavier as she fell toward the wizards like a dark missile, invisible in the night. She gathered the turyn around her to create the extra flesh and bone, and her feathers withdrew, becoming thick scales.

Her batlike wings weren't as silent as before, but in the midst of a nighttime battle, there was no chance of them hearing her. The air between the wizards tore as she got closer, forming a rip in reality itself. Tabitha had seen gates before, and while this was similar, it was also different. A sense of *wrongness* emanated from it, and while her light-sensitive eyes could see well enough in the dark, the place the elves had opened up gave off no light at all.

Her wings snapped out with a sound like the crack of thunder as she flew through one of the three central wizards. The elf's neck snapped from the force of the impact, and the enemy wizard likely never had time to realize what had killed him. Tabitha rolled over him, her wings retracting and vanishing back into her wyvern-like body as she came back to her feet and leapt toward the remaining casters. The tear in reality was already beginning to collapse as their ritual failed.

A fiery missile splashed harmlessly against her side, foiled by her innate magic resistance, and she slammed into the next elf's hastily erected force-dome. More spells came at her from the others as she tore at the invisible barrier with her claws, but all of them were as useless as the fire spell had been. One of them thought to use an earth spell, and that stung a little, but her thick hide still shrugged it off.

The force spell broke, and the frightened wizard died before he could recover from the feedback, a scythe-like claw ripping him open from neck to navel. Some of the closer elven warriors were turning around to face the threat from behind, but most of them had their hands full dealing with the human knights that had completely encircled their position.

Realizing she'd lost the element of surprise, Tabitha knew she had to fight smarter now. With a feeling of tension, she clamped down on the turyn in the air, crippling the remaining wizards. They wouldn't be able to recover their turyn, or cast anything but force spells now, but before she could leap at the next one, an elven warrior cut into her flank with a sword sharp enough to wound her. Spinning, she sent the elf flying with a powerful blow from one foreleg. His armor held, but the impact sent the warrior flying thirty feet through the air. He crashed into some of his comrades and didn't rise after he fell.

Chaos descended, and Tabitha lost track of her original targets as she found herself embroiled in a bloody conflict with the armored warriors.

She spun and slashed, using her mass to knock them about like toy figures, and when the space around her had become too great, she would leap across the distance to bowl more of them over. The magnitude of her blows was such that few moved after she struck. Bones broke and brains bled inside their nearly impregnable armor.

Tabitha didn't care, so long as they died.

She took dozens of wounds—their magical blades and spears were lethal and masterfully made, but it hardly mattered. She healed almost as fast as they could wound her, and with every movement, she crushed and maimed more of them. The Iron Knights were taking full advantage of the confusion, and the elves would have routed—if they had anywhere to run.

As the battle drew to a messy close, Tabitha realized she was in danger of being attacked by the Iron Knights, as many of them weren't sure whether she was friend or foe. A brief pause came as the last of the elves fell, and she took the opportunity to launch herself back into the air, wings growing and catching the air as she reached the top of her arc and began to fly.

She returned to her owl form; the smaller size was less costly in terms of turyn, and she was able to recover faster. One nice thing about flying was that it made it easy to absorb turyn. Rather than waiting for the magical energy to come to her, she flew through the densest currents, actively absorbing it as she went.

Although the wounds she had received were already gone, they weren't without some cost. Transformation was her talent, something she did with almost perfect efficiency, but deep cuts still caused terrible pain, and the damage to her flesh took considerable effort to heal, both in will strain and turyn. From the outside, it looked as though she was an unstoppable force, but Tabitha knew she had limits. She also worried what would happen if she received a wound that damaged her brain or rendered her unconscious—she'd never dared to deliberately test herself with that sort of injury.

By the time she reached the other side of the city, a span of just minutes, she'd recovered as much turyn as she could hold, and as she passed over Nerril's other gate, she saw that things hadn't gone so well with the other ambush. Nearly all the elves were still fighting. Something had spoiled the ambush, and their wizards had reacted in time to prevent effective sniping from the Driven. The Arcane Corps' artillery spells had similarly failed against the defensive magics of the elven wizards, and now the Iron Knights were embroiled in a desperate battle in front of the city gates.

Worse, the elves had additional allies. Heavy set forms with black, glistening skin leapt over the elves and landed amongst the Iron Knights. Individually, they were smaller than Tabitha's wyvern form had been, but they were large and heavy enough to throw the Terabinian soldiers into disarray as they knocked men into one another and ignored the spells thrown at them by the Arcane Corps wizards.

The city gate was closing to prevent a complete loss since it was apparent that the ambush had failed. The Iron Knights might have been destroyed already, but a lone figure hovered farther back behind the Terabinians, moving swiftly atop an elemental travel-disk.

As she drew closer, Tabitha could feel Emory's hand on the turyn in the area, stifling any attempt to draw or manipulate it. Her old friend was actively suppressing the elven wizards while allowing the Arcane Corps the freedom to cast elemental spells. More than that, thick vines grew wherever Lord Tallowen directed his attention, ensnaring the black beasts and hindering their movements while the Iron Knights tried to eliminate them.

Emory's response was all that had kept the Terabinians from falling into disaster, but things were growing steadily worse. Behind the elven frontlines, Tabitha could see another ritual had been completed, and a much larger tear in reality stood open, an ugly gash in the night air. More of the alien monsters were streaming through, and if the portal wasn't closed, they would soon overwhelm the human defenders.

Something had to be done, and no one else could reach the elves maintaining the ritual in time except her, but Tabitha didn't like her odds. Scanning the battle with her keen eyes, she spotted the familiar metal form of the Black Duke. Tiny was stalking through the Terabinian formation, cutting down the strange monsters wherever he found them. Although they were similar in size to his golem, his demon-steel body out-massed them by several times, and his greatsword burned with black flame as he cut them apart.

To avoid making a target of herself, Tabitha shifted down into the form of a smaller nocturnal bird, the nightjar, and then she flew down to circle just above Tiny's position. Her voice was shrill and loud as it cut through the pandemonium. "This is Tabitha. The elves have a portal and they're bringing in more monsters. I'm going to stop them, but I'm not sure I can do it alone. Join me if you can." The golem continued to chop and hew, and its metal face was immobile, so she had no idea if Tiny had heard her.

Flying up once more, Tabitha gathered more turyn and began shifting into the heavier wyvern form. Emory was unaware of her presence, so she had to overcome his control, but since the strength of their wills was similar and she was much closer to the turyn currents she flew through, that wasn't a problem. She increased her size and customized it to the task. Her last dive attack had given her ideas to improve upon it.

She was twice as large when she dropped, and this time her wings were longer, and the front edge was layered with a ridge of sharp horn. Rather than land, she curved her flight near the bottom and came in level with the ground, dropping the last few feet just as she reached the ritualists. Her plan almost worked as she'd intended.

The edges of her wings weren't as sharp as she had hoped, and the wizards wore some armor. Rather than taking off their heads, her wings struck like a battering ram. Four died instantly, though the fifth managed to drop to the ground just in time. The heavy impacts cost Tabitha some of her momentum, and she was forced to land. She shifted, making herself more compact, adopting her wingless, saurian form as she moved to finish the last wizard-ritualist.

That notable fled, and Tabitha couldn't give chase, for she was mobbed by the strange, damp monsters still streaming out of the now-shrinking portal. What followed was a bloody struggle.

The monsters were smooth, with thick blubbery skin and wide mouths that opened to display far too many teeth for any terrestrial animal. When their jaws opened, strange, high-pitched screams emerged, sending shivers down the spines of any who heard them. The monsters' main weapon seemed to be their wide, toothy mouths. Tabitha had already seen them biting into the Terabinian knights and soldiers with lethal effectiveness. Mail wasn't sufficient, and even the enchanted plate of the Iron Knights only delayed the inevitable as men were crushed inside terrible jaws.

The weird black beasts also had long, slender tails that were prehensile, agile, and tipped with a deadly spike. They could impale targets more than ten feet from the monster with those flexible weapons, and although most armor would stop them, the creatures were extremely precise, slamming their tail spikes into any gaps or weak points in their foes' protective gear. The monsters ran on four legs when charging but reared up to fight on their hindlegs, the forelegs were more human-like, muscular and equipped with broad strong hands that could grapple and hold their prey in place so they could bring their wide jaws in to finish their enemies.

It was the hands that caused Tabitha the most trouble. She spun, and her long dagger-like claws nearly bisected the first two that approached her, but there were many others to replace them, and they came at her from every direction. The strange monsters showed no fear as they threw themselves at her, and though she killed several their hands gripped her from every side and their sheer weight began to bear her down.

As her head dropped below them, Tabitha caught a glimpse of the Black Duke struggling to reach her. Tiny's golem seemed practically immune to their teeth and tails, but he was also mired down by the endless press of bodies. Their heavy hands gripped his metal arms and legs and forced him to a fiercely contested halt.

If Tabitha had actually *been* the reptilian monster whose form she had created, she would have died there, unable to escape the grapple. Fighting to control a rising sense of panic, she did something she had never done before and surrendered any reasonable concept of natural form. Her body shifted so rapidly it almost seemed liquid as she avoided biting jaws one moment, and turned her flesh into a weapon the next, driving spikes into the grasping hands that tried to hold her. For a long, nightmarish minute, she became an amorphous mass, constantly extruding giant bone spikes to impale the bodies around her.

Her sanity was close to crumbling, but Tabitha mentally caught herself and shifted back into her saurian form once the enemies holding her had fallen away, and then she leapt over the nearest ones to assist Tiny. She tore into those around him, her body moving with the frenzied speed of an apex predator.

Moments later, he was free, and the two of them fought together to keep from being overwhelmed again. Not far away, the battle continued between the Terabinians and the elves. The Iron Knights continued to contest with the black beasts and elven warriors, assisted by ordinary Terabinian soldiers. Emory and the Arcane Corps kept the elven wizards in check, and his offensive vines caused no end of trouble to the elves whenever they tried to take advantage of weak points in the human lines. With Tabitha and Tiny keeping a sizeable mass of the newly arrived monsters occupied, the battle seemed to teeter on a knife's edge.

The strange portal was slowly shrinking, but it was still quite large, stretching more than forty feet across. The bizarre allies the elves had summoned seemed to have run out, though, for no more were crossing over. Tabitha dared to hope they might have run out, but then something large moved, and a massive snout began to emerge.

No, no, no, please, Mother, no! she thought desperately, but Tabitha's wish went unheard as a vast, alien beast came through. The thing was so large it almost wouldn't fit, for it stood taller than most houses, on four tree trunk-sized legs. Its skin was dark and glistening, like the smaller ones, and there was a certain resemblance to its toothy head, but the similarities ended there.

It had no tail, but its body was covered in a multitude of long tentacles, each almost twice the length of the creature's body. They were as thick as a man's torso at the base and tapered to the width of a forearm near the end. The monster started forward, walking ponderously on its huge legs while the soldiers in its path scattered in fear. Tentacles lashed out in every direction, acting independently to snatch men from the ground. Tabitha had trouble comprehending the coordination necessary until she saw that the appendages each had an eye of their own close to the tip. The colossal monster's tentacles lifted those it grabbed, holding them over its back, where a toothy pit opened up, waiting to be fed. Gravity did the rest as it released its victims one by one, feeding the hungry maw.

Pandemonium ensued as the Terabinian defenders knew despair and began to rout. The elves took advantage and surged forward, cutting down those exposed by their frightened companions. The Arcane Corps focused their attacks on the behemoth, but its body seemed to simply absorb magical attacks. Meanwhile, the elven mages were once again free to pick their targets and the human wizards began to die.

Tabitha barely avoided being stepped on as the giant walked ponderously through. The size of its body made it seem slow, but the behemoth's long legs carried it forward twenty feet with every step as it ate and devoured men, creating an empty swath as it headed directly for the city gates. She recovered quickly and leapt into the air, but before she could reach it, three tentacles swept across, slamming into her head. Spinning, she was thrown to one side and crashed hard against the ground, dazed.

Tiny charged toward it but found himself the target of four more tentacles. His sword cut one apart, but the other three seized him and seconds later, lifted his heavy, metal body from the ground. He was tossed aside, and Tabitha couldn't see where he landed as she struggled to retain consciousness.

Emory was the first to stop the monster as he dropped his efforts against the elves and focused his full attention on the giant. Vines as thick as trees sprouted from the ground around it and swarmed up the large legs before growing even farther and wrapping around the beast's torso. A battle was waged between the monster's tentacles and Emory's vines, but the wizard seemed to be winning. Massive thorns emerged from the vines, piercing the creature's sides and causing yellow fluids to seep from its wounds.

Emory grimaced as he struggled to halt the behemoth's advance. The air was emptied of ambient turyn as all of it was converted into his ironwood brambles, and his face paled as the strain began to test his limits. Snarling, he clenched his fists, and the vines contracted, beginning to tear through the beast's body, threatening to pinch it into separate pieces. A hush fell over the battlefield, and for a moment, the only sounds were the monster's keening scream and the creak of Emory's powerful vines as they kept constricting.

The quiet ended when an armored elf knocked aside one of the last of the Iron Knights that hadn't run. Sidestepping another defender, the elven warrior dove forward, sword outstretched in front of him like a spear. The point struck Emory in the chest, and despite his enchanted mail, it tore through, sliding in between his ribs.

The elven warrior died an instant later as the Iron Knight brought a heavy mace down on his head, but it was too late. The color drained from Emory's face, and his body crumpled. The powerful vines around the behemoth went limp, and it began tearing itself free.

Tabitha had regained her wits, at least in part, and she saw the sword slide home through Emory's mail. She was wobbling back to her feet, a furious scream erupting from her saurian throat. She saw Tiny's golem returning, but he was bogged down by the smaller monsters that were savaging the Terabinian soldiers and the Iron Knights. Tiny's demon-steel body tore through the beasts as he fought to stop the carnage and rally his men.

His efforts might have worked, but the behemoth had struck terror in everyone's hearts, and with Emory's fall, there was nothing stopping it now. It had torn free of the brambles, and with a few more steps, it slammed into the city gates, staving them in with a single blow.

Black despair washed over Tabitha as it seemed everything was lost. Her vision darkened for a moment, but she ignored it and leapt to the sky, sprouting wings and shrinking in size. She needed speed, and Emory had exhausted the turyn around the battlefield. Taking the form of a falcon, she climbed higher into the air.

She hadn't forgotten what had happened to her during her first attempt at stopping the monster. *I need speed, speed and mass,* she thought. A plan had formed in her mind, one that she might have rejected if she hadn't already been pushed beyond reason and the instinct for self-preservation.

Higher, ever higher, she ascended until the behemoth seemed small and the townsfolk that it was beginning to eat seemed like ants. At that altitude, there was still plenty of turyn, and she absorbed it like a sponge, her body growing to enormous proportions as she leaned over and angled her head straight down. She was no longer a bird. Tabitha had transformed back into a wyvern, though her proportions were so large that she seemed more like a dragon.

Streamlining her body, she fell like an arrow, straight down. As the air rushed by, she was inspired to take the transformation even further, forsaking a regular form for something more like a heavy spear. Her head became long and pointed, almost entirely composed of dense bone, while the rest of her lengthened into a thick, heavy body and her arms and legs shrank down, becoming little more than vestigial limbs.

Gravity increased her fall until she reached blistering speed. Tabitha struck the center of the alien behemoth with unthinkable force, and then she knew no more. The world vanished, and oblivion swept her rage away.

CHAPTER 20

Why are you still here? asked Lognion silently. *Your part is done.*

Selene had surrendered her ruined body and rejoined her father's massive form after he had swallowed her with a single bite. Leaving the soon-to-be digested corpse behind, she was once again trapped in a small corner of his draconic brain. After a short rest, he'd used his newly regained power to open a new portal and return to Hercynia. Oliver rode silently on his back.

I want to make sure you live up to your word, she answered after a moment.

If you are foolish and continue to delay, I may decide you have reneged on our deal. In that case, you will no longer have to wonder. You know I do not lie.

Where are you flying to, then? she asked.

Ignorance is bliss, my child. With an exercise of will, the dragon created a portal in the air and flew through it.

It was night, and the passage from one empty, dark sky to another gave no clue as to where they were, but after a few minutes, her father began to aim downward, falling into a steep dive. After they passed through some dark clouds, Selene saw lights far below. They seemed familiar, and as they grew larger, she began to recognize the shape of buildings and the layout of streets.

It was her home, the capital city Cerria.

You said you would leave them alone! she accused, panic coloring her thoughts.

I said I would restrict my retribution to William's family, excluding his son.

This is the capital!

Lognion's thoughts carried a hint of amusement. *I know my city better than you realize. Pay attention to my target below.* They were rushing straight down, but at a certain point, the dragon spread his wings, and they unfurled with a thundering clap. Beating down with powerful strokes, they slowed and then hovered just a hundred feet above one particular house located in one of the wealthier districts of Cerria.

Horror filled Selene as she recognized the house, the dwelling place of the Wellings family, the home of Will's sister Tabitha. Lognion let them drop even closer, and soon Selene could count the slate tiles on its roof. Beneath them would be Tabitha, her husband James, and their four children, all peacefully asleep, unsuspecting.

In the dark night sky, no one had seen the massive dragon descend, although now the sound of his wings had caused a few late-night pedestrians to look up. A scream echoed through the air from one of them as Lognion began filling his lungs.

Selene went mad with fury. Even if she hadn't married Will, Tabitha was dear to her heart. Mark Nerrow had often kept her in his household when she was a child, treating her as though she were his own daughter. Tabitha and Laina had been like sisters to her, and despite the estrangement of the last decade, Tabitha represented one last link to the only part of her childhood that she had cherished.

NO! she screamed, and then she threw caution to the wind. Selene had always been known for keeping her bargains, but in that moment, she no longer cared. Mentally, she fought against her father with every ounce of her being, trying to seize control of their shared body. Desperation gave her strength, and for an instant, she held the dragon's jaws tightly closed.

Laughter rang out in her mind as Lognion laughed at her. *Is that all you have, child? Try harder!* His power grew, and then his mouth began to open.

Selene could feel the flames rising, and she went wild, snapping the jaws shut once more.

Better, said Lognion condescendingly. *But your soul is burdened by a thousand heart-stone enchantments, not to mention the binding that keeps you alive. Your will cannot hope to stop me.*

She understood in a flash, and hope surged. The elementals bound to her with the heart-stone enchantment did indeed weigh on her, putting a drain on her will. It was small, but if it would make a difference…

As rapidly as she could, she began releasing elementals by the dozen. Her strength did increase, and for a moment, it seemed like it might be enough. But Lognion kept increasing the pressure, and slowly, his jaws opened anyway. Selene worked faster, trying to release all the elementals as quickly as she could, but their numbers seemed endless.

The struggle went on in silence for several minutes, while Oliver wondered what was occurring. He wasn't privy to their silent conversation, and he hadn't realized where they were yet.

Selene and Lognion seemed to have reached a stalemate, and Selene continued releasing elementals. Spirits appeared around them, glowing with elemental turyn, fading and streaming away as they discovered their freedom. Eventually, the last one faded out and Selene felt as though a weight had been lifted. Her will was stronger than ever, and she was determined to reestablish dominion over the dragon's body. She regretted the fear that had kept her from abandoning the elementals sooner. Will had been right all along.

And then her father's laugh sounded again in their shared head. *You are a little stronger now, but that necromantic binding still cripples you.* Unbelievably, he shrugged off her attempts and easily opened his jaws.

He'd been pretending to struggle all along, silently mocking her and waiting for her to give up the last of her elementals.

Observe my gift for William's family—death! A blaze of dragonfire erupted from his jaws, streaming down to cover the Wellings' home. Protective wards flared and failed as the dragonfire ate through them. Nothing could deny the flame. In seconds, the wards collapsed, and the shale roof caught fire as though it was made of paper rather than stone. Brilliant white flames ate through everything, and in half a minute the building was burning everywhere, a hollow husk filled with incredible heat. Smoke poured out on all sides, but Lognion did not relent. The river of fire flowing from his mouth continued, while the walls fell in, and the interior of the building turned to ash. The dragonfire ate through everything and continued on, carving into the stone foundations and basement.

The basement was where James had built his final redoubt, the fortified saferoom that had once protected his family when they had been attacked by assassins. Another brief second passed as the flames were diverted, but then more turyn flashed into the air, released by failing enchantments as the saferoom disintegrated under the onslaught of divine fire.

And through it all, Selene cried impotently, her soul keening with a sorrow so great that she wished for nothing more than to open the green door in her mind and seek oblivion.

Exhausted of all thought or emotion, Selene sank into herself, retreating from the world as Lognion began to fly higher and turn south. They'd been flying for half an hour before she thought to check on Oliver and found him missing from the dragon's back. Shaking herself from her apathy, she asked her father where her stepson had gone.

I didn't notice he was gone until after it was over, answered the dragon. *Perhaps he doesn't enjoy suffering the way you do.*

***

The wards protecting the Wellings' home might have done him serious harm if they weren't already keyed to allow Oliver's passage when he tried the front door. It was locked, but that was a relative term for him. Since the defensive magic hadn't engaged, Oliver forewent knocking and tried to smash it from its hinges with his shoulder.

Unfortunately for him, he didn't account for the fact that James and Tabitha had not only spared no expense or effort on their magical defenses, but had also spared no expense on installing the most sturdy of doors. Although it looked ornate and fragile, it was solid oak bound with iron, and the hinges were bolted through massive framing beams. The door didn't budge.

It opened a second later. "Oliver?" asked Rob, standing in the doorway.

Oliver almost bowled the vampire over as he rushed in. "Dragon!" He pointed at the ceiling.

James looked into the hall from the parlor. "Oliver, is that you?"

"Dragon!" repeated Oliver, struggling to find words. "He's here. You have to get out!"

James Wellings blinked once, then went into action. He touched a ring on his right hand, then a second ring on his middle finger. Protective wards sprang into being as his action overrode the default settings. He motioned to the stairs. "Help me get them down to the basement. We must be quick!"

Oliver sprang past the man, taking the stairs three at a time as he yelled back, "The basement won't do. Dragonfire—it will burn through anything." When he reached the top of the stairs, he saw that his cousins were already emerging from their rooms. Each wore a ring with a glowing gem on their respective hands.

James was beside him then, and he motioned. "Down, down, run! Get in the safe room. There's no time." The teens, Edward and Elaina, and twelve-year-old Christopher immediately began to run, followed almost as quickly by the youngest, Talia, who had just turned ten.

"The basement is no good!" repeated Oliver. "Listen to me!"

James was right behind his children, but he stopped on the stairs. "I know, Olly. Trust me." He pointed at Talia as the older children ran ahead, and Rob snatched her up with lightning speed, moving faster than anyone else could, aside from perhaps Oliver.

Despairing, Oliver followed them, trying to convince James to change his plan with every step, but before he realized it, they were at the basement door and down the next set of stairs. The safe room door was already open as they started down. Light washed over them, and a sound like a rushing river filled the air. Oliver realized that Lognion had already begun.

He was too late. Stricken, he paused on the stairs.

James slapped him lightly. "Down you go. Hurry up!" He tugged on Oliver's arm, urging him on.

Unsure what else to do at that point, Oliver went along, though he was certain that they were already dead. Seconds later, he was inside the safe room with everyone else. Flames filled the basement even as they closed the door. Oliver's sense of turyn was almost non-existent, but he felt something as the door closed, and a second after that, he felt dizzy. The roaring sound of the dragonfire vanished.

"What's happening, Daddy?" asked Talia urgently, and the other kids quickly chimed in with similar questions. Oliver didn't have the heart to answer, for he knew they were all dead.

James' reply was the last thing Oliver expected. "Who wants to see Granddad?"

"Now?" asked Edward, confused. At fifteen, he wasn't so easily distracted from the fact that they'd just been rudely awoken. Edward held up his own ring, the gem still glowing. "You said these were for emergencies. We can't leave here."

Elaina addressed their father next. "Didn't you see the flames in the basement, right before the door shut?"

James sighed. "Well, yes. There was an emergency, but we're all safe and sound, and on the plus side we get to visit your Granddad Nerrow! Think of it as a holiday trip."

Christopher wasn't buying it. "Did our house just burn down? Is it gone?" Talia began to cry.

Frowning, James gave Christopher a disapproving look. "Now look at what you've done." Leaning forward, he picked up the ten-year-old girl and gave her a bounce. "It's all right, Tally, we can get a new house."

"But my dolls!" continued the girl.

"Don't be a brat, Tally," said Elaina. "We all lost our rooms. You're not the only one."

Still holding onto his youngest, James moved to the door and deactivated the ward. To Oliver's surprise, he opened it, and outside, the fire had vanished. Oliver stared at his uncle in amazement. "What happened?" Then, he realized that the area beyond the door wasn't the same as the basement they had left. It was dank and musty with a dirt floor. Across from the doorway, he saw baskets lined up against the wall. They appeared to be filled with turnips, carrots, and parsnips. A root cellar? "Where are we?"

James gave him his best smile. "Welcome to Myrsta! Have you ever been here before?"

Before Oliver could get over his stunned surprise, Elaina asked, "Where's Momma?"

James' face darkened for an instant, but the expression vanished almost too quickly to be noticed. "Your mother is helping the queen with some business in Nerril. Not to worry, she's perfectly fine. I'll send her a message letting her know where we are as soon as we let your granddad know we're here."

CHAPTER 21

Emory Tallowen struggled to stay asleep. Someone was making a lot of noise, and flashes of light irritated him even through closed lids. *What is Cedric thinking?* he thought angrily, blaming his chamberlain. *He knows better than to let anyone make this sort of noise while I'm sleeping!*

He squeezed his eyes shut, but as the noise and lights continued, his anger eventually got the better of him, and he opened them. He was not in bed—not even close. Pain and fatigue came to him in equal measures as Emory recalled the event before he had lost consciousness. Reflexively, he put his hand to his chest to check the place where he had been stabbed—or rather, he tried to do so. His right arm was caught underneath the heavy weight of a man in full plate. Emory tried to shove the man off, but the other's weight was considerable, and Emory's strength was lacking. He was tired, so tired he felt ready to die, as his father liked to say.

"Get off of me, fool. I can barely breathe," he wheezed, but the man atop him didn't respond. Then, Emory heard the strange whining roar of one of the black beasts that they'd been fighting. Its heavy footsteps reached his ears, the sound of armor shifting and groaning under the monster's feet.

His mind was still foggy, but adrenaline shot through him, helping to clear his thoughts as Emory realized fully what his situation was. He was still where he had fallen, and the man he had just cussed was dead. *Men,* he corrected himself. He was mostly covered by one of the Iron Knights, but there were other bodies on his lower legs. Dead soldiers and knights surrounded him on every side, while cold, wet ground supported him from beneath. *Wet?* It had been dry earlier, meaning the moisture was likely blood, his and that of the men around and on top of him.

The big question was why was he alive? His memory was fairly clear; he had been run completely through. He remembered being focused on the giant monstrosity, to the exclusion of almost everything else, right before one of the enemies had slipped past his defenders.

Screams came to him then, from both the city and from closer by. The beast that had walked past had found someone alive among the fallen. A man begged incoherently as the creature pulled him free, then bit off one of the unknown soldier's legs. A chill ran down Emory's spine, pure terror, and for a moment his nobility was gone. All the finer things that made him a man of honor, they vanished in the face of unadulterated horror as he realized he would probably be next, eaten alive, one limb at a time.

Reason gone, he wanted nothing more than to run screaming. But the reality of his circumstances would allow for neither of those things. He was trapped and too weak to pull himself free. Screaming was technically possible, but his instinct for survival overrode the panic that urged him to do so.

Seconds passed, and his reason reasserted itself. His fear, and the shame of his ignoble reactions brought anger and that gave him a little more strength. *I won't die like this,* he told himself silently. Fighting down his panic, he tried wiggling his fingers and toes. They all seemed to respond, and although he hurt all over, he seemed to be intact. He was still weak, though, weak and unbelievably tired. Battle usually had that effect, but this was something more. The facts clicked together, and he realized he must have been given a regeneration potion. There was one in his belt pouch, but he knew he hadn't had a chance to use it.

Looking around, he saw an empty vial in a gauntleted hand not far from his head. His dead guard had given it to him. *It might have saved him, but he gave it to me instead.* Emory closed his eyes tightly. If he hadn't been so afraid, he might have shed tears of gratitude and shame, but that would have to wait. He resolved to identify the knights who had tried in vain to protect him. *No, not in vain. I yet live,* he reminded himself.

A fresh sound came to him, movement from a different direction. Another survivor? The beast stopped, then turned. The man it was currently devouring had already died, so it reoriented on the new prey. Metal on metal, the other man was up on his feet, staggering away, but there was no way he would make it. Straining with everything he had, Emory got his head up, nudging aside the arm blocking his sight.

The black beast was rushing over, maw wide to greet its new prey. The man, another of the Iron Knights, was barely able to keep his feet, and he struggled to raise his arms as he stumbled back. Remembering a dark moment from the past, when William had come to help them against the trolls, Emory realized he had the same choice in front of him. Without power, he could do nothing, and the area around him was almost devoid of turyn. He had used it up. The only turyn to be had was in the bodies of those still living.

Not pausing to think, Emory created a source-link, attaching to the weakened knight, and then he ripped the man's turyn free. The knight collapsed, and the approaching monster stopped and turned, following the course of the turyn. It had been searching for the living by sniffing out the still-active sources producing turyn among the bodies.

Emory was now the richest concentration of energy in the vicinity, although it still wasn't a great quantity of turyn that he held, not compared to what he usually operated with. It was barely enough for a small spell. With scant seconds to decide, Emory made a choice.

He'd seen the behemoth and the smaller monsters absorb elemental spells. Logically, force spells shouldn't be affected by something like that, but he couldn't be sure. A force-lance straight to the head at close range should be enough to kill the monster bearing down on him, but if it failed, he wouldn't have the energy for a second shot. The one thing he knew worked for certain were physical attacks. Tabitha's claws, the swords of the Iron Knights, and his own talent with plants—all those he had seen produce visible results.

But did he have enough turyn for that?

He committed himself, and vines shot up from the ground and caught the beast's legs, then raced up the rest of its body. The thing was above him now, a few feet away and leaning over as it tried to reach his exposed head and neck. Emory was treated to a closeup view of its maw, with thick saliva dripping from a frankly ridiculous number of teeth. He grunted as the monster pushed harder, trying even harder to reach him. One of his vines snapped, and Emory felt fresh beads of sweat springing from the temples of his head. Fear and fury screamed silently within his mind as he felt his magic begin to give way. Desperate, he pulled at everything around him, creating a void as every wisp of ambient turyn reinforced his efforts, flowing not to him, but directly into his vines. His lips pulled away from his own teeth as he involuntarily began snarling back at the hideous horror threatening to devour him.

His vines thickened, throttling the monster. Tighter, ever tighter, while Emory strove to maintain not just his spell, but consciousness. Everything he had left went into his talent. Something heavy was approaching from behind, from the direction he couldn't see. A second beast, come to share the feast.

Determined to see at least one of them die, Emory felt a defiant scream erupt from his throat as he glared at the toothy abomination right before his face. And then it fell apart, the sound of flesh and tissue tearing as the vines squeezed its massive, neckless head completely off the rest of its body.

The world grew dim, and Emory's head sagged back down. There was nothing left for him but death now. He hoped it wouldn't take long. Something dark overshadowed him, and then the body of the knight on top of him was pushed aside. A massive hand covered in black flames reached down and slipped behind his shoulders, lifting him up. It burned for a moment, but Emory's body was already reflexively absorbing and converting the demonic turyn.

His vision cleared, and he realized it was the Black Duke. With a feeling of gratitude and relief, he wanted to cry, but instead he said, "I've never been so glad to see something so ugly in all my life." After a pause, he added, "Your Grace."

Tiny's voice was deep and metallic as he responded, "Are you wounded?"

Relief warred with guilt as Emory looked over to the body of the man who had saved him. Now that he could see the knight's crest, he realized it was Sir Percy, a young knight who had been assigned to guard him for the first time just hours ago. He had barely known the man, yet Percy, barely old enough to have grown a beard, had died for him. "Sadly no," answered Emory. "Better men than me lie dead instead."

The golem's impassive face stared at him, unable to show any expression. "Save those feelings for later. The battle is still being waged." To highlight that statement, a fresh outcry of screams came from the direction of the city. "Can you fight?"

"I can barely sit," admitted Emory. "The potion took everything I had. Where is Tabitha?"

"Unknown," said Tiny. "I was tossed a considerable distance, and she disappeared. Then the big one collapsed. I think she did something to it, but I haven't seen sign of her since." The golem straightened up. "I need to move. Other than the wounded out here, all the living, friend and foe alike, are inside the city. Can you walk?"

"Go," said Emory. "Help them. I'll join you as soon as I can." He summoned two turyn elixirs from his limnthal. It had been years since he'd used one, but now he was glad that he had them. Each carried roughly the turyn of a healthy normal person. He drank the first in one go and followed it with the second, feeling a warm glow as his turyn reserves refilled slightly. It was far from what he had been holding when the fight began, but it was enough to get his body moving, with some left over for a few spells.

With a groan, Emory Tallowen climbed to his feet, feeling older than he could ever remember. Despite the turyn elixirs, his eyes were half-lidded, and he knew he could be asleep in an instant if he allowed himself. The regeneration potion took more than just the body's turyn, and he would need a full day's rest to feel like himself again.

He surveyed the area, but all he could see in every direction were the fallen. There were areas with slightly more turyn, possibly indicating wounded survivors. He would never have counted on that as a detection method under normal circumstances, but he had pretty well exhausted all the turyn in the area. More was drifting in from the periphery, but for now, the battlefield was still fairly barren, but for the turyn seeping from those still living.

Emory headed for the remains of the behemoth. The great monster almost looked as though it had exploded, but on closer inspection it seemed that something had struck it dead center from above, creating a crater of blubbery flesh and yellow liquids. Wisps of turyn hovered above the center of the apocalyptic strike. *How did she do that?* he wondered, for there was no doubt in his mind it must have been Tabitha.

Climbing over a small hill of torn flesh, Emory looked down into the crater and saw something dark there. It didn't seem as if it was part of the monster, but his brain struggled to make sense of the shape. It wasn't until it breathed that he realized it was some sort of reptilian creature, a bizarre variation of the forms Tabitha had been using to fight. This one still had arms and legs, but they were folded against the body and the head was hidden by an enormous extrusion of pointed bone or horn. As weird as it appeared, his first impression was of a dragon that had somehow compressed itself into the shape of gigantic bone dart.

It was intimidating trying to approach the creature she had transformed herself into. If Tabitha woke and reacted badly, she might kill him simply by rolling over, or swinging one of her oddly misshapen limbs, and he certainly didn't have the means to defend himself currently. Emory paused, but the sight of red blood running down to mingle with the yellow fluids of the behemoth made the decision for him. Tabitha was unconscious and wounded, which meant she couldn't heal or transform until she woke—and even then, she would need the energy to do so.

Emory tried to keep his balance as he descended the steep meat-slope, but his unwillingness to use his hands proved to be his undoing. Slipping, he tumbled down until he fetched up against Tabitha's inert form. He was now just as covered in blood, slime, and unidentifiable goo as she was.

Forcing down the bile that rose in his throat, Emory reached into his belt pouch and retrieved the regeneration potion that he still hadn't used, since his own savior had given him one. Finding Tabitha's mouth wasn't practical; if she even had one currently, it was hidden by bone. He couldn't find where she was bleeding from either, so he was forced to make his own entrance.

Her armored hide was so thick and tough that it took him ten minutes to work one of the scales up and wedge his enchanted dagger through the not-so-soft skin that lay beneath. Eventually he got the blade in, creating an incision several inches deep and two inches wide. Then, he poured the regeneration potion in and used a small force spell to keep the excess from dribbling away.

Not much happened, and he worried that she didn't have enough turyn for the potion to work, so Emory used a source-link spell to connect himself to her. After attuning what turyn he had to her natural frequency, he gave her what little energy he had. That proved to be too much for him, and he passed out immediately after.

Sometime later—he couldn't be sure how long, for it was still dark—he awoke. The turyn in the air had returned to something close to normal, and his body had regained enough to function normally, but he was still so tired that he wanted nothing more than to go back to sleep. He might not have woken at all, but his body was cold, soaked through with Tabitha's blood and the behemoth's strange yellow fluids.

Suddenly anxious, he tried to listen for her heartbeat, but could hear nothing. Again, it was the slow expansion of her barrel-like chest that finally showed him Tabitha was still alive. Emory slumped back down into the muck, resting his back against her side, but he couldn't sleep there. The night air was chilly, and his wet body had cooled down until his bones ached from it.

There was also the matter of safety. He had no idea how the battle was going, or whether it was over, but if the enemy returned while he slept, both of their lives would be forfeit. Thinking about it, even if it was the Terabinians that discovered them, they might easily mistake Tabitha's dark, scaled form for one of the abominations the elves had unleashed.

Using some of his own, plus the ambient turyn in the air, Emory grew vines beneath them, lifting and cupping Tabitha's strange body until it was out of the blood and viscera. The vines had openings between them, so the fluids that clung to her could drip through and allow her to dry. He made a smaller bed from vines for himself, adding a thick cushion of soft grass, and then pulled yet more turyn in to encase them both in a giant, thorny cocoon. It would take several men and good axes to get in now, and hopefully the noise would wake him if anyone tried.

Emory used several simple cleaning spells to get the grime out of his hair, skin, and clothes. Learning Selene's Solution had required far too much time and effort, and as a nobleman he'd never lacked for baths; in fact, he preferred them. Now he wished he had made the effort, for the spells he knew were grossly inadequate. *Emphasis on 'grossly,'* he thought wryly.

Having done what he could, he lay back onto his grassy pillow, and within seconds of closing his lids, consciousness left him.

CHAPTER 22

The demon-steel golem that housed Tiny's consciousness moved through the streets of Nerril, hunting the black beasts the elves had brought. Janice's voice was in his ear, relaying information and instructions. While his body was helpless back in Cerria, she sat beside him, speaking calmly into his ear. Still stuck in her role as queen, she had been forced to remain in the capital, but the practical benefit was that she could receive reports and messages from enchanted tablets and share information with her husband even as he continued to fight.

"The Driven are being hard-pressed on Givens Street. The beasts resist most magic," relayed Janice. The Driven and Iron Knights from the successful side of the battle had returned to Nerril through the opposite gate and had been fighting house-to-house against the invaders through the dark hours of the night.

"I don't know where that is," he replied, frustration showing in his voice. Tiny wasn't familiar with the layout of Nerril, but again, their unique situation was an advantage. Janice had a map out as well as assistants to help her parse the information and unfamiliar layout quickly.

After a half-second pause, she answered, "Two streets north of where you are now, then west for a block and you should see them."

"I can't see the sun, Jan," reminded Tiny. "It's dark."

"If you haven't turned, then you're still going east on Lion Street. If so, the road ahead of you is Slovell. Turn left on it and you'll be heading north. Two streets then left again will see you through to the fighting."

There was no sign, or at least none he could spot, so Tiny couldn't confirm the street name, but he followed her directions, nonetheless. His heavy metal body wasn't black anymore. The last creature he had fought had lived too long, latching on and draining away the demonic turyn and causing his golem to lighten to a dark grey color.

Ordinarily, during combat, blows from the enemy caused the demon-steel to build up turyn. It used that energy to power the enchantments that moved it, and if it built up enough, black flames would cover it. If Tiny couldn't use up enough of it, he sometimes had to use a fire-breathing enchantment that Janice had built in to keep the golem from exploding.

Today, that wasn't his problem. The weird monsters seemed to drain or negate magic, including the demonic turyn that infused his golem. Worse, demon-steel, ordinarily almost impossibly hard, became softer when it was completely drained of turyn. That was how mage-smiths were able to work with it, by continually keeping it free of turyn. In that state, the metal was softer than steel or iron, being closer to copper in terms of malleability.

Deep scratches and large dents in his chest testified to that fact. Nothing short of a dragon had ever damaged the Black Duke's golem before that night.

Tiny didn't care about damage, though. Janice had helped design the golem, along with Selene, and she knew everything necessary to repair it, so long as the scrap was recovered. What did worry him was being rendered unable to fight. A sizeable portion of the Driven, the Iron Knights, and most of the Arcane Corps had survived, primarily those from the successful side of the battle for Nerril, and they would be more than enough to finish the elves—if he could hunt down and get rid of the last of their monstrous allies.

Emory still hadn't returned, and given what Tiny had seen, the commander of the Arcane Corps was likely unconscious. Tabitha hadn't shown up either, meaning she was either dead or incapacitated, and since the powerful creatures were mostly unbothered by conventional spells, that left the task up to him.

John Shaw was more than willing, so long as the enchantments that kept his golem body moving continued to work. The deep scratch down his chest made him nervous. On the other side of that massive plate were many of the complex runes that kept everything working. If something cut deeper and disrupted them, it was anyone's guess what would happen. It might cause him to lose some function, an arm or leg, or it might completely disable him.

"What happens if the enchantments inscribed inside the front plate get scratched?" he asked as he kept the golem running down the street.

"The front plate is the thickest piece of metal on it. There's no way to damage the runes on the inside," his wife answered. "Why?"

"I've already got several big scratches and a lot of dents," explained Tiny.

Janice's voice was unequivocal as she replied, "That isn't possible."

"I'll be happy to show you when I get back. Do you think I'm in the habit of telling stories?" he demanded, his weariness and frustration making him snap at her.

"No, John, I believe you. How did it happen?" After he described the continual loss of turyn, Janice gave him an answer. "Depending on where the front plate gets cut, it could completely disable you. In fact, there's not many places on that front plate that won't render you completely immobile. The master enchantment takes up most of the space there."

"I won't blow up, will I?"

"No," she reassured him, "if they're absorbing your turyn then there's no chance of that."

"Is there anything I can do to stop them from leeching it like that?" he asked.

After a long pause, she replied, "No. We would need to rework the entire rune structure. I have ideas that might do the trick, but it would be an entirely new design."

"Can you do it after we win this?"

"It will take months at a minimum."

Ahead, he saw a building on the corner that was ablaze. As far as Tiny knew, the elves and their monstrous allies weren't setting fire to anything, but it was likely that the desperate soldiers and citizens were trying everything possible to stop the bizarre creatures eating them. He was already running, but he wished he could get there quicker. People were jumping from the second-floor windows, and as he got closer, he saw a woman leap down with a child in each arm.

It was a twenty-foot drop, and she screamed in pain when she landed. The two children, toddlers by their size, were likely all right, but her legs wouldn't be carrying her any farther. Even so, she tried to crawl toward the closest alleyway. The children were in shock, so she dragged them along as best she could. Tiny saw the bones sticking out through the skin of one leg, and he knew the pain had to be intolerable.

A shriek from the building spoke to the horrors the mother had fled, and Tiny was torn between the desire to help the woman and hurry inside. The screams told him the beast was still feeding, making his choice for him. He headed for the sundered streetside door.

He'd just reached it when a thud sounded behind him, and when he turned, he beheld the abomination standing atop the wounded mother. It had leapt from the window to get to her, fixated on its prey with single-minded cruelty.

He wanted to roar in rage and dismay, but while his metal body could speak and shout to communicate and relay orders, it was emotionally unsatisfying without lungs or a throat. Turning as rapidly as he could, Tiny charged back, massive sword sweeping around to cleave the terrible monster in twain.

The black demon-steel turned grey as it cut into the monster, and although it finished the cut it was badly bent before it emerged on the other side. Tiny dropped it and used his metal hands to pull the two halves back and away before they could land on the mother or her children. The woman continued to crawl, terrified, though she never stopped pulling her children along with her. "Don't be afraid. If you can remain still, I'll carry you and the—"

The mother's face turned up to stare at him, relieved to hear a human voice, but her eyes went wide before the Black Duke could finish his sentence, and then a powerful force catapulted him forward, directly toward her. He might have crushed them, but Tiny managed to place his hands on either side of her as he fell, and instead he rolled harmlessly over the three innocents before crashing into the wooden front of what looked to be a shop. The wood wall next to its front door disappeared in a thunder of broken boards. Sharp flinders of wood clattered to the ground a half second later, but none of that mattered to the three people in the street as a second, even larger monstrous abomination loomed over them, dripping foul-smelling saliva from its open mouth.

The children were probably around two and three respectively, and far too heavy for even their sturdy-framed mother to lift one-handed, but with a strength born of fear and desperation she did so anyway. Rising to her knees, she took each by the back of their shirts and threw them toward the distant alley, and despite the terror gripping her heart, she turned back to face the beast that threatened them. Frustrated tears stained her cheeks as she cursed it, "Go ahead, eat me, you bastard—I hope you choke on my bones!"

The abomination seemed to pause, its enormous maw gaping wider as it prepared to lunge, but then a massive wooden timber seemed to sprout from the side of its head. The metal golem stepped out of the ruined shop, having just thrown the conveniently pointed beam like an oversized spear. He held a second beam in his other hand, and he swept it across like a club to hammer the beast into the ground. The monster twitched, but its ruined body didn't rise again.

His metal body now bore even more dents, but the metal had darkened to black again. The massive impact with the store had done much of the damage but had also caused the demon-steel to regain turyn, becoming harder than steel once more. Leaning down, he used one hand to lift the woman, who had sagged back to the ground. She grimaced in pain at the rough movement, but there was no time for better treatment. "Let me help move you," he told her after the fact.

"The fighting on Givens isn't going well, John," intoned Janice in his ear. "They've broken the defensive formation, and the Driven aren't having any success with their magic. The casualties are mounting fast."

"I can only fix what's in front of me, Jan. I can't leave her on the street."

"Who?" she asked, unaware of what had just happened.

"I ran across a mother and some children. She's injured," he replied tersely.

Janice's voice was tight when she replied seconds later, "The entire city is going to face the same if something doesn't change quickly."

"Why haven't my knights reached them yet? Weren't they coming from the other side of the city?" he asked.

"They haven't reported in over a quarter of an hour. Something must have delayed them, or worse."

Tiny deposited the woman next to her children, who were watching him with wide eyes. "Find a hole and crawl into it," he told her. "Nowhere is safe until this is over." He'd spotted a dead soldier nearby, so he went over and opened the man's potion case. The vials seemed impossibly tiny in his huge hands, so he brought it over to her, then pointed to the center potion. "This will heal you, but you'll sleep half a day or more after you take it. Don't touch the other vials or they might kill you. Wait until you've found a good place before taking it, or wait until this is over."

It broke his heart to turn away and leave her, but the golem's ears picked up a quiet 'thank you' as he left. He wondered if they would survive and doubted he would ever know the outcome. In the dark shadows of his heart, Tiny feared something else would likely find them, but he couldn't afford to dwell on it. Continuing his journey, he spotted an iron lamp post and stopped to rip it free. The ten-foot iron pole would serve him better as a weapon than the wooden club, and unlike his ruined sword, the iron wouldn't soften after coming in contact with the otherworldly monsters the elves had summoned.

Flames and smoke turned the sky ahead of him orange as he approached the site of a chaotic battle. As Tiny's dark form entered the city square, he saw bodies littering the ground in every direction. Citizens, city guards, the Driven—men and women of all sorts had fought and died, and yet more were still fighting, but there was no line. They had lost cohesion, and the battle had devolved into pure chaos as some ran and others were overwhelmed. The monsters roamed freely, feasting in the confusion as they tore into humans with brutal abandon.

Tiny raised his golem's voice to its loudest volume. "To those who can hear, heed my commands. This is the Black Duke. If you can move, retreat to the east. We have reinforcements coming from that direction. Head for the river! If you can still fight, retreat anyway." Stepping forward, he slammed the iron post into the nearest beast, crushing its head.

He fought and killed several more, repeating his commands continuously as he fought, and slowly, things began to change. Those that could were moving in one direction, a modest improvement over the random scattering that had reigned previously, and the abominations took notice of the dark form that had already killed those that were too preoccupied with eating to see him until it was too late.

"What's happening?" asked Janice in his ear.

"I've ordered a retreat toward the river, and I'm doing my best to distract the monsters."

"You need to rally them!" she said anxiously.

The iron pole blurred in his hands as he crushed yet another monster. "Trust me, Jan. That wasn't possible. This is the best I can do. If I can gather the attention of enough of these things, I think at least a portion of these people can make it out. Hopefully they'll meet up with the Iron Knights." He whipped the pole back, then thrust the end forward like a spear, caving in the chest of another beast.

"How many are there?" she asked.

"Too many to count."

"Are you venting turyn? If they surround you—the golem might—"

...Explode, he finished mentally, knowing what she was warning of. After the troll battles, she had added a few new and extremely offensive ways to use up the demonic turyn his golem accumulated when it was being relentlessly pounded on. "I can't," he answered.

"John. If the golem is destroyed, there won't be anyone left to lead. Most of the officers have stopped reporting."

"You misunderstand. Every time one of them bumps into me, it drains turyn. There's no chance of exploding *or* using the new enchantments. I probably look like a beat-up tin pot." He continued to fight as he talked to her in a normal voice, a strange experience that was only possible while he was using the golem. The iron pole whistled through the air as he whipped it back and forth, and it served him far better than the demon-steel sword had. With more mass in the weapon and the strength of his golem body behind it, his strikes not only crushed his opponents but sometimes even tore through them, practically liquefying their tough, rubbery flesh through sheer kinetic force.

The area was mostly empty of humans now—living ones at least—and many of the abominations had turned away from hunting those that ran in order to deal with the metal foe that was killing them. The golem was now surrounded by a growing number of the creatures. It was impossible to count accurately, but he guessed there were several dozen at least. He used the iron pole more defensively, spinning it like a staff to keep them from touching his metal frame and draining his remaining strength. He'd already slain eight or nine, but without being able to go fully offensive anymore, he wasn't able to do much other than inflict minor wounds on those that got too close. *The goal now is just to buy time, keep them busy,* he told himself silently.

His delaying tactics kept them occupied, but after a short time, perhaps five or ten minutes, they began to get organized—lunging at him from opposite sides simultaneously. He made them pay for it, killing or maiming one each time, but his enemies were still successful in touching him. The turyn that sustained his golem dropped lower and lower. It wouldn't be long before it was rendered inanimate, impotent.

To forestall that, the Black Duke shifted his position, forcing the encircling opponents to move with him as he got close to a building with a tall stone front. His plan involved using it to guard his back, or failing that—

Since there were too many of the large abominations to get at him all at once, some of those on the fringes moved into the building and pushed outward while others tore through the wooden beams and interior framework. The stone wall teetered forward, collapsing onto Tiny.

He welcomed the falling stones. The first few caused more dents, but the force of the stone blocks enabled the demon-steel to produce more turyn, enough to turn the metal black again. He emerged from the rocky avalanche somewhat restored, and as the chaos disrupted the strange beasts' formation, he killed two more. Back in Terabinia, his human face smiled at the success. Leaping up and forward, he left the piled rubble to find solid footing and killed a third monster before his foes could reorganize.

This time, he didn't attempt to continue the fight. Instead, he ran. Driving forward, he smashed down another of the abominations and rushed through a gap in their encirclement. His goal was the doorway of a large, multistory building. Charging across the distance, he rammed his way through the too-small doorway.

"What's happening?" asked Janice.

"I'm retreating into a building."

Her reply came with a sound of some relief in her voice. "Think you'll be able to rejoin our forces to the east?"

"Not like this," he answered honestly. "The golem is too vulnerable to their energy drain. If I get swarmed, I'll be disabled in seconds. I need to be there myself." As he spoke, he was going up the building's stairs, trying to enlarge the space around them without collapsing them and dropping himself back to the ground floor. After the initial few seconds, he had to do it while moving backwards since the monsters had followed him in and were harrying his backside.

"John, there's no way for you to get there in time. Even the secret beacon we used to move the troops is a half an hour's ride from Nerril."

Tiny smashed another of the creatures, buying himself a moment while they were tangled up with the corpse below him. He'd made it to the second floor and had to back around a corner to reach the next flight of stairs up. The problem was made more complicated by the fact that the ceiling was too low for his height. It was tempting to just let the golem's head tear up the ceiling, but he found it was more effective to stoop, leaving the monsters with the same problem inhibiting their movement. Although they were roughly the same size, they were less than half his mass, and it wasn't as easy for them to rip through the wood and joists.

Backing onto the stairs to the third floor, he processed his wife's statement. She was referring to Project Chrysalis, Terabinia's most closely guarded state secret. While the teleport beacons in Cerria and Myrsta were public knowledge, Selene had ordered smaller, strategic beacons be built near strategic towns and cities around Terabinia and Darrow to enable the rapid transport of military forces in times of war. Many of those beacons were still unfinished, but priority had been given to port cities like Nerril. That was how they'd moved the Driven and the Iron Knights there quickly enough to set up the ambush. But Project Chrysalis had involved a few other details.

One had been a method for transportation of certain critical personnel. Given the correct rune keys, some wizards could teleport to the beacons, but not every spellcaster had the necessary skill—in fact most of the officers didn't—and that ignored the fact that the Black Duke himself was a mundane. An enchantment had been designed for incorporation into armor that might allow the Iron Knights to teleport themselves to pre-designated beacons, but numerous problems made that solution impractical. Chiefly, finding an appropriate source of turyn to power the costly teleportation.

Selene wanted to develop a golem corps, training the Iron Knights to pilot golems similar to Tiny's, but the idea had been hindered by the lack of demon-steel. Without the rare hell-metal, it was difficult to store and maintain the necessary energy to keep a golem operating. Tiny's demon-steel golem could store vast amounts of turyn, and every time it was struck, it generated more. Consequently, only one example of the personal teleportation enchantment had been placed and tested, and rather than using a predesignated location, it had been deemed better to link two small and very specific teleport beacons.

One was located within the golem, while the other was in Tiny's personal enchanted armor. Ideally, he could wear the armor and accompany the army like any ordinary commander would, but in the case of an unexpected emergency, he could activate the enchantment and swap places with the golem. One moment, the enemy would face a large but still human warrior, and the next they would find themselves in the presence of the unstoppable demon-steel golem. Terabinia's Royal Marshal would be simultaneously whisked to safety while his enemies would be in for a world of hurt.

"John, I'm still confused. What did you mean? You can't get there yourself," asked Janice.

"If I can get enough turyn, I'm going to trigger the golem's teleport," he answered. "I can do more in person than I can this way."

"Absolutely not! It's far too dangerous. That's exactly the opposite of what we created the enchantment for."

"Demon-steel is next to useless against these things," he complained. "Once they drain the magic, it's as soft as copper. Speaking of which, will you replace the weapons on my belt? And put the elf-steel greatsword in my hands?"

"No. I'm not going to allow this."

"I'm doing it, Jan. You don't want me to show up here with nothing but demon-steel weapons. Normal steel, or elf-steel."

"John, this is madness," she argued, but when he didn't answer, a long pause followed. Then she spoke again. "Let me check the straps. You didn't tighten anything when you put your armor on." A second later, he could hear her barking orders to others in the room. "You! I need you to fetch his other weapons, the elf-steel. It looks white." Seconds later, she added, "I don't care. Look, damn you! You, go help. Move, damn your eyes!"

More commands and some choice cursing ensued before she spoke to Tiny again. "John, I need a few minutes. It's not easy moving your body to switch the belts and harness."

Still fighting, he answered, "I'm too big for you, Jan. The servants should do it."

"They're trying, damn you! We're all working at it. You're as big as a damned bull."

He'd reached the top floor but didn't know if there was any place to access the roof, so he simply smashed the ceiling above his head with the iron pole. It took numerous swings to break the joists and rafter after he'd torn through the plaster, and in between he had to fend off the monsters trying to come up the stairs after him, but eventually he had cleared an opening into the attic space and beyond, allowing him to see the stars through the roof decking above. Several more swings sent the newest abomination falling back down into its companions, and then he leapt skyward.

Naturally, he still got caught on the jagged boards that jutted toward his makeshift exit, but he didn't fall back down. Catching them with his hands, he continued pulling himself up, breaking more wood as he forced his massive bulk through the opening. The roof's pitch was a steep forty-five-degree angle, so he had to lean against it and use both hands to crawl, otherwise he'd have immediately rolled and fallen to the ground. "I'm about to do it, Jan."

"Not yet! Not unless you want to show up with your armor all a mess."

Tiny could see one of the creatures coming through his hole, and they were obviously much better suited to the rooftop than his heavy, metal body. His iron pole was already gone; he'd lost it while climbing through. Not that he could have used it anyway. He needed both hands just to crawl across the roof's slanted surface. Scrabbling, he punched holes in the slate tiles with his metal fingers as he crawled. That was the only way he could get enough purchase to keep from sliding. "I have to do it now or I'll lose the chance."

"One second." His wife sounded frantic, but then she spoke again just seconds later. "All right, it's done, but this is madness. Are you in a safe place?"

"No. There isn't one."

"You can't use the potions, you realize that? Not unless you've almost won. You're alone and you'll be helpless when it wears off."

"I know, Jan. I've fought a few battles before this. I know how a Dragon's Heart potion works. It's a last resort."

"You have to lead, John. You can't do that if you're dead. Don't use the potions. Doing this is pointless if you can't reach your men."

The warnings would never end, and she would never accept what he really intended, so Tiny did something he almost never did. He lied, "I can see them from up here. Once I switch, I'll run straight to the reinforcements. It's a clear shot."

"Really?" she asked, voice doubtful and hopeful at the same time. "I've got my hand on the keystone in your armor. It won't work if I interfere."

"This will work," he reassured her. "I can turn this around." He was spider-crawling across the roof as quickly as he could to get distance between him and the emerging creatures. The roof peak was only a few feet away now. "Let me do this. These are the people responsible for William's death. We can't let them win."

Elven assassins had killed a lot of nobles when they had attempted to foment war between Terabinia and Trendham. Their son William had been among the victims. Janice's desire for vengeance bordered on obsessive and was nearly matched by his own. Bringing it up when he was about to risk his own life wasn't fair, and it told her everything about the truth of his previous statements. Gritting her teeth, Janice pulled her hand back from his armored chest. "You better come back safe to me."

"I will," he answered. "This is it." Pushing off with his hands, Tiny's golem stood briefly on bent legs, and then launched itself into the air and out over the cobblestone street. Spread-eagle, he fell like a boulder and hit the hard stones without making any attempt to cushion the fall. The powerful impact sent a surge of turyn into the golem as the demon-steel converted the kinetic energy into turyn. The closest enemies were thirty yards away, but Tiny didn't pause. He used the brief surplus of energy to trigger the teleport.

His armored body in Cerria vanished, replaced by the bent and battered golem, while his armored human form appeared on the street in Nerril. Pushing off from the ground with both arms, Tiny leapt up and began to run, checking his armor and gear as best he could without taking his eyes off the street in front of him. The straps were good, though they pinched him in a few places. He could deal with that. His body felt light, quick, and powerful. The Black Duke trained daily to maintain his body's strength, and the enchantments worked into his plate armor did much to enhance that.

The beasts were already adjusting to chase after him, but he paused a moment to unstrap the white metal of his elf-steel greatsword. Then, he took it in hand and resumed his run.

Back in Cerria, Janice was alone. She had sent all the servants out while she stared down at the demon-steel golem. It had been battered and bent to such a degree that it was almost unrecognizable. She'd never seen it in such a state. Even after the battle against Lognion, it hadn't been so damaged—and her husband had just sent himself into the midst of the monsters that had done that damage. In her mind, she replayed his last words, and angry tears began to well in her eyes. "You're a terrible liar," she whispered. "You better make them pay or I'll hunt you down in Hell myself."

She hated herself for letting him go, but she hated the elves even more.

CHAPTER 23

Moving rapidly through the streets of Nerril, a giant of a man in steel armor prowled. The sword in his hands was nearly seven feet in length from tip to pommel, and its blade was an unusual metallic color that often appeared nearly white, as though it were made of pure silver, or some more exotic material. The Black Duke himself was somewhere close to seven feet in height, but he still looked small beside the slick, wet-seeming dark monstrosities he battled. They towered over him as he spun and cut through their numbers.

Only continued motion and his momentum kept him from being overwhelmed. If just one of them managed to get a clawed hand on his body, he would be done. Not from the turyn drain, but simply from the loss of mobility. The abominations were bigger and stronger. If a grapple started, he would be dead.

Fortunately, the blade in his hands was incredibly sharp and even longer than his usual steel greatsword. The elf-steel was lighter than iron, making it easier to wield. The size had been increased in part because it was possible, and in part because it was necessary in order to give it a proper amount of mass. It still only weighed seven and a half pounds despite the length, and with Tiny's strong frame behind it, the metal was a white blur in the air.

Despite their seemingly bestial nature, the creatures *were* intelligent. Their single-minded hunger and simple tactics were mainly the result of not needing to fear their human opponents. Most of the townspeople were defenseless against them, and the occasional spear or crossbow that they used wasn't much of a threat to the otherworldly monsters. Similarly, the magic of the Driven and the Arcane Corps had proven to be mostly ineffective. Direct magical attacks were rendered useless. One of the few things that worked was using magic to hurl physical objects, but the monsters' dense, blubbery bodies were difficult to injure.

As Tiny cut and danced his way along the street, however, they began to learn. No longer did they wait fearlessly for him to arrive with a sweeping cut that would bisect even their large forms; now they were ducking and dodging, and some were using makeshift missiles, throwing broken boards, loose masonry, and in one case an entire cart still partly loaded with turnips. Tiny had to turn constantly to keep watch behind himself, for unlike the golem, his human body was far more fragile when faced with heavy impacts.

The big warrior ran in a zig-zag pattern as he made his way toward the eastern gate, but he didn't focus solely on covering ground as quickly as possible. Instead, he hunted monsters opportunistically as he went. The Black Duke wasn't trying to escape. He was on a rampage that took him in the direction of his allies. The city was in chaos, and the only tool left to him was violence, so he used it with deliberate intention. The monsters he had left behind had been left confused by his change and rapid exit. Many hadn't realized the direction he'd gone, so they'd spread out instead of chasing him together.

Meanwhile, the few that had continued chasing the retreating soldiers and townsfolk were forced to turn and face him as he hunted them from behind. Tiny's legs propelled his heavy body forward with the vitality of a much younger man. Despite his regular exercise, running for so long in full armor would ordinarily have exhausted him by then, but the enchantments in his armor went a long way to make up for ordinary human limitations. They made him faster and stronger, but they were limited by the amount of turyn stored in the crystal mounted on the inside of his breastplate. While his golem could recharge by taking blows from the enemy, his steel plate didn't have that convenient property.

He could have accepted a few elementals to address that limitation, but Tiny had always refused on moral grounds. Leaping over an overturned cart, Tiny cut the legs out from under one monster and dodged a heavy missile thrown by another. Taking three giant steps down an alley, he jigged to one side to avoid a second missile before cutting down the creature throwing them. It was only after the fact that his mind registered that it had been throwing dead citizens at him.

Tiny glanced at the inside of his right vambrace, where ten small stones were mounted near his wrist. Eight still glowed while two had gone dark. Twenty percent of his stored turyn had been used already, and he still hadn't found the Iron Knights that were supposed to be fighting their way in from the east. Despite what Jan had said, he knew that when the last gem went dark, he'd be forced to use the Dragon's Heart potion if he was still fighting, and once he'd done that, he would have thirty minutes or less before it ran out, leaving him exhausted and helpless.

Many years ago, before the golem and before the enchanted armor, he'd trained using the potions. While under the influence, he wouldn't notice injuries, and more than once he'd found himself on the verge of death when the alchemical concoction exhausted itself. Alone and surrounded by enemies, he had no doubt that a grisly end would soon follow if that happened.

Tiny proceeded down the alley and was just emerging onto another street when his world abruptly went white, followed by a jarring impact. Momentarily dazed, Tiny struggled to recover. His vision returned as the magic that had cushioned his armor disappeared. It took a massive shock to trigger the magical failsafe. Something had hit him so hard that without it he would likely have died purely from the shock of the blow.

In front of him, he saw one of the creatures draw back to hit him again, a massive club in its hands. It had waited around the corner to ambush him with the makeshift weapon. Tiny didn't know how much turyn the emergency shield and air cushion had cost him, but he knew his armor couldn't do that too many times before it would be completely drained. He'd lost his sword, and the club was coming back at him again, so he did the only thing he could; he dropped down and fell forward, spoiling his opponent's aim. The club glanced off his left shoulder, but it was robbed of some of its force and didn't set off his armor's failsafe that time.

His left arm was numb as he fell to the ground and drew a dagger from his belt and drove it into the area he would have called the ankle on a human. The anatomy didn't look the same on these things, but they still had to support weight, and he levered the hilt to one side, cutting through a significant portion of the dense flesh. The monster stumbled and fell to one side. One clawed hand grabbed his shoulder, pulling him along with it, and a desperate wrestling match ensued.

Its maw clamped down on his head and shoulders while he used his free arm to stab and cut. The pressure steadily increased as it bit down, and only luck saved him when he managed to cut into the jaw muscle. The bite lost its force and metal screeched as he dragged his helm out from between the creature's teeth. One of its arms caught his knife-wielding hand and twisted until the blade fell from his grasp, but by then his left arm was working. As it lifted him into the air by his right arm, he awkwardly drew the war hammer from his belt with his left and drove the spiked end into the thing's eye.

It dropped him, and Tiny had a moment to recover. Seeing his greatsword, he snatched it up, and before the monster could stagger back, he swept the sword across and half severed one of the creature's legs. The fight ended predictably after that, though it took him several messy cuts to finish the thing. Then, he studied his surroundings, worried that more would come to finish him, but thankfully, he was alone. Tiny checked the stones on his vambrace. Seven were dark. *Only three-tenths left,* he noted mentally. *That club took a lot out of the armor.*

He'd killed his attacker, but if he ran out of turyn and was forced to use the potion it would be the monster at his feet that deserved the credit for his eventual death. Tiny recovered his dagger and rehung the hammer at his waist. "If I die, you'd best hope we don't meet in Hell," he said, addressing the monstrous corpse. "I'll make it twice as painful next time."

Greatsword in hand once more, the big man resumed jogging down the street, this time with more of an eye out for creatures lying in wait. He couldn't afford any more mistakes.

At the next street intersection, he came upon a scene that made no sense. Dead men were lined up in rows, but they hadn't been dragged there. The lines were too even, too perfect, and the dead all wore the dark leather of either the Driven or the enchanted plate armor of Tiny's Iron Knights. It would have been even more confusing if he'd gotten there later, but only the first three rows were dead, their blood still leaking out to trickle into the gutters. Behind them, four more rows, mainly Iron Knights, were kneeling with their helmets on the ground. The soldiers stared straight ahead with empty eyes while someone moved slowly down the line, a bloody knife in hand.

The executioner wore a dark blue tunic of finely woven linen with silver trim. Beneath were dark trousers and expensive-looking black leather boots. Long, white hair covered the killer's shoulders, and Tiny could see a gleam of silver that indicated a silver circlet on his head. It was hard to tell since the man was facing away from him.

A larger, armored knight walked beside the slender man, clearly a guard or assistant of some sort, and by the white metal of his armor Tiny knew without doubt that it was an elven warrior. Unsure what was happening, Tiny moved directly toward them. "By the Mother!" he swore. "What devilry is this?"

The armored warrior moved to interpose himself between Tiny and the blue tunic, but the man turned and held up a hand to stop the guardian from attacking. It was then that Tiny saw that it was an elven woman in the blue tunic. Her beauty was startling, but the bloody knife in her hand spoiled it. She smiled and beckoned him forward. "Welcome, warrior," she greeted him in accented

Darrowan. "Please, remove your helm and take your rest over there with the others." She gestured toward the end of the front row.

Tiny felt something pass over him, a strange feeling, as though someone else's thoughts were overlaying his own. It made him dizzy, and he put one hand to his head as he continued forward. Deeper down, he understood she was using some sort of magic, but he had no way of knowing the particulars. *She's trying to control me somehow.*

He walked toward her on unsteady feet. "You're so beautiful," he murmured, mesmerized by her features.

The look on the elven woman's face registered annoyance. "I'm aware. Take your place over there." She seemed wary, so Tiny stopped a few feet away, and he heard the armored elf say something, but he couldn't understand the language. She nodded in response to her guard, then spoke to Tiny again, "You don't need the sword, my friend."

The dizziness swept through him once more and Tiny answered with confusion in his voice. "Huh?" He let the sword fall from his hands.

"Take off your helm and move over there." She pointed again, and a look of concentration furrowed her brow.

He lifted his hands to his head and pulled, but the straps held his helmet firmly in place, but Tiny knew that would be the case. Removing it would require some work. His gauntlets would need to come off first, and then he'd need to reach under his aventail to loosen it. "It's stuck."

"Just move to your place. You can work on it there," she ordered, but when he continued to fiddle with the helm without moving, she took another step forward. "Are you daft? Move over there first."

"I don't understand," said Tiny.

The elven warrior said something, but she ignored him. "Are you from a poor family that couldn't afford bluet for lamps? The connection feels weak." Another step forward and she was now within a few feet of Tiny, gesturing once more toward the end of the row.

"What?" Tiny staggered, then took a step toward her and to the right, as though heading in that direction. Then, his steel-gauntleted left hand came up and struck with blinding speed. His metal-encased fist hit the elf squarely beneath her right eye, breaking bone as it lifted her from her feet and sent her body falling straight back. Her arms and legs were stiff as she hit the ground, already unconscious if not dead from the brutal impact.

The elven guard had already been suspicious and consequently reacted quickly despite his surprise. He leapt back, drawing a thick, short sword with one hand. In his other, the elven warrior held a misericorde, a specialized dagger with a long triangular blade. It was slender, but strong since it didn't have a cutting edge. The weapon was tailor-made for driving into gaps, and the point was ideal for bursting rings and piercing mail.

The elf's armor was well made, and thanks to the strange metal the elves used, also lighter than Tiny's. Although his greatsword lay nearby, Tiny pulled his war hammer free from its hanger and took his own dagger into his off hand. They were better tools for the job at hand. Without pausing, he stepped forward, his anger evident in his stride.

The enemy's sword lashed out, sending sparks down the Black Duke's arm as its enchanted edge met hard steel. Trusting his armor, Tiny let the attack slide off and stepped even closer to slam the hammer head into the side of the elf's helmet. The weapon was deceptively small. A slender metal bound wooden haft only two and a half feet in length led to the business end, which only weighed an ounce over three pounds. All told, the thing weighed less than five pounds, making it easy to carry and maneuver, but just like the elf's misericorde, it was a devilish thing, designed to kill men in heavy armor.

Tiny's opponent staggered sideways, rocked by the blow and raising his dagger to ward away a second strike while he stepped back and tried to recover. Moving quickly, the Black Duke stepped forward, but his foot came down on something unexpected, and he stumbled. The elven warrior was back at him in an instant, his dagger driving up at Tiny's throat. The point hit his breastplate just above the stoprib meant to deflect such things and went upward, catching in the mail and padded gorget protecting his neck.

The point was slender enough to slip through mail rings, but the triangular blade could only get an inch in before its width was caught and stopped. Even so, the point found flesh, and Tiny felt a sharp pain as it pierced his throat. The elf was no fool and didn't withdraw. He'd dropped the sword in his right hand and now clasped the back of Tiny's helm with it while continuing to push on the dagger with his left. The two men were locked in a clench, one that would soon be fatal for Tiny.

The elf was strong, whether from desperation or some magic, Tiny didn't know. Although he was probably more than double his opponent's mass, he couldn't break away. He'd dropped his own dagger and caught the elf's wrist in his left hand. Desperate to stop the elf's inexorable pressure from popping the rings and going completely through, he nearly dropped his hammer to hold the elf off with both hands. Instead, he braced his elbow against his foe, using his forearm to reinforce the distance between them as he continued to hold the elf's wrist.

That kept his right arm, and crucially the war hammer, free to communicate his feelings about the matter. The angle was awkward, but Tiny didn't lack for strength. He brought the blunt side over and down onto the elf's helm, once, then again, trying to stun him. The maneuver cost him. He could feel the point sliding deeper into his neck.

The third blow rattled the elf, and Tiny felt the other warrior's muscles slacken a bit, though the elf still held on with frenzied desperation. Unable to push the point farther in, the elf levered it from side to side, hoping to do more damage or tear through an artery or vein. Hot blood began to run, staining Tiny's armor.

His fourth blow finally made the difference. The elf's grip slipped, and Tiny pushed him back. The next swing of the hammer sent the other warrior reeling, and the following blow sent him tumbling to the ground. The Black Duke stepped on one arm to keep him there as he turned the hammer over in his hand and used both hands to swing the spike at the elf's helmeted head.

The elven armor was well made. His first strike glanced away from the obdurate metal, but it left a dent. The elf jerked his head to spoil his next attack, but Tiny knocked him senseless with the impact and was able to carefully aim after that. The hammer spike found the dent in the enchanted armor, and Tiny's powerful shoulders drove it through. All three inches of the spike went in, and the skull beneath offered far less resistance.

The elf began to jerk and twist, his muscles spasming uncontrollably. The war hammer was caught, and Tiny struggled to remove it, but the elf's seizure made it difficult to hold the helm still beneath his boot so he could lever the spike free.

Then, the world went white again as Tiny's armor activated once more to save him from a massive, unseen attack. His body was thrown forward, and he suddenly felt the weight of the armor more heavily as the magic protecting him failed. The last of the gems on his vambrace had gone dark, devoid of turyn. Falling forward, he tried to use the momentum to roll and escape his unknown attacker, but one of the Iron Knights blocked his path. Before Tiny could recover, the man lifted a sword and swung it across, hitting him on one pauldron and sending him sideways.

"Are you mad? I'm not your enemy!" Tiny shouted, but then he saw the knight's eyes. They were glazed, empty of comprehension, as were the eyes of the rest of his men—all rising to their feet to face him.

In a flash, he understood. *The elf-witch is still conscious.* Leaping up and turning, he knew he had to reach her before he was overwhelmed.

Just fifteen feet away, he saw her, half sitting, propped up on one arm. Blood dripped from her broken and swollen face, but he could see the spite glaring back at him from the woman's one good eye. Tiny charged toward her—and received her second spell, another force-lance, directly in the chest.

It felt like he'd been hit by a troll wielding a maul, but somehow he kept his feet, and after a second, he began moving forward again. Shock showed in her visage. Another spell followed, but panic spoiled her aim. She managed one last spell, hitting him in the shoulder before he finally reached her. Lacking weapons and unsure if his arms were even working, the Black Duke kicked her in the head, then stepped on her neck after she collapsed. All of his considerable weight pressed down, and he felt bones pop and crack as his armored boot crushed her throat.

Flushed with anger and adrenaline, John Shaw stared down at the fallen spellcaster. "That's for my son. May you and all your accursed race rot in hell." Turning back, he saw the Iron Knights looking on in confusion. "What are you waiting for?" he asked. "Put your helmets back on. This isn't a damned holiday! There's a city to save and foes to be slain!"

"Sir?" The closest man still showed uncertainty.

Wondering why they didn't recognize the crest on his breastplate, Tiny looked down and saw that his breastplate had crumpled inward. The pauldron that had protected his left shoulder was entirely missing, ripped free of the rivets and straps that had connected it to his rerebrace and breastplate. The mail and gambeson beneath were bloodied and torn, and he suddenly became aware of the pain of broken bones rubbing as he moved.

Realizing he'd been badly injured, Tiny reached up with his right hand, the only one that would move, and fumbled a moment to unclasp and raise his visor. "It's me, damn you all!" he roared, ignoring the pain in his chest. Glaring at the nearest knight, he ordered, "You can see my face. Tell them who I am."

"The Black Duke," said the man. "But you were here in the golem, how…?"

"Say it louder! They need to hear you. We can discuss particulars later," commanded Tiny.

"It's the Black Duke!"

Tiny would have preferred the man simply say the 'Royal Marshal,' but it was the substance that was important. He knew what they called him, and everyone would recognize the reference. Looking at the insignia of those nearest, he chose the most junior knights and pointed them out. "You, you, you, and you—each of you take a street and keep watch until we've reestablished the command structure here." A second later, he admonished them, "No, fools, put your helmets on first. Make sure you've got your weapons as well." By the time he'd done that, the officers were stepping forward, and he recognized their faces.

Within moments they began reorganizing and the sergeants and lieutenants were barking commands. The Driven were few in number, and none of their officers had survived, so Tiny split them up and spread them among the squads of knights. Once the hierarchy had been reestablished, complete squads were moved to guard the perimeter—and just in time, as a few lone abominations stumbled upon them while instructions were still being given out.

Working together, the Iron Knights cut them down with ease. Despite the monsters' intelligence, they tended to operate independently, and their teamwork was rudimentary at best. After fighting his way through the streets and being hunted by them, the Black Duke had a good feel for their limitations and weaknesses. "We'll modify the city fighting procedures we trained with, but only slightly," he informed the officers. "Keep the minimum group size to two squads, three if one of them is missing too many men. I want no fewer than fifteen in each group, and make sure one of the Driven is with each group, so limit the number of independent units based on that. The sorcerers will limit themselves to serving as magical sentries. I don't want any more men to fall prey to elven infiltrators like this. If they find another elf, withdraw and notify me. It's obvious we have a serious weakness to whatever mind magic they are using."

He continued talking at a rapid pace, stopping to answer questions and clarify their priorities, until finally the most senior of the officers present, Lord Paryon, a knight captain, spoke up. "Your Grace, you need to retire from the field. Your wounds…"

Tiny could see worry written in the man's features. "This is a city, Captain Paryon, not a field."

"Sir, your injuries are serious," responded the captain. "Do you still have your regeneration potion? If not, take mine. The—"

"I can't afford to sleep, Captain," said Tiny.

The knight captain was insistent. "The eastern gate should still be clear behind us. I'll send a squad to escort or carry you back while you recover. You cannot continue in this state."

A dangerous glint showed in Tiny's eyes. "Careful with your words, Captain. Insubordination is a serious crime."

"I'm required to relieve a superior from duty if they are no longer fit to command, Your Grace."

"Then address me as Marshal, Captain Paryon." Tiny leaned closer, looming over the nobleman and gazing down. "Be aware I won't cooperate if that's what you decide to do. Try to remove me and you'll be the one heading to the east gate, and it won't be on your own two feet. Do you think this is a good time for dissension?" Lifting his eyes, he gave the other officers a hard stare. "That goes for the rest of you as well."

"At least let one of the Driven look at you," pled the captain.

Tiny nodded. "I intended to do that regardless. I will also stay with the main body as we progress toward the city center. If I weaken or lose consciousness, feel free to give me the potion. That good enough for you?"

"Yes, sir."

He glanced around once more. "You have your orders. Time is blood today. Move!"

CHAPTER 24

Although there was no light, with sound and movement came vision, for the void was no longer empty. The existence of anything required some amount of turyn, and Will could see that. Creatures moved within the darkness, and while they were almost entirely devoid of turyn, there was still enough for him to see. His perception improved with each passing second as Will adapted to the strange, turyn-starved environment.

Calling his sword-staff to hand, he prepared to defend himself as a weird, multi-limbed *thing* slithered toward him. The creature moved like a slug, a fat, gelatinous mass with sharp, insect-like arms protruding out from it in every conceivable direction. The creature was nearly his height, and if its spindly, chitinous limbs were stretched out from the central body, it could probably span a distance of more than fifteen feet.

With a thought, Will reflex cast a minor spell, creating a small glowing light above his head, allowing him to see the approaching monstrosity in clearer detail. Its surface was a disgusting texture of dark hair and glittering scales, mixed together with little rhyme or reason. He set the blade of his staff vibrating and removed the first of the pointed appendages as they reached tentatively toward him.

The thing must've been blind, for it reacted with fearful surprise, first pulling back before surging forward once more. Its legs whipped at him, but Will's blade cut through them in spite of their hard surfaces, and those he couldn't cut in time, he blocked with the quick use of various force spells. The point-defense spell would have been his preference, but the attacks came at him from too many directions at once. Fortunately, his repertoire had greatly expanded over the years, and he could reflex cast force spells of many different shapes and sizes. Each time, he used only what was necessary, conserving his turyn by limiting the shape, distance, and duration of his shields.

Even Arrogan would have been impressed if he'd been alive to see him fight. Although Will couldn't know it, in the history of Hercynia, throughout its many ages, no wizard—or magic user of any kind— had ever been placed into so many conflicts as he had. Those that might have been usually died early in their careers, and of those that survived, none had faced as many trials, nor trained as religiously, as William Cartwright.

Men? He had slain thousands with both spells and his own hands—thousands more had died at his orders. Sorcerers, warlocks, and even wizards, he had faced those. Monsters, trolls, and vampires? All were familiar to him. He had fought them in every sort of circumstance, often from a position of great disadvantage. Demons and demon-lords? They and their ilk were practically extinct after antagonizing him and receiving his retribution.

Even Grim Talek, an undead lich and former First Wizard, hadn't fought in as many direct conflicts, despite his many millennia of existence. The lich had devoted himself to defeating Lognion, but where the ancient lord of the undead had failed, Will had actually slain the dragon.

Will dissected this new foe with surgical precision, and although with each cut it siphoned away some of the limited turyn he had imbued his staff with, he never faltered. He remained focused, and when he had finally cut through the quivering mass and rendered it dead—or at least helpless—he reclaimed as much of his energy as remained in it, drawing it out of the dying flesh. When that was done, and in the absence of a continuing threat, he extinguished his light spell to conserve turyn.

He was deep in thought, considering his options, when a voice found his ears. "You do not fear the darkness."

The voice was feminine, and familiar. It had been in his dreams many times, but today was no dream. An electric shiver of fear ran down Will's spine. "Who are you?"

"You already know me. You must. You used my spell to arrive here, did you not?"

Will's eyes were straining as he tried to catch sight of her, but they found nothing. No hint of turyn that he could see. "Do you wish to talk, or play at riddles?"

"After such a long acquaintance, I thought you'd be more affable. Perhaps you'd prefer me to leave you alone? The void is endless, and even time fails here. Even madness cannot save you. Your own thoughts will devour you. Trust me, I know," the voice replied. Silence followed, for Will didn't reply. At last, the voice asked, "You won't talk to me?"

"Conversation should involve a meaningful exchange of information. You've only responded to my question with more questions. There's no point in talking if you're playing games."

"Such discourtesy. I might kill you for such impudence."

Will remained unfazed. "Courtesy requires an introduction, and you've not given one."

A tense pause stretched on for some time, until finally the voice returned, "Some call me the Watcher. I have no need for other names anymore."

He mulled that over, then replied, "My name is Will Cartwright, and I'd prefer conversation to solitude, unless you plan to kill me in the near term." After a second, he added, "That's my answer to your first question."

Amusement tinged her voice. "You have a peculiar attention to details. Are you always so meticulous with your speech?"

"I don't know you, and I learned early on to watch my words. Words can bring more misery than blades, especially when dealing with unknown entities. My first unexpected meeting like this was with the fae, so you can understand my caution. That's two answers I've given you, by the way. You owe me an answer."

"I am not fae," she replied, "and you have not asked a second question."

Will wasted no time. "How do I leave this place?"

Laughter answered him. "You don't. You've trapped yourself. I see no reason to send you back so you can butcher more of my servants."

"The elves serve you?"

"They do, and by the rules of your game, it was my turn to ask a question."

"You told me you were not fae."

She laughed. "I am not *anything*. I am surprised it has been so long since you were attacked. I thought our conversation would have been interrupted by now."

Will grimaced. "You've called more monsters to attack me?" Even as he asked the question, he heard the sound of leathery skin sliding across dry stone. Something was drawing closer, something large, and he could see faint hints of turyn through the darkness.

"Survive this one and I'll consider answering that question."

He paid her no heed, all his attention already focused on the massive black dragon rushing toward him, a cloud of poisonous turyn expanding around it like an evil wind. Will's sonic shield sprang up instantly while his sword-staff vanished into the limnthal. The weapon was too small to be useful against a monster so large, so instead he rushed forward, spoiling its aim and slipping beneath the enormous jaws as it attempted to snap him up. With singular intent, he used a force-based travel-disk to lift himself so he could drive straight into the dragon's chest. A human weapon, his sonic shield tore through the armored flesh, and gouts of red blood and liquefied viscera flowed around him in a sanguine torrent as he burrowed deeper.

The dragon roared, but only briefly, for he passed through its windpipe and into the chest. The sonic shield disintegrated flesh and tissue but wasn't tuned well for bone, so he moved around those as he progressed, destroying organs, arteries, and veins as he went. Walking wasn't really possible, and he remembered the gory, fleshy festival of his first trip through a body, back when he had slain Lognion. This time, he was calmer and had better control of himself, using a small force travel-disk to propel himself and an elemental water spell to shunt the bulk of the fluid mess away from his body and guide his path.

Unlike Lognion, this dragon died quickly, like any ordinary beast. Its flesh also required much less energy from him to destroy. He'd feared he wouldn't have the turyn necessary, and the thing didn't seem to have a blazing source like a true dragon would. Emerging from its back, Will descended along one side and stood beside the gigantic corpse, reclaiming and absorbing every bit of the turyn that remained in the air, both from his magic and the monster's dead flesh.

All told, he finished with slightly more than he had started with, a good sign if he was going to be faced with more random attacks. Almost as soon as that occurred to him, he heard a rushing of wings, and a swarm of flying, spider-like creatures roughly the size of squirrels descended upon him. Hairy central bodies were surrounded by ugly legs, but he saw no mouths or fangs. Instead, they attacked with prehensile tails that were tipped with venomous stingers several inches in length.

It was the stuff of nightmares, and Will wasted an excess of his strength creating a wind-wall spell to tear them apart and clear a space around himself. He acted with thoughtful deliberation after that, using the more efficient light-darts spell to take the creatures down with surgical precision. When the last was dead and he had gathered the turyn residue from the area, he was only slightly down from his starting point. If he hadn't wasted so much on the first panic-wrought wind-wall, he might have come out ahead. *I have to be more careful,* he thought, *since this seems to be a war of attrition.*

As long as he had turyn for magic, he could continue, but there was no ambient turyn available in the void; therefore, efficiency was paramount. That and harvesting what he could from fallen foes.

"You're doing well," complimented the Watcher.

By her tone, she sounded genuinely admiring, but Will had no reason not to think she was simply mocking him. "What's the point of this? Are you enjoying this?"

"No point, and yes—I think I am enjoying it. This is more entertainment than I've had in quite some time," she answered.

"I thought it might be a test, but you're willing to waste your minions for malicious enjoyment? How many do you have?"

There was a smile in the Watcher's voice. "Legions, but you're mistaken if you think these are mine."

"What does that mean?" he demanded, but he could already sense more of the beasts approaching.

"You'd better pay attention," she told him. "I don't want the show to end too soon."

Vampire dogs was the best description he had for the rotting hounds that attacked next, and after that, it was diminutive trolls of a similar size to human men. Will destroyed them all as efficiently as possible and then incinerated the cloud of alien insects that attacked immediately afterward. At the end of it all, his turyn stores had grown.

"I can do this all day," Will announced. "You're killing them for no gain."

"Day doesn't exist here," the Watcher told him, "and no matter how much turyn you hoard, it will never be enough to fill the void. You will tire eventually. One mistake and they'll devour your flesh, but that won't be the end. There's no end here, either. No relief from either boredom or torment."

"You make no sense."

"You'll see," she said simply. "They all will."

More things were gathering in the darkness, just beyond his ability to see them, but they were hesitating. Had they learned caution after what he'd done to the others? Was it possible for these things to experience fear? He didn't know, but Will enjoyed the reprieve. Deep down, he wasn't too surprised. Deep within his subconscious, the Stormking stirred, and Will drew confidence from that. Over the past year, he'd learned to accept his powerful alter ego as an essential facet of himself rather than a stranger. He was *the* First Wizard, and he embodied many roles and complex pieces like any other mortal man. The Stormking was the embodiment of his arrogance, power, and confidence. All of that was fine, so long as he didn't allow it to overrule his wisdom and humanity.

At his core, the Stormking knew a certain primal truth. The creatures hiding in the dark could sense his presence, and they feared him. Slinking, nocturnal hunters, they feared a greater predator— him. No matter what their numbers, they wouldn't attack until he allowed it.

Understanding he had time, Will asked, "Who is *they*, and what is it that you want them to see?"

A pause followed, then the Watcher replied, "Don't you think you should focus on the next onslaught?"

"It will come when I am ready," he said simply. "I'm more interested in our conversation. Illuminate me." As he said the words, their truth seemed to solidify within him.

"Don't fool yourself, thinking you understand this place," she warned.

"An endless war against my own anxieties and insecurities? It doesn't seem much different than the real world. How about we try something more original? Let's talk."

Dark laughter fell on his ears. "You learn quickly, I'll grant you that. I look forward to devouring your essence. I hope your death doesn't come too soon. I want to crack your pride slowly, then draw you out in tender morsels, like a dog eating marrow from bones." The void began to seethe with movement and activity as the uncountable hordes surged in toward him.

Snarling, the Stormking met them.

CHAPTER 25

Block by block, the Black Duke and his Iron Knights cleared the streets of Nerril. The strange monsters they fought weren't stupid, and one-on-one they were often too much for the men in enchanted plate, but the monsters had only a crude understanding of how to fight together, and true teamwork was an entirely foreign concept for them.

Tiny stayed in the rear, but his presence mainly served as a morale booster. His officers knew what to do, and now that the shock and strangeness of their new foes had worn off, they began taking their oversized enemies down with ruthless efficiency. The men worked in squads, and tactics that worked well were quickly communicated to other units as the night wore on. Single squads would move forward to draw out several foes, while backup squads would move to flank. The Driven used their magic for scouting and mobility, preventing unwelcome surprises and enabling the Terabinians to keep abreast of the enemy's movements.

Listening to the reports that were relayed back, Tiny felt a sense of pride in his men, though it was increasingly hard to focus on what was being said. One of the Driven had helped close and dress his wounds, but the magic used had been crude. The man wasn't versed in much beyond the basics, which mainly revolved around stopping bleeds and sealing cuts. Realigning and fusing broken bones had been beyond the sorcerer's comfort zone, and things like bruising and damage to tissue and organs weren't within the man's education, either.

He kept his head high and his chin up as he strode along, but his vision was growing blurry, and things seemed to swim around him. The oddest sensation was the wet clicking he felt in his chest. It seemed to follow the timing of his heartbeat, but he was still conscious, so Tiny thought his heart must be all right, otherwise he'd have been dead already.

Jeremy Paryon, the most senior captain and the knight actually in charge now that Tiny was simply trying to stay conscious, had been watching him with a look of serious concern for some time now, but the man had vanished. Tiny's thoughts were muddled, but someone had said something about finding another elf, or perhaps a nest of them. *I should have gone with him,* he realized, then swallowed. His mouth was dry. *Why am I so thirsty?*

He saw Jeremy returning and tried to form a reasonable question. *Did you find any elves?* But what came out of his mouth was, "I need some water."

"I have better news, Your Grace," replied the captain. "You won't need water soon." There was a strange look in the knight's eyes as he drew his sword. "We found the elves."

Despite his muzzy head, a jolt of adrenaline roused Tiny. He saw the captain's sword point slide up the side of his breastplate, toward the mail at his armpit. Jeremy had one gauntleted hand gripping the midpoint of the blade and the other on the hilt, a technique called 'halfswording'. Essentially it made the weapon function better for close-up stabbing, such as when driving the point through mail when fighting a heavily armored opponent.

Without thinking, Tiny twisted, spoiling Jeremy's target, and swung his right hand, slapping the captain's helmet and sending the officer stumbling to one side. Glancing around, he saw two more knights with weapons in hand, while the rest of the command unit had vanished. Jeremy had probably ordered them away—or sent them to visit his new elf-friend.

How easily they subvert us, thought Tiny, but he had no time for lamenting his situation. He was about to die. The three knights were well equipped, and their armor still gave them an excess of strength and speed, while Tiny's was merely a protective weight. He had them in size and mass, but in his current state, that only made him an easier target. He couldn't outrun them, and his brain had already shown him how the fight would end—they'd trip him, and he'd die squirming while they stabbed repeatedly through the gaps and joints in his armor.

He backed away. His hand fumbled with the potion case at his hip and he lifted a black glass vial to his lips. The liquid within was deadly, both to those who used it, and to those who faced them, a Dragon's Heart potion. Energy surged in him, and the small veins in the whites of Tiny's eyes turned black as the magic took hold. He felt a popping in his chest, but if there was pain, he was unable to feel it.

The Black Duke's left hand caught the wrist of the closest knight, who was swinging at him with a flanged mace. Roaring, he attempted to crush the man's arm, but the enchanted steel resisted him. Something slammed into him from the other side, but he ignored it as he jerked the knight's arm down and twisted, turning and ducking his entire body as he put the wrist through a greater than three-hundred-and-sixty-degree rotation. The mace dropped out of the knight's grip, and Tiny caught it with his other hand as he released the now crippled man.

Continuing his turn, he slammed the metal head of the mace into the other knight's knee. Something else struck him in return, but again, it didn't stop his attack, or even slow him in the slightest. The mace dented the wing of the knight's knee cop, but more importantly, it swept the man cleanly from his feet. He brought the mace down on the fallen knight's helm three times before the other stopped trying to get up. Whether he'd killed the man or just stunned him, he didn't know.

Again, something caused his balance to shift, and a grating noise reached his ears. Something had gone in at an angle under the back edge of his left pauldron. He felt no pain, which ordinarily would mean the point hadn't gotten through, but Tiny had used the Dragon's Heart potion before and knew he probably wouldn't feel anything even if it had. Reacting on pure instinct, he spun clockwise and swung at the captain, who had moved in behind him.

His subordinate tried to step back, but Tiny's speed was superhuman, and even the knight's training and armor wasn't enough to make up the difference. The mace struck a glancing blow, but with the Black Duke's massive form behind it, it was enough to make the captain stumble. The next strike stunned his opponent, but Tiny was unwilling to kill the man, so he dropped the mace and caught the other man's arm. As he had done before, he twisted until he felt a pop, and the captain began to scream—then, he repeated with the other arm.

Ordinarily, even with his size, such a feat wouldn't have been easy, but with the potion enhancing him, the wounded man didn't have a hope of fending him off. "Where are the elves?" demanded the Royal Marshal, but the captain wouldn't answer. The knight was still painfully conscious, but very likely the magic clouding his mind wouldn't allow him to betray his new master. Tiny fought down a bloodthirsty impulse, then stalked off in the direction the captain had come from.

Ahead, he caught the sound of metal on metal, and he sped up. After turning the next corner he saw the rest of the command squad moving down the street with purpose. Jogging, he caught up to them. "Where are you going?" He hoped they hadn't met the elves yet, or he'd likely be in for another fight.

Fortunately, they turned to him without drawing arms. "Captain Jeremy told us to secure the cellar of that tavern," answered one of the men.

"There's an elf sorcerer in there," Tiny responded. "Captain Jeremy fell under their influence, as did two of your fellows. Go back and render aid. I had to hurt them pretty badly. Under no circumstance should you believe anything they say, not until I find the one controlling them. Keep them under guard."

"Where will you be, Your Grace?" asked the knight.

Tiny pointed at the tavern. "Probably in the cellar. Don't follow me. For whatever reason, I seem to be the only one immune to their charms."

"Sir! You can't go in there alone!"

"I can and I will. I don't have much time. If I don't come out in half an hour, barricade the building and set it on fire," ordered the duke. Then, ignoring his men's complaints, he headed straight for the place they'd pointed out to him. A painted sign near the front door proudly proclaimed its name, both in script and with a picture, 'The Blue Pony.'

Tiny paused just outside the door and let his body go still for a moment. The Dragon's Heart potion also heightened his senses, and if he paid attention, his hearing was good enough to hear things as subtle as the beating hearts of those in hiding. It took a few seconds to tune out the other sounds in the area, but then he heard it, the quickened breathing of someone waiting in ambush. There was one, no, it was two—there were two men waiting for him on either side of the front door.

Supernatural speed aside, if he stepped through that doorway, he would almost certainly be struck by whatever weapons they had waiting. Depending on their plan, his armor might be sufficient, but it had seen better days, and his breastplate was dented and even torn in places. Glancing around, Tiny decided the top railing of the fence that served as a decorative boundary for outdoor seating would be the perfect tool. He grabbed hold of it, and with a sudden jerk pulled one end loose, nails and all. It was a simple matter to lever it up and down until the other end came free.

The heavy board was eight feet in length and perfectly square. At least four inches thick, it was a formidable piece of lumber, and when he ran forward, holding it like a lance, it smashed through the protective wooden shutters covering the tavern's main front window. Glass and wood shattered as he withdrew and swung the wood post like a club to clear out more space. Then, he dropped his makeshift tool, took hold of the mace, and entered through the door.

The thing about smashing windows was that it made people look and refocus their attention. If you made a sudden opening in one, people expected you to use it, not enter through the perfectly clear doorway that you should be trying to avoid. Tiny came in to find the man on the left facing the window and the one who had been on the right was already moving to flank the other side of the window. Both were surprised when he appeared in the doorway and smashed the right-hand ambusher in the face with his mace. The one on the left died only a second later.

The men looked to be civilians, probably thralls to the elf in the cellar, and seeing them dead didn't make Tiny feel any better. It just stoked his rage.

One of them was holding an arming sword that had been obviously salvaged from one of the Iron Knights. Tiny picked it up and sheathed it in his empty scabbard, then he started looking for the cellar stairs. As expected, he found them in the main storeroom to the right behind the bar. He paused and listened.

There were numerous people below, though whether they were elf or man, he couldn't say. Either way, they'd all be trying to kill him. A flutter in his chest told him it wouldn't be long before the potion ran out. *I've got ten minutes left at best.*

His course of action was never in doubt. Even one elven magic user could spell doom for the battle. They'd subverted his knights once and now had almost done so a second time. Opening his potion case, he took out a second black vial.

The Iron Knights carried only one each, for emergency use only, but command had its perks. Janice wouldn't have approved of him having it, but he hadn't asked for permission. The knights were taught to immediately use a regeneration potion when the Dragon's Heart potion began to run out. The reason for that was that it put an incredible strain on the body, and even in training situations, the warriors often discovered they'd broken or dislocated their own bones while fighting with alchemical enhancements. Even if they hadn't, their bodies were bruised and in bad shape.

Will had told him once that a second Dragon's Heart potion wouldn't last as long. Rather than an extra thirty minutes, it would likely be half that. Worse, the strain that a second potion would put on the body had a high chance of leaving the user dead once it wore off. Tiny popped the stopper and downed it, then removed the final two potions from his case. Moving the mace to his left hand, he tucked one vial in between his teeth and kept the other in his right hand.

Then, he went to the top of the stairs.

There was no door at the bottom, and the part of the cellar he could see from the top was well lit. The people below were taking good care to remain out of sight, though. Tiny's heart was pounding in his chest, and all the veins in his face had turned black. Reaching back, he found something lodged in his backplate and pulled it free—an axe with fresh blood decorating the edge—his blood. Dropping it to the floor, he rechecked the potion in his hand. It had a red seal around the neck, identifying it as alchemist's fire. He started to go ahead with his plan when something better occurred to him. Walking back to the bar, he found two large bottles of spirits, then smiled.

Returning to the cellar stairs, he threw both bottles down, then followed with the alchemist's fire. The enchanted red seal around its neck made sure it broke, and the instant its contents met fresh air, it blazed into white flame. By itself, it would have easily started a fire to burn down the building, but the alcohol greatly accelerated the spread.

He had planned to run down and toss the vial at his enemies, but this was much better. Seeing the fire spread, he stepped back and eyed a large cask of ale. If he could roll it over, the top of the stairs it would be difficult for anyone to escape. The fire would take five or ten minutes to really get going, and the elf and whoever was with him would certainly try to get out.

Before he could do anything, the flames parted—no doubt as the result of some spell—and men with a variety of weapons began charging up the stairs.

Tiny would have loved to let them live, but the magic user controlling them wasn't about to allow that. Like madmen, they hurled themselves at him. Drawing the sword he had found with his right hand and using the mace in his left, the Black Duke beat them down. Cutting and smashing, he sent them tumbling into their comrades. Some fell into the flames on either side of the steps, screaming as their clothes caught fire, while others were fortunate enough to avoid the points of the weapons below and get back up again.

Feverishly, they fought to climb and clear the way, and even with the Dragon's Heart potion raging in his blood, Tiny felt pity for them. Eventually, one hooked his ankle with a poleaxe, and he fell. Although Tiny rolled and was back on his feet a second later, the desperate men were now all around him. It was then that the slaughter began in earnest. And make no mistake, it was a slaughter, not a fight.

Moving with speed and precision, Tiny cut and stabbed. Armored as he was, he didn't bother dodging, and he parried only when it was convenient. Swords and axes glanced away from the steel plate covering his body while his unarmored foes suffered terrible injuries. The luckiest fell with wounds that wouldn't allow them to continue fighting—the rest died painfully.

Things proceeded like that for several minutes, when suddenly Tiny found himself facing an elven warrior in elf-steel plate. They were visor-to-visor, and when Tiny pushed his foe away he saw the elf's sword was bright with blood. It had already pierced him once without him even noticing. Still, he felt no pain.

Only a few civilians were left, so the elven warrior was his main concern. Behind his foe, he could see the cellar stairs, and another elf was on it, still only part way up. The other elf was dressed in an austere dark blue robe. Tiny marked him as the one probably controlling the townsfolk that were attacking him. He threw himself forward, hoping to surprise the elf warrior with sheer speed.

Tiny's opponent reacted with confident grace. Unable to match the Black Duke's sheer size and mass, the elf took a half step to one side and used his hand and foot to trip him and send him sprawling to one side—or that was the intent. Tiny stumbled, but experience saved him as he had half expected the maneuver. Turning, he caught a large ale cask with his left hand and shoved off, recovering his balance before he fell. His sword swung back to strike the elf's leg, but the swing lacked enough power to do much. The elf-mage emerged from the stairwell and moved back to the opposite side of the storeroom.

His heart was pounding in his ears, and despite the second potion, Tiny felt his strength beginning to flag. It hadn't been long enough, but he'd suffered numerous wounds and had probably lost a considerable amount of blood. The fact that he was beginning to feel weak despite the potion meant he was close to collapse.

Two more exchanges with the elf-knight proved unfruitful. His opponent had both skill and experience, not to mention incredible quickness and dexterity. If Tiny had been fresh and rested, facing him in a one-on-one duel, he probably could have bested him, but war never worked like that. If the elf was foolish enough to let him get into a grapple, he might still win by pinning his enemy down and using his strength and size advantage to keep the elf down while he stabbed through a gap with his rondel dagger.

But he already knew the elven warrior wasn't that stupid. They'd both figured out how the fight was going and how it would almost certainly end. Despite the Dragon's Heart potion, Tiny was leaking blood from dozens of wounds he hadn't noticed earlier. The elf only had to hold him off for a minute or two longer and nature would take its course. Even if he could get his wily foe into a grapple, the mage would then have an easy opportunity to hit him with a spell.

A plan formed in his mind. Edging around the room, he deliberately tried to get closer to the mage, but as expected, the warrior blocked his path, and as their positions shifted, the mage would adjust to stay behind his guardian. Tiny repeated that pattern twice before exploiting it. The elven fighter couldn't see behind himself, and so was subconsciously relying on Tiny's movements to inform him of where his friend was. With a helm on, his eyes were hard to see, so Tiny jerked his head slightly and started to move left, even though the mage hadn't shifted in that direction.

When the bodyguard moved to follow, he turned right and threw the mace as if an opportunity had suddenly presented itself. The elf leapt back to intervene, using his body to block the thrown weapon—a weapon that had been thrown at nothing. The mage had already moved in the other direction to stay behind his protector—a protector that had now jumped aside—leaving him exposed.

Tiny's blade had gone into motion even as the other warrior moved, and it swept across and down, cleaving into the mage's shoulder and partway into the torso. It stuck when he tried to remove it, but it didn't matter. The mage was dead. His goal was accomplished.

The Black Duke had nothing left to defend himself with, but it hardly mattered. Defeating the elven knight was unnecessary. With the elven spellcaster removed, there was nothing left to prevent Tiny's men from finishing their task. The battle would be won, whether he was there to see it or not. The strength was already leaving his body as he heard the elf-warrior shout in dismay. Something hit him hard under the chin, slamming his helm back and breaking the clasp that held his visor shut. Tiny felt something snap, and he fell sideways.

It had been his own mace that had struck him. The elf had snatched it up and was already swinging it at him again, this time aiming for Tiny's exposed face. The Black Duke smiled at his opponent, showing bloody teeth and cut lips as he sagged to the floor. He'd have saluted his foe, but his arms seemed to be made of lead, and there was no time anyway. Two and a half pounds of forged steel hit him square in the mouth, and the world went red, then black.

He'd expected nothingness, but instead light returned, and Tiny found himself in an unknown place, though it felt familiar. The light was so bright he couldn't see, but it gradually dimmed as a dark figure approached. It was a man, and for a moment he hoped it was his friend. "Will?"

"No, I'm afraid not." The voice was that of a stranger, and now that the light had become bearable, Tiny could see that the man had dark hair and a sharp, aggressively cut beard. Black leathers with blood-red trim and accents gave the man a dangerous look.

"Where am I?" asked Tiny, but he was afraid he already knew. His memory of recent events was beginning to return to him. He didn't feel any malice from the newcomer, but there was only one answer that made sense. "Marduke?" He sighed. "I suppose I've seen too much blood for the Mother to take me."

The Lord of the Underworld grimaced. "I hear that entirely too often. Does no one pay attention in church? Even the confusing doctrines of your faith teach that I escort everyone to the afterlife, whether they've been good or bad."

"You're taking me to Hell, right?"

"There is no Hell, unless you want there to be, but I don't recommend it."

Tiny frowned in confusion. "But that's where you're from. You're the ruler there, aren't you?"

The other man rubbed his face tiredly. "This really gets old. No, and before you say anything else stupid, I'm not evil either—well, at least no more evil than you are. Everyone thinks Penny is all goodness and light, but trust me, if you ever saw her angry, you'd realize I'm the nice one."

"Penny?"

"Temarah. I wish for once someone would invent a religion that could get the names right." The stranger held out his hand, and when Tiny took it, he helped him to his feet. "By the way, my friends call me Mordecai, so no more of that 'Marduke' business please."

"I'm dead." Tiny stared down at his hands, then glanced back up. "What happens next?"

"Well—"

"Jan!" interrupted Tiny. "She's going to be devastated. How could I leave her alone?"

Mordecai's face took on a wry expression. "She's going to be furious with you. I wouldn't want to be in your shoes when she catches up with you."

"Catches up? What does that mean?" asked Tiny, suddenly apprehensive. "We won, didn't we? Is she in danger?"

The god held up a hand to forestall Tiny's panic. "That was just a turn of phrase, and anyway, death is just an illusion. Trust me. We all share one soul. You'll see her again. But I didn't come here to philosophize. I thought you might want to see someone." A figure appeared, stepping out from behind Mordecai.

"Dad?"

"William?" Tiny's heart jumped, and his eyes went wide at the sound of his eldest son's voice. The man standing before him now was fully grown, though his son had been murdered as a teen, but his features were unmistakable. "How is this possible? How did you get so tall?" His arms had already gone around his lost boy.

"I thought you'd like to see me as I would have been, if—well, if I hadn't left."

The big man struggled to keep from crushing his son as his emotions overwhelmed him. "You didn't leave, you were taken from us. Gods! I've missed you so much!"

"I'll give you two some privacy to catch up," said Mordecai, stepping back. Meanwhile, they were now in a grassy glen. A table and chairs stood nearby. "Take your time."

CHAPTER 26

Flying over a city at war, Selene observed the battle through eyes that were more akin to the windows of a prison cell. Still trapped within the body of a dragon, she felt numb as Lognion's keen senses picked out details that should have made her feel… something. Her mind was still filled with the memory of Tabitha's burning home.

She'd grown up wishing she could be a real part of Mark Nerrow's family, and they had responded in kind. Lord Nerrow had been the nearest thing to a real father to her and Laina and Tabitha had made her feel welcome—like a true sister. The pain of Laina's death had never gone away completely, but to be directly responsible for murdering not just Tabitha, but her children and husband—it was too much to comprehend.

Selene had already considered herself well and truly damned, but this was too much. Even if she could escape her father's body, she couldn't face William. Not after incinerating the precious few family members he had left. Even if he could forgive her, she couldn't forgive herself.

It didn't matter that she hadn't been in control. She had been the one to unwittingly bring her father back from his well-deserved death. And Lognion *was* her father, as much as she hated it there was no denying that anymore. Dragon or human, it didn't matter. It had been his hand on the tiller throughout her childhood, his presence, his decisions, and ultimately his cruelty that had shaped her into becoming the woman she was now.

The dark of night offered no concealment from dragon eyes, and Selene watched the final conflict play out as Lognion circled high above. The eastern side was largely untouched, for it appeared the Terabinian forces had preempted the attack on that front, but an ugly battle was now playing out near the center of the city as Tiny and a sizeable number of the Iron Knights strove to eliminate a type of monster she'd never seen before. The western gates were ruined, and the field outside the city there was littered with the bodies of elves, men, and more of the strange, hulking monsters.

A strange cocoon of vines protected something large, and she recognized Emory's turyn in its creation. More turyn was present inside, and as Lognion focused his attention on the thorny egg, she could see traces of turyn from two distinct individuals leaking from within. One matched Emory, indicating he had taken refuge within the living defense, but the other belonged to someone else. *Tabitha?*

"His sister!" bellowed Lognion in a voice that was more roar than words. He had little care for whether he alerted the people below to his presence. "She wasn't at home, then. How fortunate that we stumbled upon her here."

Father, no! She yelled within the skull they shared.

She could feel his delight as he addressed her in return. *You should already be gone. Remaining to watch this hunt only hurts you. You know her fate is inevitable, and after I swallow her down, I will find the others—all of them.* Lognion waited, and when she didn't respond, he continued, *Perhaps you had some small hope that some of her family wasn't home, as she wasn't. You should know me better, or have the claws and scales made you forget? I am not careless.*

I will spend years making certain they're dead. Every living relative that bears even a drop of William's blood will perish. Root and branch, I will burn them out. But never fear, per our agreement, Oliver will be spared. A sense of evil glee washed over her, making Selene's soul itself feel dirty. *Now it is time to burn this annoying bug I missed before.*

Emory Tallowen is there, interjected Selene. Her brain was finally beginning to work again. *You promised not to hurt my people. He's one of my subjects.*

I said I'd leave them alone unless they tried to protect one of William's blood. That dome of vines is obviously a protective shell. His life is forfeit.

She felt the dragon's body shift, angling forward as Lognion adjusted his wings, preparing to dive. Again, she fought him, but as before, her struggles were for naught. Her father's will was as iron. Together, they descended with frightful speed, but this time, instead of hovering, the dragon landed and inspected the thorny cocoon up close. Then, he reached out and nipped at it with massive jaws, tearing the vines apart with almost gentle precision.

Inside, Selene could see Emory's unconscious body, along with a strange, monstrous form that must have belonged to Tabitha. At the same time, she could feel her father's malice building as he savored the moment. He inhaled, and she felt intense power building in his chest as he prepared to burn them both to cinders and ash.

All her life, Selene had protected herself against her father's cruelty with logic and reason, carefully controlling her emotions. She'd had no choice; it was that or collapse into madness. She'd also known it was what he wanted, training her to always choose according to reason while ignoring the dictates of her heart. Once, she had believed it to be a critical skill for a ruler, something he had taught her out of some deeper concern for the future of Terabinia, but later she'd learned it was nothing more than a game to him.

Logic told her to hold on, to keep suffering. That sometime later she might have another chance to salvage some good or undo the damage her father was doing—but she no longer cared. She'd lost almost everything already. There was no place left in her for hope for the future. Lognion was right. She was only staying to suffer. Perhaps deep down she thought that the pain was some form of atonement, but no longer.

You were right, Father, she announced, putting emphasis on the last word.

The dragon paused, sensing a shift in her mood. *Tell me, Daughter. It would please me to know if you truly learned before your final moment.*

I always wanted your approval, even as I hated you, she responded. *Even this drawn-out misery has been some misguided attempt to impress you, but I finally understand.* After a brief pause, she finished, *I am your daughter, your true heir, and I no longer give a damn what you think.*

With that final announcement, she threw open the green door that led to freedom—and dissolution. The chains that bound her soul to her phylactery, to the mortal plane, cracked and fell apart as the enchantment sustaining them unraveled. No more was she an immortal lich. Now she was only herself, a dying wizard, a woman with only her heart and her desire left—with a will that had been forged by years living as a soul without a source. She might be dying, but in that moment, she truly was a fourth-order wizard.

Lashing out, she seized control of the dragon's body and turned away from Tabitha and Emory. *This ends now,* she declared.

Lognion struggled, and pain lanced through her as Selene felt her very soul start to rip from the strain of their conflict. *You cannot win. This is pointless,* he told her. *Even if you could contain me, your victory wouldn't last. After your passing, I will simply resume what I was about to do.*

For as long as I am here, you will do nothing. What you do after is nothing to me, for I won't exist, but you—you will live with the knowledge that I bested you, that for as long as I lived, you were the lesser. In spite of the pain it caused her, she bore down on Lognion's soul, tightly crushing it into a tiny space. She did it not for some advantage, but merely because she knew how much it would hurt. *I hope you like feeling small, because that is what you truly are,* she told him.

At the same time, she could feel him in a way she never had before. Without the enchantment binding her soul to the phylactery, she was no longer untouchable. William had once described the sensation to her, from the time when he and Laina had accidentally let their souls touch and intermingle. What had he told her then? That all souls were one? Or that they would become one? Did that hold true for dragon souls too?

It didn't matter. She understood the truth now. She'd spent her life wanting to deny their connection. Finding out that Lognion had been a dragon all along had merely been a convenient excuse to deny her parentage. Dragon or human, brilliant leader or cruel sadist—he was her father. She owed much of what she had become to his influence, but that didn't mean she had to accept his philosophy or follow his path. *I am the daughter of the dragon, and I will choose my own way.* Her resolution rang out like a bell within her soul.

Lognion's thoughts were inside her now, no longer separate. The slick, oily malice, the evil of his existence was part of her, but it no longer felt foreign, or evil. It simply was. *Am I changing? Am I becoming him, or is he becoming me?*

Did it matter? Even then, she felt reality nibbling away at the fringes of her existence. Only her stubborn will kept the end at bay. The current stalemate couldn't last forever. Would she see Laina if she died? Had her best friend wondered something similar in her last moments? She'd died in a similar way. Will had described the painful moment to her, along with his own self-doubts, *"Sometimes I wonder if she's still there. I hear her voice, and sometimes we converse. It makes me wonder which of us truly survived."*

The Mother, Temarah, had already told her she was damned. Her soul wouldn't be welcome when she finally died. Only nothingness awaited her. The biting cold eating away at her soul only confirmed what the goddess had said. At the same time, she could acutely feel the agony her pressure was inflicting on Lognion. She felt the pain just as he did, and it wouldn't end until one of them gave in—or perhaps not until she finally vanished. As their souls continued to intermingle, she was more and more becoming a dragon at war with herself.

Then again, perhaps that was what she had been all along.

Live or die, there was only one way to save those she loved. That was the true difference between them. Selene fought for family, for her people, but Lognion only fought for himself. Opening her heart, she embraced her father's tortured soul, ending the struggle.

Rage flashed through her, consuming everything as he took control once again, screaming, *I am Lognion. I am the dragon!* Their jaws opened, and a roar emerged with such volume and ferocity that it seemed to shake the world. *I am eternal,* he repeated mentally.

But then Lognion's legs went weak, and he sank to the ground. His mouth opened, and the dragon's voice emerged. "No. I am the Daughter of the Dragon. Today I die, and you die with me, as you should have millennia ago."

What? Lognion's panic flared up. *What is this?* He could no longer feel his power, the ineffable essence that refused to die. The raging fire of an undying star that had fueled his existence was now gone. A cold wind blew through his heart, and their conjoined soul began to disintegrate.

"This is death," she told him in a deep, rumbling voice. "Enjoy the novelty."

The dragon's eyes closed, and its head settled to the earth as its breathing stopped and its massive heart slowed to a gentle stop. For the first time, Lognion knew peace, and Selene didn't mind the nothingness that was beginning to swallow her up. It would be better than remembering what she had lost. Darkness was a warm and welcome blanket.

***

Her Grace, Janice Shaw, lady of the realm and currently an imposter acting as the queen of Terabinia, had abandoned her duty. Some minutes after her husband had switched places with his demon-steel golem, she had sat motionless. Staring at the impossible damage the nearly indestructible construct had suffered only reinforced her feeling of impending doom. No man could withstand the forces that had wrought such destruction, yet she had willingly allowed John to step into the eye of the storm.

Her hatred for the elves still burned strong within her, but she was about to lose the love of her life. Things had been tense between them after their son's death, but she still loved him. Was vengeance worth it? Over the years, she had come to accept the painful fact that she'd lose her husband long before her own death. Watching him age over the last fifteen years had made that clear, but it also made plain how precious those years were. She didn't want to squander the time they had left.

And now she had let him walk alone into war's hungry maw, knowing he would almost certainly die.

Those thoughts had quietly built within her, until at last she jumped to her feet and went running from the room, leaving the messengers, couriers, and servants who attended her behind. They called out to her as she ran, and some tried to follow, but when her feet were no longer fast enough, she cast a force-travel-disk and began skimming along as fast as her skill would allow, and though she was only a second-order wizard, Janice's magical skill was considerable. She zipped down the palace corridors almost too quickly to be identified, slowing down only to turn corners and open doors.

She had a specific destination in mind, a destination unknown to most and classified as a state secret under the name 'Project Chrysalis.' The project involved building teleport beacons at numerous secret sites scattered across Terabinia and Darrow, or what was now commonly referred to as Greater Terabinia. The locations were primarily chosen for strategic defense purposes and included all major cities and important coastal cities—anywhere the queen might want to send troops on short notice.

Many of the sites were still under construction, as teleport beacons required extensive work and expensive materials to build. Cerria and Myrsta had both had public beacons built, although the term 'public' was a bit of a misnomer when only a mage could use them, but they were known to everyone, and anyone could pay to use them. Selene had set up a special department to oversee the two public beacons and set fair prices so that private citizens and traders could pay reasonable rates for transportation between the two major cities.

Project Chrysalis would almost certainly become public knowledge with time, especially now that it had seen its first use, transporting thousands of soldiers. The secrecy was primarily intended to provide an additional advantage of surprise, as well as to make it less likely for outside interests to try and sabotage the effort. Selene and Janice had already worked on plans to transition the private government project to public use once secrecy was no longer possible. The economic gains from the fast trade between Cerria and Myrsta had already shown themselves to be massive, and the royal coffers were overflowing with the additional taxes collected. Expanding to a system that allowed fast trade between all major ports and cities would yield benefits they had no way to calculate yet.

For now, all Janice cared about was reaching Nerril as quickly as humanly possible. She raced for the city center. Cerria had been rebuilt after a significant portion of the city was destroyed during the vampire assault decades ago. The central square had been rebuilt again when Selene had started the project to build teleport beacons in both Cerria and Myrsta. The army had relocated its main garrison to a complex that took up a full city block bordering the northern side of the central city square. That had been done on purpose, for an underground passage had been built connecting the marshalling grounds to a large, open room beneath the teleport beacon. This allowed the military to use the same beacon as the connecting point for the capital; they simply had a secret location beneath it for arrivals and departures.

Janice made it there in minutes and streaked past the guards, stopping only to identify herself for the Driven who might conceivably interfere with her using the beacon if they didn't recognize her authority. Reaching the center of the room, she cast the teleport spell as quickly as possible. The wizards entrusted with operating the beacons for Project Chrysalis all utilized specially enchanted key tokens. Tabitha's husband James had been instrumental in creating the tokens and the system of encrypted keys. Each user had a token that would work only for them, and the user was required to add one of several extra runes when used, runes that would signify whether the beacons were being accessed normally or under duress. Depending on what they added, the system would record their usage, identity, and might even potentially disable the entire teleport network.

Janice did not have a token. Acting as queen, she was one of only three people who had been given knowledge of a special rune sequence that would allow use of the beacon without a token. The other two were Selene, and James, since he was the architect of the system.

After casting her spell, she reappeared at the central hub for Project Chrysalis, a secret military site that had been built in a nearly inaccessible location in the mountains near Barrowden. An intersection of ley lines there made powering the beacon a trivial matter, and the remoteness made it difficult to attack using conventional modes of travel. The pass leading to it was unusable except during the warmest parts of summer, and the hub had been built underground using earth elementals.

She wasted no time there. The guards and sorcerer posted at the platform tried to ask questions, but they knew the face of their queen, and when she ignored them, they didn't press her. Casting a second teleport spell, Janice sent herself to the hidden staging area near the city of Nerril. Again, she ignored the few men left on guard there and immediately headed out, speeding through the night toward the city itself, three miles distant.

A night-vision spell made it possible for her to see as she sped down the hidden path and onto the road. Her turyn was low, as teleport spells were energy intensive, but she removed an elixir of turyn from a pouch at her side, wishing for the millionth time that Will had given her a limnthal like the third-order wizards had. Despite their closeness, he had been unwilling to bend the tradition, and not even the queen had dared to cross him on the matter, though none of them knew of a reason that it shouldn't be done.

Downing the potion, she felt her energy return to middling levels. Being only second-order it took her longer to absorb and replenish her reserves from ambient turyn, so keeping a supply of the elixirs had been something she'd started doing many years ago, and today she was glad of it. She had no time left to be wasted. Speeding along the road, she took a second elixir to top herself up and offset the losses from pushing her travel-disk spell beyond its regular, more efficient speeds.

She entered Nerril through the eastern gate, and although it was the side of the city that had mostly been spared, she still saw signs of fighting, passing the occasional dead body, be it knight or abomination. From the sounds, the main conflict was up ahead, west of her. That was where she would find John. *If he's alive, he'll be in the thick of it. Damn his sense of duty.* She made a point of not thinking about the fact that she'd allowed him to go.

Minutes later, she found the first squad of knights, and after they recovered from the shock of seeing the queen, they offered to escort her to the central command location, presumably where the Royal Marshal was coordinating things. Janice had no time for walking, or even running. After listening to a quick set of directions, she sped off alone.

Along the way, she did encounter one of the abominations, but she never slowed. Gliding to the opposite side of the street, she sped past, sending a force-lance at the creature. The spell didn't do much damage, but she didn't wait around to see; she was already speeding onward. Only one goal occupied her mind, finding John.

Smoke was billowing from the doors and windows of the tavern, and a small crowd of townsfolk stood around it. Most of them held weapons in hand, but none of them threatened her. Likely they didn't even recognize the face she wore, but seeing the magic propelling her along, they quickly moved out of her way. Janice approached a pair of men before they could avoid her and addressed them directly, "What happened here?"

"I'm not sure," one of them started to answer.

The other man was more sure of himself. "We were taking shelter when someone came in, an elf, and his orders seemed to make sense, but now I'm a bit confused."

The smoke coming from the building made her nervous, so Janice wasn't feeling patient. "Is there anyone still inside? What happened to the elf?"

"He's dead. A knight came in and they fought. He set fire to the cellar, and we tried to get out." The man rubbed his forehead. "He killed a lot of people, and the elf, but I think he's dead. If he isn't, the fire will take him for sure—"

"Where is he now?" she demanded.

Both men pointed toward the smoke-filled tavern, and Janice had her answer. Ignoring them, she cast a water-breathing spell on herself and sped into the smoke-filled doorway. Despite not needing to breathe, the smoke stung her eyes, and between the pain and the way her eyes watered it was difficult to see anything. She also immediately regretted the water-breathing spell. It worked by storing a magically compressed air supply within the upper airways, but it also prevented normal speech. She couldn't call out, so if her husband was still conscious, he wouldn't know she was searching for him.

They mentioned the cellar, she reflected, heading straight past the bar and into the rooms beyond. She found no one in the kitchen, but the storeroom was right next to it, and she found a multitude of bodies there. If she'd been walking, she would have tripped, for they were all over the floor. Dismissing the travel-disk, she stepped down and then knelt, trying to get her head below the smoke so she could see. Crawling and using her hands to search among the dead, she found more townsfolk and a lot of blood. Most of the bodies had suffered grievous wounds and in some cases were entirely missing limbs.

She found a man—no an elf—in what had previously been a high-quality robe, but the sword still buried in his chest had spoiled it. It wasn't John's sword, but it definitely belonged to one of the Iron Knights. Janice's anxiety worsened as she feared she might be close to finding the wrong knight.

Her hand found metal, and her eyes saw legs encased in steel greaves. It was one of the Iron Knights, and by the size of the limbs she knew it had to be John. Moving up his body, she would have cried out upon seeing his bruised and bloody flesh through the terrible holes in his armor. The breastplate had been torn open in the middle, and she could see the broken end of a rib poking out. Black veins spiderwebbed across the ravaged flesh, making it clear he had used potions to keep fighting despite the injuries.

You idiot! she cursed mentally. *Why didn't you leave this to someone else?* She already knew why, and she probably would have made the same decision herself, but in that moment she didn't care. Fury and fear had robbed her of rationality. Was he alive? It didn't seem possible, and the more she saw of his body, the less likely it became. Her husband had been hacked, cut, and stabbed in multiple places, and she couldn't even see the other side of him. The visor of his helm was bent and stuck open, and within she could see that his face was a ruinous mess. John's beautiful features were practically unrecognizable.

Along with the thick smoke, flames were also jetting up from the cellar stairs, and even the floor beneath her was hot to the touch. It wouldn't be long before the floor collapsed and the ground level of the tavern became an inferno. Dead or alive, she had no intention of surrendering her husband's body to the flame.

A flat plane of force would be simplest, and she already knew an appropriate spell, but it would require rolling his body over since there was no gap between him and the floor. An air spell could lift him up, but it would buffet his body, and if he was still alive it might be enough to kill him all on its own. There was no time for planning, and the heat was growing worse, so Janice compromised. Using both spells, she briefly lifted his body, then used a force spell to create a flat plane beneath him. John's body experienced a brief jerk from the initial motion, but afterward she was able to move him without doing any further harm.

Moving quickly, Janice got to her feet and navigated back to the main door, towing John's massive body behind her. Some of the confused townsfolk were still outside, watching, but as she moved to put more distance between herself and the burning building, an armored form stepped out.

It wasn't steel armor. A faint difference in its sheen, as well as something about the sound it made as the warrior moved, made it clear that it was elven plate. Janice felt her anger rise as the elf stepped in front of her, somehow unafraid despite the evidence of her power as she used magic to move John's body.

"Put him down, woman," the elf ordered flatly, the breeze carrying the smell of blood, metal, and something undefinable toward her. Janice felt her heart speed up slightly as her body began to react in an uncharacteristic way. The elf wasn't using magic, but just the scent of him was doing something strange to her.

It didn't stop her rage, though. In fact, it made it far worse. Cognizant of the fact that she couldn't use force spells while supporting John on one, she instead used elemental magic. Prior research had shown that the enchanted armor the elves used was proof against most simple attacks, magical or otherwise, so she didn't bother with simple. Her fury required more anyway. Looking up at him, she felt her nostrils flare as her traitorous body tried to inhale more of the enemy's scent, and then she snarled and used an earth spell to open up the cobblestoned street beneath the elf's feet.

The elf fell two feet before she reversed the spell, and although he attempted to leap out, she drove him back down with an air spell as the earth and broken stone closed around his armored knees. Then, she used a small spell usually employed to start fires, creating a thumb sized flame on the ground in front of the warrior.

It wasn't a battle spell, being somewhat slow and less focused than something like a firebolt, but it was perfect for her purpose in this case, for the spell was designed with a variable input for turyn. Ordinarily, that would mean using a small amount of energy to light a fireplace or something similar, but Janice began pouring her power into the spell. The flame bloomed, growing rapidly.

The elf, now fearful, began yelling in his native tongue, but Janice ignored his cries. The intoxicating scent he gave off vanished as the fire surrounded the warrior, and while the armor's enchantment kept the flames out, the elf still had to breathe. Smoke would be filtered out, but the air was too hot for lungs, whether it was clean or not. Her eyes lit up with pleasure as she heard the elf choke, trying not to inhale. Meanwhile, the sustained heat began to cause the metal armor itself to reach temperatures that would burn skin.

Eventually, the elf's resolve failed, and he gave out an abrupt scream from the pain. It didn't last long, for when he inhaled, the superheated air ruined his lungs. Janice happily watched as her hated enemy was baked alive inside his magical armor. The sight sickened her, but at that moment she didn't care. The elves had taken her son, and now her husband from her. Given the option, she would see them all burn.

A small movement beside her caused her to turn, and she saw John's lips move. His nose had regained its shape, and she could see the swelling had decreased. Was he healing? Something sparkled, and she spotted bloody shards of glass near his mouth.

Her heart leapt into her throat.

Lowering him to the ground, she traded the force-plane for a force-dome to protect the two of them while she examined her husband.   Her fingers moved with frantic speed as she tried to remove his helmet and breastplate. Haste made her clumsy, and when the straps refused to cooperate, she used an air spell to cut the tough leather. The spell was meant for surgery, but it served her well in the absence of a knife. She continued on to remove his pauldrons, rerebraces, vambraces—every bit of armor she could easily access—and then she was forced to deal with the magically enhanced mail shirt that lay beneath the plate. Her air scalpel wasn't strong enough to cut the tough steel rings.

Reaching in from the bottom, she lifted the mail and the gambeson beneath while using a spell intended for metalsmithing and crafting to slowly heat and cut the mail along a line. It was slow going, and she suffered minor burns using the spell so close to her hands without any protection, but the only thing that mattered was making sure she didn't do any additional damage to John.

Though Janice was a second-order wizard, her skill and finesse with magic was among the best in Terabinia. Working with Selene, she'd learned a lot regarding the healing arts, though her greatest talents were primarily in spell design and artificing. Much of the work that had gone into the Black Duke's golem had been hers, but she had also helped with designing the human interfaces that enabled him to control the magical construct. She wasn't a doctor, but she was confident in her ability to provide first aid and heal a wide variety of injuries.

What she saw as she peeled back the mail and blood-soaked linen brought an involuntary gasp, and tears sprung up at the corner of her eyes. Her husband's flesh was torn and macerated in places where the mail had been driven through the gambeson and had ground into his skin. Where the skin was intact, it was crisscrossed by black veins, evidence that he was still under the influence of a Dragon Heart potion. She counted multiple stab wounds and could see that his ribs, clavicle, and sternum had all been broken.

He had already lost so much blood that his wounds seemed to have stopped bleeding and they weren't closing. Opening his mouth, she dug out more glass and discovered why his face had healed as she smelled the pungent odor of a regeneration potion. *He must have had it in his mouth,* she realized. Janice felt her throat tighten. *He was trying to live, despite his suicidal plan.*

And he *was* alive, barely.

But aside from the changes to his face, her husband's body wasn't healing. The wounds on his chest and elsewhere remained open. She took a moment to study the turyn around him. It wasn't the best way to assess a patient, since she could only see the energy in his skin and just above it, but it could provide a rough gauge for what might be happening.

What she could see wasn't encouraging. The influence of the Dragon's Heart potion was visible, but the turyn radiating from his body was barely more than what she would expect from inanimate stone. To someone with eyes sensitive to magic, he appeared dead, or nearly dead—his head showed a bit of energy, but even that was very subdued compared to normal.

Knowing the potions he'd taken, she had rough guess at what had happened. The Dragon's Heart potion had kept him going far longer than it should have and had exhausted his body's turyn reserves. She'd seen him train with them in the past, but this was well beyond what she would expect from what she'd seen then. That meant he'd either somehow surpassed the potion's limit through sheer stubbornness, or more likely he'd taken a second one. *Which he wasn't supposed to have,* she thought bitterly. The regeneration potion was working, but his body simply had nothing left for it to use. By the time it had broken in his mouth, it had been about the same as pouring it over a corpse.

Desperate, Janice tried matching his natural turyn frequency and pushing turyn into his body, but it didn't seem to make a difference. Tiny wasn't a wizard, and his body had never been trained to absorb turyn from the environment. Even if it had, she wasn't sure it would have responded given his current state. Her mind shut down, but she didn't stop. She examined the largest wound in the middle of his chest, then opened it to examine the flesh within. The mess was so terrible that she could barely understand what she was seeing, but she thought it had missed his heart. She tried closing the skin, though it felt like a waste of time given the damage inside.

Hopeless and despairing, she pushed more turyn at him, then tried closing smaller wounds. "Please, John, you can't die. Don't do this to me." Minutes passed as she continued attempting to heal him, but she knew her efforts were futile. "I'm sorry. I shouldn't have let you go. Please, you have to live." Her vision blurred, but she wiped away the tears and kept working. Would fixing some of the bones help? Maybe something was in the way.

She didn't know the right spells, though. She could set a simple fracture and she knew the spell to fuse bone ends together, but the damage to John's chest was extensive. There was an eighth-order spell that would allow her to see bones within the body, but she didn't have it memorized. She'd never even used it before. She fixed one rib, but the rest was beyond her. Choking back tears, she returned to trying to get some turyn into him somehow. "John, this isn't good. If you can hear me, you have to fight. You can't leave. Do you hear me?"

The turyn around his head seemed to have grown dimmer. "Someone find the Iron Knights!" she yelled without looking to see if anyone was near. "Get his men! There are healers with them."

A soft masculine voice spoke beside her. "Your Majesty, I've already sent men to find one."

Looking up, she saw a captain kneeling a few feet away. "Well, where are they?"

"I'm not sure, Your Majesty. A few of the Driven are with us, but their medical skills are limited. The Arcane Corps has a few well-trained wizard-physicians, but we've lost contact with them. Hopefully, we'll rejoin them on the other side of Nerril, but we're still fighting our way through these cursed beasts."

She needed help. She needed someone. Her husband was dying in front of her—she could see the turyn around even his head beginning to dim. Fighting the urge to scream, Janice kept trying, while tears trickled steadily down her cheeks.

CHAPTER 27

A warm light suffused the area, and Selene felt as though she was floating within a cloud as the darkness around her withdrew. *I'm dead, aren't I?* she thought idly. *This doesn't seem like the nothingness I was expecting.*

She waited, expecting her awareness to fade away, but nothing changed. Eventually, her thoughts began to wander, and naturally they turned to William, to Oliver, to Terabinia. Had she really defeated Lognion? What if he hadn't died? It was possible that she had passed and he had somehow stayed behind to reawaken. Even if he had passed away with her, what about the elves? Knowing nothing of the outcome was frustrating.

"Why am I still here?" Selene complained.

A gentle voice answered, "You surprised me."

Selene recognized it immediately this time. The Mother, Temarah. *No, she told me to call her Penny,* she remembered. "You said I would dissolve into nothingness."

"That was one possibility. I also said I would forgive you if you made the right decision," answered the Mother. "Please sit up. This conversation will be less awkward."

Realizing she had a body and was actually lying down, Selene did as she was asked. Rising to her knees, she found herself looking at the goddess, who was sitting in a similar position next to her. The floor beneath them seemed solid, although it was obscured by mist. For a moment, she felt like a child, sitting on the floor with a friend. "Shouldn't you be on a throne?" asked Selene. "This seems beneath you."

"I was born a commoner in my old life," said Penny.

Selene grimaced. "Even more reason for you to dislike me. Am I to be punished?"

"You think we are so different?" asked Penny.

"The circumstances of birth are probably the least of our differences."

The goddess nodded. "You aren't entirely wrong. I was a mother, and now the people of your nation worship me as a goddess of creation, life, and rebirth. While you—"

"—never had children. In fact, I murdered and enslaved the souls of children to give myself immortality," finished Selene. She no longer had any urge to justify her choices. "I had reasons I felt were important, but it's obvious to me at this point that I was rationalizing my own selfishness. Now I see you here and I realize that even hoping for dissolution was probably selfish of me." Lowering her eyes, Selene folded her hands in her lap.

"You wish to be punished?" asked Penny.

"It is what I deserve."

The goddess sighed. "You had good intentions, and you accomplished much good, but I won't play devil's advocate and pretend I agreed with your choices. Nor am I here to punish you." Selene waited without responding, so Penny continued, "I came to make an offer."

Selene finally looked up. "An offer?"

Penny nodded. "I won't let you disappear. The moment you chose to end the evil that kept you alive, I forgave you. Your soul will rejoin us, and a new life awaits you. I don't know what it will be, but given the one you just lived, I would say your chances of having a better experience this time are almost guaranteed."

"That is more than I expected."

The goddess shook her head. "That's not the offer. If you prefer—"

"Please," interrupted Selene. "I don't deserve anything. The most I would ask is to know whether my people survived, and whether William will be happy."

Penny's eyes took on a predatory expression, and a malicious gleam showed in them. "You ask for answers that will punish you. The soul is eternal, and death means nothing. Your release of the souls you were holding—that was important—but the death of your people, your friends, your family, that is not. They will return and live again, like you."

"I still would like to know," reiterated Selene.

"You ask for punishment," said the goddess flatly.

"I need to know."

"Your husband is gone already. His soul is cut off from me, and I can see nothing regarding him. I can only presume he has been devoured by the void." Selene flinched at the answer, so Penny paused and asked, "Is this the kind of knowledge you seek? Should I continue?"

Selene nodded silently.

"John Shaw, your Royal Marshal, is dying and his wife has abandoned her post in a failed attempt to save him. She will almost certainly follow him to the grave, and without a ruler Terabinia will ultimately lose the war. Your people will be enslaved, and the other nations of Hercynia will also fall in the years to come."

Selene frowned. "What about Tabitha, or the other wizards? Surely—"

"Dead," said Penny. "Lognion will kill them all, and he no longer cares to protect Terabinia. Once his vengeance is finished, he will depart and leave the humans to their fate."

"But—"

"No," interrupted Penny. "You failed. Lognion was correct. You've made an impression on him, but he will reawaken."

"How could you allow such suffering? You speak of the enslavement of all humanity."

"Misery for your people and a golden age for the elves who will restore Hercynia in the aftermath. Even this is not the end; the cycle will turn again. Mortal choices are by their very nature ephemeral. Lognion, however, will continue to act as he wishes, and at best, the good he does will be balanced by an equal amount of suffering."

Selene met the goddess's eye. "You created him! How can you be so cruel?"

"You do not understand dragons, or the reason for them," said Penny. "The alternative is far worse."

Anger flared in Selene's heart. "I understand enough to see that Lognion has more freedom than you. You claim to be good, while he is cruel and evil, yet you allow him to do whatever he pleases. Either you are too weak to stop him, or you are an accomplice to his wickedness."

"Would you like to know how I became like this, how my husband ascended to godhood?" asked Penny calmly. She continued without waiting, "Don't answer, for I will tell you regardless.

"In our universe, my husband grew too powerful, and not only did he wield magic and the positive powers that come from magic, but he touched the void. The power to destroy everything infected him, and in the push and pull between that and the forces of creation, he became steadily more powerful until eventually the universe died to birth him. The old creator was overthrown, and a new reality was born—*this reality*.

"But the same can happen again, if Mort and I allow it. That is why we have dragons."

Confused, Selene spoke up. "What? Who is Mort?"

"Mordecai, or Marduke as your people call him—he is my husband, or my other half depending on how you look at it. That part doesn't matter," explained Penny. "The important thing to know is that over the endless ages, individuals of great power still arise, and sometimes they go so far as to reach beyond the boundary and touch the void. When that happens, they begin to destroy everything. The universe begins to unravel. To stop that, they must either be destroyed before they become too powerful, or harnessed in a way that makes the universe stronger rather than weaker."

"Dragons?" asked Selene.

Penny nodded. "Lognion's ancestor was one such, and he came from a world of such massive creatures. There have been countless others, in various forms and bodies. They truly are as countless as the stars now, and each one expands the universe, but no matter how large it becomes, the void is always endless, while the light of creation is finite."

"So, they aren't all dragons?"

"Physically, no. Their original species doesn't matter at all, though Lognion and his ilk are the only ones I know of who pass the power on to their offspring."

Dozens of questions rose in Selene's mind, but she asked the most important question first, "Why are you telling me this?"

"You need to be informed if you're to make the choice," said Penny.

"What choice?"

The goddess leaned in, until they were almost nose to nose, then spoke softly, as though they were two girls passing secrets. "I despise cruelty. Lognion is repugnant, and destroying him isn't an option, but you've created another possibility. Live and take his place."

Selene's eyes widened. "Would he die instead?"

Penny shook her head. "No, you would have to absorb him. You already started the process. If you go back, instead of passing on, your souls will merge permanently." Bile rose in the back of her throat, and Selene blanched at the thought, but the goddess continued, "You've seen an example of this before, in your husband. He and Laina merged in a similar fashion."

"But he's not Laina," Selene protested. "This doesn't make sense."

"All souls are pieces of me," explained the goddess. "After death, they return to me. Instead of passing on, Laina's soul merged with Will's, but he remained dominant. The same is possible here, but the outcome is less certain. Laina loved her brother, whereas Lognion has no desire to give up his place."

"I have no desire to spend eternity watching his cruelty," said Selene.

"You would only rise to awareness occasionally if he remains in control," explained Penny. "But even in that worst case, you'd likely serve as a moderating influence. In the best case, you would be dominant, and *he* would be the one sleeping through the ages. It isn't as bad as it sounds."

"You're not the one being asked to meld with someone else," argued Selene.

Penny's eyes softened. "I already have. That is why you'll never see Mordecai and me at the same time."

"What?"

"I made a sacrifice to save him, but it cost me. The person I love most is the one I can never see again, for only one of us is awake at any given time and place."

Selene frowned. "You're saying you merged with your husband's soul, the same way Laina and Will did?"

"Reality was different back then, and it has changed yet again after we ascended, so the circumstances are slightly different," said Penny.

"Will talks to Laina sometimes," added Selene, "though she doesn't always reply."

"You, Will, his sister, even Lognion, you are all parts of a whole. I *am* the whole, as is Mordecai. Only one of us is aware at any given moment. The universe itself would have to divide in two for us to stand face to face again. What will happen to you might be far better. If you remain in control, then Lognion will be little more than an annoying whisper in the back of your mind," explained the goddess.

"So, I could see Will again?"

"If he still exists. He passed into the void. What happens to him now is very much in doubt."

Selene thought for a moment, then asked, "What do you think will happen?"

"I would not wish to give you false hope. Although this is rare for you, I have watched scenes like this play out countless times over the eons. Most perish and are never heard from. William was already on the path to dissolution or dragonhood, so it is possible he will survive, though still unlikely. Less than one in a billion successfully return—and this is not blind conjecture, this is based on an eternity of observation. Few have the strength of mind and spirit to retain their sanity and identity." Penny's voice communicated a deep sense of empathy and compassion.

Lowering her eyes, Selene stared at her hands. "So my options are—"

"Die and live again, as all people do. This life has not been kind to you, the next will surely be better—or alternatively—you can return and try to take Lognion's place. You cannot count on anyone else to save your people, your world, or your family. If you are willing to face eternity without closing your eyes, you may be able to save them yourself," said Penny.

"With the power of a dragon?"

"Eventually. That power is not as you think. Even victorious and in control, you will only be yourself. The power itself is not so easy to claim. With time you will have few limits, but in the beginning you will be relatively weak and there will always be the risk of being devoured by someone stronger who desires to assume your strength."

Selene raised her head, meeting the goddess's eyes with an even gaze. "Most of my life has been like that. I am the daughter of a dragon, after all. I do have one request, if it is possible…"

CHAPTER 28

Time passed—an instant, a day, a year? Selene had no way of knowing, she merely felt that it had, and though she had no recollection of it, she had survived a battle of some sort. A dream was fading from her mind, breaking into fragments that dissolved no matter how hard she tried to hold onto them. She'd spoken with someone. The Mother? It was hard to recall, but despite the muzziness of her head, certain things were clear to her. *I'm alive. Truly alive!*

She hadn't died. Her father had, and somehow, she had taken his place. *No, not dead. He may haunt me still,* she reminded herself, though exactly how she knew that, she wasn't sure. Opening her eyes, she was blinded by an intense light that was just beginning to fade. Her body, her old body, or rather Lognion's, was burning away, leaving her behind—her true self, or how she thought of herself, anyway.

It wouldn't have happened on its own, but she had asked for this. Hadn't she? *I wanted to be myself again,* she thought, though she wasn't sure who she had spoken to.

Everything seemed far away, including the most recent events. It felt as though she'd awakened from a nightmare, but rather than feeling drained, she was clear and calm. Renewed. She felt revitalized, and more herself than she had in many years. The world was crisp, and her experience of it was so powerful she could almost taste it. She could definitely smell it, for smoke and death were everywhere.

Taking a step forward, she looked down and saw her leg beneath what looked to be simple light-grey cloth. She was wearing her favorite attire, a simple dress made of tough yet well-spun wool. The length wasn't overlong, reaching only mid-calf and allowing her freedom of movement. It was the same dress she'd worn when pretending to be a nurse serving the Terabinian army. She'd longed for such utilitarian clothing often while serving as queen.

Focusing on the present, she examined the scene in front of her. A few quick diagnostic spells confirmed that Emory was in no danger of expiring. The regeneration potion had done its work, and his body was in a deep sleep. Tabitha was more difficult to assess. Her strange form didn't seem to be in danger of dying, but it was anyone's guess as to what the state of her mind would be when she awoke, or if she would awaken. Taking on such strange shapes and forms was risky. If it was too different, or if she stayed in it too long, Tabitha might lose her human identity, or even forget who she had been. It was one of the many reasons that shapeshifting magics were almost never practiced by human spellcasters. Not only was the magic unbelievably complex and difficult, but the side effects were hard to predict.

Most shapeshifting magic was done by the fae, who usually used wild magic rather than spells. Selene didn't know if there had been other third-order wizards with a natural talent like Tabitha's, so she had no idea whether the risks were the same. For now, there was little she could do. Using a quick earth spell, Selene created an earthen wall to block off the exposed portion of the protective cocoon. She couldn't afford to stay and guard them while others still needed her. Tiny was dying. While the details of her conversation with the goddess were already fading, she remembered that with an intense sense of urgency.

Around her were mainly the dead and dying. The fight had moved into the city of Nerrill, and while she likely could have saved the lives of a few that she passed by, her priorities wouldn't allow her to pause. Running toward the ruined gates, she regretted giving up the dragon form immediately. With wings, she could have flown, and with the dragon's keen senses, she would have likely found Tiny and Janice much quicker. *If he dies, it will be because of my selfishness for wanting to be human again.* The thought brought a short flash of guilt, but Selene pushed it aside. As a ruler, she already had a mountain of past choices and regrets to bury herself with, but one thing she had gained from her psychopathic father's upbringing was pragmatism.

You are my daughter, after all, came Lognion's voice in her mind. *The problems of the chattel are nothing to us.*

Shut up, old man, she replied immediately. It wasn't until a moment later that she wondered if she was just talking to herself or if it had actually been her father's ghost, but Lognion's voice didn't return.

She passed through the ruined gates and along the main street, and everywhere Selene saw evidence of the recent battle. Bodies were strewn about, as though tossed at random by the hand of a mad god, tired of his playthings. Some were dead monstrosities, but far too many were human, whether civilian or soldier. A quiet anger built in Selene's chest as she progressed, and being fully alive, she felt it more keenly than before. *They will pay for this.*

A flicker of motion from the edge of her vision was the only warning she got as a massive wooden beam swung toward her. She'd just passed a building and entered a street crossing, and her confidence nearly became her undoing as one of the abominations ambushed her. She failed to get a shield up in time, and only poor aim on the monster's part saved her from a crushing blow. Instead, the tip of the massive timber clipped her shoulder, breaking bones and spinning her around in a violent circle.

The pain was profound, stealing her breath away and wiping away all rationality for a moment. She hadn't felt anything like that in—decades—if ever. Selene had been undead so long she had forgotten what true pain was, not to mention the need for caution. Her body was vulnerable in ways it hadn't been for a long time. Stumbling, she fell, and when she looked up, the shadow of the beast was over her. It had dropped the makeshift weapon and was reaching for her with the delight of a starving man who'd found a fresh meat pie placed in front of him.

Reacting at last, she sent a reflex-cast force-lance slamming into the creature, but the effect was less than she'd hoped for. The thing's blubbery body absorbed the kinetic force of the spell with only minor damage, and it caught her in its grasp with hardly a pause. More pain shivered along her spine as Selene's fractured bones shifted. The world dimmed as consciousness threatened to leave her, but something deep within rose up. She snarled, her jaw clenched, and she fell back on some of her oldest and most familiar magic, an elemental water spell.

She pulled moisture from the air, and a circular blade of water appeared next to the creature's arm. In less than a second it had spun up to unthinkable speed before slicing into the rubbery flesh. Unlike the force-lance, it worked to devastating effect, cutting through the skin and sinewy tissues underneath like a surgeon's scalpel. Seeing the water blade's success, she created a second blade and took the abomination apart as though it were little more than a child's toy.

She'd learned from her disastrous lack of caution, so she quickly scanned the side street for more enemies before doing anything else. Twenty yards away, she saw a man crying over a child's limp form, but no threats were apparent. She'd fallen to the ground after cutting the beast apart, and thanks to her broken bones she wouldn't be able to stand. It wasn't a safe location for healing, but Selene didn't have any other options, so she got started.

As a lich, she'd built and rebuilt her dead form many times, as well as reshaping living bodies to disguise or alter her appearance, but being undead had put her at a remove from the sensations that came with truly being alive. After a quick succession of diagnostic spells, she attempted to realign her broken clavicle, sternum, ribs, and humerus all in one go without accounting for the pain that would inevitably result.

Blinding agony nearly rendered her unconscious, forcing her to choose a more moderate course of treatment. *I have to think of myself like one of my living patients,* she reminded herself, applying several nerve blocks. Pain wasn't just an inconvenience anymore; it could be dangerous in and of itself. Overwhelming her body's tolerance could send her into shock or even result in death. She wasn't sure what death meant for her now, but today wasn't the day to find out.

With steady determination, she set and aligned and fused her shattered bones, repaired torn ligaments and tendons, and then finally sealed up the cuts and lacerations. By sheer luck, none of her large blood vessels had been damaged, but the abuse had ruptured tiny veins all across her arm, back, shoulder and chest. Bruising was one of the most difficult and time-consuming things to heal, so much so that few healers had the skill. She was capable enough, but time was not her friend. Growling at the aching pain, Selene pushed herself up and back onto her feet again.

Everything hurt, but not to the point of stopping her. Ignoring the discomfort, Selene marched onward, this time with a steady pace rather than a headlong rush. Her caution paid off when she met another pair of the monsters a block further on. One lifted a heavy paving stone and threw it her way before both of them charged at her. She caught it with a quick point-defense shield and cut them apart with water blades when they closed on her. Knowing her enemy made them much easier to fight.

Walking as quickly as she could, it was hard not to hobble or limp along given all the aches and pains, but she managed, and eventually she came in sight of some of her knights. Alert, they spotted her movement and watched warily until it was apparent that she wasn't a threat, and by the time she'd come within speaking distance, they'd largely discounted her presence. *Of course, I look like one of the townspeople,* she realized. One of them gestured toward her, then pointed eastward in the direction she'd already been heading. "It will be safer that way. We think the city is largely in our hands beyond this point."

"Do you recognize me?" asked Selene without preamble.

"No, ma'am, should I?" asked the knight, displaying some courtesy despite the stressful circumstances.

Armored as he was, even with the visor up, she had little hope of identifying the knight either, but she had the advantage of seeing the coat of arms emblazoned on his surcoat. As one of the Iron Knights, it bore her colors, but knights from noble families (as most were) were allowed a small designator on the right shoulder. From early childhood, she had memorized them all, as did everyone raised within the nobility. While most commoners could be forgiven for ignorance regarding heraldry other than their own local lord, such was not the case for the upper classes.

Her gaze had already taken in the crest and her eyes met his with a surety that immediately communicated her importance. "Tibald," she intoned, stating his surname. "Your family will be proud you served in Nerril this day. I'm looking for Duke Shaw, or the queen, though I expect she may already be with him. Can you assist me?"

"Milady? Forgive me for not knowing how to address you," said the knight, realizing he was speaking to a noblewoman of unknown status and rank. "The battle still rages, I'm afraid His Grace is indisposed, and Her Majesty may not be free to meet with anyone for some time. If you'll provide me with your name, I'll try to find you an escort to…"

Selene held up a hand, cutting him off. "Forgive my lack of introduction," she began, "but I'm a special assistant employed directly by Her Majesty. I'm not at liberty to disclose the particulars, but I was told the marshal is in dire need of medical aid. There is no one in Nerril more experienced in the healing arts aside from the queen herself. If she is with the duke she will have need of me, and if she is not present, he will need my help even more."

The knight's expression froze, and his eyes studied her carefully. To his credit, his mind worked quickly. After a brief pause, he motioned her forward. "Follow me." The other soldiers moved aside, and he began leading the way for her. As he went, he said to one, "Notify Captain Devers, and have him join me where the marshal is being treated."

Recognizing the officer's name, Selene commented, "Sir Balin is a good man, despite what some think of his background." Captain Balin Devers was one of those who had risen to his rank through merit alone, having been knighted on the battlefield during the war with Darrow. She'd confirmed his new rank personally after the war.

"You know him?" asked the knight. After she nodded, he continued, "He can confirm your words then?"

"He will know me," she answered without further detail, and a few minutes later when they reached the site of a still-burning building, they were met by a number of knights and a large contingent of soldiers. She was led through and saw a number of wounded men being kept under close guard, and she spotted Captain Paryon among them.

Armored men stood in a square facing outward, forming a makeshift privacy wall. Two of them stepped aside to allow Selene and her escort inside, and there she saw Janice kneeling beside Tiny's broken body.

Captain Devers looked a question at the knight escorting her, then his eyes met hers, and he went still, confusion showing on his face. He glanced at her twin, then back at her.

At the same time, Janice looked up, and seeing the queen, she felt renewed hope. "Speak of this to no one," she ordered the captain and the younger knight who had escorted Selene. His face was just beginning to turn quizzical as he realized there were two identical women in front of him. He hadn't known the queen on sight before, but he'd made the connection quickly. "Keep everyone facing outward and erect a privacy screen as soon as you can. One of us will create an illusory barrier in a moment," added Selene.

The two men stepped out immediately, and Selene created a temporary sound- and sight-screen with a quick spell. She knelt beside Janice and began a series of diagnostic spells without waiting. She'd used the spells so many times in the past that she was able to talk as she worked, though she waited for Janice to speak first.

Janice's eyes showed desperation, and she ignored all the obvious questions she might have had. John was all that mattered now. "If anyone can save him, it's you. Just tell me what to do, and I'll assist any way I can."

Selene felt a cold despair as her spells gave specific information regarding the state of Tiny's body. The spells she used were the cutting edge of Terabinian medical research and showed a variety of information to her as overlays on top of the big man's body. She could see his bones and vasculature, the way blood was moving, and the temperature and oxygen levels of his core, head, and extremities. None of it was good.

To say that Tiny was alive was merely a technicality. His heart had stopped, and even if she forced it to beat it would do little good, for there wasn't enough blood left for it to pump. The tissues that made up his organs were already beginning to die from lack of blood, and his extremities were cold lumps of flesh that would soon begin to necrose. The only thing showing some life was the big man's head, as the effects of what was probably a regeneration potion somehow kept his brain alive, and it was doing that by using every bit of vitality and turyn remaining in Tiny's head and neck.

As always, Selene projected calm in her features and demeanor, but inwardly she quailed at what she saw. Relying on the clinical detachment she'd adopted while working with patients in the capital, she tried to prepare Janice. "He must've fought fiercely, but his body is too far gone, Janice. You should—"

"No!" shouted Janice. "You'll save him! I know you can do it!"

"Jan, you can see the state he's in, there's no way—"

"Don't fucking lie to me! Look at yourself and say that to me again. Don't let him die."

"Jan…"

Janice shook her head violently. "No! He's served you loyally through everything. Even when he had to march into Trendham against William—*your husband,* his best friend! You owe him, you owe me! I've done everything you asked and sacrificed far more than you should have asked of me. You'll save him and damn the cost."

"I can't—" began Selene.

"Make him like you."

"That took preparation, and sacrifices—human sacrifices. There's no time for that."

Janice glared back at her. "Then do something else. I've seen enough to know there are other possibilities—like Rob, or something similar."

Selene frowned. "You think he would want something like that? You know him better than that."

"I know enough to destroy everything. Think about that before you refuse," spat Janice bitterly. Her next words emerged in a cold hiss. "Save him."

Selene ignored the threat. She'd been threatened by far worse, and she knew Janice would regret her behavior later. "His body is mostly dead. Some of the things I've learned could keep him here, but he would suffer horribly. The best options left at this point involve soul-binding magics, and anything involving the soul requires consent."

"I'm his wife. I consent," answered Janice immediately.

"*His consent,*" replied Selene, motioning to Janice to move. "Sit on the other side. Before we can do anything, I need to stabilize what's left." She was already using a spell to rapidly cool the Royal Marshal's body and brain down to a temperature just a few degrees shy of freezing.

"But what…"

"Shhh!" hissed Selene, another spell-construct already forming above one of her hands. She finished the spell a second later and began a duplicate spell even as the first began working on one of Tiny's legs, sealing off the arteries and killing the nerves. Janice watched with a growing sense of horror as Selene began selectively killing and isolating the big warrior's limbs and then started on his internal organs.

"This is too much, you're destroying it all," complained Janice, though she made no move to stop her queen.

"His limbs were dying already, the same with most of his internal organs. If I'm to save anything, I have to isolate the healthy tissue.

There's no chance at all if we waste his dwindling resources trying to keep dead flesh alive." Her next spell stopped the heart, which had been spasming as it tried to pump the tiny amount of blood left in the big man's chest.

Janice started to protest, "That was—"

Selene cut her off. "I need blood. Ask for volunteers. Five or more at minimum since we'll need to test for compatibility." As she spoke, Selene was using yet another specialized water element spell to draw the remaining blood from the limbs and trap it within the much smaller vascular space she had isolated for the heart, lungs, and most importantly, the head. It wasn't enough, and the clock was ticking.

Janice was up and issuing a quick series of orders in mere seconds. The captain's voice rang out a moment later. "The Black Duke is dying but our queen can save him if someone has the right kind of blood. I need volunteers—now!" A pause came next, and then murmurs among the knights, but a soldier from the back stepped forward, and the noblemen were shamed by the example set forth by a commoner. More than ten were ready and willing to give blood for the Royal Marshal after just a short minute or two of discussion.

Selene showed Janice the spell construct for the initial blood test, and they began checking the volunteers one by one. The first was good, as were the third and fourth, so it appeared blood wouldn't be an issue, but Selene followed with a more comprehensive test, mixing the blood of each with a small sample she took from Tiny's tiny reserve. One began to clot after only a minute, leaving just two of the first volunteers tested as viable candidates.

It was enough, and time was too precious to test the other six men.

"Lay down, here and here," indicated Selene, pointing to the ground near Tiny's head. As soon as the men were prone, she put them to sleep and began the complex seventh-order spell that Dr. Morris had created for field transfusions. Though she had used the spell many times in the past, it wasn't something she'd learned to reflex cast, so it took her a couple of minutes to prepare, but when finished, blood began flowing between the men through invisible tubes in the air. When enough was present, she used another spell to compress the heart, creating an artificial beat to pump the new and old blood through Tiny's arteries and veins.

The regeneration potion was still active, and as blood began to flow, it started working again, drawing on Tiny's small amount of remaining turyn to heal not just his face and head but tissues and organs in his chest and neck. It was only making things worse at this point, though.

The great man's vital reserve was dwindling, and his source was only providing a trickle of turyn to replace what was taken. Selene watched with clinical detachment as her diagnostic spells showed her the disaster unfolding within her most loyal commander. Despite the drastic choices she'd already made, Tiny's life was fading away and there was no practical way to stop the action of the potions already in his system.

His options were narrowing with each passing second.

Healing and necromancy were two sides of a coin, two different perspectives on what was essentially the same magic. Up to that point, Selene had used spells that, while extreme, were still within what most wizards considered the medical tradition. Now she was about to cross the line—yet again.

Amongst the extant practitioners of the modern age, she was second to none but Grim Talek when it came to knowledge and skill in the healing and necromantic arts. The ancient lich had spent some time tutoring her in magic, but he hadn't shared much about necromancy, or the secrets to how he'd become a lich or created his vampire servants. No, she'd studied the gaps in his teaching, the things he'd deliberately left out. A brilliant student, she'd reverse engineered the secrets to his immortality and then created her own method to achieve the same thing. She hadn't put a lot of time into figuring out how the vampires were created but she'd done some cursory study. Most of her personal efforts over the previous decade had focused on using some of the more heretical and ignored techniques of necromancy to improve medicine and the outcomes of her patients—things like integrating and restoring lost function within previously dead flesh.

She couldn't revive dead tissue, but she could turn it into something like a machine. With the right magic, muscles could be made to operate after death via several different methods. Some allowed them to function using only turyn as an input, and others required blood or other additional materials. In every case, there was a trade-off between efficiency, complexity, and the difficulty of the material requirements. As a general rule, the closer the tissue was to its original state, the easier and more efficient animating it was.

Selene wasn't worried about muscles currently, however. She needed to keep Tiny's brain—and if possible—his entire head alive, because failing that, the choices beyond that point would become increasingly repugnant. And she had to do it in the middle of a battlefield, with only a single assistant and no advance preparation.

Give him some blood, suggested her father's voice.

I am human, she returned, *my blood doesn't work like yours did.*

You are a dragon, and even weak as you are, it will work like mine did—if you wish it to.

She remembered how Lognion's blood had nearly destroyed her stepson's sanity—indeed it still might. There were too many unknowns. *I'll do this my own way. If you know a spell that will help me, share it. Otherwise, stay out of my way.*

There was no reply from Lognion.

Pushing aside her doubts, Selene began to work. She formed a spell to reanimate the lungs while issuing an order to Janice. "I need a constant supply of turyn. I can match it to your husband's, but it would be easier for me if someone else could do that while I attend to other things. Can you do it?"

The lungs began to move as the big warrior's chest rose and fell slowly. The muscles of Tiny's chest and diaphragm were dead, and the spell animating them worked purely on turyn alone. The blood moving through the lungs was being oxygenated, but it flowed only to the heart and then on to the warrior's head and brain. Selene's next spell focused on the liver. She intended to use similar spells to animate all of Tiny's organs. Once things were stable, she could reorganize his blood supply so that some of them could benefit from the living blood, making them more efficient, but for now her only goal was to create a stable environment that would keep Tiny's mind alive.

Acting as a transducer to convert turyn from one frequency to another was possible for second-order wizards, but it was a more difficult task than for those of the third-order. Janice had already been doing her best before the queen arrived, but she nodded affirmatively. "I'll do everything I can. How is this?" She projected the turyn carefully toward Selene.

Selene's eyes focused on her for a moment, then back on Tiny. "Close, but not quite a match. Still, it will make things considerably easier." Casting a source-link spell, she connected to Janice and began pulling the excess turyn into herself. "Pay attention as I work. If you can refine what you're doing, it will make things simpler. Just make sure the supply is uninterrupted."

Time passed while she individually reanimated the dead organs and restored their functions. Selene reopened certain arteries as more blood became available, and before long it appeared almost as though the Royal Marshal was returning to life. Nothing could be further from the truth, though. Only Tiny's head was alive. Everything else from the neck down was thoroughly dead, and his torso was little more than a necromantic conglomeration of undead organs processing his blood to make it possible for his head to remain alive. The arms and legs were worse, but given their relative simplicity, she had stopped their decay and soon would restore blood flow to them as well. With some luck she'd be able to return control of them to him, but that would have to wait for another day.

Janice, despite knowing Selene's darker secrets, was still unsure what exactly had been done. "It looks like you saved him—all of him," she muttered.

Selene's expression was a warning. "No," she said quietly. "Far from it. Only his head is alive, the rest is…"

"Will he be like you were?" asked Janice.

"No. He would have to do that to himself, and he'd have to be a wizard first. And before you ask, no, he's not a vampire either. I don't know how they were created."

"Then what is he? Part man, part zombie?" asked Janice.

It was an apt comparison, but the term didn't really fit. Though she'd never seen one, Selene knew much about zombies, mindless undead animated by trapped souls or other spirits. "He's more akin to a golem, a living mind grafted onto a flesh machine. But for now, he's not even that. He'll perish the moment these spells expire. I need to get him back to the capital. More work will be needed to make this last, and more still to restore function to his limbs. After he's conscious, it will be his decision as to what comes next, or whether he wants us to let him go."

"He has to live," reiterated Janice. "I don't care what he decides. I won't let him go."

Selene felt her right eye twitch. *Am I annoyed?* Her emotions were definitely stronger than they'd been before being returned to life. Schooling herself, she used the habits of a lifetime to relax her facial muscles. "We will discuss that later. For now, you need to get your husband back to Cerria. I'll remain here to oversee the end of this, but first we need to fix your appearance…"

CHAPTER 29

Tiny answered an endless litany of questions from his son William, who wanted to know everything that had happened with his family since his death. How long they talked was hard to tell, but after too short a time he realized a woman had entered and was watching them quietly. No. Not a woman, he could tell by her presence she was something more.

With a sense of awe, Tiny lowered his head. "Mother, please forgive me for not seeing you sooner."

The goddess chuckled faintly, then beckoned him to lift his head again. "No need for that. Your time here is almost done."

The big knight frowned. "What do you mean?"

"You aren't dead," she explained, "just nearly so. Your wife reached your side, and Selene is helping her keep you alive."

Considering recent events, that made him somewhat anxious, but worse, he didn't want to return. He looked at his son, then back to the goddess, "I don't want to leave him."

Penny's visage softened. "No one can compel you, but your wife won't give up."

"What does that mean?"

"She'll keep your body alive for as long as possible. If you refuse to return it will never reawaken. Essentially you will be dead, but she will be stuck in limbo, caring for a body she won't allow to die. You also have someone else to consider."

Emmet, thought Tiny. His younger son still needed him.

William put a hand on his shoulder. "It's all right, Dad. Time isn't an issue here. Go. They need you. We'll all be together eventually."

Feeling as though his heart was being torn in two, Tiny turned and embraced his son again. Tears ran freely down his cheeks as he answered the goddess without breaking the hug. "Send me back then." He squeezed William tightly. "How long do I have before…?" His question tapered off as everything faded away and his son vanished from his arms.

***

Will looked out across a green field, gently swaying in the breeze. It extended almost as far as he could see, and at the distant edge it was bounded by an enormous stone wall. Everything within that wall was his—the dirt, stones, even the air—all of it was a product of his mind. It still wasn't easy for him; this new world he'd carved out within the void was fiendishly malleable and would shift and change quickly depending on his moods. The years he'd spent managing his emotions to avoid storms came in handy now, as the same skills helped him to maintain a stable environment here where any stray thought could change the landscape or create a monster.

He sat in a rocking chair on the porch of a small wooden house. Things were peaceful, but far from perfect. Despite the distance to the boundary wall, he could still hear the pounding of the Watcher's minions as they tried to force their way in. They were unceasing in their efforts.

It was important that he did not give that fact much of his attention. Anytime he thought too long and hard on the assault, they inevitably broke through, leading to another pitched battle. The strength of his wall depended upon how much he *believed* in it. It worked best when he never even considered the possibility that they might break through. Instead, he focused his attention on the flower bed in front of the house.

The tulips and daffodils kept vanishing when he looked away. Will sighed in frustration. Sometimes it seemed as though paying attention made it more difficult, while at others it was the opposite, and the flowers would disappear the moment he looked directly *at* them. Like everything else in the void, it made little sense.

It was impossible for him to tell how much time had passed. Night and day were dependent on his whims. He never truly grew hungry either. Will cooked when he felt like doing something different. When he did, he generally used real magic and real food to do so, as opposed to simply imagining food. Maintaining his practice with normal magic felt important, and he often noticed improvements in his control over the dreamlike elements of the void after he'd spent some time using real spells.

The two skills were separate yet linked somehow. Or perhaps that was yet another effect of his subconscious on the local environment.

A bell chimed.

Forgetting the flower bed, Will stepped away from the porch and began walking down the long path that led from his front door to the boundary wall. How long it took to get there was difficult to gauge, but he didn't worry about it. Once he reached the wall, he glanced at it and a small window appeared. The Watcher, a beautiful woman with blond hair and hazel eyes, stood on the other side. "Let's talk," she announced.

"I'm listening."

The Watcher pursed her lips. "This is awkward. Let me in so we can speak more comfortably, perhaps over tea?" When Will didn't respond, she added, "I'll offer you no violence."

"You said the same thing last time."

She answered with a huff. "I promise."

Will's eyes remained cynical. "You promised last time."

"That wasn't my fault. You provoked me," she responded.

"Refusing to let you devour my soul isn't provocation, it's a reasonable response to a ridiculous demand. Unless you have something different to say, go away. I have flowers to grow."

"I want tea," said the Watcher.

"Make your own," he replied. "I know you can. You've created endless hordes of monsters. A cup of tea should be simple for you."

"Just let me in. I won't start a fight this time."

Will stared into her eyes. He didn't believe her, but after a moment, he dissolved part of the wall, replacing it with an open door. He was bored. "Follow me." She walked beside him, and he noticed she wore a dress. In the past she'd simply gone naked, and her form varied—from demonic to bestial, but it always included claws, horns, or at least unusual teeth. At the moment she looked like an ordinary woman. She'd even kept her height normal rather than towering over him as she usually did. "Is this what you used to look like?"

"I'm not sure," she answered with seeming honesty. "Maybe."

"You don't remember?"

"Truth doesn't exist here, and even the past changes."

"Your memories of the past," he corrected.

She looked up and her eyes locked onto his. "You sound so confident. Is there a difference between the two?"

"Here, I'm not certain, but in the real world there's a difference between reality and imagination." They stopped at his porch, and he summoned Arrogan's old silver tea service from the limnthal. Using a selection of his cooking spells that manipulated elemental air and water, he heated water and began steeping the tea leaves. He also created furniture, a table and chairs for them to sit upon, and rather than simply imagine them, he again used elemental spells, adding some illusion to give his 'air' furniture pleasing visual elements to go along with its solidity.

The Watcher seemed amused by his efforts, but she didn't comment on them. Instead, she continued their previous conversation. "You claim there is something called *reality* in your former world, but I think you're wrong. The only difference between there and here, is that someone else controls everything."

"You mean the Mother?"

His adversary nodded. "Or Marduke, they're one and the same."

Will recognized the truth of that statement. He'd spoken to both versions of the deity, though he always had trouble remembering the conversations. It seemed easier to remember them now, whether because he had changed or because of the nature of the void itself.

They sat quietly, waiting on the tea to steep, until Will broke the silence with a question. "Can I call you Erica?"

"The last I checked, it's still rude to call a lady by her first name without permission."

And murder isn't rude? thought Will, but he held that thought back. "I never learned your full name, just that you were the tenth First Wizard, and your first name."

"Do you think speaking this way will earn my forbearance?"

A flicker of sparks around his eyes betrayed his annoyance. Will took a moment to calm his spirit. With a thought, he directed the vessel holding the steeping tea and poured it into two porcelain cups before adding milk and sugar. Once finished, he passed one cup to the Watcher. "You came for tea. I thought we'd have a civilized conversation."

Her eyes studied the cup, then lifted it to her mouth for a sip. The temperature was perfect, hot but not enough to burn. "Sayer."

"Pardon?"

"My full name back then was Erica Sayer, not that it matters now. Just call me Erica if that's the game you wish to play."

He smiled. "Call me Will, then."

She sipped her cup again. "You remembered how I like it. We've only had tea like this once before."

"My teacher was a stickler for details, not to mention it seemed worth the effort."

Her eyes remained on the tea. "You'll play nice like this, but you won't let me help you."

"You mean devour me."

"It would be painless. I'm offering you a mercy. This place will slowly destroy your sanity. I've watched it a thousand times. Give yourself to me, and I will end your suffering."

"Thus far, things seem to be improving. I'll have flowers soon, and after that I'm thinking of adding a garden. Is this what you call suffering?"

"It's a temporary reprieve."

Will took a swallow, then replied, "You say everyone who comes here falls into madness or dies quickly, yet you're still here."

Erica shook her head. "They don't die. They're eaten by one of the other denizens or they go mad *and then* get eaten."

"Yet you're still here."

"I'm not trapped anymore," she answered, arching one brow.

"But you were," he insisted. "So which one happened to you?"

She gave him a feral smile. "First I went mad, then I began eating the others lost here." She pointed at her chest. "They're all still here, and with each one I've gained knowledge and power. You have no chance, none at all."

"That isn't how you escaped, though," stated Will. He'd been mulling over the Tenth's twisted existence for some time, and certain truths were slowly becoming clear to him.

Her eyes dropped to the teacup she held for the briefest second, then back to him. "There is no escape."

Will shook his head, then took another sip. "There is, otherwise you'd never have been able to return."

Erica laughed. "As much as I'd like to claim credit, it was rude luck that was my reprieve when the elves began experimenting with forbidden magics and made contact with me. There is no such escape waiting for you."

"That's what you'd like me to believe," he returned, "but it's a coincidence too unlikely to believe. If the elves had been testing such dangerous magic before you were trapped, they'd have already destroyed themselves before. If they started sometime after you came here, there's little chance they'd have made enough progress to accidentally contact you before it was too late. You made a way out for yourself."

She waved a hand dismissively. "Believe what you wish. You're only tormenting yourself with false hope. That's not what I came here to talk about. Would you like to see how things are progressing for your loved ones?"

You weren't in a hurry to discuss it before, but now you want to speed the conversation up. You really want to change the subject, don't you? he observed. Ignoring her question, he asked, "Would you like a scone with your tea?" He'd made some fresh a few days prior, and they were still warm and fresh within the limnthal. He activated it and summoned one to his hand as he spoke, but his attention was fully on her gaze. The Watcher had looked away from him, suddenly interested in studying his house.

"You're fooling yourself if you think I truly came here for tea and sweets," she replied dourly. "Your people are dying, and I was considering offering you a way to help them."

And you're fooling yourself, thought Will. *You looked away to draw my attention away from the answer you fear I will discover. The answer I already have in hand.* "All from the goodness of your heart, I suppose," answered Will, not hiding his sarcasm.

"My armies have landed in Terabinia and Darrow. Your wife's kingdom is falling apart quicker than a house of cards. Give me what I want, and I'll let the ones you care about escape to Trendham. I'll even offer to leave Trendham as a free state governed by humans," she offered.

"I don't believe you've been that successful, and even if I did, I'd have no reason to expect you to keep your word," said Will.

Erica sighed. "If you don't take my offer, I'll still get what I want, and there will be no chance that I'll spare any of them. You've already lost everything. Your distrust does you a disservice."

Finishing his tea with a long swallow, Will spread his hands wide. "I have nothing you need. Devouring me, absorbing my soul, whatever it is you plan to do to me won't actually grant you any special power or knowledge. You already know everything I do and more besides. The only reason you keep making this offer is because you're afraid of what I'll do."

"Again, you delude yourself," said the Watcher. "Your talent with storms would be very useful to me."

"More lies."

Erica finished her tea and stood, looking down on him. "Perhaps you'll reevaluate your decision when I begin bringing you the heads of people you love, one by one." Her flesh was beginning to change as her anger came to the fore, her skin thickening and her fingernails becoming long claws.

"If you could, you'd be doing so already." The teacup held by the Watcher dropped, falling from fingers no longer suited for holding small objects. Will caught it without moving, using an instinctive telekinetic spell. "Finished with your tea? Time for you to go, then."

With a snarl, she lunged, sweeping powerful claws toward his face. Summoning the limnthal, Will swapped the cup for his sword-staff, and with a thought set the blade to humming. It sliced off her outstretched digits as he leaned away, sending a spray of crimson blood across his porch.

The injury did nothing to dissuade her, and the Tenth's skill with magic was formidable. She continued her attack, recreating her claws while simultaneously sending a barrage of elemental and force spells at Will. The porch was torn apart as their spells collided and the contest began in earnest. Between two wizards of such power, many spells were pointless. Their wills were almost evenly matched, and close to their bodies, their magic resistance was such that most hostile spells would inevitably fail. The trick was in knowing which spells offered genuine threats and countering them in time while ignoring those that were harmless. Flame and lightning meant nothing, while stone spikes and water blades could still cause grievous wounds.

With her madness and loss of humanity, physical wounds meant less to the Watcher. She could recreate her form after most injuries, and pain was nothing to her. The Tenth had survived eons of agony and torment in the void, and reality itself was constantly revising itself to match her expectations.

For Will, things were not so simple. His ability to manipulate the void was still a work in progress. As tough as he was, pain could still potentially overwhelm his senses, and injuries were harder to deal with. He was human, and sudden death was a major concern, not to mention wounds that might destroy his concentration. Even worse for him, her will matched or possibly even exceeded the strength of his own. That was not something he was used to having to worry about anymore. Strangely, although the Tenth was older by centuries and should have been far more experienced, Will's biggest advantage was his skill with spells and battle magic. Though he was far younger, Will had never stopped practicing. Decades of daily drills and continual training had paid off, and it was apparent that he'd also fought more real battles.

The world swirled around them, sending a constant barrage of random projectiles toward him, but Will dodged, deflected, or parried each and every one—all while remaining calm. He returned the favor with a bewildering variety of combat spells, many of which were original spells of his own creation. Some of them looked harmless but were not, like razor-sharp chains of volcanic glass cloaked within flames.

That particular spell cost the Watcher an arm and a leg before she realized the ruse, and after that, she was forced to guard against many more of his spells on the off chance that something physical might be hidden within flames. Meanwhile, Will always seemed able to tell the difference between her attacks.

And he taunted her constantly.

A faint smile or even a wink after he'd caught her with a swing from his staff—all of it served to further provoke her temper.

Chaos raged at her whim, but nothing seemed to touch him. Furious, she continued her efforts. She could afford mistakes, while he could not. Time was on her side. Eventually, Will slipped up, and distracted by the projectiles flying at him from the maelstrom, he missed seeing one of her claws. It slipped past his guard, ripping through his tunic and the brigandine beneath it as though they were nothing, tearing open his belly and sending a shower of hot blood over her.

Erica licked her lips, enjoying the salty taste while Will leapt back to create more distance between them. Yet, for some reason he failed to display the look of fear and horror she had hoped for. Then, she felt his turyn move an instant later and an unexpected spell came to life within the blood that coated her. Sanguine threads formed and sliced through her body from every direction. The pain was white hot, and for an instant she nearly lost consciousness. With a thought, her control over the void rewrote the present and she was whole once more. She had lost track of the fight, though, and valuable seconds had slipped past.

It took a moment to find him, but finally her eyes spotted a distant figure. Will had used a travel disk to create a large distance between them, a space of some hundred yards or so—far enough for his own control of both magic and the void to be greater than hers. She saw a smile flicker across his features as a new wall grew up to divide them. Lifting one hand, Will waved to her, and Erica saw that the cut on his abdomen had already closed. Seconds later, he was gone from view, and the boundary of his domain was complete—he had escaped her once again.

Safe within his private world once more, Will touched his stomach, probing the tender new skin. Then, he walked back to his new home, an exact duplicate of the one that had been destroyed just a few minutes before. Or perhaps it was the same one. Such definitions were hard to pin down in the void. He kept his emotions calm and put the violence from his mind—otherwise the boundary might crumble and then the fight would resume.

In his bedroom, he removed his clothes and armor so he could examine his body in front of a mirror. The wound on his stomach was now little more than a thin grey line of scar tissue. It wasn't as fine a job of healing as Selene might have done if she'd been there, but it was good.

Standing naked in the light, he studied the runes and lines tattooed into his skin. They were delicate and hard to see, as he'd intended, unlike the thick, bold lines his son Oliver had. Wardsmen wanted people to see their tattoos. They served as a warning, like bright colors on a snake.

Will preferred anonymity, so he'd made sure his were subtly done and he kept them hidden under his clothing as much as possible. Other than Selene, none of his family and friends knew about the tattoos, or the metal plate implanted in his chest over his heart. The enchantment on it was identical to the one he'd given his son. He smiled. *And some people thought I was risking Oliver's life with unproven magic. Obviously, I'd never put such a thing into my child without testing it first.* He winced as he remembered the pain of breaking one of his bones during one such test.

The tattoo enchantments didn't really do much for him since he could produce all of the same effects with either standard spells or his wild magic talents, but the skin-and-bone healing functions were handy in battle. He could do as much on his own, if he was conscious and had the time, but the tattoos worked whether he was awake or not, and more importantly, would heal him even while he continued to fight. Plus, the tattoos allowed him to do at least one thing he couldn't manage on his own. Glancing down, Will activated the phase-spider shield, watching the silvery grey turyn envelop his body. He'd never used it in battle. He hadn't needed it yet, but it was always good to have more surprises hidden away.

Will dismissed the spider shield and chuckled. Erica had certainly been surprised by his blood-razor spell. He'd come up with that spell ruse years ago, but that was his first time using it in an actual fight. "It worked well, but I doubt she'll fall for it twice," he muttered. Fighting an opponent like the Watcher took everything he had, and now he was down one more trick. If he kept engaging her on such uneven terms, he would eventually fail to escape, and then she would have him. He needed to find a way to defeat her or escape the void, or preferably—both.

He had a strong clue now, though. The Tenth's eyes had confirmed his theory. Will activated his limnthal and studied the rune construct once more.

When Arrogan had first given him his limnthal, he'd been an apprentice and had barely even cast his first spell. He'd known very little about enchantments and rune constructs back then. Will had grown so used to using the limnthal that it had become something he hardly thought about, and it was put together very differently from most spell constructs. But Will had learned a wide variety of specialized magics since the day he'd first received it. Now, he could tell that it shared certain features with the forbidden heart-stone enchantment as well as elements of the magics kept hidden by the Wayfarer Society. It was linked to his soul and yet also functioned in some way like a gate spell. The fact that he could still use it despite having stepped outside of reality and into the void meant that it was keeping some sort of linkage between him and the realm where his items were stored.

What didn't make sense to him was how the link functioned. It shouldn't be able to simply link to a place, not in another dimension. The runes weren't designed to operate with anything like a beacon, the way teleport circles did. Everything he could see indicated a link between his soul and that of someone else. *Does that mean the limnthal is binding someone over there, similar to an elemental? Or does it mean that the limnthal is itself alive?*

He had a lot of work to do, and not for the first time he wished his sister's husband James was there with him. His brother-in-law was only a second-order wizard, but there was no finer mind when it came to designing and understanding the workings of enchantments. James didn't know some of the secrets Will did, but he had no doubt the other man would have been able to provide numerous insights.

Those thoughts led him to Tabitha, the rest of his family, and inevitably back to Selene. He hoped they were all doing well. The Watcher's threats had unsettled him more than he had shown. He did believe she was lying, but he wasn't sure to what degree. For the millionth time, he tried to reach one of them via his astral bond, but he found nothing. While he was in the void, it was as though they didn't exist, or perhaps worse, it meant that for them *he* didn't exist.

Selene might think I'm dead. That worried him. The last time she'd thought he was dead, she'd made some rather extreme decisions. There was nothing he could do, however, other than get to work on figuring out a way home.

He focused on the runes hovering in the air above his palm.

CHAPTER 30

Rob was the first to step into the dank cellar, followed close behind by Oliver. James studied the space for a second before motioning for his children to step out with him.

"Are we really going to see Grandad?" asked Talia.

Seconds later Christopher added, "Where are we?"

Oliver had already put things together, but it was still a bit of a shock when James once again confirmed it. "We're in Myrsta, in Darrow. This root cellar is beneath a house your mother and I bought a few years ago. It's just a block from the governor's palace."

"But we always stay with Grandad when we visit," reminded Christopher.

Ever quick, the oldest, Edward, shushed the others. "Obviously they bought the house for a different reason. Probably just for the cellar, right, Dad?"

James nodded. "That wasn't the only reason, but it was what prompted us to buy it. Your Grandad may not be the governor here forever, so we did want to make sure we would always have a place to stay. Having a separate home also makes it a little more private. Plus, this house is a little closer to the main public teleport beacon, which saved me some effort."

Rob had been silent until then, using his nose and sharp eyes to search every corner of their location, but he had been paying attention to the conversation. "Effort? How did your saferoom send us here at all? If it's using the city beacon, we should have arrived there."

The technical details of how the teleport beacons worked were still considered state secrets, and even the theoretical details of how the magic operated were kept to a select few individuals, but James had been one of the main architects involved in implementing the teleport beacon system. "It's too complicated to explain here, but suffice it to say the saferoom here includes a small sub-beacon. The short distance means it can be very small—we're only a few blocks away from the city beacon. I designed the saferoom back home with an interesting enchantment that allows it to teleport us using the city beacon in Cerria.

We've actually been through three separate teleport 'jumps,' if you want to call them that. From home to the capital beacon, from there to the Myrsta beacon, and then here, to this location. The hardest part was getting the necessary materials here through the public system so I could assemble the—"

"There are people above us," interrupted Oliver. "Shouldn't the house be empty?"

Rob glanced at him in surprise. "Probably staff. I'm surprised you could hear that." As a vampire, it was rare that a human could match his hearing.

"There's a housekeeper and groundskeeper here to keep things shipshape," said James. "They'll be surprised to see us, though. Follow me." He led them out the cellar door and around to the kitchen door of the house.

After a brief meeting with the staff, which involved a few wholly unbelievable white lies regarding their sudden arrival, James decided they should head to the governor's palace and stay there. The children would be safer under a well-guarded roof with their grandfather. They took to the streets, and despite the late hour, managed to convince the night guard (who initially didn't recognize them) that they should be admitted to see the governor. They passed through the outer gate and two stout inner doors, and then they were escorted along a hall and into a small sitting room.

"Wait here," said their escort, leaving without further explanation. Another man appeared ten minutes later, Mark Nerrow's chamberlain Guy Tidwell. The chamberlain looked tired and out of sorts, but he recognized James and the children from previous visits.

"His Excellency will be with you as soon as he can," Guy announced without preamble.

Oliver felt bad for showing up suddenly in the middle of the night, but James was of noble birth and wasn't bothered by potentially having disturbed the chamberlain at such an hour. James did worry about offending his father-in-law, though. "Please tell Lord Nerrow I wouldn't have awakened him at such an hour if it weren't necessary."

The chamberlain rubbed tired eyes. "Oh, he was already awake. Something happened in Terabinia. He's been working in his office for at least an hour now, and some of the military officers are waiting on him. We've had messengers in and out all evening."

"Oh. I didn't realize," replied James. He wondered if the operation in Nerril was going well and if matters in Darrow had been quiet. From Tabitha, he knew that the queen had been monitoring the situation in all the coastal cities and ports, but from what he'd heard, it was only Nerril that had reported any activity.

Despite their close relation to the governor, it was more than an hour before Mark Nerrow appeared. Talia was the first from her seat when she saw him enter through the door. "Grampa!" she squealed, leaping to her feet and crossing the room to leap at the grey-haired count. Talia's excitement was mirrored by her siblings, who all ran to greet their grandfather, though their alacrity varied with age. Edward and Elaina were last, showing some decorum, while Christopher hurried over almost as quickly as Talia. James smiled patiently, while Mark took several minutes to hug and respond to each of them.

"Tally! When did you get so tall? Chris, you're sturdy as ever and growing like a weed. Elly, you're more lovely than ever, and Edward— let me look at you." Mark hugged them individually and all in a gaggle before holding his oldest grandson out at arm's length for a second. "You've got your father's eyes," he announced after a second. "Now, I know you're all excited, but I'm afraid you all need to be in bed. It's very late, and I've lots of work tonight." The governor glanced at James, who nodded in agreement.

It was a very brief greeting, but they were all tired. "You heard your grandfather," he told his children, motioning toward the chamberlain, who stood waiting by the door. "Guy will take you to our suite."

They'd stayed before, so the children were familiar with the room they'd be in, a bedroom sized and outfitted for all six of the members of the family. It held three beds, one each for the boys and girls and a third bed for their mother and father. It was located right next to the governor's rooms. They had fond memories there, since it was always a special occasion when they visited. Plus, they were normally split up in separate rooms at home. "It'll be like a slumber party," Christopher declared with a grin.

"You need to sleep," warned James. "I'll be along later, after I've caught your grandfather up on what's happened."

"Our house burned down," said Talia mournfully as she was ushered away.

Mark turned to James with a worried look. "What happened?" He already knew about Tabitha's mission with the military. "Cerria is a long way from Nerril."

"Dragonfire," said James. "I think something's happened to the queen. Oliver here knows more than I do. He was with her right before the attack on our home."

"Does Tabitha know? Never mind. It's a silly question given where she is currently." The count's eyes locked onto Oliver. "Speak up, Oliver. I need to understand all this."

Much of what Oliver told his grandfather was old news. Mark had already heard numerous times from Tabitha what she thought about the queen's unique condition, but he'd been unaware that she had kept Lognion's dragon body. "She possessed it?" asked the count incredulously. "She can do that? I'm not sure I understand how this works."

"Essentially, she's a lich, like Grim Talek, so her spirit is tied to an object, and she possesses bodies. She can switch back and forth between whatever bodies are most useful to her."

"Just dead bodies?"

"She can use living volunteers too, but that's not important in this case."

Lord Nerrow shivered, rubbing his shoulders with his hands. "It damn well feels important."

James stepped in to steer the conversation back to the present. "What matters is that she's no longer in control. Lognion has somehow resurrected himself and now he's possessing *her*. The dragon very nearly killed me and every one of your grandchildren."

Nerrow nodded, then focused on Oliver again. "You're sure it's Lognion? She could simply be mad. How can you be sure it's really him in there?"

"She talks to herself," said Oliver. "If she's only pretending, then her acting is so good I can't tell the difference. My best evidence is that when we were in Hell, she separated from Lognion to help fight the younger dragon. They were completely separate then, and only re-merged after things were finished."

Mark Nerrow blinked. "Hell? You didn't mention that. Explain."

"It was a tangent," said Oliver. "Lognion took us there so he could reclaim part of his power from one of his children." He spent more long minutes explaining what he knew of that part of the story. That inevitably led to more questions, and the conversation continued for more than an hour.

Eventually, Mark had heard enough and bid them all to get some rest. "It's late, and you've been through an ordeal. The reports I'm receiving show no elven activity on the Darrowan coast, so you should be safe here, and even if that damn dragon could fly all the way here in a single night, there's no way he knows where you are currently. Go to bed. I'll likely sleep late if I'm ever allowed to rest, so I'll catch you up on events here tomorrow afternoon."

The three of them left and headed toward the room where James' hoped his children were sleeping. It was a short walk from the sitting room they'd been in. Four armored knights passed them on the way, heading to meet with the governor. Their expressions were dour, and they moved at a fast clip, indicating their news must be important.

Rob frowned after they passed but continued to walk behind James and Oliver until they had turned a corner and reached the door to their quarters. "That's not right," he muttered finally.

James looked a question at the vampire, but Oliver nodded. "Something's wrong, but I can't figure out what it is."

The vampire tapped his nose. "Their smell. Those men had their blood up. They were expecting violence."

"You can smell that?" asked James, bewildered. Then, he added, "Given the night's doings, they're probably just anxious about the possibility of war."

Rob shook his head. "No. Anxiety smells different. They were expecting a fight any second."

"Or they were about to start one," said Oliver. His eyes lit up at the realization, and a split second later, he exploded into motion, running back the way they had come. The young warrior moved so quickly that he took even the vampire by surprise. To James' eyes, it almost seemed as though Oliver blurred and then vanished.

"Where's he going?" asked James.

Rob had been acting as a family bodyguard for the Wellings family for years at that point, and his mind naturally followed the unsettling evidence to the worst conclusion. "They're after Lord Nerrow!" He started to run after Oliver, then paused, his duty divided. "Check on the children and then barricade yourself in with them."

Rob only waited long enough for James to open the door and confirm that his family was safe before the vampire bolted down the hall the same way Oliver had gone.

***

Oliver was twenty feet away from the door to the sitting room, which was just swinging shut in front of him. He could hear his grandfather's voice, the tone surprised. He hadn't expected the knights who had entered. A click informed him that the door's latch had locked just before he got his hand on it, not that it mattered. Oliver braced his left foot against the wall and took hold of the door handle with his right arm, then he pulled.

The muscles in his back and shoulders flexed, and the door came open with a tinkle of falling metal and a loud crack as the bolt ripped free of the door and the wooden doorframe split. Three of the knights started to turn, and the governor's eyes snapped up to see what had happened. The fourth knight had already moved into the nobleman's blind spot and slammed his gauntleted fist into the older man's head. Nerrow dropped as though dead, and given the force of the blow, he might well have been.

Though he was moving faster than any human had a right to move, Oliver seemed to glide into the room, stepping directly into the midst of the armored men before they had fully registered what he'd done to the door. Every movement was deliberate as he placed one foot carefully and shoved the nearest knight with his left hand, sending the man tumbling backward into a fall. At almost the same time, Oliver's right hand closed around the dagger hilt of the knight on his other side. It was free of the sheath and plunging into the mail that covered the man's right hip, just above the plate thigh guard that could have stopped the strike.

The knights were no slouches in combat. The other two attacked as the young wardsman ripped the blade free. His back was exposed to them, and though he was turning quickly, there were limits to his speed. The phase-spider shield flared to life, covering his body in a grey shield as the first blow landed between his shoulders.

Finishing his turn, Oliver dismissed his defense and drove the still-bloody knife into one of the men, targeting the one place that neither of them had armor—the face. The force of his strike drove the blade through the knight's cheek and deep into the man's mouth and throat. It caught on something, so he released it while simultaneously swatting away his other opponent's dagger.

Weaponless, he dodged another strike, then activated his iron-skin enchantment. He did so not to protect himself, though that was an additional benefit, but his main purpose was to reinforce his hands to keep from breaking his bones when he took the next opportunity that presented itself. His last foe was quicker than most and had obviously trained extensively, but he was no match for Oliver.

Moving with seemingly effortless grace and dexterity, the young wardsman leapt back to avoid a rapid-fire series of knife thrusts, then stepped forward again, leaning to one side to slip past a fresh attack before slamming his right fist into the other man's jaw. A resounding *clack* echoed as the unfortunate warrior's teeth slammed together, and he fell limply to the floor.

A sound from behind alerted Oliver, and he turned, whipping his bare fist around to strike the newcomer approaching him from behind. His eyes locked onto Rob's face, and Oliver caught himself at the last second, stopping his attack only inches from the vampire's throat.

Rob stared at him for a moment, eyes wide. "Damn, Olly, remind me never to surprise you. I thought you might need help with the last one, but I guess I was wrong." Sidestepping the wardsman, Rob knelt and checked the man Oliver had just felled. The knight's jaw had been broken, his teeth shattered, and his skull cracked. The vampire could still hear the man's heart beating, but that wouldn't be the case for much longer. "He's dying. Do you have a regeneration potion?"

Not one that I can give you, thought Oliver, thinking of his modified tattoos. "No. Why?"

"You dispatched the others so thoroughly there's no chance they'll be answering questions. This one is our only hope of getting direct answers," explained the vampire.

"Oh."

"I have a few." Mark Nerrow had regained consciousness and was gingerly touching his head, probing his injury. "Damn, that stings! He hit me hard. Help me up, Oliver."

Oliver did, treating the older man with considerable gentleness compared to the violence he'd displayed just a minute before. "Can you sit, Grandfather?" asked Oliver.

"I can stand if you—oh, never mind." The governor wobbled briefly, then took a seat. He looked pale. "I feel nauseous." Once he was in a chair, he studied the room. "These men aren't strangers. I don't know their names, but I've seen them at other posts. Why would they turn traitor?"

"The regeneration potion, milord?" prompted Rob, still kneeling beside the dying assassin. "This fellow won't last much longer." As he said it, a bell sounded the alarm, though it only rang a few times before going mysteriously silent. "What does that signify?"

Mark grimaced. "An attack within the city, and it should still be ringing if that's the case. This must be part of a coordinated attack." He rose unsteadily to his feet. "I need more information, and I need to get back to the council room for that. If the palace hasn't already fallen, that's where the messengers will be coming to find me."

Oliver started to assist him, but his grandfather waved him away, gesturing for Rob instead. "You need your hands free." When Oliver started to protest, Mark asked a question. "Rob, which one of you is more suited to playing the roles of guard and nursemaid?"

Rob chuckled. "Ordinarily, I'd say let me do the fighting, but I wasn't trained like Olly here. I might be strong—immortal, and all that—but your grandson is a demon. I caught the tail end of the fight here, and I've never seen anything like what he just did. He trounced these men as handily as you could wish. They looked like toddlers fighting a grownup."

Oliver started to argue, opening his mouth briefly, but he closed it again without saying anything. False humility would serve no one. "I'll lead the way. Just direct me as we go, Grandfather."

"Call me Grandpa," said the governor. "I know we've not spent much time together, but you're being too formal, especially given the situation. We're going out the door and down the hall to the right. The council room isn't far." Oliver blinked at him, processing what he'd just heard, so Mark continued, "Don't get emotional on me now. There'll be time later."

They proceeded down the hall, their footsteps muffled by the carpet, but before they got far, the sound of fighting reached their ears. Mark continued motioning Oliver forward, so they hurried as quickly as they could. Oliver went farther ahead to look around the corner, and when he did, he spied a group of six men with axes chopping away at the heavy oaken doors to the council room. Rob and Mark caught up to him a moment later.

"More traitors," said the governor. "Someone loyal must've barricaded the doors from inside. We need to help them but—" He was about to finish with *there's too many to take on by ourselves*, but Oliver hadn't waited to hear the rest. The young wardsman raced forward with breathtaking speed.

"Wait!" came the governor's belated warning, but the fight was already in motion. Oliver stepped into the first man's swing, taking hold of his axe and twisting as he threw the man over his shoulder. The axe wielder let go of the axe when he slammed into the floor, and Oliver used the newly liberated weapon to kill one of the other men chopping at the door. The axe head buried itself deep into the man's shoulder, and the battle began in earnest.

It didn't last long. These foes weren't armored, and in fact looked like ordinary court officials who'd suddenly lost their minds and decided that becoming axe-wielding murderers was a better career choice. Less than a minute had passed, and the conflict was done, leaving Oliver standing over six very dead and exceedingly bloody men.

His companions caught up, and his grandfather gave him an appraising look. "I'd tell you not to rush in without an order, but your instincts were good, and I'd rather not handicap you with my hesitation at a time like this, but—make sure you think before you leap." Then, he called out to the door, "This is Lord Nerrow. My men have secured the hall. Open up for me." A long pause followed, likely because the officials and administrators inside were still trying to process whether they could trust the voice outside.

Seeing that the door was already in terrible shape, Oliver took hold of it and pulled. It turned out to be in better shape than he'd realized, and he was forced to brace himself before the iron hinges surrendered and the door came loose. To the credit of the craftsmen who'd made it, the hinges hadn't ripped free from the frame or the door, but instead had sheared through their pins. Even Rob raised a brow when he saw what Oliver had done, but he didn't comment.

Inside the room, seven very frightened people stared at them from the other side of the council chamber. Mark Nerrow could understand why, since Oliver was covered in blood and still had an axe in his left hand. He stepped past his grandson and tried to reassure the functionaries. "It's me. What happened?"

Donald Blaise, his senior military advisor, was the first to recover his wits, and he immediately blurted out, "There's an army at the gates! Reggie and the others went berserk right after we got the report from Alan here." He pointed at a messenger standing to his left, presumably Alan, though Mark didn't recognize the man.

The governor was still sharp as ever, despite his age and recent head wound. His gaze locked onto Alan. "You, repeat that report for me."

"T-th-there's an army at the gate, milord!" stammered the nervous messenger.

"Be specific! An army could be twenty soldiers or a host of men. What did you see?" snapped the governor.

"I'm not sure, milord, but they were elves. Hundreds at least, thousands maybe!" Alan's wide, frightened eyes underscored his declaration.

Mark Nerrow, the Governor of Darrow and a well-respected noble of Terabinia, went still, then calmly unleashed a distinctly nautical sentence. "Well, fuck me backwards on a bed of rusty nails and beat me with belaying pins."

CHAPTER 31

The governor's colorful language wouldn't have done much for morale, but he and been a leader of men his entire life and had also served in times of war. He followed his brief lapse of decorum with a steady stream of commands. "You, you, you, and you"—he pointed at individual councilors as he spoke—"get out there and find your people. We need to restore order and get more information." His eyes went to his military advisor. "Find the barracks commander, or whoever the most senior officer is that you can find. Have them issue a full alert and secure this building. I want runners sent to every gate and guard post. We need men on the walls."

Lord Nerrow started to address the others but then stopped, looking at those he'd already spoken to. "Get moving! There's no time to waste. Don't wait on me to give everyone else their orders!" They jumped and cleared out of the room. "Where is my chamberlain? Has anyone seen Guy?"

"Here, Your Excellency." Guy was standing just inside the doorway.

"Where were you?" asked Nerrow.

"I hid in a closet when I saw them grabbing axes," said the old man without an ounce of embarrassment.

The governor nodded. "Get me the messaging tablet. I need to send notice to Her Majesty."

Thinking he meant Selene, Oliver tried to interject, "But—"

His grandfather silenced him with a look. "I haven't forgotten. Don't distract me." The chamberlain was already handing over the enchanted tablet, and he accepted it while holding Oliver's gaze. "You're my guard today. Stand by and be still until I give you an order. Any questions?"

"No, sir," answered Oliver.

Tense minutes passed as they waited for councilors and messengers to return. Rob went back to join James and help guard the children while Oliver remained with his grandfather. Nerrow sent some sort of missive to the queen, but he didn't share the contents with Oliver. After what was probably only a quarter hour but felt more like an eternity, messengers began returning, and the council chamber became a hive of activity. Most of the posts had nothing unusual to report, but several guard stations had been deserted, though there was no sign of violence, and no bodies were found. Being unfamiliar with the layout of the city and the posts they were talking about, Oliver couldn't see the pattern, but Mark Nerrow spotted it almost immediately.

"They've cleared all the posts secondary to the main gate, but not the gate posts themselves. That's strange, since you'd think they'd want to empty the guards on the gate and walls. They've also removed all guards around the teleport beacon," observed the governor.

One of his advisors, a man named Grant Argyll, asked, "They had to know we would spot them from the walls, and we did—that's where the first report came from."

Donald Blaise, the chief military advisor, had just returned minutes earlier, and he added, "The teleport beacon is a strategic target, but they can't use it without knowing the keys. I'd guess they mean to disable it to prevent reinforcements from coming from Cerria."

Mark Nerrow rubbed his chin. "They already had men inside the city working for them, and judging by the men that tried to kill me and those that turned on their fellow councilors, they've managed to subvert some fairly high-ranking officials as well. If they could suborn the loyalty of guards as easily as they appear to have done, and with this much specificity, then why the guard posts inside the city near the main gates?" A pause followed, but before anyone else made a suggestion, Lord Nerrow's brows went up, and he snapped his fingers. "They've got the beacon codes! Send reinforcements to the teleport beacon—now!"

Lord Blaise seemed confused, but sent a runner, then asked, "What do you think they're planning?"

Nerrow's answer was immediate. "They plan to use the beacon against us. They'll send a strike force through our beacon and head for the gate. Without warning, they could easily overpower the gate guards and let their army into the city without much of a fight." He paused, then made a chilling observation. "In fact, since we don't know their timing or how many they plan to send, they may already have the beacon under their control. Send everyone we have to spare." He turned to his grandson. "Oliver—"

"Which way is the beacon?" asked the young wardsman.

Mark Nerrow's face was shadowed by dark resignation, knowing his next words might send his grandson directly into an unwinnable fight, but the fate of the city was hanging in the balance. He turned to Lord Blaise. "Give him an officer's sash."

"Why?" asked the other man.

"Now, Donald!" barked Nerrow. "Give him your own sash and insignia if you don't have an extra. I don't want any of our own people standing in his way, and if he finds help, he'll need to be able to give orders." Facing Oliver once more, the governor began giving directions. "Down this hall, then left. You'll see the main hall and there's a guard posted there. Tell them to let you through, then turn right on the street. Two blocks from there you'll see a massive stone building with a ten-foot-wide gate set in a massive stone arch. After the alert went out, the gate should be closed, but this sash will give you enough authority to order the guards there to open the postern door and let you in."

Oliver was gone almost before Nerrow finished, ripping the sash from Lord Blaise's hand as he ran out the door. He was grateful when he saw that the door guard for the governor's palace was still alive and well. The two men there let him pass without question when they saw the maroon-and-silver embroidered cloth across his shoulder, though they did raise their brows at his impatience. One of them offered his wisdom. "I know your orders must be important lad but take my advice and slow down. When war looms, it's the cautious heads that survive."

Oliver likely had more combat experience than either of them, but he nodded respectfully. "Thanks," he told the man, but the moment the door opened, he dashed out.

"Holy Mother!" exclaimed one of the guards behind him. "Did you see that? The kid moved so fast that if I'd blinked, I would have thought he vanished into thin air!" Oliver was down the street and too far away to hear the rest, but he couldn't help but grin to himself at the reaction. He covered the distance to the city beacon building in almost no time at all, and he was relieved to see that the gate was closed rather than open.

That could mean it's under the control of either grandfather's men or the elves, he cautioned himself. Approaching the gate, he called up to the wall above it. "I bear orders from the governor! Let me in!" He saw no one for a minute, but then a head appeared and looked down at him.

"There's been an alarm. The beacon is closed," said the guard.

Holding up his sash, Oliver repeated his words. "The governor sent me with orders. I need to see the officer in charge."

Another head appeared almost before he could finish. "That would be me, lad. Tell me your orders."

"First, you need to let me in. I won't shout them from the street," responded the wardsman. He shook his sash again. "I was given authority that outranks yours."

"Probably stole it," said the guard commander. He lifted a loaded crossbow. "Move along or you'll regret it." The second guard showed a similar weapon, and both looked fully ready to use them.

Something was off about their demeanor, and Oliver had made up his mind. He hoped he wasn't mistaken. The street there, like most of the streets in Myrsta, was cobblestone, and like most such roads, it had a few loose stones at the verge. Bending down, Oliver pried three of them loose with his fingers. Each stone was roughly a four-inch cube weighing several pounds. Not ideal, but they'd do for his purposes. Looking up again, he judged the distance to the two men staring down at him—they were roughly twenty feet up from street level by his best guess. The wall was cut stone, but the mortared gaps weren't smooth. A person with sufficient finger strength could probably climb it, given a few minutes, though it would be tricky.

The guard commander showed Oliver the crossbow again, though he kept it pointed at the sky. "See this, lad? You try throwing stones up here, and I'll turn you into a tailor's pincushion. Do you understand me?"

Oliver nodded, then drew back his arm and threw the first cobblestone so that it arced up toward them. Despite his speed, both men were watching him, and they still had time to duck, not that it mattered. The stone smashed into the wall just half a foot below where the commander had been standing. Cursing, the commander and his subordinate popped back up and started to aim their weapons.

What they didn't know was that Oliver's first throw hadn't been aimed at them. The young warrior had had two purposes for it: one, it caused them to duck down and lose sight of him, and two, it allowed him to judge his aim. As their heads reappeared, Oliver's second and third stones crashed into them with lethal force. Not hesitating, the young wardsman ran forward and leapt as high as he could and caught a handhold fifteen feet above with just his fingertips. From there, he climbed with calm efficiency, and in less than half a minute from the time he'd thrown the stones, he was atop the wall.

It was only a moment later that Oliver remembered he could have used the climbing tattoos to simplify his ascent, but on second thought, he decided it was better he'd gone up the way he had. His way had been quicker, and while the tattoos might be safer, they weren't always the best solution.

The two guards lay still on the walkway with blood pooling on the stone around their heads. They looked dead. If they weren't dead, it was at least a certainty they wouldn't be eating solid food ever again, much less trying to put up a fight. Oliver felt a twinge of guilt, but he pushed it aside and quickly rifled the bodies. He'd come without a single weapon, so he rectified that by taking the commander's arming sword. Since he assumed he was about to use it, he didn't bother with the sheath and belt, instead shoving the naked steel through his own belt. He wanted his hands free to carry the two crossbows, which were still loaded.

Glancing over the wall, he saw no sign yet of the reinforcements his grandfather had ordered to be sent to the city beacon, but that was no surprise. It would take at least fifteen minutes to round up squads and dispatch them, even if they were already on alert, while Oliver had run straight to the target. *I'm on my own for the foreseeable future,* he told himself.

The thought didn't bother him.

Running to the end of the wall, he made his way quickly down the stairs and then back along the base of the wall until he reached the gate. A figure stood by the massive oak doors and looked up when Oliver approached.

It was an elf. "Did he leave?"

He doesn't even recognize the people under his thrall, Oliver realized. *He thinks I'm one of his.*

The elven knight was well armored, but he held his helm under one arm. Oliver's first crossbow quarrel punched through the elf's cheekbone and kept going. The elf fell, and Oliver could see the point sticking out the back of his enemy's skull.

The area behind the gate was a small, roofed courtyard. A set of wide double doors led into the main beacon chamber, and more guards should have been posted there, but the area was empty. As Oliver studied the area, the doors opened, and another person stepped out, this one human. He shot the unsuspecting man as soon as the doors closed fully behind him. He hoped it would be a quick kill since the man was unarmored, but the bolt missed the heart and buried itself in the newcomer's shoulder. It missed the lungs too, because the man let out a hearty scream of pain and outrage.

So much for the element of surprise.

The screaming man was twenty feet away and unarmed. Oliver's first instinct was to finish him, but he could hear armored boots running inside the main building. He could only run or fight a pitched battle while outnumbered. The goal was to stop the elves from using the beacon to send out a strike force to the city gate, and it was unlikely he could do that alone. Running wouldn't lead to success either, though it might keep him alive. Making his choice, Oliver turned, unbarred the gates, and started pushing. When the governor's reinforcements finally arrived, they would at least be able to get inside and retake the beacon—if he could keep the gates open.

Drawing the sword he'd stolen from his belt, Oliver waited.

Seconds later, the double doors flew open, and fully armed and armored elves came streaming through. He'd hoped it would be regular guards, but these were the elite knights, fully equipped with enchanted plate and greatswords that never dulled and were sharp enough to cut through anything but steel armor.

He'd expected to feel fear. This was well beyond what he could handle, but with his decision had come calm resignation. With just an arming sword in hand and only simple clothes to protect his skin, Oliver emptied his mind of words and conscious thought and allowed his body to flow into motion.

The big, two-handed swords the elves wielded were an ideal weapon for a strike team that would be entering a heavily defended stronghold since they wouldn't be fighting in formation or on an open field, but the large weapons made it difficult for more than two or three of them to approach the wardsman at the same time, and while the magics on their enchanted plate made them fast and strong, they still weren't a match for Oliver's natural talent and reflexes.

They swung at him from both sides, as he stepped forward, one aiming high, the other low. It was a calculated maneuver to make it impossible for him to dodge both blades—so he didn't. Oliver crouched, letting one attack swing over his head while compacting his body and using his shorter sword as a defensive bar braced by both his arms and legs to stop the low swing cold. As the larger blade rebounded, the elf used the change in momentum to turn his back cut into a spin that would bring the blade back around to strike Oliver from the other side.

The wardsman had fully expected that. As the blade rebounded, he sprang up and entered the armored elf's space just in time to grab his foe from behind. He spun with him, and while the sweep of the elf's weapon kept Oliver's other enemies at bay, he reached around and pulled the rondel dagger from the warrior's belt and drove it upward, under the knight's helm. The gorget and mail protecting the elf's throat failed to stop his thrust, and the triangular spike of the dagger pierced the knight's chin and went up into his skull. Oliver continued following the momentum of their spin, almost seeming to dance with the dead elf as he slid his arms out to take the greatsword into his own hands.

The fight had been going for a fraction of a minute, and already one of his foes was dead, and Oliver was now better armed. Dodging another knight's swing, he took a step back and used the toe of his boot to kick the hilt of his discarded arming sword into the air and into the face of the elf leaping in from his right side. The other fighter flinched, trying to duck instinctively even though the awkward missile offered no real threat. He used the extra moment of freedom to sweep the feet out from under the one who had swung at him from the other side.

For a couple of minutes, the battle turned into an elaborate dance as the elven knights attempted to take him down with skill and swordplay, but he knew that would change soon. He could tell by the way they fought that they trained without armor, since they behaved as though their weapons offered a real threat to someone in plate. They dodged and parried his swings even though they wouldn't have done any real damage considering their armor.

The advantage of a large sword for a single fighter against a mass of lightly armored enemies was huge, but it dwindled to nothing in a fight like this. Most fights between men in heavy armor devolved into a grapple followed by a blade through a visor or other gap, and Oliver didn't even have the benefit of such armor. Any time now, they'd give up trying fancy swordplay and rush him. Although he was strong, so were these elves, and sheer mass would bear him to the ground. His lack of armor would see him dead only moments later.

The phase spider shield would save him for a while, but he couldn't keep it up forever, and they didn't need to kill him anyway. They needed to immobilize him so they could exit the gate and head for their objective.

His surroundings provided no advantages. There were no convenient oil lamps or other flammables he could use to create chaos. Terabinia hadn't skimped on costs in construction, and the beacon facility was lit with enchanted lamps that needed no fuel. The gate opening was too wide to serve as a chokepoint for him since his enemy's armor made slashing attacks with the greatsword ineffective. He started to back out into the street; perhaps he could delay them there, where at least he would have room to avoid being swarmed, but then he got a brief glimpse of the teleport beacon.

The doors had just opened as more armored elves came out, and as they did, he spotted the beacon in the center. It was a massive clear crystal that stood taller than a man with metal plates set into the floor around it, engraved with a complex array of runes. Normally, it would be enclosed within a protective structure, but the metal plates encasing the sides of this one had been removed and a robed elf stood beside it with an unknown metallic cube in his hands, which he held up to the crystal itself.

I don't know what that is, but I'd bet that's how they've gotten past the beacon's security so they can use it for themselves, realized Oliver, and with that thought, his priorities shifted. Reversing direction, he dove forward into a roll and slipped past the warriors facing him. Those behind weren't prepared for such a move, and with a quick series of ducks and dodges, he raced through the elven knights before shouldering past another just exiting the doors to the beacon room.

Once they realized where he was heading, all hell broke loose. The elves closest swung wildly, even at the risk of hitting their comrades, while the mage standing at the beacon panicked and released a powerful attack spell that filled the room with flames.

The fire didn't hurt the men in enchanted armor, though they shouted and cleared out of the room, something Oliver was grateful for. It also didn't hurt him, since his magic resistance proved to be sufficient to stop it from burning him, though some of his hair was singed. Grinning madly, he charged at the mage, then activated his phase-spider shield just in time to stop a more deadly attack. Razor-sharp stones filled the room, bouncing off of him hundreds of times as he closed the distance.

Seeing that his spells weren't working, the mage created a force-dome to protect himself, which Oliver then pushed through, courtesy once again of his phase-spider shield. A force-lance slammed into him as he entered the elf's space, but that was the last danger to him as Oliver drove his new greatsword through the mage's midsection and ripped it free again. The elf collapsed, leaving his strange device attached to the side of the beacon. Using the pommel of his sword, Oliver knocked it free, causing it to clatter to the floor. Lifting a booted foot, he prepared to smash it when a voice called out, "Stop!"

Looking back, he saw an elf in more decorated armor standing in the doorway. Given the gold filigree and other ornamentation, he assumed the elf was an officer of some sort. He was surprised to hear the elf using heavily accented Darrowan to speak to him.

"Why should I?" Oliver asked with a malicious grin.

"It will explode. Kill us both," said the elf.

He shrugged. "It will stop you. Do you think I care? I was not afraid to take on this hopeless battle, was I?" More warriors started to crowd into the room behind their commander, but he waved them back.

"You have already stopped it working. Fight me, one on one, with honor. If you win, you may do as you please. If you lose, I will take it back."

Oliver considered him, then replied, "Why should I bother? I already have what I need. All I need to do is smash it and I win." He raised his boot menacingly once more.

"I warned you it is deadly. I did not have to," said the elf. He barked more orders in his language and the doors closed, leaving the two of them alone. "Fight me and you can win *and* live. They will honor my commands. But if you lose, then I can win. If you smash it, we all die."

Sizing up the elven knight, Oliver felt something strange—a faint anxiety. Just the subtle movements of the officer's hands communicated something to him. This was no ordinary opponent, and combined with the elf's apparent confidence, he wondered if he could win against the elf in a one-on-one fight. He gestured to the officer with his stolen sword. "You think you can win against me? You saw how I fought just now."

The elf smiled. "I wouldn't make the offer if I didn't think I could win, and you, you would not refuse it unless you think you can lose. What will you choose?"

"Your armor gives you an advantage."

"You have secrets as well. I saw your strange shield."

"And you still want to try me?"

The elf nodded. "You are like me. I can see it in the way you move. You do not believe you can lose." The officer tapped his breastplate. "I also believe I cannot lose. There is only one way to find the answer."

His enemy was hiding secrets, but the truth resonated in his words. Oliver tipped his head briefly in acknowledgement. "Very well." Pointing his sword at the knight, he stepped forward. "Let's find the answer."

The officer smiled, then lowered his visor, hiding his face. "What is your name, human? I will honor your memory after I kill you."

"Oliver Cartwright. What is yours?"

"Tiandrel Insperten, first of my name."

Oliver supposed that meant the elf had been a commoner before gaining his rank, but it hardly mattered. The elf drew two blades, an arming sword in his right hand and a rondel dagger in his left. They looked rather ordinary, despite being made of lightweight elven steel, but he could see runes on both hilts, mostly hidden by the knight's gauntleted hands. Not that it mattered—since Oliver had no armor on, he couldn't afford to get hit. Whatever the magic was, any blow that landed would likely end the fight for him.

They crossed blades a second later, creating a flurry of sparks, but unlike the ones Oliver fought before, this opponent knew exactly what his advantages were. The elf ignored some of Oliver's attacks, letting them glance off his armor and closing the distance, which forced Oliver to dance back. Testing each other with a blazing array of high-speed feints and parries, they circled the room.

Kept on the backfoot by his foe's speed and skill, Oliver knew he was at a serious disadvantage. Close up, the elf's dagger and sword would rapidly eviscerate him, while his larger sword's reach advantage was nullified by the elf's armor. Their respective speed and skill were evenly matched, and it was difficult for him to block the other's multiple attacks with his more cumbersome weapon. Death would be the result the moment he made a mistake.

Tiandrel's incredible ability was not just an effect of his armor. The elf was a granling, a natural like Oliver. That also meant some of the tricks Oliver might have used against an ordinary fighter in such a situation would probably not work, or worse, get him killed. As the fight dragged on, he began to wonder if he'd made a mistake. It might turn out that his best option was to go for a draw and accept a lethal blow in exchange for killing his enemy.

If so, it's no worse than the odds I had before we started the duel. He made sure not to look at the magical device on the floor, lest his eyes give away his thoughts.

"Do you regret fighting me?" asked Tiandrel, excitement and bloodlust clear in his tone, while his weapons never slowed their pace.

"No. I'm glad to finally have a challenge!" Metal clashed and sparks flew as they continued the lethal dance without pause or respite.

CHAPTER 32

"You think I'll someday be good enough to beat you?" asked Oliver, panting at the end of a long training session.

His teacher, the Viper, was a wardsman of legendary reputation. The older man's face was flat as he replied, "You already think you're good enough to beat me. What you're really asking is whether I agree with you." Oliver's cheeks flushed slightly, but after a moment, he nodded. The Viper gave him a feral grin. "If we fought for real, I would make sure to kill you before you could beat me."

Before Oliver had been his student, he'd once fought the Viper to escape a prison. Even in that first fight, he'd managed to break the older man's ribs, and that had been without tattoos or the experience he had now. His teacher's statement might sound like boasting to some, but he knew the man to be realistic. The Viper wasn't one to brag. "How?"

"If I told you, you would be able to stop me."

"Aren't you supposed to teach me everything you know?"

The wardsman reached out and tapped Oliver's bare shoulders with the rod he often carried. "I teach you to kill other people. I teach you to make you a better wardsman. I teach you what was taught to me, but I have no duty to teach you the tricks I created on my own."

"Because I could use them against you?"

"Because then I could not use them against *you*," clarified his instructor. Oliver stared back at him, and after a minute the Viper explained, "The fighting manuals say little of people like us. There are things we can do that others cannot. This means there are techniques that do not exist in the manuals. I have found tricks that can kill someone else, even if they are my equal, but they will not work if they know them as well. So, I will not teach them to you."

"How many do you know?" asked Oliver, intensely curious now.

The Viper studied him a moment, then replied, "Against you? Three."

"Teach me one, then."

A long silence followed as Oliver met the older man's stare without flinching. Finally, his teacher answered, "I will teach you one, but only one. You must devise your own techniques from now on. Pay careful attention."

Fighting against Tiandrel brought back memories of his days with the Viper, and he worried the elf might have come up with his own lethal tricks, but he got the sense that the knight had never trained with anyone with the same level of ability. He hoped not, otherwise Oliver's next ploy would only get him killed.

Still retreating up to that point, Oliver reversed course, launching a blinding flurry of attacks. Tiandrel countered them easily with his sword and dagger, but the greater weight and reach of Oliver's sword meant the elf was forced to deflect rather than use hard blocks. Either that, or he'd have to take hits with his armor, which was the smarter course, given the situation. In the end, he chose a combination of the two tactics, but it didn't really matter to Oliver.

Let him think I have a weapon stratagem. That will only make it simpler, thought Oliver. He kept up the attacks, striving to put the elven knight off balance, as though he had some way to bypass the armor if given a chance. Eventually, the elf went along with it, stumbling slightly as though Oliver's latest swing had knocked him out of line. Oliver knew it was a trap, and he went with it, whipping his sword around as though he would use the opportunity to knock his opponent's legs out from under him. If Tiandrel fell, it would be his best chance at getting a thrust into a joint or gap.

The elf sprang back, driving past the long, two-handed sword's blade and coming in close against Oliver's side, where he would drive his dagger.

Oliver had hoped for an easier exchange, but the elven knight's speed and skill made that a vain wish. Accepting his part, he gave up his chance at escape and launched his gambit. With two odd steps, he turned his feet and stepped around and behind the knight, so that they were now standing back-to-back. It was a seemingly pointless maneuver, as Tiandrel was easily able to adjust his dagger's aim and drive it into the human behind him. *Got you,* thought Oliver.

Everything happened in an instant.

Releasing his weapon, Oliver reached up and behind himself with both hands, catching hold of the armored elf's head just below the chin. Then, he jerked the knight up and over, as though he was trying a ridiculous shoulder throw. Ordinarily, such a move would be pointless, since a normal person without proper leverage couldn't hope to pull a grown man up and over from such a position, but Oliver's strength was anything but normal, and it didn't matter if

Tiandrel was just as strong, for he'd left himself open to the awkward yet unexpected throw. The elf's armor wouldn't protect him either; it was made to prevent cuts and concussive blows. It did nothing to protect against upward jerks to the head.

As Oliver's hands clamped around Tiandrel's chin, the elf's dagger flared with a green glow. Oliver activated his phase-spider shield and hoped it would be enough.

An instant later, the knight was airborne, not that his landing would matter, for his neck was already broken. The elf was dead before he hit the floor. Meanwhile, Oliver dismissed his shield and looked down. He'd felt nothing, but he saw the rondel dagger lodged in his abdomen, still burning. He pulled it out, and the glow vanished. Blood ran freely down his side. Ironically, the strike would likely have killed him but for the fact that he'd stretched up onto his toes to reach behind himself just before it went through his shield. The extra couple of inches had caused it to enter just below his ribs. His skin closed up and the bleeding stopped, but he wondered about the internal damage.

Of more concern to him was what the late commander's subordinates would do once they saw their leader had lost the fight. Would they honor his command? *Unlikely.* Oliver picked up the knight's sword and studied the hilt. It had the same strange rune markings as the dagger.

He'd never learned to cast spells despite his father's efforts, but Oliver did possess some small ability to control the turyn outside his body, even if he could barely perceive it. His father would probably think his next action was reckless since he didn't understand the enchantment on the weapons, but he didn't care. He'd just survived a near lethal encounter. Throwing caution to the wind, he tried to push some of his turyn into the hilt of the sword to see if it would do something.

Many magical devices wouldn't work unless they were supplied with the proper frequency of turyn. Before Will had come along, that meant enchanted items had to be matched to the user, or they had to have a transducer enchantment included. Newer enchanted items created using methods developed by his Uncle James had micro-arrays that would convert the turyn automatically so they could be used by anyone, and some of the older magical relics had similar techniques, but it was anyone's guess about elven magics. The sword in his hand might simply explode.

It didn't.

A deadly green glow sprang up around the sword blade, and when Oliver tried the dagger, the same appeared there. When the doors opened and the elves looked in, they saw him standing in the middle of the room with their commander's weapons glowing in his hands. He gave them a mad grin and motioned to them with the sword. "I'm ready for more."

The elves hesitated, but the sounds of battle were echoing back from the street. Lord Nerrow's reinforcements had arrived, and the small elven force was fighting a pitched battle outside. They might be better armed and equipped, but they were badly outnumbered. Their only escape lay with the teleport beacon in the chamber where Oliver now stood.

He pointed at the device they had used to override the beacon's security. It was still lying on the floor at the back of the room. "Is that what you want?" Oliver growled. "Come and get it."

A second passed, and then they charged in. Oliver met them with sword and dagger, and although he had a disadvantage in reach, his shorter weapons made it easier to target gaps when he got close enough. The first one in received a dagger to the hip, and although the blade was glowing, Oliver didn't notice much of a difference in the force needed to punch through the mail covering the gap there. Regardless, his foe cried and bled. Oliver jerked the dagger out and blocked a swing from a second knight, backing farther into the teleport chamber.

He fought like a demon, and the desperate elves matched his commitment to violence as they had no other option for survival. Oliver slew another and wounded two more before his sword got caught in a bind and he was forced to release it. If the elves thought that would make him less deadly, they were sadly mistaken. Without a long blade, he was forced to rely on his phase-spider shield frequently as greatsword blows came at him from every direction. But if anything, his own attacks became more lethal. Closing whenever possible, he stabbed at every opportunity, aiming for necks, armpits, hips, and occasionally the backs of knees. He was so hard-pressed that many of his attacks lacked the power or precision to find tender flesh, but the elves had learned to fear him, so they treated every one of his attacks as a lethal threat.

But eventually, the dagger was caught in a tight gap, and he didn't have time to wrench it free. Weaponless, he continued fighting, and even now he used the spider shield as sparingly as possible since he needed to fully lay hands on his enemies to hurt them. Plate armor did nothing to prevent arms from being twisted and dislocated, or necks broken, as the elves soon learned.

Bodies and blood littered the chamber, making the floor treacherous, but Oliver danced upon the slaughterhouse floor as though born there. At least twenty of the armored elites were dead and more had retreated to the edges of the room with injuries that made it impossible to continue.

The end was nearing, however. From the sounds outside, the Darrowan reinforcements were nowhere near close enough to reach him in time, and despite the young wardsman's incredible endurance, his strength was beginning to wane. He relied on the spider shield to save him more often as he began to slow.

Out of the corner of one eye, he saw a wounded elf pick up the device he'd removed and start to place it back against the teleport beacon. Oliver ducked low and dove across the floor, sliding past two knights' legs so that he could grab the one with the security-defeating construct. He broke the elf's neck, but his desperate action cost him as he felt a sharp pain in his back. Activating the spider shield, he turned and drove the elf back with a palm strike.

Then, he was falling—someone had swept his legs out from under him.

Bodies piled on, and daggers came at him from every direction. He tried to push up from the floor, but the weight on his back was too great. His turyn was low as well, and the spider shield faded out. Oliver activated his iron-body enchantment, hardening his skin, but the enchanted elven blades cut him anyway. Pain and blood were his world now.

He was dead, but he had no regrets. Being a wardsman had always been his dream, and their motto felt particularly true to him then. *Fight hard, die young. I had a good run, and if there's any justice in the world, this fight will inspire a song to make men shout and women cry.* It was a selfish thought, but Oliver figured he deserved it since he'd just given his life to save a city. In his ears, he heard elves screaming still, and it made him smile. More screams came and then he realized the stabbing had stopped. It hadn't lasted long. *Did they think three or four pokes would be enough to slay me?*

The screaming increased in pitch and fervor. Light returned as the elves on top of him leapt up and tried to get away. Oliver couldn't understand why, until he heard a familiar feminine voice. "Your death warrants were signed the moment you came here, but even worse, you tried to kill my precious boy. Don't scream and beg for mercy. Your deaths will be as painful as I can make them—be grateful I don't have the luxury of time to make your punishment last."

Standing before the teleport beacon, Oliver saw his stepmother, Selene Maligant, the Queen of Terabinia, and her visage spoke of malice and misery unending as she gazed on the remaining elven knights.

CHAPTER 33

The fight in Nerril was over, but the city was still in chaos. Selene directed her forces, the Iron Knights, the Arcane Corps, and the Driven as they tried to restore order and save the living. Thousands had died, and while most of those deaths were soldiers and others serving Her Majesty, several hundred were ordinary citizens who had been caught by the abominations when they first flooded into the city.

The damage could be repaired, and the city would be able to recover relatively quickly, but there would be scars in the hearts and minds of those who had lost loved ones. Selene could easily have spent days or weeks there personally supervising the situation, but less than two hours after she'd stabilized Tiny and sent him back to Cerria under his wife's care, she received an urgent message via the enchanted tablet she had reclaimed from Janice—the tablet used for priority communications with Terabinia's monarch.

The message chilled her.

An elven army has appeared at the gates of Myrsta. Unsure how they got this far without alerting the inland posts. Still no reports from the coastal cities. The situation may be dire, as it is apparent we have traitors working within the city to ensure its fall. Currently, I believe the elves are targeting our teleport beacon, either to cut us off from support or to suborn it for their own purposes.

Request immediate reinforcement and assistance. I cannot overstate the urgency, as I am still not fully aware of the extent of the elven forces or how much they have committed to this attack.

Your Loyal Servant,

Mark Nerrow, Governor of Darrow

Selene didn't waste any time. "Sir Kyle, I am appointing you as the acting Royal Marshal and commander of my armies until such time as Duke Shaw can return to his duties or I find a suitable replacement."

She'd been in the midst of overseeing arrangements to have the wounded, along with Tabitha's strange and unresponsive body sent back to the capital. Kyle Barrentine, knight of the realm and one of her most trusted retainers merely nodded. Despite her sudden shift in tone, the appointment was practical and expected. "Your Majesty."

Selene handed him the tablet, allowing him half a minute to read it, then commanded, "I will go now. Have as many men as you can spare meet me at the waypoint beacon."

"I should come with you, Your Majesty," protested the knight commander.

"With Lord Tallowen unconscious and Duke Shaw wounded you are the only one here I can entrust with overall command," she answered cooly.

Sir Kyle's expression showed adamant disagreement. "Respectfully, you should send me and remain here yourself, Majesty."

"Given what I've seen I believe this will need my personal attention. I respect your opinion, Sir Kyle, but you will take charge here. Send most of those who can fight, and as soon as you have established order, send the rest unless I send word otherwise." Studying those closest to her, she made eye contact with one of the Driven. "You can use a travel disk?" It was a foolish question, and she berated herself for wasting time as soon as the words left her lips. "I want you and as many Driven as are here now to come with me. Each of you, bring a knight with you. We're heading to Myrsta immediately."

"We need a minute to see who we have to send," remarked one of the officers present, panic apparent in his tone as she started to leave then.

Selene shook her head. "Those who can, follow me now. Sir Kyle, send the rest as quickly as you can. You've a quarter hour to have them organized and on the way." Summoning a travel disk, she left at speed, causing a stir as the elite Driven rushed to cast their own travel spells and follow her. Some managed to find a knight to travel with them, while others simply followed.

She finished the three miles to reach the beacon site in less than ten minutes, and once there, she realized she'd left her escort behind. They would probably reach her in a minute or two, but she still felt a sense of urgency that drove her to continue without them. As a queen, it was foolish to act so hastily, but she teleported by herself anyway, first to the Project Chrysalis main beacon, which acted as a central hub for the military's secret teleport network, and then from there to the main city beacon in Myrsta. Or rather, that's what she tried to do.

Her teleport spell failed.

Selene wasn't prone to mistakes, even with complex spells, but she assumed she had somehow misremembered the rune keys. Working more slowly, she recreated the teleport spell construct, checking and rechecking the security keys at the end before activating it. It accepted her turyn normally, so she knew the spell construct was properly done, but nothing happened. Raising her voice, she yelled for the operator on duty; there were always at least two wizards from the Arcane Corps on site to manage operations and monitor the network.

The senior wizard on duty was an artificer specialist named Calvin, and he'd already spotted the queen and had been quietly watching her for a solid minute. He jumped at her call and nervously responded, "Your Majesty?"

"I can't teleport to Myrsta. Why?"

"E-everything looked fine a bit ago," stammered Calvin.

Selene's eyes locked onto him like a predator sensing blood. "How long ago was 'a bit'?"

"M-m-maybe a quarter hour, Your Majesty…"

"You're supposed to keep eyes on the indicators around the clock. Why are you standing here? Is someone watching it now?" she demanded.

"W-well I saw your arrival, so I stepped out to greet you—"

"Which means you aren't monitoring it. More importantly, why aren't you running to check it now?" she asked mercilessly.

"U-um, my assistant, Jonathan is watch—"

The door to the monitoring station flew open, and a young, balding man poked his head out. "The Myrsta beacon is down! Oh!" The younger man blinked at Selene, his face showing no sign of recognition. "I didn't realize we had company. My apologies miss. Calvin, something's happening."

The senior wizard paled at his assistant's failure to realize who was among them. "Jonathan, please bow, this is Her Maj—"

Selene cut him off. "Silence. Go help him figure out what's wrong. Now. I need that beacon working sooner than five minutes ago."

Jonathan turned red and almost fell trying to bow. Calvin pushed him back into the monitoring room, and after a second, the door closed. Selene went after them, though she waited a minute before entering to give them a moment to collect their thoughts. From past experience, she knew people sometimes folded under pressure if she surprised them and pushed too hard. When she opened the door, she found them both bent over a polished wooden table with gold rune inlays and numerous gems set into its surface. Though she hadn't studied the enchanting designs, she knew that one of the three most prominent gems, a ruby, was meant to represent Myrsta's city beacon. The rest of the jewels were glowing, while Myrsta's was dark. "Do you know what's wrong?" she asked.

Jonathan jumped, and Calvin nearly fell down as he spun to face her. "N-not yet, Your Majesty," answered Jonathan. Seeing the shadow in her brows, Calvin hurried to add, "I'm sending a message to them to see what's happening. I think Chris is on duty there currently." The senior wizard held up the stylus he was using to write on a communications tablet built into the table.

Selene crossed her arms and waited. After a minute, she asked, "How long should this take?"

"I sent the message just before you came in, Your Majesty. Unless he's stepped out, he should see it immediately."

"Stepped out?"

"He should have seen it already, but sometimes the body makes demands of its own," explained Calvin.

"I won't take offense if you mention bodily functions, Supervisor," replied Selene. "However, it is for this reason that there are always two wizards on duty at each beacon. Are you implying that you and your associate here both step away occasionally?"

"N-n-no, Your Majesty, certainly not," said the senior wizard hastily.

"Then either someone is derelict of duty, or the elves have removed them forcibly," she concluded.

"Oh! There it is!" exclaimed Jonathan, pointing to the ruby, which was now glowing brightly. "He must've seen your message and acted to fix the problem before replying."

Selene stepped out and recast her spell without bothering to reply, but being suspicious she made certain she was ready to defend herself if the situation called for it. The world changed, and after a split second of disorientation, she found herself in a room full of armored combatants—all of them elves. They were piling onto someone, presumably the lone defender of the beacon. An instant later, she recognized the turyn of the underdog, just as one of them drove a dagger into him.

Her power flared, filling the room as she cast one of the spells she'd prepared and stored in advance. In her haste, she put more power into it than she'd intended, but she did at least remember to exclude Oliver from the effect. His magic resistance might have saved him, but now that she was no longer bound to the phylactery, her will was far stronger than before, and it wasn't a risk she wanted to take.

The room was filled with screams of pain and horror as many of the elves felt their bones dissolve, and the few that managed to resist the spell watched their comrades collapse in agony. Seeing Oliver on the ground and bleeding filled her with anger, and since she was new to life again, the intensity of feeling almost overwhelmed her ability to reason. She spoke to them, pronouncing her decree of death, but she wasn't fully conscious of what she said, for the wave of emotions made it hard to remember the words. She hadn't raised Oliver, and in truth, he would never really feel like a son to her, but he was representative of the one untarnished thing that was hers alone—the one thing her father had never corrupted.

The stench of death was overpowering as the dying and amorphous elves voided themselves in a room already slick with blood from Oliver's battle. The few knights with enough magical resistance to escape the effects of Selene's spell had little hope of reaching her in time to stop her next spells, for most of those still capable of combat were now struggling to rise from a dogpile of oozing armor and dying allies. The enraged queen's eyes moved from target to target as she sent blades of water scything into them, and when the cutting spells failed to work against enchanted plate, she switched to binding ropes of liquid that caught, pulled, and twisted, breaking arms and legs until there were none left who were able to stand.

Still lost in her fury, she solemnly walked to each of the crippled knights one by one. Though she was clad in a light grey dress, her demeanor gave the impression of a vengeful shadow as she calmly slew them. Her merciless eyes were the last thing the remaining knights saw, before she gave each of them an agonizing death. Since these were the ones with enough resistance to keep her previous spell from warping their flesh, she instead lifted their visors and reached in with one finger and used a long forbidden and almost forgotten necromantic spell known as 'fleshroot.' She'd never cast it before, but her memory was sharp, and she constructed the spell construct flawlessly time and again, causing her index finger to elongate as she pressed it into the terrified eyes of her crippled enemies. From there, it would extend, growing and spreading into multitudes of hard, chitinous, roots of flesh. She controlled the spreading roots, making sure to avoid vital organs. The elves screamed themselves hoarse, enduring what seemed an eternity of pain for that last minute until she allowed them to die.

Those outside the teleport chamber were still being pressed back, but she cast a force-wall to block entry to the room and give herself the freedom she needed to examine her stepson. Oliver seemed barely conscious, which concerned her, but her diagnostic spells found his body to be in a fairly stable condition. The enchantments she had designed for him had already stopped the bleeding and sealed his wounds. Only one of his internal injuries had exceeded the capabilities of the formulaic magic that had been built into his tattoos—a deep stab wound that had gone straight through his liver. Even so, he would have probably recovered from it, but the internal scar tissue that resulted might have brought other problems later in life. Selene repaired the wounded organ with a series of skillful spells that would ensure he had no lasting problems.

The young wardsman still seemed weak, but after finishing her examination, Selene understood the cause. *It's just turyn exhaustion. Like a normal wizard overextending themselves, he fought using his natural talents and the tattoos until his body had nothing left in it.* Oliver was struggling to rise, but she gently pushed him back down. "Rest. You've done all you had to do." She used a force spell designed to act as a stretcher to help move him to one side of the room. "Rest here."

Oliver shook his head weakly, then pointed across the room at a strange rune-inscribed cube. "That's what they used to take control of the teleport beacon. I knocked it free, but their leader said it would explode if destroyed. I'm not sure if he was lying or not."

"Which one was the leader?" she asked, and after he pointed the elven commander out, she added, "How did you get here?"

He was too tired to give a proper explanation. "James Wellings. He had an extra safeguard at home. It got us to Myrsta."

Selene blinked. Since her return to life, she hadn't had time to process the memories of the last few days while she had been held hostage by Lognion. Remembering the destruction of Tabitha's home hit her in the gut like a blow from a smith's hammer. It felt as though she couldn't draw air, but she finally managed to ask the most terrifying question. "Did they? When you say us—who exactly? Did everyone—?"

"I'm not sure about the servants, but James and the children all came here with me. Rob as well." Watching her face, Oliver found it hard to reconcile the vulnerable eyes blinking back tears with the harrowing memory of just moments before when his stepmother had calmly and coldly tortured the remaining elves to death.

"Where are they?"

"At the governor's palace, with Grandfather," he answered quickly. "They're safe."

She nodded, blinking once more before wiping her face. As he watched, the color of her cheeks faded, and her facial expressions smoothed out. The anxious woman faded away, replaced by the demeanor of a queen, calm and in perfect control. "Rest," she told him.

Straightening her back, Selene went to the doorway and removed her barrier. The elves had their backs to her as their frontline fought to defend against the governor's reinforcements. She slew them in the most efficient way possible, by using a powerful wind spell to sweep their feet from the stone floor and send them tumbling awkwardly to the ground. With their formation disrupted, the prone knights died quickly as the human guards moved in and took advantage of the situation.

It took a minute after that for her to assert control, but two of the officers recognized her face, and with Oliver's ready endorsement, they accepted her authority. The queen of Terabinia wasted no time. "Inform the governor of my arrival and have him meet me as soon as he is able. I'm informed that James Wellings is at the palace—have him sent here immediately." She lifted the elven device. "I need his counsel regarding this clever bit of treachery."

She then had crossbowmen posted around the teleport chamber with other guards to protect them. The Driven and their Iron Knight companions had arrived by then, and she arranged them as well. Oliver was moved out of the room and she handed the elven device to one of her Driven. "Place this against the beacon and leave it there, but be ready to remove it should I give the command." Lifting her voice, she addressed the others, "If they are unaware of the doings here, more of them will use the beacon, but they can only teleport in groups of twenty at a time. Show no mercy to any that appear."

One of the Driven spoke up, "I do not think this is a safe course, Your Majesty."

Her voice was cold as she replied, "Every dead elf is a step forward for us. Do it." Once they had obeyed, she pointed to two of the guards, and then at the elven knight commander's body. "Move that into the outer corridor where my stepson is resting." They appeared confused, so she clarified, "The wardsman with the officer's sash. He's the governor's grandson, in case you didn't realize."

"Yes, Your Majesty." They moved to do as she said with alacrity.

In the outer corridor, she lowered herself to sit cross-legged next to the dead elf, a distinctly non-regal thing to do, but she had more important matters to concern her than her image at that point. She intended to possess the commander's brain and rifle through his last memories, but it was only at the last moment that she wondered if she was still capable of such a feat. She was no longer a lich. Her soul now had a true home, a living body. Could she still possess a dead one, and if so, what would that do to her?

After learning so much from Grim Talek, she had gone through the restricted books on necromancy that were locked away at Wurthaven. Her goal had been primarily to learn spells and techniques to improve modern healing magic, but her study had led her to many other less palatable spells as well, such as the fleshroot spell she had just used. In general, the prevailing opinion among those brave enough to research such dangerous topics had been that any magic involving the soul brought with it the most extreme risks. The inadvertent mingling of souls that sometimes occurred in tests with living subjects underscored that danger, as most went irretrievably insane. Will's successful merger with his sister was almost unheard of. Likewise, none of the authors of those texts had had any personal experience as an undead existence. Selene and Grim Talek were the only two wizards who had ever successfully become liches, and she was certain she was the only one to ever return from that condition.

Will frequently traveled away from his body to communicate at a distance or to teleport to those with whom he had a personal connection. She had never been able to replicate that feat while alive, and as a lich, she was bound to remain close to either her phylactery or whatever body she was currently using.

Aside from her more intense emotions and vitality, Selene didn't feel that anything fundamentally would stop her from doing some of the things she'd done before. She just didn't know if there would be side effects or consequences. *There's no soul in this dead flesh, so I don't have to worry about madness, do I?* She'd thought the same about her father's draconic body and been wrong, but this was just an elf. She needed information. Otherwise, her entire kingdom might be at risk of falling.

Setting aside her doubts, she did as she had done before, moving herself in that peculiar sideways direction that wasn't physical but astral, and although she'd feared some unexpected barrier, none appeared. As smoothly as when she'd been undead, her soul slipped free and into the dead knight's head, which was currently tightly clasped between her hands.

Her eyes popped open, offering her the disconcerting view of her body from an outside perspective. It had gone limp and was slowly sagging down. Her lips were slack and in a sudden panic, she shot back to her proper self. For a moment, she felt as though she was suffocating, but after drawing several loud, heaving breaths, her heart calmed down again.

Based on that short test, what she wanted to do was possible, as long as she could maintain her bodily functions while she was absent.

Will did something similar when he teleported, but she'd never been able to replicate the way he somehow split his focus enough to keep his body functioning while his attention was in another part of the world. Fortunately, she didn't need to. Modern medical magic had a spell that would solve the problem without much fuss, one that would keep a patient's breathing constant and their heart beating despite a plethora of factors that might cause them to stop ordinarily. Selene used it frequently, although until then it had always been on someone else. As a lich, breathing had been optional.

She constructed the spell and put it in place before returning to the dead elf, and then she wasted no time delving into the knight's recent memories. It didn't take long, since what she wanted was recent, and he'd been mindful of his orders up until the point that Oliver had nearly ripped his head from his shoulders.

The knowledge she found was disconcerting, but as she considered it, new possibilities came to mind. Knowing the enemy's plans and their contingencies would enable her to exploit them. Before returning to her body, she drew on her turyn and animated the dead elf briefly. Turning his left arm so that the forearm was up, she unclasped a latch on the vambrace, exposing a hidden piece of metal roughly two inches square. Elven runes decorated its border, and six large symbols were prominently displayed. She touched one on the upper right with the index finger of the elf's right hand. She wasn't sure if it would activate, since she didn't know the dead officer's unique turyn frequency, but she suspected the enchantment was keyed simply to his physical body, since many of the other officers weren't magically trained and would be unable to express their turyn.

She smiled mentally when she felt the enchantment respond, sending a signal to the elf's superiors, a message that simply meant, 'area clear, proceed.' Abandoning the dead body, she returned to her own, and seconds later, she heard the sounds of combat as more elves teleported in to be met with massed crossbow fire and alert guards. Despite that advantage, their armor was excellent, and they were well trained. Only lucky shots would find gaps that crossbow quarrels could penetrate, and the elves didn't panic.

Selene quickly opened the door and rejoined her men. Twenty elven knights had appeared, and while four were down with bolts sticking out of their visors or armpits, the other sixteen had rallied and were now forcing the guards protecting the crossbowmen back. Several of her men were dead, and the fight was definitely shifting in the elves' favor.

Rather than do anything dramatic, she chose to make a few selective kills, allowing the Darrowan guards to regain control and then defeat the elves seemingly without much help. A cheer went up as they forced the last few knights back and began using polearms to hook their legs to make them fall. Once downed, the humans fell on them in numbers great enough to keep them on the stone floor while stabbing into gaps with sharp daggers.

As soon as it was over, she began issuing orders. "Switch them out. These men need rest. Another group will appear within a minute." Once she was sure the soldiers would be rotated to keep fresh, untired men at the ready, she addressed the sergeant who was leading the governor's men, "Where is James Wellings? I need him here."

The sergeant had no answer. "I've sent messengers, Your Majesty."

"Send another, then."

CHAPTER 34

The sergeant was about to obey her command and send another messenger when the action became pointless. A smaller contingent of guardsmen arrived, led by Lord Nerrow himself, with James Wellings beside him. Selene felt a surge of relief at the sight of them, and although it was James she needed at the moment, it was Mark Nerrow who actually made her feel reassured. He'd been a surrogate father to her during her formative years and his confident presence made her feel safer whether he could actually do anything or not.

None of this showed on her features, however. As always, she maintained her controlled demeanor. "Lord Nerrow," she said, acknowledging him. "I received your message."

The governor's eyes had already taken in the numbers present, noting the handful of Driven and Iron Knights that were with her. Almost all the others there were the men he'd sent to reinforce the teleport beacon. With a brief but respectful bow, he began, "Your Majesty, I am grateful you've arrived so quickly, *and* in person. Are there more coming? We have an army at the gates."

The question bordered on rudeness, but the situation left little time for dancing around the subject. "Not at this time," she responded bluntly. "For now, we will have to work with what you have and what you see here." Without waiting for his reply, she nodded to James. "Lord Wellings, I need you to look at this device they attached to the teleport beacon. As far as I can tell, it has disconnected it from our network and given them access to it."

A loud cacophony arose as another group of elven elites arrived and were promptly ambushed. This time, the humans were better prepared, and several Driven assisted. The fight was bloody, and a few more casualties resulted, but the elves were all dispatched within a couple of minutes. Selene went to the hall outside the teleport chamber to explain the circumstances, but before she could say a word, Nerrow rushed to Oliver's side. She let them have a moment while she led James into the teleport chamber and showed him the device the elves had put on the beacon.

"Why haven't you removed it?" asked James, though his eyes never left the foreign artifact.

"Oliver already removed it once, but I intend to use it to our advantage," she told him.

James' eyes were distant, as though he only half heard her, but he replied quickly, "We can't use the beacon for ourselves while this is attached."

She nodded. "The real question is whether we can activate the beacon defenses while their breaching device is subverting the beacon's other enchantments."

James blinked, his mind shifting course as her suggestion registered in his ears. He stared at the floor, then the ceiling, then the doorway leading to the monitoring room. His eyes stopped on the defenders forming up again in preparation for the next batch of elves. "It would kill everyone in the chamber," he muttered.

Selene nodded in agreement. "Obviously, I intend to remove our people first. Can you do it?"

James' eyes returned to hers, focusing fully as his mind finished its thoughts. "Yes, Your Majesty. It will take a few minutes. I'll have to make some quick and frankly crude adjustments to the security enchantments and how they're linked. It will also make the beacon unsafe for anyone to use, even after we remove their override device, so keep that in mind."

"You can repair it then, correct?" she asked.

James nodded. "It will take me longer to restore proper function and undo the modifications if we do this."

"How long?"

"A day, possibly longer. I'll have to re-engrave one of the plates, and I don't have my luxpress here, so the work will be roughly done," said James.

Mark Nerrow had just rejoined them. "What work?"

Selene explained the conversation up until that point, then added, "I intend to use their trickery against them, but another question is how well your men can take advantage of this. With some help from your men, I think I can keep them from realizing what's happening to their knights as they send them through, but it won't be enough on its own. Eventually, they'll give up and attempt a conventional assault on the gates."

The governor's mind was already working through the possibilities, and a malicious light had appeared in his eyes. "They'll continue sending them if they think they're making progress. Is that what you intend, Majesty?" At her nod, he continued, "Then we'll need smoke, and sound, the clash of arms. How long do you think they'll keep trying the portal?"

She smiled. "They have contingencies planned, but they'll continue sending them until they're sure it has failed. We might be able to get nearly half their available force, but I'm sure they'll switch to a more conventional plan before then."

"And then?" asked the governor.

Selene's eyes darkened, seeming to draw all the warmth from the room. "Their plan was to open the gates and allow their army into the city without a costly fight on the walls. They'll think they've succeeded when their men open the gates."

"Their men?"

"We will have a lot of unused elven armor by then. Our men won't be able to use it properly, but they won't need to—they just have to help confuse the enemy," she told him.

Nerrow's brows furrowed. "They must have some means of communicating. The lack of proper responses from these elves will make them too suspicious—"

"The dead have no secrets from me, Lord Nerrow," said Selene. "They'll receive exactly the signals they expect. What I need from you is a plan to capitalize on the situation once they enter the city thinking victory is already theirs. Do they have any abominations with them, or is this army composed of purely elven troops?"

"Everyone we can see from the walls appears to be either elven or human," he answered.

She nodded. "That's another thing. We have to change up our systems to account for the men who have been secretly subverted."

Nerrow's face flashed with irritation. "I've begun sending messengers in groups of three and had their roster reshuffled. Several times now I've had one turn on the others, with little rhyme or reason to it."

"It's the bluet," she told him, sharing a conclusion she'd reached after sorting through some of the elves' memories.

"We haven't had much of that here," argued the governor, "and none since your orders to stop allowing the trade."

"Anyone who has had lengthy exposure is highly susceptible to their mind affecting magics," she explained, "and from what I've gathered, they can implant commands without leaving any conscious memory in the victim's mind. Your idea of mixing the rosters and sending men in groups was a good one."

"Is there any way of telling who has been bespelled?" asked Nerrow.

"Possibly, but I don't know it," Selene replied. "If I have an extended period of time to search through the memories of one of their mages, I might be able to find that out, but events have moved too quickly for that."

Sounds of another battle in the beacon room reached them, prompting James to speak up. "Do you still want me to force start the defense enchantments, Your Majesty?"

Selene glanced at Nerrow. "If we do this, do you think we can capitalize on it properly?"

The governor nodded, determination written in his eyes. "I'll see to it."

She turned to James. "Do it."

"I'll have to wait until this group is finished and we clear the room, Your Majesty." James' eyes flicked to his father-in-law. "Also, I have some ideas that might make your plan more efficacious, Governor."

Mark Nerrow grinned. "Good. I was going to enlist your help anyway. We're woefully short of wizards here. It's a shame we can't delay the beacon trap long enough to bring in more reinforcements first."

Selene felt the same. "I wish so as well, but the forces in Nerril are exhausted and in disarray after the battle there. Sir Kyle is reorganizing, but it will be at least a day before he has a significant force ready." The teleport chamber was beginning to quiet down. "James, you should get started. The governor and I will begin making plans for the second stage. You can advise him on your ideas after you get those defenses working again."

***

Force-walls appeared, sealing every entrance to the teleport chamber, while a strange hissing noise informed Selene's ears that the air was being removed. She had seen a demonstration years before, when James had first suggested the system, but this was the first time it would be used to actually take lives.

Some of the details of how it operated had escaped her in the intervening years, so she asked, "Remind me again, James, how does the beacon work if the room is sealed?"

The renowned artificer and enchanter warmed up to the subject quickly. "The force-walls only seal the doorways. The rest of the room is encased in solid stone, which is just about completely airtight. Actually, the stone isn't completely impermeable, but it's a negligible effect that doesn't really affect the vacuum we create inside." One of the gems in the monitoring board lit up, and James tapped it with one finger. "There, they've sent in a group. I imagine they aren't enjoying themselves."

"I don't hear anything," said the governor.

James nodded. "You won't. Sound needs something to travel through. Their deaths will happen in complete silence." He shivered. "It's disconcerting even for me, and I thought it up."

"They'll just suffocate. Similar to drowning, right?" asked the governor.

Selene shook her head. "The lack of air pressure will cause them to bleed from their eyes and ears. If they try to hold their breath, their lungs will pop. If they don't, their lungs will begin to bleed inside them, filling with blood. I'm not even sure what will kill them first, lack of air or the injuries created by the vacuum. We haven't tested it on actual people."

"But you know it works?" asked Nerrow.

James nodded. "Pigs. We tested on pigs. It wasn't pretty."

Straightening her shoulders, Selene ended the moment. "You two have work to do. I'll be interrogating the dead between teleport groups. If anything significant changes, I'll use the tablet to send a message."

The governor gave a quick bow, then responded, "Understood, Your Majesty."

The two men started to leave, but James turned back. "You know the circumstances of my arrival in Myrsta, and yet..." His sentence tapered off as he searched for words.

Why did I burn down your home? Selene finished mentally. *Or are you wondering if I'm actually Janice?* They had no time for a proper discussion, but James and Tabitha deserved the answers. She could see the same questions in Mark Nerrow's eyes. "Oliver told me how you and your children escaped, and I am very grateful to know that neither you nor your children were hurt. There is much to say, and this is a poor place for it. I will tell you this for now: The dragon has been dealt with; you need not fear *his* vengeance any longer. Once our nation is safe, I will do everything possible to recompense you and your family for the strife you've been through."

They nodded, then Mark added, "I'll have Oliver taken to the palace to recover."

Selene waved him away. "My son is fine, merely tired. He will be safer with me where I can keep an eye on him."

An expression of guilt flashed across the governor's face. "I sent him ahead when I feared this site would fall before reinforcements could arrive. If he has any lasting injuries, they are on my head for asking too much of him."

She hadn't heard all the details yet, so she had only guesses as to how Oliver had wound up acting as a one-man army to stop the elves, but she'd had her suspicions. Nerrow's statement confirmed them, and Selene felt a flush of anger, which she quickly suppressed. "As ever before, you acted in accordance with your duty to Terabinia. As much as I would like to condemn your choice, I myself have chosen duty over family time and time again."

Mark Nerrow bowed his head in contrition. "I am grateful for your mercy and understanding, Your Majesty."

"I said that I understood, not that I have forgiven," she corrected. "I will pray to the Mother that I find the strength to forgive you, as well as myself. Now go."

Once they had left, she reset the chamber and sent two men in to bring out the body of the officer in charge. Then, she reactivated the defensive measure and put herself to the task of possessing and examining the dead elf's recent memories. She would need to send a confirmation message back and check to see what the elven commanders were currently thinking.

CHAPTER 35

An hour passed, and hundreds of elven knights bled, choked, and died in agonizing silence without ever knowing what caused their deaths. Selene continued interrogating the dead officers and sending back confirmations to proceed from each of them. Meanwhile, the governor had bonfires set in multiple locations. Damp rugs and wet wood were thrown on the fires to create as much smoke as possible, while at the same time the Darrowan guardsmen shouted and clashed in mock combat to try and create as much noise as possible.

From outside the walls, it was easy to believe a major conflict was underway, which bought them as much time as possible for the rest of the governor's men to create barriers and set up a special area to welcome the 'victorious' invaders. Despite their best efforts, however, the elves were growing suspicious, as Selene saw from the thoughts of the dead officers she examined after each group teleported in and subsequently died.

They weren't expecting to need so many to get to the gates and get them open. This won't go on much longer before they give up and focus on a different strategy, she thought. It was about then that Lord Nerrow and James returned.

"We have a problem," began the governor.

James interrupted before he could finish, "I may have a solution, Your Majesty."

Mark's features flashed annoyance at the discourtesy. "We have a significant difference of opinion."

"State the problem first, then I'll consider your differing opinions," said Selene.

"My men have built quick barricades inside the city in the region near the main gate, but they aren't robust enough to hold for long. The Driven would like to attempt using earth spells to create a muddy region just beneath the streets, but we don't have enough wizards or sorcerers to handle the area required to make that tactic effective, and even if we did, we would need more still to capitalize on the moment and eliminate most of them before they could escape. I also don't have enough crossbowmen to pick up the slack," explained Nerrow.

James started to speak, but Selene held up her hand to forestall him. "What about the wall defenders? This is a risky stratagem to begin with. We could take most of the men off the walls knowing we are about to let them in anyway."

The governor shook his head. "I'm already doing that. The garrison here is just too small. We never expected an army of this size, and the assumption was always that there would be enough warning to use the teleport beacon to bring in Terabinia's army if a serious attack was attempted. The army outside the gates is easily twice our numbers, even after what you've been doing here, and we've seen how good their armor is. Our current plan is good, but we don't have the soldiers or magic to make it work without a miracle." He paused, then after a moment said, "I don't suppose you know where William is?"

Selene blanched inwardly. She would dearly love to know that herself. "I do not," she said plainly, then turned to James, who seemed to be fairly bursting to speak. "Speak, Lord Wellings. I need all the counsel I can get."

James almost sputtered as he rushed to get the words out. "Lord Nerrow is right. We need the Stormking, or a dragon, but without either of those, we need a dragon killer." He paused, giving her a meaningful look that made it seem as though his eyes were about to pop out of his skull. When Selene just stared at him, he repeated the last words with extra emphasis, "A *dragon killer.*"

"Please explain, Lord Wellings. I don't have time for guessing games," she told him.

"Haven't you seen my reports?" asked James. "Nevermind. What I mean is this, a dragon, or your husband, either one, they're powers on a scale I would describe as catastrophic. But lacking that sort of power, we could use something designed to kill them—well, not William—but a dragon. Do you see what I mean?"

She sighed. "Not at all. Do we have something that can kill a dragon?"

"Yes!" James exclaimed. "Well, maybe. Have you *really* not read my reports? I submitted them to the duchess just as you asked."

"As I asked?" questioned Selene, but it was becoming clear to her this was something she hadn't been involved in.

"When you first asked me to design a solution, you told me to coordinate with Her Grace, Janice Shaw. She's been looking over my ideas for the past year. She told me you were being kept informed," he explained.

So she intended to keep this from me? Selene was surprised, but she would deal with that later. "Remind me, what was the solution for?"

"It was more of a mandate, to seek methods and weapons that could be used to eliminate powers on the level of a dragon, or perhaps Grim Talek, for example. I shouldn't have mentioned your husband before, but he would certainly count as such."

"And you have such a weapon?"

James nodded, then glanced at the governor as if unsure if he should proceed. Selene waved at him with impatience. "I need details. How does it work, and can we actually use it here? The governor has my complete trust. Continue."

"It's based on the spell you and William designed for a sword or a mace. It causes an explosion by forcing two objects to exist in the same space at the same time. First, it—"

Selene cut him off. "That won't kill a dragon. They exist in two dimensions simultaneously, and real damage has to occur on both for wounds to have any lasting impact. That spell works by creating an explosion on one plane while the caster is teleported to safely to the ethereal at the same time."

James nodded impatiently. "I'm aware, Your Majesty. This is done with a device that addresses those limitations, if you'll allow me to continue?" He raised his brows, waiting until she nodded. "I only have one prototype, and it works by moving four heavy steel balls into specific positions with incredibly precise timing. You might find this surprising, but the timing was the most difficult part, since any discrepancy in the timing would cause a complete failure to detonate in either the material or the coterminal plane, or even both. As I'm sure you're aware, rune timing is notoriously unreliable because of the subjective and relative nature of time with regard to human observers. To get around that, I used the vibrations of a specific crystal instead to get an objective measurement to keep all the parts of the device in sync even after half of it is shifted to the coterminal phase—"

Selene held up a hand to stop him. "First, what do you mean by coterminal phase?"

"Oh! The ethereal plane, Your Majesty. I find precise language to be more useful when designing enchantments, and common parlance can be confusing." James paused. "Where was I? Oh! The timing! So, it turns out that quartz has this interesting property—"

"James, let's stick to the points pertinent to our current situation. Do you have this device here, and if so, is it useable?" Selene prompted.

His face changed, going from curious and excited to serious and calm in an instant. "Yes. It's in the cellar of my house."

"Your home was in Cerria, and if I recall it was just destroyed," she reminded him.

James winced but then explained, "Yes, it was in that cellar, but now it's in this one. I kept it in the safest place possible, our safe room. When we escaped here, the room and all its contents came with us. I have the prototype, and with a few minutes and some modifications, I think I can make it do something."

"I'm assuming it's supposed to explode," said Selene dryly, "but the question is how big the explosion will be and how we intend to use it. Also, I hope you realize the elves have shown us repeatedly that they are very comfortable using the ethereal plane for defensive purposes. In the conflict in Trendham, they kept a contingent in the ethereal just to prevent William from retreating there."

Jamed nodded. "That's the beauty of it. I made this to deal with a dragon threat. Since they exist in both dimensions simultaneously, I created this device to create an explosion in both planes at the same time. That's why the quartz was crucial to make sure the timing was perfect."

"How does it do that exactly?" she asked.

"Like I said, there are four steel balls. When activated, the inner casing and two of the balls transition to the ethereal, then the mechanism moves them into the position that was occupied by the other two balls in the material plane. Then, it shifts again and—"

Mark Nerrow was frowning and he broke in then, "Wait, if they both shift back it will only be on one plane, the material."

James shook his head. "No, only one shifts back. At the same time, one of the others on the material plane shifts to the ethereal. That's why the timing has to be exact, otherwise one side will be destroyed before the other can shift, but if it works properly, you get a powerful blast in both the material plane and the coterminal plane at the same time. It's meant to do damage to higher-dimensional beings like dragons, but it should wreak havoc with the elves too if they have escape spells in place, or if they have some troops hidden in the ethereal."

"If it works properly?" said Selene, repeating the words that bothered her.

"I haven't tested it yet. I was waiting on word from you for a good place to do so safely," answered James.

"How big will the explosion be?" asked the governor. "I assume you're thinking we set it and let the elves in. How much of the city are we going to lose? You know we still haven't finished rebuilding everything from when William decided to blow that demon-lord to hell and back."

"That wasn't from an ethereal/material collision device," corrected James. "He did use the spell that inspired this device outside the city, but the explosion that devastated Myrsta was caused by a demon-steel overload when he sabotaged their demonic turyn generator."

"There's still going to be a big boom," argued Nerrow. "How big? Do we need to evacuate the entire city? There's no time."

James smiled. "It's tuneable. That's part of the genius of the design. Depending on the size of the steel balls, you can get different explosive yields."

Sensing a problem with his statement, Selene asked, "Do you have several sets of four identical steel balls?"

"Well, no," said James, "but since it's a test device, I used small balls. Each one is only three quarters of an ounce, so the explosion should be limited to something like a city block. Just so you know, the final version—the one meant for a dragon, that is—was going to have demon-steel casings that would overload from the initial explosion, similar to what happened when William went to Hell and killed the entire demon-lord council. Thankfully, this prototype isn't built to those specifications, or it would put the entire city at risk."

Nerrow looked thoughtful as he met Selene's gaze. "The area we've barricaded will keep them within an area of roughly six city blocks. Even if we wait until they're all within, we won't get more than a quarter of them. Can't we sneak this out and hit them out there? If it does enough damage, it might demoralize them."

Selene had already been briefed on the disposition of the elven army. "You'll get even less of them that way, and I don't think you *can* demoralize them. Their leaders control them just as effectively as they do humans. However, I think you've underestimated what an explosion that size will do."

James jumped back in. "Exactly, Your Majesty. Those within the proximal blast will die instantly, but those a block farther out will be badly wounded by the pressure wave and even those two blocks away may suffer badly with burst ear drums, nausea, and shock. We should consider pulling the defenders from the barricades and retreating as far as possible just before we detonate it." He glanced down then. "That brings me to the real problem."

"We have enough of those," interjected the governor.

"What is it?" asked Selene.

"There's no remote activator for the prototype," answered James abashedly.

"How did you expect to test it, then?" said Selene.

"With a timer enchantment, a simpler version of the one that keeps the device itself in sync," he answered, "but I haven't made it yet."

"Well, get busy!" exclaimed Nerrow.

"I don't have my luxpress here, and even with my tools, it would take half a day. I haven't even made a template for it yet." James waited a moment, then continued, "I can do it myself. I just ask that you swear to protect my family from this day forward, since I'll be—"

Selene put her hand on the table between them. "Absolutely not." She saw Nerrow's mouth open, but she cut him off, "And not you either. I will do this. Besides, it will be more believable if the elves think I've come out to surrender and beg mercy for the city."

"That's insane! You're the queen, Selene! Don't be stupid, girl!" exploded the older nobleman, abandoning etiquette entirely.

She gazed evenly back at the two men. "I'm not sure what rumors you've heard, but I'm sure you both know I'm not exactly normal anymore. What happened in Trendham wasn't a trick or a ruse. William destroyed my body. Of the three of us, I'm the only one who can survive this." The statement was a half-truth at best. She was no longer a lich, but she wasn't strictly just human anymore either. Like Lognion, she knew she could probably recover from wounds that might kill others, but she had never tested the theory. Dragons *could* die, or at least be devoured by others, and the device James described would likely vaporize her entirely on both planes. She was still young and untested. She didn't truly expect to survive such a blast, but neither of them knew that. Even so, she didn't intend to commit suicide.

James and Mark were both looking less uncertain, so she continued, "Surely you can add a time delay, James. It doesn't have to be accurate like the crystal mechanism you were talking about, just a few seconds so I can teleport."

"I can, but the delay won't be consistent," replied James.

"I'll have the teleport prepared in advance. I'll only need a second."

"If I try to make sure it's at least ten seconds, the delay could be too long. It could vary between ten seconds and a few minutes. The older methods of specifying time with runes are notoriously subjective."

"I'll need just one," she reassured him.

"You're able to keep a spell like that prepared in advance?" asked Nerrow. Having been trained as a sorcerer before the return of true of wizardry, the emphasis when he had been at school had been less on preparation and more on focus and direction of one's elementals.

James answered for her, "These days, all the students at Wurthaven are encouraged to practice and stretch their capacity for maintaining prepared spells." He didn't add that only talented minds like Selene, or his own, would attempt to prepare spells as complex as the teleport spell in advance. "Students are expected to be able to maintain at least two prepared spells before they graduate."

Selene had been able to manage three before she finished school, and that had also been before the change in curriculum. After learning that William could manage four, she had begun practicing again until she could match him, but none of that was pertinent to the conversation at hand. "James, you need to fetch your device and get it ready. Lord Nerrow, you need to brief your men on what to do when we open the gates. I have spells to prepare."

CHAPTER 36

The main gates on the southern side of Myrsta opened onto the main street, which ran in a north-south direction through the city. The governor's palace, which had formerly belonged to their prophet before Terabinia had overthrown him, was also on the main street, but it was more on the northern end of the city. The south gate opened onto the heavily traveled road and a large market square sat just two corners away from it, so when the battle for the gates concluded and they were thrown open by the tired, yet victorious elven knights, the square was easily visible.

Tragically, the brave elves who had fought from within to reach and open the gates suffered massive losses. The last of them, an unknown figure who gave the final push to the unbarred gates, fell as they opened. Crossbow bolts stuck out from the elf's armor in various places.

Cries went up from the human defenders as they abandoned the walls and retreated, while the elven host marched forward without resistance. It was obvious the humans had been demoralized, for now that the gates were open the fight had gone out of them. Ahead in the market square, a force of men could be seen, but it was easy to see they were badly outnumbered.

Liambrell, first of his name, rode forward with five mounted knights on either side of him. The rest of his force were afoot and a group of twenty marched in advance of him. They entered the square as most of the human soldiers withdrew in shame, leaving a lone woman behind. Surprisingly, Liambrell recognized her face. It was the human who had been sent to live among them for a year, the one who had later become a queen. He hadn't expected to find her there. The reports had claimed she was still in Cerria.

Back then, he had held a lesser rank, and he'd been given the ignoble task of babysitting the human while she lived among them. He'd enjoyed tormenting her, watching as his scent had sent her into lustful heat time and time again. He would have bred her, but for the fact that their agreement with the fae had forbidden it. Now, it seemed that the universe had conspired to right that wrong. Today, he would take their queen, and once the sun had set, he would finally put her to the only proper use for any human—carrying elven progeny.

His men fanned out as they approached her, alert for any sign of counterattack, but it seemed that the cowardly humans had indeed abandoned their queen. Liambrell was not surprised. Throughout his life, he'd watched as the humans in his household repeatedly failed to display the nobler traits found in his own race. They had no sense of honor and would betray one another for any reason at all. It was no wonder they were a slave race. They were born to it. He waited until the scouts came back before approaching her.

"They've completely withdrawn, milord," said Telnir. "Some have erected makeshift barriers, but it's clear they're afraid to face us now that the gates are open."

Liambrell nodded, then walked his force forward without dismounting, giving him an even greater height advantage over the human queen. He remembered that she was a spellcaster of some sort, but he was skilled with magic in his own right and two of the men flanking him were also wizards, so he wasn't afraid of her potentially attacking him with magic. Removing his helm, he met her gaze and imagined he could see defeat in her eyes, or was it anticipation? She probably remembered her time among them and longed to host his child within her womb. "This day was fated to come," he told her without preamble, speaking in his native tongue.

Looking up, Selene saw his face, recognizing the elf who had brought her so much shame during her time apart from William. At the time, she'd feared something was wrong with her, until she had later learned about the power of their pheromones. Knowing the elf would make her next task even easier, not that she had any sympathy for their race to begin with. "Agreed. I am glad I am here to see it."

Liambrell hid a smirk at her poorly accented elvish. "I remember hearing you had died, and then finding out you had faked your own death. You would have done better to continue working with us. If you expect mercy, you would do well to kneel."

"You think I would do so for my own sake?" she asked.

"Unless you would rather I give you to one of my lowest-ranked soldiers. Your life will be easier if I claim you for my own household."

"I will not kneel for myself, but if you will promise leniency to my people, I will gladly bow down," she answered.

"Your servants have fled. Whether I promise or not is immaterial. Kneel or I will grind your face into the dirt with my own hands." Dismounting, he towered over her and stepped closer, so that her eyes were level with his chin.

Selene didn't flinch, staring coldly back at him, but after a long pause, she began lowering herself. The prototype was between her feet, hidden by the long skirt of the more formal dress she had changed into. As she did, she saw a flash of dark metal, causing her to freeze a moment. *Is that what I think it is? Is he wearing demon-steel?* If so, the device she was about to activate would potentially trigger an even bigger explosion. Depending on the size, people just outside the area that they thought would be safe might be injured or killed, not to mention destroying a much larger portion of the city. One block was bad enough, but any increase in the blast radius would drastically increase the total area of buildings and structures ruined.

With hardly any time for conscious thought, she altered her plan. She had two teleport spells prepared. At the center of the square, she only had line of sight to the rooftops of nearby buildings, not far enough to be safe, so she had intended to teleport once to a higher vantage point on the edge of the square, and then a second time in quick succession to a rooftop much farther away. Her plan would still work, but she would have to take along a passenger. Her hand touched the prototype, and she sent a small pulse of turyn, activating the external delay enchantment that James had hastily put together.

Only seconds were left now.

Rising quickly, she reached out to lay her hand on Liambrell's arm, then teleported. For an instant, she felt as though she was pressing against a stone wall. The elven wizard's magic resistance was fighting the influence of her spell, but in the end there could only be one outcome. Her will prevailed, and the two of them appeared atop the slate roof of a large building, one that was much closer to the city's southern gates. The distance was short enough that the blast would still be lethal, but she hoped it wouldn't have enough force to overload the elf's demon-steel equipment.

Releasing his arm, she was about to teleport again, but she'd underestimated the elf-lord's reflexes. Liambrell didn't bother with spells or anything complicated; instead, his gauntleted fist slammed into her face with bone-crushing force. A flash of intense pain overwhelmed her, and then Selene's vision went black as she fell. She wasn't unconscious, for she could feel herself beginning to slide down the slate roof tiles, but then Liambrell's fingers caught hold of her hair, jerking her to a painful halt. With the inhuman strength granted by the magic of his armor, the elf lifted her into the air in front of him until her feet dangled.

The fresh pain helped focus her mind, and though she still couldn't see, Selene batted at the armored elf with her right arm. She felt his surcoat under her fingers, then metal as her fingers scrabbled, seeking skin. And all the while, he laughed. "Bitch! Did you think—"

The elf-lord's words cut off as her hand found his lips. The magic of her spell shredded his will and deformed his body with such casual speed he might as well have been a child, rather than a second-order wizard. Liambrell died in agony as his bones dissolved and his body collapsed, never fully understanding what his mistake had been.

But Selene still couldn't see.

She needed to see in order to teleport. *The device should have gone off by now.* The makeshift timing enchantment was known to be less than reliable, but by now it surely should have activated and killed her. She could hear shouting in elven as Liambrell's subordinates spotted her and realized she had killed their leader. After his collapse, she had fallen with him, but now she got shakily back to her feet and rubbed at her eyes. Pain lanced through her as her hand touched her nose. *That was a mistake,* she realized. The nose was definitely broken, but she could see some light. One or both eyes had swollen shut, but it was likely blood in them that kept her from seeing clearly.

The shouting grew louder, and she heard feet on the roof slate as someone raced toward her. *I'm dead.* Then, a body slammed into her, and strong arms closed around her torso. Expecting another blow, she curled into a ball to protect herself and was about to try and find skin to kill her attacker when she heard a familiar voice.

"Stay still. I've got you." It was Oliver.

We're both dead, Selene thought despairingly. Then, she felt his feet leave the rooftop and they were falling. Oliver's turyn shifted as he used one of his tattoos, and then it felt as though something kicked her in the back. Consciousness fled, and oblivion took her.

***

The Watcher in the Void was frustrated. She'd kept the pressure on the new self-proclaimed 'First Wizard' for weeks now, and he seemed no closer to cracking than he had when she had first trapped him. If anything, he had grown more comfortable as he learned to manipulate the nothingness around him.

Erica couldn't help but admire his competence, but it was still annoying. From what she could see, Will was one of the rare individuals who might actually survive the madness of the void on his own, but that didn't fit with her goals.

Making matters worse, she'd just learned of the previous day's failure, as the humans had defeated the attack on Nerril. That wasn't too bad, though. The elven commander, Liambrell, had proposed the strategy, cleverly telegraphing their move toward Nerril and thus Cerria in order to keep the Terabinian forces focused there. Meanwhile, their main army was quietly slipping through Darrow, avoiding smaller towns and cities to assault Myrsta.

It wouldn't have been possible to move such a large force without alerting the human leaders but for the efficacy of elven mind magic. The bluet trade had been cut off, but it had already done its job, creating vulnerabilities in large portions of the populations of both Darrow and Terabinia.

She had hoped for a victory in both Nerril and Myrsta, but ultimately, only Myrsta mattered. Once they had taken one of the two great cities, the rest would simply be a matter of time. Her elves were better equipped and trained, and it was all too easy to subvert and control humans who had used bluet in their homes for any length of time. The loss in Nerril would just mean it took longer.

Hoping for good news, she left the void and returned to her throne in Tienelle, the main elven city. Truth be told, it was their only large city. The elven plane was mostly barren. The elves had received it as a refuge to flee Hercynia after the arrival of the dragon, thousands of years ago, but they had been cheated. The demons had sucked it dry long before trading it to them. The turyn left in it had been barely enough to sustain life.

The elves had been fighting a long, slow decline ever since. Retaking Hercynia would be the key to revitalizing their race, and the fact that it held an enormous population of brood mares to carry their future generations was a big bonus.

Erica had been human herself once, and she might have objected to their methods when she had been the First Wizard, but such concerns were long behind her. Her people had abandoned and forgotten her long ago, and she no longer cared. Even the elves were simply a tool.

A highly effective tool, she thought with a smile.

Assuming an elven form, she signaled to one of the servants, and both food and drink were brought to her. Once she had finished, a messenger arrived. His face looked nervous.

"Spit it out," she commanded.

Casting his eyes downward, the messenger answered without stammering, but his body trembled as he spoke. "Your Magnificence, Liambrell is dead. The attack on Myrsta has failed."

The air grew still, as though the world itself waited on her response. Finally, she said, "Details. Explain this to me."

"The sleepers did their work. The beacon's security was bypassed, and a large force was sent into the city. It took hours, but eventually they opened the gates, or so we thought. A trap had been prepared. The army entered, and it appeared as though the queen herself had come to offer their surrender, but instead she killed Liambrell and set off an explosion that destroyed a part of the city and killed many of our soldiers. Those left were stunned or badly injured, easy prey for the humans," explained the nervous elf.

"How many were lost?"

"All but the reserve force that was left outside the city. They are retreating now. Fortunately, the humans didn't have sufficient numbers to pursue."

Her temper snapped then. "Fortunately?" The Watcher's eyes were furious, and in spite of her intent to remain calm, her emotions got the better of her. The messenger collapsed into a pile of fine grey dust as her anger swept over him.

It would take decades to replace the army that had just been lost. She'd lived in the depressing wastes the elves called home for far too long. With the dragon's death, she'd had hopes of returning to her old home and claiming the veritable paradise that Hercynia represented. She had wanted to keep it relatively intact, but that dream was dead now.

As she rose to her feet, black flames expanded around her, racing across the floor to consume tables and furniture. The flames turned all the furnishings to dust as the servants fled the room, knowing it would do the same to them if it touched their skin. "I tried to be merciful," hissed the Watcher. "No more. If the land must be purged, then so be it. After my flame clears the way, I will tend Hercynia like a garden, until is more beautiful than ever."

Seeing that her minions had fled, she suppressed her flames and called them back. "Open the void gates, and clear the path to the sea gate. I am done with war. I will annihilate them."

CHAPTER 37

A familiar face was looking down on her as Selene opened her eyes. She expected pain, but strangely felt nothing. Her heart jumped. *Am I undead again?* The racing heart dispelled that fear, but she still wasn't sure what had happened.

"How do you feel?"

The deeply masculine voice reminded her of Will, as did the face itself. Mark Nerrow was studying her with a look of concern. "Lord Nerrow," she began slowly. "Did it work?"

"Other than you nearly killing yourself, it worked beautifully," answered the governor.

"The elves?"

"The explosion killed at least a quarter of them, and the rest were easily dispatched. Half weren't even able to stand, and the rest were badly stunned. Only a small force that remained beyond the gates escaped."

"What about the city?"

Nerrow smiled. "The explosion was slightly smaller than even James expected. The market square and the buildings around it were destroyed, but beyond that, everything not made of flesh and blood was fine, aside from broken pottery and glassware. Even the gates were fine, which made securing the city a simple task."

"My stepson?"

"Oliver is fine. I thought he'd lost his mind when he raced out to get you, but he made it in time. He got you beyond the first line of buildings, and although you were both battered pretty badly by the blast, that odd shield of his protected him from the worst of it. You were a terrible sight to see, though."

Feeling suddenly self-conscious, she reached up to carefully touch her nose. It was whole, and there was no pain there either. "My nose?"

"Your everything," said the governor. "Oliver's shield only covered him, but he kept himself between you and the worst of it. Even so, you looked half dead. You were bleeding from your eyes, nose, ears, and your skin was badly burned in places and bruised everywhere else."

"Who tended me? Is Doctor Morris here? He must have done a skin graft. Fetch a mirror. I need to see what I look like." She'd tended enough burn victims to know she probably looked bad. With flesh shaping, she could probably restore her old face if it had finished healing, but she was saddened nonetheless. After the Mother's gift, she'd truly been her old self, physically at least. She'd wanted Will to see her. Now, he would only see a close copy, for despite all her skill, he'd always been able to detect subtle differences.

"No one," said the governor. He gestured to someone at the edge of the room, and they brought over the polished silver mirror that had been standing next to the wash basin. "Your healing is a mystery. Did you take a regeneration potion right before the blast?"

Selene's old face stared back at her from the metal surface. The skin was unblemished, and the only flaw she could see was the faint bend in her nose that had always bothered her. Will would be happy to see that, but she still didn't understand. "No. Besides, you said I was burned. Regeneration potions don't handle burns this well, if at all."

"Your body was healing already when they brought you here," said the governor. "Except for this." He pulled the blankets away from the far end of the bed, exposing her feet. One was fine, while the other was a strangely shaped lump of flesh, as though it had been half amputated and the skin had grown back oddly. "Oliver thinks that foot was sticking out enough to get the full force of the blast, but unlike the rest of you, it hasn't healed, except to regrow skin."

Finally, she understood. Like Lognion, she must fully occupy both the material and ethereal planes. The parts of her shielded by Oliver's body had mended, but the part exposed had been obliterated on both planes, and thus hadn't been able to restore itself. It was a hard lesson to learn, but she was still fascinated by the miracle she was seeing and experiencing. The foot didn't really bother her either. She could manage that with prosthetics, and given some time a necromantic flesh graft would probably enable her to create a fully functional foot.

"How long have I been in this bed?" she asked after a moment. "Did Sir Kyle send reinforcements? We're still vulnerable until we know for certain how many there were."

Mark shook his head. "No, Your Majesty, we haven't been able to send anyone in either direction yet. James is still repairing the beacon enchantment. It's been a night and half a day since you were hurt, but I've been in communication with Sir Kyle, as well as Duchess Shaw in

Cerria. So far, everything is calm. There have been no further elven attacks, and the dragon seems to have disappeared."

"What about Tabitha?"

The governor's face blanched at the mention of his daughter's name. "I'm told she still hasn't regained consciousness or human form, but they say she hasn't gotten any worse. I'm hopeful you can help her once the beacon is operational again."

Selene reached over to put her hand against his face. "Mark, I will do everything I can to help her. You have my word on that."

"I know things have been tense between you in recent years, but—"

She cut him off. "I don't blame her, and in any case, I count you both as family. I would do everything in my power even if she never forgives me. You always treated me as if I were one of your own children when I was young. I've never forgotten that, Father."

Mark blinked. Technically he was her father-in-law, but it wasn't common knowledge, and she'd never publicly acknowledged the fact. "I'm honored, Your Majesty, though I'm not sure if its wise of you to say that with so many ears around."

"I'm tired of secrets. Just when you planned to acknowledge him as your son, everyone thought he was dead—thanks to me. Now he's alive, but no one knows whether we're friends or enemies. I had planned to give up the crown for him, but that doesn't seem practical either. Going forward, I intend to make no secret of the fact that he's my husband still, as well as your son. People can make what they will of that."

"But the political ramifications…"

"Mean nothing," she replied. "No house would dare challenge me now, and with the Stormking as my husband, they would be doubly fools to do so."

"They can still find all manner of ways to cause you trouble without directly challenging you," cautioned the governor.

"They should know me well enough not to try, but if they do, so be it. Some of the houses would probably benefit from having new blood to lead them," she responded.

"If you don't mind me asking," began Nerrow, "where is William? He would have been handy in either Nerril or here in Myrsta."

"Your son retired from public life when he moved to Trendham."

"That's not an answer," returned her father-in-law. "If he'd been able, I'm certain he would have helped. What's happened to him? If anyone knows, you must. Even Oliver couldn't tell me anything."

Uncomfortable for the first time since waking, Selene took a deep breath before answering, "I don't know. He decided to find the gate the elves are using to visit our world. We were communicating now and again, but I haven't received any word from him for weeks now. My tablet won't send messages, and he hasn't visited me astrally. To be honest, I'm worried."

"Since you're determined to put me in the spotlight, can I dispense with proper etiquette for a moment?" he asked. Selene nodded, and he reached over to hold her hand. "You aren't alone, Selene. Whatever happens, we'll get through this together."

She felt something strange wash over her, and then something ran down her cheek. Mystified, Selene reached up with her other hand to find something wet there. Tears? She couldn't recall the last time she had shed actual tears. More fell as she glanced back at Will's father. "Thank you."

***

An elegant yet small grey housecat threaded its way between trees and tall tufts of grass as she made her way back to what some would call her home, a modest cottage on the outskirts of Lystal, in the nation of Trendham. She had white hair on her belly and feet, giving the impression that she wore stockings, and while her long, magnificent coat was relatively clean, there were bits of leaf litter stuck in her tail. She would get those out later. Evie had been gone for days, wandering and hunting, but such short spans of time meant little to her. Everyone had left except Will's mother, Erisa, not that she minded. Independent and self-contained, Evie didn't become anxious about separations in time or space, whether those separations were composed of decades or thousands of miles.

But although Will's comings and goings didn't really concern her, something else did—she could no longer feel his presence. That had happened before, almost nightly, whenever he shielded himself against whatever it was that caused his night terrors. Even worse, her human had kept himself blocked off for the better part of a decade while he hid from his mate, but thankfully that was no longer the case. Recently, the only time he'd bother to completely isolate his soul had been while sleeping, but she hadn't felt him reappear for several weeks now.

Worry was almost a foreign concept for the feline demigod, but it was probably the best label for the discomfiting feeling that plagued her now. Something was wrong, and anything that could be bad enough to force her human into perpetual hiding had to be bad indeed. Over the past few years, she had come to understand that despite his ape-like foolishness and human stupidity, there weren't many things that could threaten Will Cartwright.

As she approached the back door of the house, Evie's sharp nose caught the scent of something she didn't like—death. Something was dead inside, and unlike one of Selene's bodies, it was beginning the process of normal decay. Pausing, she sniffed the air and felt some relief since she didn't detect Will or Oliver. Erisa was in the house, however, and there weren't any strangers present.

Ignoring the door, she jumped onto Will's bedroom windowsill and entered as she usually did. Now inside, she detected the aroma of blood that had dried but wasn't particularly old. Evie was now uncomfortably aware of what she would find, and as she entered the main living room, her eyes confirmed what she'd suspected. Erisa was sprawled out on the floor, with a long streak of blood behind her stretching from the direction of the kitchen.

On silent paws, Evie circled the room and checked the kitchen. The hardwood counter there had blood on the edge and on the floor. She didn't detect any sign of foul play, for there were no foreign smells. The old woman had slipped, or possibly fainted, and struck her head. She'd awoken later and pulled herself along with her hands, moving from the kitchen into the living area before giving up.

Back in the living room, Evie thought the old woman's leg had probably been broken, but she couldn't be sure without changing forms and adjusting the body. Not that it mattered. Erisa was dead, and knowing which bones had broken and which had not wouldn't bring her back.

Evie paused, unsure what to do. Her chest was tight with a feeling she didn't quite understand. Death was part of nature for most creatures, she knew that, and she experienced it closely when she hunted. Will's mother had lived a fair number of years, more than was typical for many of her kind. Even so, she felt a strange pain within, and a long, low mew escaped her lips.

What should she do? For most beings, nothing, but she knew humans had strange customs and Will would probably want his mother buried in the earth. It was a waste of flesh in her opinion, but other things would still find a use for the body.

I should find him, she thought, though she had no idea where to look. Oliver was somewhere far distant while Sammy was much closer, probably in Bondgrad. She would go to her first before searching elsewhere.

With that decision made, she felt the urge to leave immediately, but she couldn't. Another long, mewling noise escaped despite her best efforts. *I will bury her for him.* But the thought of taking human form to accomplish the task was unpleasant. *Not yet.* Circling, she drew closer to Erisa's cold form.

She's been dead for almost a day, but she spent several on the floor before that. A lonely, painful death— Evie didn't finish the thought. Instead, she moved closer, curling up against the old woman's neck and wrapping her tail around so that it shielded her green eyes against the light. She'd napped with Will's mother in the past, and it felt like the right thing to do.

She couldn't make Erisa feel better, and her own heart ached as she smelled the scent of the old woman's hair, but she didn't want to move. Not yet. It was too soon. She would find Sammy and Will tomorrow, after burying the old woman.

The afternoon sun created a pool of light on the two of them, cat and dead mother, and in its warmth, Evie eventually fell asleep. Tomorrow would be soon enough to face the pain of loss.

EPILOGUE

The emptiness beyond Will's boundary wall had been quiet for longer than ever before. He assumed that meant the Watcher was preoccupied with something else. Either way, the important thing was that he devote none of his attention to it. Only his domain existed, and the void beyond was nothing. The less he allowed his thoughts to drift to it, the less power it had to disrupt his world.

In front of him was the limnthal, its runes glowing quietly as he studied it. He'd mapped out the entire rune construct, written it down, and analyzed it a dozen times over. It bore many structural similarities to the heart-stone enchantment, which explained the greatest anomaly— the fact that fully half of it was missing.

It was hard to believe he'd taken it for granted so long, but now that he'd given it a thorough examination, it seemed abundantly clear that the enchantment operated on the principles of soul magic. It wasn't a well-studied area of magic, and in fact, the only other example of a rune construct using soul magic that he knew of was the heart-stone enchantment. The fact that only half of it was visible made perfect sense now, for the other half would be with another soul.

From what he could tell, there were no compulsions or command components built into the enchantment, at least not on his end. It did contain simple control runes, but they were being used purely for communication, to carry his wishes to the other soul. Whether it acted upon them or not seemed to be purely voluntary, at least from this end. He couldn't discount the possibility that the other half of the enchantment might contain unwholesome functions that enslaved the other soul, but it might just as easily have rune functions that could torture him.

The entire thing seemed like a magical contract that did little more than establish a connection and enable easy communication of simple requests to withdraw or store items. Did that mean the limnthal was nothing more than a soul-bound relay to some archivist in another dimension? Will imagined an elderly caretaker dutifully removing and replacing items for wizards across the centuries. Or was it more than one?

Either way, the limnthal represented a possible escape route. It still worked, providing him with whatever items he had previously placed within it, and that meant he had a connection to a real place, a place not smothered by the endless emptiness of the void.

He'd seen the way Erica's eyes had lingered on the enchantment each time he summoned or sent something away. As the tenth First Wizard, she should have had a limnthal of her own, but he'd never seen her use it. Did she lack one? Had they been created after her time?

Will didn't think so. *She was trapped in the void for a long time, but she eventually escaped to enslave the elves. It's possible she used her limnthal to do so.* The idea was intriguing, and it could also explain why she might not have the enchantment anymore. If she'd inverted its function in order to store herself in that other realm as a means of escape, the action might have caused the rune structure to fracture and fail.

Unfortunately for him, the limnthal only transmitted very specific pieces of information, in particular the information needed for requesting or storing items. It wasn't designed to allow for two-way communication or more abstract things like questions or prose.

Some time ago, it was impossible for him to know how long, but it felt like a week or more, he had summoned one of his journals, torn out a blank page, and written a long message on it that detailed his name, the fact that he was the current First Wizard, and the predicament he had fallen into. After folding it up, he'd written 'To the Limnthal Keeper: Please read and reply' in large bold letters on the outside.

He'd summoned the page back just moments ago, and it now sat on the desktop in front of him. To his disappointment, there had been no reply inside, but after studying, it he noticed one subtle difference. Two of the lines he had folded it on were no longer sharp and clean, as if someone had opened it and then refolded it imperfectly.

They didn't write a reply, though. Will took that to mean it was either against the rules they operated under, or that they didn't want to get involved. The lack of a written response was an obvious 'no,' but Will hadn't survived and grown into his power with a lack of stubbornness— quite the opposite.

Leaning back in his comfy chair, Will studied the wood paneling of his study, painfully recreated from memory. His ability to manipulate the void had gotten much better, as evidenced by the many intricate details that no longer shifted whenever his attention wandered. Scratches and blemishes in the wood remained where he had put them, at least as far as he could tell. It was possible his memory was flawed or shifting, but he didn't think so.

"After being trapped for an unknown time, fighting and being tormented, she lost her mind. That's easy enough to see," he muttered aloud. "But then she had the same thought and realized she might have a way out." Will scratched at his chin. "Except she didn't know of anyone else who had done it, and she probably only knew one way to twist the enchantment to her needs." He *really* didn't want to tinker with his limnthal and ruin it, although he could see how it might be done. "I have another option, though, one that she probably didn't have."

In her time, the Wayfarer Society had still maintained a monopoly on teleportation and gate magic. As First Wizard, it was possible she was allowed to know their secrets, but he doubted it, and even if she had, it was likely that learning to teleport the way he did was even rarer. From his previous studies, Will knew that becoming astrally perceptive was pretty uncommon—not unheard of, but uncommon. To be able to directly teleport to unseen friends using an astral connection also required the caster to be able to consciously unseat themselves from their corporeal form *and* learn how to split their awareness between two places in order to cast the spell.

It was a lot to ask of anyone, and while the records did show that some members of the Wayfarer Society were able to teleport to faraway places without using a beacon, it was almost certainly a small number of practitioners that were capable of it. Chances were, Erica hadn't been one of them, and if so, that meant she hadn't been able to try what he was considering.

With a building sense of excitement, he sat up straight and let his soul slip just a little, loosening the connection between his body and spirit. Somehow, everything changed without changing. More in tune with the astral, he could see that nothing was real, even his own creations—everything lacked substance. The astral itself was almost nonexistent, but for himself and a thin connection representing the limnthal.

Will didn't know the soul on the other side of it, but the limnthal itself created an artificial bond between them. Forming his intent, he followed it. Instantly, he recognized the presence of another person, but halfway between places, he also saw his void domain crumbling. Looking into the astral had broken his control, and now the monsters were flooding across his former borders.

In that moment, he only had two choices: return and take up the battle to reassert control over the nearby void, or commit fully and teleport. For him, it was no choice at all.

Gathering his turyn, Will teleported out of the void and into the unknown.

Books by Michael G. Manning:

Mageborn
The Blacksmith's Son
The Line of Illeniel
The Archmage Unbound
The God-Stone War
The Final Redemption

Embers of Illeniel (a prequel series)
The Mountains Rise
The Silent Tempest
Betrayer's Bane

Champions of the Dawning Dragons
Thornbear
Centyr Dominance
Demonhome

The Riven Gates:
Mordecai
The Severed Realm
Transcendence and Rebellion

Standalone Novels:
Thomas

Art of the Adept
The Choice of Magic
Secrets and Spellcraft
Scholar of Magic
Disciple of War
The Wizard's Crown

Wrath of the Stormking
Wizard in Exile
Daughter of the Dragon
Watcher of the Void

About the Author

Michael Manning was born in Cleveland, Texas and spent his formative years there, reading fantasy and science fiction, concocting home grown experiments in his backyard, and generally avoiding schoolwork.

Eventually he went to college, starting at Sam Houston State University, where his love of beer blossomed and his obsession with playing role-playing games led him to what he calls 'his best year ever' and what most of his family calls 'the lost year'.

Several years and a few crappy jobs later, he decided to pursue college again and was somehow accepted into the University of Houston Honors program (we won't get into the particulars of that miracle). This led to a degree in pharmacy and it followed from there that he wound up with a license to practice said profession.

Unfortunately, Michael was not a very good pharmacist. Being relatively lawless and free spirited were not particularly good traits to possess in a career focused on perfection, patient safety, and the letter-of-the-law. Nevertheless, he persisted and after a stint as a hospital pharmacy manager wound up as a pharmacist working in correctional managed care for the State of Texas.

He gave drugs to prisoners.

After a year or two at UTMB he became bored and taught himself entirely too much about networking, programming, and database design and administration. At first his supervisors warned him (repeatedly) to do his assigned tasks and stop designing programs to help his coworkers do theirs, but eventually they gave up and just let him do whatever he liked since it seemed to be generally working out well for them.

Ten or eleven years later and he got bored with that too. So he wrote a book. We won't talk about where he was when he wrote 'The Blacksmith's Son', but let's just assume he was probably supposed to be doing something else at the time.

Some people liked the book and told other people. Now they won't leave him alone.

After another year or two, he decided to just give up and stop pretending to be a pharmacist/programmer, much to the chagrin of his mother (who had only ever wanted him to grow up to be a doctor and had finally become content with the fact that he had settled on pharmacy instead).

Today he lives at home with his teenage twins, a feral cat familiar, two yorkies, more cats, and a head full of imaginary people. There used to be some fish, but the cats deny any involvement in their disappearance.